Praise for Anne Emery

Praise for *Lament for Bonnie*
"You know you are in the thick of a good mystery novel when you start becoming suspicious of characters you consider shady in the parking lot of your very own town. Anne Emery's latest, *Lament for Bonnie*, will leave readers spooked and wary of their surroundings." — *Atlantic Books Today*

"*Lament for Bonnie* is a good mystery in this entertaining series set in eastern Canada." — Glenn Perrett, All Things Entertainment

"The author's ability to say more with less invites readers along for the dark ride, and the island's Celtic culture serves as a stage to both the story's soaring narrative arc and a quirky cast of characters, providing a glimpse into the Atlantic Canadian communities settled by Scots over two hundred years ago." — *Celtic Life*

"The novel is ingeniously plotted." — Reviewing the Evidence

Praise for *Ruined Abbey*
"The eighth in the series, this winning mystery stands on its own . . . fans of Emery's earlier works will enjoy seeing Father Brennan in the bosom of his feisty Irish family." — *Booklist*, starred review

"True to the Irish tradition of great storytelling, this is a mesmerizing tale full of twists that will keep readers riveted from the first page to the last." — *Publishers Weekly*, starred review

"This is a really tightly plotted historical with solid characters and the elegant style we expect from Emery." — *Globe and Mail*

"Suspenseful to the final page." — *Winnipeg Free Press*

Praise for *Blood on a Saint*
"As intelligent as it is entertaining . . . The writing bustles with energy, and with smart, wry dialogue and astute observations about crime and religion." — *Ellery Queen*

"Emery skilfully blends homicide with wit, music, theology, and quirky characters." — *Kirkus Reviews*

Praise for *Death at Christy Burke's*
"Emery's sixth mystery (after 2010's *Children in the Morning*) makes excellent use of its early 1990s Dublin setting and the period's endemic violence between Protestants and Catholics."
— *Publishers Weekly*, starred review

"Halifax lawyer Anne Emery's terrific series featuring lawyer Monty Collins and priest Brennan Burke gets better with every book."
— *Globe and Mail*

Praise for *Children in the Morning*
"This [fifth] Monty Collins book by Halifax lawyer Emery is the best of the series. It has a solid plot, good characters, and a very strange child who has visions."
— *Globe and Mail*

"Not since Robert K. Tanenbaum's Lucy Karp, a young woman who talks with saints, have we seen a more poignant rendering of a female child with unusual powers."
— *Library Journal*

Praise for *Cecilian Vespers*
"Slick, smart, and populated with lively characters." — *Globe and Mail*

"This remarkable mystery is flawlessly composed, intricately plotted, and will have readers hooked to the very last page." — *The Chronicle Herald*

Praise for *Barrington Street Blues*
"Anne Emery has given readers so much to feast upon . . . The core of characters, common to all three of her novels, has become almost as important to the reader as the plots. She is becoming known for her complexity and subtlety in her story construction." — *The Chronicle Herald*

Praise for *Obit*
"Emery tops her vivid story of past political intrigue that could destroy the present with a surprising conclusion." — *Publishers Weekly*

"Strong characters and a vivid depiction of Irish American family life make Emery's second mystery as outstanding as her first."

—*Library Journal*, starred review

Praise for *Sign of the Cross*
"A complex, multilayered mystery that goes far beyond what you'd expect from a first-time novelist." — *Quill & Quire*

"Snappy dialogue, a terrific feel for Halifax, characters you really do care about, and a great plot make this one a keeper."

—*Waterloo Region Record*

"Anne Emery has produced a stunning first novel that is at once a mystery, a thriller, and a love story. *Sign of the Cross* is well written, exciting, and unforgettable." —*The Chronicle Herald*

THOUGH
the HEAVENS
FALL

THE COLLINS-BURKE MYSTERY SERIES

Sign of the Cross
Obit
Barrington Street Blues
Cecilian Vespers
Children in the Morning
Death at Christy Burke's
Blood on a Saint
Ruined Abbey
Lament for Bonnie
Though the Heavens Fall

THOUGH
the HEAVENS
FALL

A Collins-Burke Mystery

ANNE EMERY

Published by ECW Press
665 Gerrard Street East, Toronto, ON M4M 1Y2
416-694-3348 / info@ecwpress.com

Cover and text design: Tania Craan
Cover image: © Mick Quinn/mqphoto.com
Author photo: Precision Photo

LIBRARY AND ARCHIVES CANADA
CATALOGUING IN PUBLICATION

Emery, Anne, author
Though the heavens fall / Anne Emery.

(A Collins-Burke mystery)

Issued in print and electronic formats.
ISBN 978-1-77041-386-3 (hardcover).
ALSO ISSUED AS: 978-1-77305-235-9 (EPUB),
978-1-77305-236-6 (PDF)

I. Title. II. Series: Emery, Anne. Collins-Burke mystery series.

PS8609.M47T57
2018   C813'.6   C2018-902531-X   C2018-902532-8

The publication of *Though the Heavens Fall* has been generously supported by the Canada Council for the Arts which last year invested $153 million to bring the arts to Canadians throughout the country, and by the Government of Canada. *Nous remercions le Conseil des arts du Canada de son soutien. L'an dernier, le Conseil a investi 153 millions de dollars pour mettre de l'art dans la vie des Canadiennes et des Canadiens de tout le pays. Ce livre est financé en partie par le gouvernement du Canada.* We also acknowledge the Ontario Arts Council (OAC), an agency of the Government of Ontario, and the contribution of the Government of Ontario through the Ontario Book Publishing Tax Credit and the Ontario Media Development Corporation.

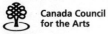

PRINTED AND BOUND IN CANADA   PRINTING: FRIESENS   5 4 3 2 1

"Counsellors, I give you the Four Courts."

That was Father Brennan Burke, giving his two friends a little tour of Dublin, his hometown. The two friends were lawyers: Monty Collins and his wife, Maura MacNeil. They stood on the south side of the River Liffey, gazing across the shining waters at a magnificent neoclassical building on the other side. It had a row of Corinthian columns along the front under a triangular pediment. The building was crowned with a circle of columns in the middle, topped by a dome.

Maura threw up her hands and turned away. "I can't live up to that. I rest my case before I even get started."

"Maybe this will bring you back down to earth. Or even below it. Many years ago there was a warren of alleys and passages along there, close to the courts. One of the lanes was so dark and obscure, it became known as Hell. 'Apartments in Hell' were advertised in the newspapers as 'suitable for lawyers.'"

"I am humbled," Maura averred.

Then they crossed the O'Donovan Rossa Bridge to Inns Quay,

admired the Four Courts again from close up, and Monty and Maura followed Brennan around the back of the building to Chancery Street, where he directed their attention to another part of the complex. They looked up; this building too had a triangular pediment. On it was inscribed the words *fiat jvstitia rvat cœlvm*. In modern letters, *fiat justitia ruat caelum*. They all gazed in silence at the ringing proclamation. Monty felt the urge to genuflect before it.

Let justice be done though the heavens fall.

Chapter I

Monty Collins

It was Tuesday, January 24, 1995, and Monty Collins was on assignment in Belfast. He was defending a lawsuit filed against a Canadian-owned company that had a large farm equipment factory on the outskirts of the city, and he had secured a temporary placement with a Belfast law firm by the name of Ellison Whiteside. Monty's office was in the city centre near Queen's Square, with a window looking out on the Gothic-style Albert Memorial Clock, which stood over one hundred feet high in the square. He did some paperwork on the farm equipment file and conferred with a couple of local clients, then left the office for lunch in the company of two fellow lawyers from Ellison Whiteside. It was their habit, and would now be his, to head over to McHughs bar, no apostrophe, for a pint and a bite to eat. Wisely, his companions had brought umbrellas for the short walk in the cold winter rain; Monty turned up the collar of his jacket and kept his head down till they reached the bar. They got the last vacant table and ordered soup, sandwiches, and pints of Guinness. It was apparent that the pub regulars had got an early start to the day. Two old fellows were having a row over the leek and potato soup, specifically about what leeks were and where they were grown.

"They're in the same family as onions. And garlic."

"In yer hole, they are! Where are we, Ireland or Italy?"

"You're not even in Ireland!" someone declared from the bar.

"Those are fightin' words, Charley. Every inch of land on this island is Ireland, and every blade of grass growin' on it."

"And every leek!" another guy chimed in. "And they're green and white. Not a patch of orange on them at all."

Soup grew cold but pints were consumed before their ideal temperature altered for the worst.

Monty enjoyed a few laughs with his colleagues until they departed for a meeting. He sat and finished his meal. When he was about to get up, he saw a man slide off his barstool and come towards him. He had a wild crop of white hair and stubble on his face, and he appeared to be in his late seventies.

"Those fellas with you were from Ellison Whiteside, am I right, sir?"

"That's right."

"You're new here."

"Yes, I am."

"What part of America are you from?"

Monty and other Canadians got that all the time. Everyone assumed they were from the United States. A very few people could discern a Canadian accent, often making the comment that it was softer than the American. Maura was recently told that hers was "sweeter." No surprise there, Monty supposed; Cape Breton speech often sounded like a mix of Scottish and Irish. He addressed the man in McHughs and said, "I'm from Canada."

"Oh, I beg your pardon. My mistake. No offence intended."

"None taken." And if offence had been taken, Monty was too much the polite Canadian to say so.

The man lowered his voice then. "You're a solicitor with Ellison's?"

"That's right."

"Well, I have a matter I'd like to discuss with you. A highly confidential matter."

"I keep all my work confidential."

"Very good, as it should be. And it's good to have somebody new in town. The solicitors here have become a wee bit cynical. Worn down by all the violence, you know."

"Town" sounded somewhere between "tine" and "tarn," "bit cynical" like "but sunnacal," "violence" like "vayalence." Monty nodded in acknowledgement.

"So could I have an appointment with you? Without delay?"

Might as well get it over with today. "Sure, come in after lunch. Ask at the desk for me. My name is Collins, Monty Collins."

"Interesting combination, sir. Sounds as if you've a Brit and a lad from County Cork in your family tree."

"I have both; you are correct."

"I'll see you this afternoon."

Monty paid for his meal and his pint and returned to his office, where he sat reading the file of a man who claimed he had tripped coming out of the loo in his local bar and had fallen on his knees. Monty could imagine how popular this man — and his solicitor — would be if they took a well-loved publican to the law over something like this. It was hardly the life-and-death legal drama he was accustomed to in the courts at home, defending clients who faced the possibility of life in prison for murder. He shook away those thoughts and started to reach for another of his files when the firm's receptionist popped her head in the door. "Mr. Malone would like to see you, Monty." She rolled her eyes.

"Sure, show him in."

She mouthed the words "good luck" and went back out to reception. Then Mr. Malone, the man from McHughs, was in his doorway. He reached around and closed the door ever so quietly and sat in one of the two client chairs in front of Monty's desk.

"So, Mr. Malone . . ."

"Hughie."

"Hughie. How can I help you?"

"You can help blow the lid off one of the biggest cover-ups the wee statelet called 'Northern Ireland' has ever known!"

"Cover-up," Monty repeated.

"A cover-up at the highest levels is what I suspect."

"I see."

Hughie sat there nodding his head.

The old cover-up story again. This was not a new experience for Monty, nor for others in his profession. In fact, in a certain kind of case, with a certain kind of client, the client typically goes through a series of lawyers as each one drops his case for lack of merit. That often results in the disgruntled client lodging a complaint with the Bar Society or commencing a lawsuit against the lawyer on completely bogus and fantastical grounds. In virtually every case, the lawyer is accused of "being in on it," that is, being part of a conspiracy with another party or parties to the complaint, along with other lawyers, the Crown prosecutors, and the judges. It is not unusual for the CIA to crop up in these allegations and, until recently, the KGB. Sometimes aliens had a hand in things as well. These cases often resulted in the client representing himself and foisting on the courts hundreds, even thousands, of pages of the claimant's ramblings, on everything from his conspiracy theories to his revelations on the meaning of life and the universe. The self-represented litigant. As the old saying goes, "He who acts as his own lawyer has a fool for a client."

"Tell me what has you concerned," Monty urged him, against his better judgment.

"In the wee hours of November the fourteenth, 1992, my niece's husband, Eamon Flanagan that was, fell off the Ammon Road Bridge and drowned. This happened the same night, and in the same vicinity, as a fatal shooting, which has never been solved. That same dark, early morning, Eamon just *happened* to *fall off* the bridge and *drown*."

"Why do you believe this was something other than just an unfortunate accident?"

"There is no justice in the artificial state known to the world as Northern Ireland."

"Yes, but in this instance, what do you think really happened to this man?"

"He was attacked and then thrown or pushed off the bridge."

"What evidence do you have of that?"

"If you don't mind me saying so, Mr. Collins, you sound like all the rest of them." *Signed lake all the rust o' thum.*

"This happened over two years ago. If things went as you believe they did, why has nothing been done before now?"

"Others have refused to take on the case." Of course. That's why he homed in on Monty, the new solicitor in town. The blow-in from away. "They're afraid of losing their livelihood. Or worse."

"That doesn't exactly encourage me, Mr. Malone."

"This statelet, this wee bastard of a political entity, is kept in place by fear. Terror from above."

Monty had no desire to open that particular door, so he tried to steer the conversation back to the facts. If there were any. "What is it you know, which makes you think this was not an accident?"

"The injuries on the body."

"Oh?"

"Blunt force trauma to his leg and other parts of him."

"And that tells you what?"

"That he was struck by a powerful force before he went off that bridge."

"Or he suffered trauma in the fall. The structure of the bridge, perhaps, or rocks below? I don't have the advantage of seeing the post-mortem report, so there's nothing I can say about that."

"Katie has it."

"Who?"

"His daughter. May I send her in to see you?"

Every cell in Monty's body cried out *No!* But, trying to stifle a sigh, he said, "Sure. Send her in."

Malone nodded and stood up and left the office.

Monty got busy for the rest of the afternoon and put the Hughie Malone visit out of his mind. He would not hold his breath waiting for the dead man's daughter, if there was a daughter, to make an appearance in the offices of Ellison Whiteside, solicitors, Belfast.

†

Monty Collins and Maura MacNeil had come to Ireland because of Monty's work on behalf of Canadian Earth Equipment Inc., which was one of the biggest clients of his law firm in Halifax, Stratton Sommers. The lawsuit against the company had been launched by farmers and "agribusinesses" — Monty hated that word; it made him lose his appetite — who claimed that their equipment wore out prematurely because of manufacturing defects. It was a multi-million dollar claim. Canadian Earth insisted that the fault lay not with its processes but with the company that supplied the metal for the equipment. Monty's role would be to gather evidence and statements from the vast manufacturing complex to use in its defence and in the third party claim against the metal supplier. Stratton Sommers expected him to get this done and return home by early May. The fact that he was a Queen's Counsel at home in Nova Scotia with more than two decades of experience gave him a leg up when it came to meeting the qualifications to practise law in the North of Ireland. Monty was pleased to have been chosen for the overseas posting, but it had to be said that his partners and associates had not exactly been queuing up in the hopes of snagging this assignment. It was not Paris, not Rome, but Belfast in the midst of the Troubles. With that in the forefront of his mind, Monty had done his research; the flat he had rented was close to the university and the Botanic Gardens, a part of the city that had been spared much of the horror of the past quarter century. A ceasefire had been in place since August, but nobody knew how long it would hold.

He and Maura had agonized over whether she and the children should accompany him. They settled on Dublin for her and the two youngest kids, Normie and Dominic. Normie was eleven going on twelve and Dominic was three. The oldest boy, Tommy Douglas, was attending university at home in Halifax. Maura had arranged a leave of absence from her job as a professor at Dalhousie Law School in Halifax, and she had been taken on as a part-time lecturer at the University College of Dublin's law school. The family had been in Ireland before, but law courts and law books had not been part of the earlier trip.

Monty had spent three days in Dublin, at the little row house Maura had found on the city's north side, before he headed north to Belfast to start work. He had leased a nifty little Renault hatchback from Burke Transport, and he left the city with assurances that the family would all be together again soon. It was a pleasant two-hour drive through rolling green fields. He was stopped at a border check-point, but the army — that being the British Army — did not detain him long.

Ellison Whiteside was a firm of solicitors specializing in civil litigation, and the arrangement was that Monty would work a few cases for the firm in addition to his work for Canadian Earth. This provided an interesting change of focus. In Halifax, he was a defence lawyer trying cases in the criminal courts. Or representing defendants and their insurance companies in civil trials, taking the position that the person claiming injury was barely hurt at all, that there was nothing wrong with the plaintiff beyond a few minor aches and pains, and that he or she was not entitled to retire from the workforce at the defendant's expense. Now, here in Belfast, he worked mainly on the plaintiff side. Now he'd be the one claiming that the injured party would never work again, My Lord, because of the pain in his back, neck, leg, head, or little finger. He had to admit that the work wasn't as exciting as winning acquittals in high-profile murder trials, but the sojourn in Belfast would be an adventure, he was sure.

There was somebody else who had a hand in this whole scheme, and that was Father Brennan Burke. The priest was practically a part of the Collins-MacNeil family now. Born in Dublin, he had a big extended family in Ireland. Although he was a frequent visitor to the country, he had always wanted to spend a longer stretch of time here. Brennan had originally intended to stay in Dublin but with prompting from some of his northern Republican relations who had never recognized the border — "It's all Ireland, Brennan" — he decided on Belfast. That way, he said, "I can make sure that Monty will continue to receive the sacraments. And he'll never be alone when it's time to raise a glass after hours." So he signed on to assist the other priests at a church in the north part of the city, and he would be staying with a cousin by the name of Ronan Burke.

Monty had made plans to go for an early pub supper with Brennan. Brennan expressed an interest in seeing Monty's new residence, so they met there. He had the downstairs flat in a typical red-brick Victorian terrace house with projecting bay windows, on Camden Street near Queen's University. They headed out from there, walked through the university district, and came to the shore of the River Lagan. Fortunately, the weather had changed, as it did frequently during any one day in Belfast, and the river shone in the setting sun, reflecting the flame-coloured sky above. They kept to the Lagan's bank for a while and then turned into the streets of a neighbourhood

Brennan called the Markets. A Nationalist area of brick houses with Republican murals and the green, white, and orange Irish tricolour, which would most likely be described here as green, white, and *gold*. People were out of their houses chatting and enjoying the late afternoon warmth. Monty and Brennan greeted them and were greeted in return.

They then left the residential area and found themselves on a busy street fronted by an imposing Portland stone building with columns and multi-paned windows. Monty had had a glimpse of the building on a short trip to Belfast three years earlier; it was a sight you wouldn't forget. It was the High Court, its noble elevation marred by the enormous concrete blast wall that surrounded it. When would they be able to dismantle the wall? When would they deem it safe from car bomb attacks? Was there really a chance that peace would prevail at last?

"Some of our greatest buildings are those dedicated to the ideal of justice and the rule of law," Brennan said.

"And rightly so," Monty agreed. *"Fiat justitia ruat caelum."*

"Well, we're in a place now where justice and the rule of law have been taking a thumping for over twenty-five years."

"Longer than that, I suspect."

"Much longer indeed. Centuries. But you're an officer of the courts now, Collins. You'll put things to rights."

"Yeah, with my trip and fall cases. Those are my files these days when I'm not sorting through cartons of papers from the equipment manufacturer. At least these cases won't get me killed. Or so I would hope."

"Nothing too thrilling yet, I guess?"

"Could be worse."

He and Brennan continued on their walk, keeping an eye out for a place to enjoy some pub food for supper, and they found what they were looking for at the Garrick, a beautiful old bar with dark wood and gleaming fittings, dating back to Victorian times. As they sipped their pints and waited for their meal to be served, Monty asked, "So you're settling in at your cousin's place? You don't miss rectory life and Mrs. Kelly?" Mrs. Kelly was the priests' housekeeper in Halifax. A nervous, fussy woman, she made no secret of her disapproval of Father Burke for reasons too numerous to mention.

"I imagine the screws in the Crumlin jail would be easier to take than Mrs. Kelly," he said. "But all that aside, it's lovely staying at Ronan and Gráinne's. Plenty of room. Aideen's the youngest; she's at university in Galway. Tomás is about to be married and is living just around the corner, so he calls in for visits. Lorcan is rooming with some other lads in a flat off the Falls Road. I've a nice, comfortable room upstairs at Ronan's, so it's grand."

"I understand Ronan works for Burke Transport, northern division?"

"He does. Part-time, a few mornings a week. He used to run it but he was, well, away for a stretch of time. Or two."

"I see."

"So somebody else runs the place and he's there about half the time. His son Tomás is full-time, though. Does the books. Studied business and accounting, all that, in college. But Ronan wouldn't be able to devote all his time to the transport operation anyway. He has other activities that are taking up his energies."

"His name pops up frequently in the news."

"He's in the thick of things with the ceasefire and with some extremely delicate machinations that are going on, to try and get a peace agreement."

"Good luck to him."

"He'll be needing it. To the Unionists, any accommodation with us papists is a surrender. And one of their mottos, as you've seen on the murals, is 'No Surrender!'"

"Unionist," Monty knew, meant union with the United Kingdom, not with the rest of Ireland.

"They are already calling the process a sell-out. *Sull-ite*. But they can't have been sold too far down the river, because the Republicans are calling it a sell-out, too. Or they assume it will be, from what they've heard to this point. So you can imagine the rocky road ahead of the fellas trying to strike a deal. Here's Ronan, with the best intentions in the world, and he's getting as much resistance from his own people as he is from their age-old enemies."

"He'd better watch his back," Monty remarked.

"God bless him and keep him."

It was a familiar phrase, uttered frequently and without much thought. Not this time. Father Brennan Burke had the look of a very worried man.

Chapter II

Monty

Monty was all set to meet Ronan Burke and his family a week after arriving in Belfast. At least, he would meet them whenever he located Saint Matthew's church on the city's east side. Brennan had extended to Monty, Maura, and the kids an invitation to the wedding of Ronan's son Tomás on Saturday, January 28, and Saint Matthew's was the parish church of the bride's family. Monty had crossed the River Lagan in his Renault and found himself on the Newtownards Road. So far so good, according to the directions he had been given; this was the road. But something wasn't right. They were looking for a Catholic church, yet all they were seeing were Union Jack flags and murals celebrating Loyalist paramilitaries. The murals called death down on the Irish Republican Army, and more than one bit of graffiti vowed "No pope, no surrender!"

To state the obvious, this was not a Catholic neighbourhood. And it was Belfast, so that was no minor distinction. Monty didn't even want to roll down his window and ask for directions. Especially since, as Brennan had told him, Saint Matthew's had been the scene of one of the earliest battles of the Troubles. In 1970, Loyalist gunmen attacked the church with petrol bombs, and the Provisional IRA took up rifles and defended it, and thereby wrote themselves into the modern history of the island. It was considered the first major action by the Provisionals, who had split from the Official IRA, partly because they believed the Officials had failed to take up arms to defend Catholic neighbourhoods from attack. With all that history in mind, Monty wasn't about to stop in front of a Loyalist mural and ask for directions to an RC church.

But Brennan had said the turnoff came soon after the bridge, so perhaps Monty had missed it. He got himself turned around. There. A large stone church with a steeple on the side. Hard to miss. He must have been distracted on his first attempt by the towering yellow shipyard cranes visible from the street. The cranes loomed over the Harland and Wolff yard where the *Titanic* had been built. The turn Monty wanted was Bryson Street. He drove in and parked. They were now in the Short Strand. The flags on display here were the green, white, and *gold* Irish tricolour, the murals Nationalist-Republican. As the family walked to the church, little Dominic pointed out the nearest IRA mural with great delight.

"Boys will be boys," his mother groused. The little fellow seemed particularly interested in the barrel of a rifle, which was pointed over the heads of observers of the mural. Monty assumed the gun was pointed at the Loyalist population that surrounded this tiny Nationalist enclave in east Belfast. As if to emphasize the point, there were several men dressed in bulky jackets, standing in the churchyard looking outwards and making no move to go inside for the ceremony. It was a mild sunny afternoon so nobody else had heavy clothes on, nothing like what the Collinses and MacNeils would have been wearing for a January wedding at home in Canada.

Brennan was just inside the door as they entered the church. He was in his Roman collar and was wearing a white alb over his clerical suit. Monty knew he was one of the soloists for the wedding Mass.

"Are those extra choirboys I see out there, Brennan?"

"Let's hope we won't have to hear from them."

"Especially any bursts of percussion, eh? Are there bodyguards at every Mass at Saint Matthew's?"

"It wouldn't surprise me, given that we papists are outnumbered in this area ten to one. They could push the lot of us off the bank and into the river if they were of a mind to. But of course the muscle have to be here on this occasion anyway, for Ronan."

Monty caught Maura's eye. In her mind surely, as in his, was the word *ceasefire* followed by a question mark.

They took their seats in the middle of the church. The place was packed and there was a lot of socializing going on across the pews, hands being shaken, laughter bursting out as wisecracks were exchanged. The bridal couple came in together, the bride in a pale pink suit, the groom in a navy suit, white shirt, and tie. Tomás Burke was a young groom, young for these times, at twenty-two. His bride, Aoife, was a few years older. Brennan had said she was a widow with two little children. Tomás was tall, over six feet, with black hair and dark eyes, like his cousin Brennan. Aoife was black-haired as well, petite with a pretty, friendly face. Glorious coloured light beamed down on the congregation from the ruby, sapphire, and emerald stained glass windows.

The only thing more heavenly than the light in the church was the music. It was not difficult to detect the hand of Father Burke in the selections. The choir sang a simple, exquisitely beautiful Gregorian Mass; a soprano gave a haunting performance of the ancient Irish love song "Eibhlín a Rún," and Brennan himself sang the Bach-Gounod "Ave Maria." Father Burke's musical talents had not only landed him a job as choirmaster in his adopted home of Halifax, Nova Scotia, they had put him on the short list for a one-year stint as a choirmaster in Rome, beginning in the fall. But this was not the time for Monty to badger him for news about that. There was enough to occupy everyone's attention here and now in Belfast.

The party afterwards was at the home of Ronan Burke on the other side of the city, in Andersonstown. There was no formal reception at or near the church. In Brennan's words, "We can't have everyone loosened by drink, wandering onto the Newtownards Road." *NEWT'n'ards.* Not an option. So the father of the groom had offered to host the party. Monty drove across the city and pulled up at the given address, a two-storey red-brick house at the end of a terrace. He parked behind a black car with two men inside, and he and his family got out. Normie took Dominic by the hand and skipped ahead. Monty saw her turn and peer into the black car and raise her free hand in a wave. Monty looked at the car and took note of the stone-faced occupants. They may have waved at Normie, but there was no wave for Monty.

The door of the house opened then, and their host emerged to welcome his guests. Ronan Burke was in his mid to late forties, in good shape. His hair was a mix of black and iron grey, his eyes blue but dark, almost a navy blue. He called out, "Welcome to Andytown!" and then stood aside as the guests piled in through his front door. He appeared to take no notice of the men in the car.

Monty introduced himself and his family, and Ronan shook hands with the adults and crouched down to greet the children. He whispered something in Normie's ear. Her eyes widened, and she responded, "Yeah! I mean, yes please." He pointed her in the direction of the back of the house, and she took off like a shot, pulling her little brother along behind her.

"The little ones are all out in the back garden. One of the young fellas is in from the country with a pony and cart. Not the usual way he gets around — he usually drives a sporty little car. But he knows the children love Rocket, the pony. Now what can I get for you? Gráinne has a lovely dinner spread out, but I'm the barman. What will you have?"

Monty spied bottles of beer and stout on a table, with glasses, and said he would help himself. He poured a Smithwick's for Maura and a Guinness for himself. Ronan was empty-handed, so Monty picked up another bottle and gave him an inquiring glance.

Ronan put up his hand and said, "None for this boyo. Come and meet Gráinne, my wife."

He led them to the mother of the groom, who was just coming in with a pot of what appeared to be stew. Mrs. Burke was tall and auburn-haired, with lively brown eyes. Ronan spoke in what Monty recognized as a strong Dublin accent, and he remembered Brennan saying Ronan had left Dublin for Belfast as a young man. Gráinne sounded like Belfast, born and bred.

Monty circulated through the party, making small talk with the people around him, then wandered out back where the kids were having a grand old time. Normie was chatting with Orla Farrell. She was a relation on Gráinne's side of the family, now living in Dublin, and Brennan had arranged for her to sign on as a daytime nanny for Normie and Dominic when Maura was lecturing at the law school. Normie was very fond of the young nanny. The fact that Orla had red hair and glasses was another plus. These were features that Normie was self-conscious about at times; turns out they were not so isolating after all. Not in this part of the world. Normie and Orla had their eyes on two little girls sitting in the pony cart with a couple of toddlers on their laps; the little ones were urging Rocket the pony to go, go, go! But the ambitiously named animal would have been hard put to move, there were so many children sitting on his back. The pony's head was turned towards Monty, a stoic expression on his face.

"Sure, the creature has the patience of a saint," said a woman standing at Monty's side.

Someone called from the house, saying it was time for family pictures. This was met by a groan from all the kids outside. Debate raged back and forth, and the children won out. "All right, we'll take them out there." That was Tomás, leading his bride by the hand.

"We'll do some more inside," Aoife said, "so try not to get too much pony shite on your good suit." She gave her new husband a playful swat and came outside. Soon the yard was filled with people in their wedding finery, and they posed beside and behind the kids and the pony, and the kids laughed uproariously and the photographer snapped away.

"I just happened to be in the neighbourhood." The strong Belfast voice sounded somehow familiar. Monty turned and saw a tall bearded man with glasses. It took him a moment to realize who he was. The Sinn Féin leader, Gerry Adams.

"Is that the real Gerry or an actor playing the part of him?" a man asked.

"I'm the real thing. You're allowed to hear my voice now."

"And a powerful voice it will be, after a rest for, what, six years? How long were you banned from the airways?"

"Six years, that's right. Lot of actors out of work now."

Banned? Actors? Monty was about to ask somebody for clarification, when Ronan came by and invited Adams out into the garden.

"Get out here, Gerry. But not too close to me. I may be running against you some day, and I'll want to deny I ever knew ye."

"Story of my life," Adams joked.

"Get down there by the rear end of that animal, Gerry," said an old fellow who must have been eighty if he was a day. "Two horses' arses for the price of one."

"Have I stumbled into the Shankill by mistake?" Adams asked. "I'll have to get my glasses checked. Here I was thinking I was amongst my own people."

The ribbing continued, and Adams took it in good humour.

The weather underwent an instantaneous change, which Monty already knew was typical. It started to rain, and the party moved inside. Adams and Ronan signalled to each other with their eyes and moved off to a corner of the room. They began an intense whispered conversation, and Ronan caught the eye of Tomás and another man and beckoned them over. The deliberations continued for a few minutes, then Adams moved through the crowd, shaking a few hands and exchanging pleasantries, and took his leave.

At that point there was more picture taking, more formal arrangements of the bride and groom flanked by their respective families. Monty took the opportunity to visit the bar table and replenish his supply of Guinness. He was joined by Gráinne Burke's sister, who introduced herself as Éilis Farrell.

"You're Orla's mother?"

"I am."

"Our two are crazy about her."

"Well, I can tell you she loves looking after wee Dominic. And of course Normie, when she comes home from school. Orla plans to become a teacher, and it's the very young children she wants to teach."

Someone in the centre of the room announced that it was time for a toast or two, if people weren't too bashful to speak up. It turned out that nobody was bashful or at a loss for words, as glasses were raised and toasts offered to the happy couple. When Ronan got up to speak, his glass appeared to contain nothing but water. A little girl and boy hugged him around the legs and looked up adoringly. He began speaking in Irish. Whatever he said caused tears to well up in his wife's eyes, and she turned and put her arms around him and held him tight. He kissed her tenderly and, when they released each other, he told the crowd, "Roughly translated, I raise my glass of pure water to the lovely bride, Aoife, and to my wife, Gráinne; my daughter, Aideen; my sons Tomás and Lorcan; my new little grandchildren, Catriona and Brian; and to every one of you here. The members of my family know I love and treasure them above all things. For them I would give up anything —" he looked ruefully at his glass, and there was affectionate laughter throughout the room "— *anything*. I would give my life for them. And I thank them from the bottom of my heart for their understanding over the years, their forgiveness, and their love." The wedding guests burst into spontaneous applause.

Monty had no idea what Ronan was referring to. Typically, Brennan had not said a word about whatever troubles the family might have suffered. No ships would be sunk on Brennan Burke's watch if loose lips were indeed a causative factor in shipping disasters.

But Éilis Farrell was not as reticent. And it was not a matter of gossip for Ronan's sister-in-law; she spoke with compassion of a family she knew and loved. "They've had their troubles. Ronan was . . . involved in the situation here in Belfast, so he had her worried half to death. He had two spells in Long Kesh, but he never gave up the struggle. A strong man for the fighting, but a weak man for the drink. His drinking got so bad Gráinne took the children and moved out. So he was without his family for nearly three years. But, God be good to him, he packed himself off to a monastery, went on the dry with the help of the monks, and gave it up for good. That was four years ago, and they have been together ever since. Now you couldn't find a closer family. Or a more loving husband and father."

There was music then, a couple of traditional ballads for the bridal couple, and then the tunes got a little rowdier, as fiddles, guitars, a mandolin, and a bodhran were brought out, and various people came forward to perform a number of rebel songs. Monty knew enough Burkean history to know that, when these people sang along with "The Boys of the Old Brigade" and "Rifles of the IRA," they were no mere barstool revolutionaries.

Chapter III

Monty

Monty spent Tuesday morning at the Canadian Earth Equipment factory on the outskirts of Belfast. It was an enormous manufacturing plant with yards full of tractors, harvesters, harrowers, and all manner of farm implements at various stages of production. He had a short tour inside, where he was given ear coverings to soften the scream of metal slicing through metal. His tour guide, accustomed to the procedure, knew just how loud he had to speak to make himself heard. Monty then sat in the office with one of the managers and discussed the lawsuit, the evidence, and the thousands of documents that would be delivered to him at Ellison Whiteside.

Back in his office in the afternoon, he got saddled with another file that had tedium written all over it; the client was a shop owner engaged in a dispute with the city over the assessment of his property. Monty couldn't bring himself to open the folder. He knew there were more exciting cases in the office; anything of a criminal nature would be of greater interest than property tax and minor injuries. The firm had only one criminal lawyer, and it wasn't Monty. It was Emmet Crowley, down at the far end of the corridor. Monty knew from office chatter that not everybody was enamoured of Crowley's clients. Some of his cases involved paramilitary activity, offences under the Prevention of Terrorism Acts. Now, something like *that* would keep Monty awake in the afternoons at his desk. And probably at night in his bed as well. He got up and headed for Crowley's door.

The office was jammed with file folders and boxes. Emmet Crowley sat hunched over his desk, running his fingers through his curly brown hair. He was a short, slim man in his late thirties, with black-framed glasses that were slightly askew on his face. He had the appearance of a man under pressure. He looked up, startled, and closed the file he was reading, when Monty showed up in his doorway.

"Sorry, Emmet, didn't mean to take you by surprise."

"No worries, Monty."

"I just wanted to say — well, as you probably know, I have a criminal practice over in Canada — so, if you need help on any of your files, I'd be *very* happy to pitch in."

"Sure, thank you, Monty. If anything comes up . . . I don't see anything right now, but you never know."

"Great then, Emmet, I'll let you get on with it."

"Right. Cheers."

Monty returned to his office empty-handed. He knew a polite rebuff when he heard it. An office stuffed with overflowing files, but nary an affidavit to be taken, a witness to be interviewed, a routine court appearance? Well, if Emmet Crowley wanted to keep his criminal practice to himself, that was his prerogative.

So it was back to the property rate assessment. He was trying to impose some order on the file when he received a call from the receptionist. "Monty, a Miss Flanagan is here to see you. She doesn't have an appointment but . . ."

Good. A diversion. "That's all right. Send her in."

A young girl, in her mid-teens, walked to his office door and hesitated at the threshold. Monty stood to greet her. She was wearing a light blue suit and white blouse with a piece of silver jewellery at the neck. Her skirt was unfashionably long, and Monty formed the impression that the suit might be that of an older woman, perhaps her mother, borrowed for the occasion. She carried a small grey handbag and he tried to remember what his own mother had called bags like that. Clasp bag? He couldn't remember. The girl's long brown hair was shining and held back with a silver band. She was pretty in an understated way.

"Come in and have a seat."

She entered the room and sat down, holding the bag on her lap. She took a deep breath and let it out. Monty had the impression that she was preparing herself for an ordeal.

He sat down again behind his desk and said, "I'm Monty Collins. And your name is?"

"Katie Flanagan."

The name meant nothing. He waited but she didn't say anything else.

"What can I do for you, Katie?"

"My uncle, well grand-uncle, he was here. About what happened on the bridge."

He had it now. The old fellow with his theories of a cover-up at the highest level. Monty hadn't thought of him again in the week that had passed since their encounter.

"Right," he said.

"He . . ." She dug in her bag, pulled out a piece of paper and placed it on the desk. She attempted to smooth out the creases. "He said to give you this."

Monty picked it up. An autopsy report on Eamon Flanagan, signed by a Doctor Forster, pathologist.

"The man who died, he was your father?"

"Aye."

Monty read through the report. Eamon Flanagan was forty-nine years old when he died on November 14, 1992. The cause of death was, contrary to Hughie Malone's version of events, not drowning but fractures to his head and neck. A scribbled note said the river was shallow and the riverbed rocky where he landed. His neck was broken in the fall, and there were fractures to the occipital and parietal bones of the skull. There were several posterior rib fractures. His left leg was broken as well. The blood alcohol reading was at the "impaired" level.

Monty picked up the phone and asked his secretary to come in.

"Would you make a copy of this for me, Laura?"

"Sure. Back in two ticks."

He turned to Katie. "I'm very sorry about your father, Katie. This shows he had a terrible fall."

"He didn't fall."

"Why do you say that? Please tell me, so I'll understand."

"My mother got money."

"Oh?"

"Money came in for a while, then it stopped. Mam doesn't know why. Doesn't even know where it was coming from."

"Your mother . . ." Monty began.

"She's been poorly since Da was killed. For days on end, she just sits around and can't do anything. Can't make meals or look after the little ones. She's trying to work at two jobs, cleaning jobs, but sometimes she can't bring herself to leave the house. So I do her jobs when I can."

"I'm sorry to hear that."

"So it's up to me now to try and take care of things. I'm the oldest."

Laura returned with the copy, and Monty set it aside. Katie looked around the office, at Monty's practising certificate and the bound volumes on the shelves. "I wanted to be a solicitor," she said, "or a barrister. My teachers at school recommended the classes I should take to give myself the best chance. They said I could do it. That's what I wanted most of all."

"Wanted?" Monty smiled at her. "You're hardly over the hill yet. How old are you?"

"Sixteen."

"You've got lots of time."

"No. I've finished with school."

"Surely not. If you want to study law, go for it."

She looked at him as if he was thick in the head. Which of course he was. "We don't have that kind of money. And I have responsibilities. I've a clatter of kids to look after, you know, when Mam can't do it. My wee sister and brothers. I have to get *them* through school, or they'll just sink into . . . I have to make sure there's a future for them."

There wasn't a trace of self-pity in her voice. Monty then asked himself why he thought that way. What was it about "self-pity" that earned so much rote condemnation? He remembered a sister of Maura's talking about an aunt who had just been given a bad diagnosis and had undergone disfiguring surgery: "She's feeling sorry for herself." Why the hell shouldn't she be? But he turned his attention back to young Katie Flanagan, who had just laid out the facts of life as they pertained to her family.

"Anyway, Mam explained to me that there's a mortgage on the house, which means we have to keep paying for it. And there's the electricity rates and all that. Da didn't have a life insurance policy. If we knew who threw or pushed my father off the bridge, we could have sued them and got money to make up for him not working. I mean, for him dying and the family being without his pay. But we don't know who it was, so we couldn't. And there was nothing the police could do because there was nobody to arrest; they think he just fell off. There's no kind of victim compensation or whatever it would be, because it's down in the records as an accident.

"Mam never worked after she had me, and then she had some kind of sickness. Then it went away and she was better, so she started having babies again. So she was home with us, not out at a job. After Da died, she went out doing the cleaning. Houses and a butcher's shop. The pay from those jobs is only a few quid a week; I know because I'm doing that work myself now. I don't mind the houses but the butcher's, with all that blood and the guts of animals . . . Ach, I shouldn't complain."

You have every right to complain, Monty said to himself. A lovely young girl like this, who wanted to be a lawyer, slopping out a butcher shop.

"Our youngest is six. They're all in school but I have to be there after school, or when they're sick or on holiday, in case Mam's not up to looking after them. I can't be in university and be running back and forth, and missing classes. Well, I can't afford uni anyway. And I can't sign on for a full-time job with good pay, because I have to be there for the little ones."

"Let's back up a bit. Tell me about this money."

"Mam didn't even have a bank account before my father died. But she opened one up after. And big amounts of money starting coming into her account, and I don't know where they came from."

"What makes you think it had something to do with the . . . with your father's death?"

"It only started after he died."

"But your mother didn't have an account at all before he died, so you might not have had any records . . ."

"If somebody had been giving her big whacks of money, we would have seen them. Or seen extra things she'd have bought for us or for herself. There wasn't money in amounts like that. And there were no big payments in Da's account. All his bank statements were in the drawer at home. Nothing like that in those records."

"You've spoken to relatives, people in your extended family? Maybe somebody was helping out?"

"We don't have many relations, but the ones we do don't have that kind of money. They're gutted that they can't help us that way, but they can't. And then the money, wherever it came from, stopped coming. The social security — the government, you know — gives us money to live on but just barely. We would be entitled to more benefits but . . ."

"But?"

"Well, my mam's embarrassed about this. But she shouldn't be! This is the modern world. Or at least it's supposed to be. You can only get full benefits as a widow with children if you're married. And after Da died she told me that she and him were never really married, even though she is always called Winnie Flanagan and she and Da were together for nearly eighteen years. She felt awful telling me. But I told her she shouldn't feel bad. We're a real family even if her wedding ring isn't the real thing! She told me she got married when she was really young, and the fella was a sleekit wee bastard and she walked out on him. But she never got a divorce, or maybe never got a church divorce. I didn't want to badger her with questions, the state she was in. So, anyway, the benefits we get don't go anywhere near covering our house payments. The bank keeps giving us more time, but they'll have to put us out. Where will we go, the six of us?"

"I'm so sorry to hear it, Katie." And he was. With her mother laid low by grief and depression, Katie Flanagan had taken on the role of a single parent at the age of sixteen. If there was any way he could help, he would, but he had next to no hope that her claim for damages would see the light of day. "The police were involved?" he asked. "I mean, it was a fall but a sudden death —"

"They're useless, the peelers. Said there was nothing they could do."

"Who did they say that to?"

"My mam when it happened."

"What else did they say?"

"Just that they were sorry, but there's no evidence of anyone else being involved. All the information they have is my father lying dead under the bridge. Mam was gutted. Not only did they say they couldn't help, they put it in Mam's head that Da was on a rip that night, coming home from O'Grady's bar, and he was legless with drink and that's why he fell off. They said it in a polite way. Sympathetic, like. But . . ."

Monty thought back to what Hughie Malone had said. "Mr. Malone is your grand-uncle?"

"Aye, an uncle to my mother."

"He said there was a shooting the same night."

"Right. The police haven't solved that either."

"What can you tell me about that?"

"An IRA man was shot and killed."

"I see."

"Up the road from the bridge where Da got killed. The police found Da's body when they were investigating the murder."

Monty was not about to ask whether her father had been involved in the IRA. That was one of many questions you simply did not ask in Belfast. All he said was "And that murder was never solved."

"The UDA did it." That was a Loyalist paramilitary group, Monty knew.

"You know that?"

"It would have been them." When he didn't respond she said, as if making a comment on the frequency of rain showers in her country, "They're forever killing Catholics. And fellas in the 'RA."

Monty took Katie Flanagan's phone number before she left and told her he would look into her claim. He knew there was nothing he could do, whether he was in Belfast for five months or five years. If the police had found no indication of anyone else on the bridge that night, Monty wasn't going to find a smoking gun, speaking figuratively; he wasn't going to discover a file folder sitting on a shelf somewhere with all the details of Eamon Flanagan's demise, allowing Monty to launch a suit, win a judgment for damages from the hitherto unknown but now remorseful defendant, and see Mr. Flanagan's family live happily and prosperously ever after.

Chapter IV

Father Brennan Burke

Brennan began a new ministry on Wednesday, February 1. His new parish was on the Crumlin Road in Ardoyne, north Belfast. Holy Cross. He liked the big old stone church with its twin spires, and he found the other priests congenial. The job had an extra perk he had not anticipated: he was asked to assist in the teaching of music at Holy Cross Girls' School. Good to keep his hand in, in case he managed to snag the choir director job in Rome. But even without that prospect on the horizon, he loved doing music with children. Imprinting the great traditional music on their souls early in life, so it would be a part of them forever. He remembered hearing a story about music legend Frank Zappa: Zappa said he sometimes found himself, during a guitar solo, incorporating into it the medieval Kyrie that had been sung at his confirmation.

After spending the morning at Holy Cross, Brennan headed back to Andersonstown. He decided to cater lunch for his hosts, which he did by putting in an order at the counter of a local chipper and lugging the bags home on the bus. Ronan got home from work shortly after Brennan, and they all dug in to some very greasy, very tasty fish and chips. When they had finished, Gráinne asked Father Burke whether he had ever been to the Milltown Cemetery.

"I've been in there but never long enough to make the rounds."

"Well, I'd like to go say a prayer and lay flowers on the grave of a young girl who died fifteen years ago this week. She was the youngest daughter of a family I grew up with."

Brennan gathered up the wrappings of their meal and put them in the bin. "I'll go with you to the cemetery, if that would be all right."

"I'd like that, Brennan."

"We'll all go," said Ronan, and they made ready to depart.

Gráinne went into a back room and returned with a bouquet of white lilies. Brennan followed her out of the house and to a black car that was parked outside. She motioned to the back seat with her hand and Brennan stepped back to allow her to enter first. There was one man at the wheel and another in the front passenger seat. The driver had a shaved head, the other cropped dark brown hair; both looked fit and alert. Gráinne greeted them, though not by name, and they gave her a friendly nod. The passenger opened his door, got out, and started to walk to the house. Brennan saw Ronan emerge and look around him. He waved the security man off, and the man returned to the front seat. Ronan got into the back with his wife and cousin and spoke to the men in Irish, so fast Brennan couldn't catch it all. The men laughed, and the driver turned the key and started the car.

They drove along the Andersonstown Road. When they got to the Falls Road, the driver pulled over and parked. The front passenger got out and scanned the area. Nothing was amiss apparently, and they all disembarked, the bodyguards sticking close to their charges. They both turned at once to the sound of a motor on the road. A small, battered-looking brown hatchback had stopped behind the black car. When one of Ronan's men put his hand in his right pocket and started towards the car, it pulled out and sped away down the Glen Road. Brennan paid it no more mind. A cold, drizzling rain began to fall, but he, Gráinne, and Ronan ignored it and walked to the big stone archway with a cross on top, which marked the entrance to the cemetery.

The graveyard is one of the most potent symbols of nationalism in the country, a Catholic burial ground that holds the graves of Republicans who died in the struggle to alter the course of Irish history. Brennan recognized many of the names on the gravestones, including Bobby Sands, Kieran Doherty, and the eight other H Block hunger strikers. Irish tricolours and Republican symbols marked out the landscape. The grave marker for Deirdre Ryan showed that she was eighteen when she died in 1980, shortly after being released from the Armagh prison. One look at Gráinne's face as she tenderly laid a bouquet beside the granite marker made it clear that she was still grieving for Deirdre after all these years. Ronan whispered to Brennan, "She was imprisoned for Republican activities and never recovered from the strip searches and the beatings she received at the hands of the screws. Male screws." No one could have missed the raw anger in his voice.

"The fools, the fools, the fools," Brennan said softly.

"They have left us our Fenian dead." Ronan completed the quotation from Pádraig Pearse. "While Ireland holds these graves, Ireland unfree shall never be at peace."

It made Brennan wonder all over again at the compromises his cousin had to make, with others and himself, in order to abandon the "physical force tradition" and support the peace process.

Brennan gazed down at the grave. He made the sign of the cross and quietly recited prayers in Latin and in Irish for Deirdre Ryan.

After they had paid their respects, they headed out towards the Falls Road. The wind had picked up, driving the rain into their faces. Any time he had glanced at Ronan's bodyguards during the cemetery visit, Brennan noticed that one pair of light grey eyes and one pair of green were in constant motion as the two men scanned their surroundings. Now, as the group approached the street, one of the men moved to the front of the small procession and the other walked behind.

Brennan heard a shout before he was able to focus on its source. "Save your prayers, you fuckin' Taigs; all them Fenian scum are rotting in hell!" The brown hatchback had returned to the scene; it must have been lurking on a side street. Men screamed from the open windows of the car, their faces contorted with hate.

Ronan's two minders had both reached into their jackets and moved in front of the Burkes, but Ronan said, "They're all noise and no light." And sure enough, after spewing some more verbal abuse, they peeled away and drove out of sight.

"There's no sacred ground for some," Brennan muttered.

"We've seen worse on this holy ground," Ronan said. "I was here in '88."

Brennan knew all about '88. Thousands, including the Sinn Féin leadership, were on hand for an IRA funeral, when a lone gunman appeared and starting shooting and lobbing grenades at the mourners.

"I was limping around, useless," Ronan said, "while some of our young lads went after the killer. Unarmed our boys were, but that didn't stop them. They kept after him, and him armed with a gun and grenades. Three were killed and more than sixty wounded."

"Including this fella himself," said Gráinne. "He says he was useless, but that's because his leg was torn open by shrapnel!"

A despicable attack upon mourners at a funeral, no question. Brennan was not about to bring up the fact that the three who were buried that day, two men and a woman, had been, apparently, on their way to cause an explosion at the changing of the guard of a British Army regiment in Gibraltar when they were killed. Whatever they had been up to, they were unarmed when they were shot down on the street by members of the British Special Air Services, the SAS. Whatever their intended crimes, the remedy would have been arrest and trial, not summary execution. The entire history of these Troubles — this *war* — was a cycle of action and reaction, attack and revenge, and, if there was such a term, counter-revenge. Brennan kept his thoughts to himself.

"The Milltown killer was sentenced to something like seven hundred years for those and other murders," Ronan said.

"I suspect somebody else will come forward to fill in for him while he's away serving those centuries in the lockup."

"No doubt, Brennan. We have to get past all this. Our talks will have to lead to a future without all this fucking violence and intimidation."

On the way back to Andytown in the car, Brennan asked his cousin about the peace process.

"What they're talking about . . ."

"Don't be modest now, Ronan," his wife said and then to Brennan, "He is included in the 'they.' He's been in on the talks, behind the scenes."

They continued the conversation as they walked into the house.

"You can be sure I'm only a minor player when you consider that the talks involve us here in the North and the governments in Dublin and London. But, yes, I've had a part in it. They're hoping to publish something soon. The negotiations are paying lip service to full respect for, and protection of, the rights and identities of both traditions in Ireland. The Reverend Ian Paisley has condemned it as a 'one-way street to Dublin.' Another Unionist leader said it amounts to an eviction notice for Ulster to leave the United Kingdom. That tells me there really is something in it for our side!"

"That does speak well of the project, I'd have to say."

"It does, *go deimhin*." Ronan looked at Brennan. "What could go wrong?"

"What could go right?" The voice of Ronan's son Lorcan came to them from the dining room. Lorcan was dark like his brother Tomás, but short and wiry while Tom was tall and muscular. Brennan went in to greet him and was greeted in turn. There was another fellow with him, a few years older than Lorcan. He had short dark hair neatly combed to the side, almost a little boy's haircut, but there was nothing boyish about the pumped-up muscles or the cold grey eyes that examined Brennan before greetings were exchanged. He was introduced simply as Carrick. He stood, gave Brennan a "Hi ye" and a curt nod, then sat down again and turned his attention to a batch of newspapers on the table.

Brennan had made plans to attend a special Mass for peace later that afternoon at the Clonard Monastery, so he went up to his room and changed into a dry set of clerical clothing. While he was bent over tying the laces of his priestly black brogues, he heard raised voices from below. And when he got downstairs and started into the dining room, he walked into a firestorm. Father and son were both on their feet, glaring at one another.

"Would you catch yerself on, Da?" Lorcan was nearly shouting. "If we go down your road, partition will never end, and all our men, all our volunteers who died to unite this country, died for absolutely nothing. They didn't die for another fucking assembly at Stormont. They didn't die for the Brits and their Loyalist killing squads to keep running things in the Six Counties. They died for full independence, Brits out, and a united thirty-two county republic! Nothing less than that. And you, of all people. You've been an IRA man all your adult life. You, of all people, to be giving us up!"

Ronan kept his voice down, but there was no mistaking the iron in his tone. "I'm not saying for one minute that I'd be satisfied with less than an independent republic! The institutions they're talking about now, we'll work within them, subvert them to our own ends. We *will* have a united Ireland someday."

"A stepping stone to a full republic. Sounds as if Michael Collins has returned to life and is standing in this very room."

"Well, he was proved right, wasn't he? The Free State eventually got rid of every vestige of British rule. The Commonwealth, the oath, all done away with. An Irish Republic to the south of us."

Brennan stood on the sidelines and didn't say a word.

"I can't believe I'm hearing that out of your mouth," Lorcan continued. "They're to the *south* of *us* because the border is still here. And if you think the Unionists are going to go along peacefully with an Irish Republic, you must be back on the drink."

"Well, we can't force them the way things are now, because they're in the majority. But over time —"

"When you say they are a majority, you're recognizing the border."

"I'm recognizing reality."

"They are a minority on this island. The only reason they have a majority in the North is because the border was drawn for that very reason, drawn to include heavily Protestant-Unionist areas, so they would outnumber our people and be able to outvote us into eternity. Which is exactly what will happen."

Carrick stayed silent at the table, but his red face and clenched fists spoke volumes.

"And so," Ronan said, "the solution is to keep trying to shoot them and bomb them into submission."

"They have tried all through history to shoot us and burn us out of our homes. Finally we decided not to submit anymore. You were there when the Provisionals took up arms. You knew then it was the only way to defend our communities. Force is the only language the Brits understand. They don't respond to anything else."

"They responded to Gandhi. Nonviolent resistance got them out of India."

"Jesus Christ, what are you saying now? You're doing my head in! You've seen the Brits' response to nonviolent protest in this country: Bloody Sunday. Twenty-seven unarmed protesters were shot. Fourteen of them died. And the soldiers who did that weren't punished, were they? Some of them were promoted. Before the year was out, one of them was decorated by the Queen. Remember, Da?"

"Don't you dare lecture me about Bloody Sunday, as if I could ever, ever forget such an atrocity against our people!"

"Fine, then." Lorcan brushed past his father, and his companion did the same. They both headed for the door. Lorcan turned back and said, "Don't you be lecturing me about Gandhi. Gandhi got thrown into prison. He got partition. Sound familiar to you?"

"And," said Carrick, looking directly into Ronan's eyes, "he came to a bad end, didn't he."

Ronan Burke, the guerrilla warrior, the former second in command of the Belfast Brigade of the Provisional IRA, the reformed drunk and rededicated family man, was without words. White-faced, stricken. Brennan felt sick. Here it was all over again, father against son, brother against brother. Just like the Irish Civil War more than seventy years before.

There had been no need to spell it out. Gandhi had been assassinated.

Chapter V

Monty

Monty spent Thursday afternoon negotiating a settlement with an opposing solicitor in the case of a client who had slipped in a puddle of spilled dish detergent in MacAllister's, a Belfast grocery store, and sustained a bruised tailbone and a broken string of beads. When it was all over, Monty walked away with the sum of £1,200 for his client. The hourly rates normally charged by himself and the defence lawyer, calculated over the time it took to settle the claim, far exceeded the amount of the payout. He tried not to be snooty about it, even in his own mind. But he wouldn't even get a good story out of it. If the woman had, say, broken her rosary beads, splaying fifty-three Hail Marys and a few Glory Bes all over the floor of MacAllister's Protestant grocery shop, he might have made a barroom tale out of that. But no, it was just costume jewellery, pink plastic beads. Even the fact that what she slipped in was Fairy Liquid, as the well-known brand of washing-up detergent was called, wouldn't get him a pint of warm beer over here.

He was waiting for a new load of documents from Canadian Earth but he didn't expect them for a couple of days. So, with nothing better to do, literally, Monty got out the thin file he had opened on the Flanagan case. He had researched the law after Katie's visit and found that she was right: her mother was not entitled to a widowed mother's allowance because she was never actually married to Eamon. Now Monty looked at the photocopy of the autopsy report. There was nobody to even try to claim damages from on this one, but he perused the file. He hated that word beloved of lawyers, *perused*; did anyone else ever use the word? He doubted it. Anyway, Flanagan. Found dead in a river bank with multiple fractures. Occipital and parietal bones of the skull. Back of the head. The rib fractures were in the back, too. Posterior. So he fell backwards. Unlikely to have gone that way if he jumped. Not impossible of course. Who knows how the mind works in those last desperate seconds of a suicide? Left tibial fracture. That's the front bone of the lower leg. So, one fracture in the front, all the rest in the back. Is that something that would happen if he fell and tumbled about on the rocks? If it happened that way, why were there no other injuries to his face or the front of his body? Taking the point of view of the Flanagan family, that something had happened to Eamon before he went off that bridge, what would that have been? If someone attacked him, would the attacker go for his lower leg? Not likely. But there was another possibility. Monty had seen fractures like this in his personal injury practice at home. More than one pedestrian had been hit by a car and suffered a fracture to the tibia as a result. The bumper of a small car would hit an average size or tall man in the front of the leg below the kneecap. Had Eamon Flanagan been the victim of a hit and run that propelled him off the bridge to the riverbed below?

Monty was loath to get Katie Flanagan's hopes up, but he could not sit and do nothing if there was even a remote possibility of solving the question of her father's death. He picked up the phone and called her.

"Hello." Her voice had the hollowness of someone having a very bad day. He could hear a child crying in the background. There was a loud crash, and the crying turned to a wail.

"Hi, Katie. Monty Collins here. I can call back if this is a bad time."

"No, no, you're grand." Raised hopes were audible in her voice. "Did you find something?"

He had to "manage expectations" as the workplace expression went. The chances of the family seeing any money out of this were so remote as to be non-existent. "Not really, but I think it would be a good idea for me to see the area where your father died. Could you take me out there?"

"Em, well, I don't have a car, but . . ."

"No, no, I didn't mean . . . I have a car here. I could pick you up whenever you can get free."

"Now's not good. School's finished for the day, and I'm here with my sister and brothers, and Mam is in bed, so there's no one else . . ." Monty heard a prolonged wet cough in the background then. "Don't be spewin' that in her face, Timmy! Mr. Collins? Wait, I see Mrs. Hamill across the street. She must be off work today. She sometimes comes in when Mam's not able. I can ask her to come in. So you can collect me whenever you like."

She gave him the address and said it was in the Musgrave Park area of the city. She provided excellent directions, so he left the office and got himself on the A12, then the M1 motorway, and drove to the home of the Flanagan family in the suburbs south of the city. The family lived on Clarkson Terrace in a semi-detached house of light-brown bricks with a tiled roof. The dark-brown door and window frames were in need of paint, but it was a nice-looking street. Monty knocked on the door and heard a squeal and the patter of little feet approaching. When the door opened, he looked down to see three little kids: a blond boy of six or seven, with what looked like porridge all over his face and T-shirt, a girl of eight or nine, and another boy a year or so older. The older two were wearing school uniforms, bottle-green sweaters with the school crest, shirts and green ties on both, a grey skirt on the girl and grey trousers on the boy. Three pairs of big sky-blue eyes gazed up at Monty.

"Let the man inside!" Katie admonished them, shooing them away from the entrance.

"Who do we have here?" Monty asked. "My name is Monty."

"I'm Timmy!" the smallest boy shouted. "I'm having my birthday Saturday week! I'm going to be seven! I'm getting a cake and a bag of oranges!"

The two older kids looked shy and gave their names as Clare and Dermot.

"Go and change out of your uniforms now, so we can keep them clean, and not have this fella —" she pointed to Timmy "— spewing and spilling stuff all over them and me having to wash them again. The state of you!" she said to Timmy. The older two left and pounded up the stairs. Then Katie said, "Where's Darren?"

"He's got the football today," Dermot called down.

"All right. I'm going to ask Mrs. Hamill to come and keep watch over youse till Mam gets up. And I'm going out for a bit of fresh air."

Timmy looked pleased. "Tell her to bring us some biscuits!"

"I'll tell her no such thing. If she brings some biscuits, fine. If not, they're not to be mentioned. Right?"

"But she might forget!"

"That's a chance you'll have to take."

"Aww!"

"Why don't you go colour a picture of the kind of cake you'll be wanting next week."

"Yeah!" He made a flying leap towards the stairs, missed his landing, and fell, but got up and ascended the steps. "Do we have a brown crayon? I don't want pink like Clare's!"

Katie rolled her eyes in Monty's direction and said, "If you'll wait here a wee minute, I'll go across and fetch yer one across the street. Excuse the state of the place."

"The place is just fine, Katie."

And it was. The furniture was old and nicked, the green painted walls scuffed, and the carpet worn bare in spots, but the room was clean and well organized. There were a couple of tin whistles on the coffee table and a mandolin in the corner, battered but fully stringed. A built-in bookshelf contained books for all ages, including classics and art books and one about the law. Monty picked it up. *Hear the Other Side*, the autobiography of Dame Elizabeth Lane, who, Monty read, was the first woman appointed a judge of the British High Court. He was interested to see that she had attended McGill University in Montreal. The book was well thumbed. He remembered Katie saying she had wanted to become a solicitor, her ambition already relegated to the dust bin.

A few minutes after she left, Katie was back, with a woman of fifty or so carrying a large tin. Monty hoped it was full of biscuits.

"All right. We can go."

"God go with you," the woman said.

"Oh, Mr. Collins, this is Mrs. Hamill."

Monty said hello.

"How well do you know the place out there, Katie?" Mrs. Hamill asked.

"I'm not sure, but . . ."

"Why don't you ring Hughie and have him go with you?" the older woman suggested.

"Well . . ."

"Go on now and ring him. Or, what time is it?"

"It's half four. That means he's . . ." Katie began.

"At McCully's," Mrs. Hamill concluded. "Still, you're better off with Hughie to help you find the place if you've never been there, Katie."

"It'll be no trouble to stop by McCully's and pick up Mr. Malone," Monty assured them, "as long as you can provide directions to the . . . bar?"

"It's up on North Queen Street," Katie said. "I'll know it when I see it."

"That's good enough for me. Let's motor."

He followed Katie out of the house. When they got into his car, she said, "Oh, I have this for you. It's from Mam." She pulled a sheet of paper out of her handbag and passed it to him. It was a hand-written letter addressed to Mr. Monty Collins and signed by Winnifred (Winnie) Flanagan, thanking him for assisting the family with their difficulties and assuring him that she would provide any information he required. Well, that was good to know. He had the mother's authorization to represent the family. He had, as well, one more person to disappoint when it all came to naught.

"She said, Mam did, that we'll pay your fees on time. You don't have to worry about that."

Monty knew that a lawyer's fees were far beyond the capacity of this family, especially if, as expected, the claim went nowhere. And, unlike the situation back home in Nova Scotia, there were no contingency fees here; a solicitor couldn't arrange to take thirty percent of the proceeds as payment for his or her services. "You tell your mother this will be what we call pro bono. There are no fees when it's pro bono."

"Oh, we couldn't . . ."

"The law has spoken, young lady." He turned and smiled at her.

She laughed, a little embarrassed, and nodded her head.

He started out for the city centre. It was getting dark, and Katie directed him into a couple of wrong turns, but Monty assured her he didn't mind. "Sometimes that's the best way to get familiar with a new place."

"You'll be able to qualify as a tour guide if you keep travelling with me," she said. "I know I've seen the bar."

"We can pull over and ask somebody."

"Sure, if I don't see it soon."

"We'll ask that guy right there." Monty had looked over the pedestrians on North Queen Street and adjudged one of them in particular, a fellow with a red nose and an unsteady gait, to be a man well acquainted with establishments serving strong drink.

He stopped beside the man, and Katie rolled down her window and called out, "Excuse me, sir, could you tell me where McCully's bar is?"

"You're headed straight for it. Just keep going past McGurk's, and it'll be on your left."

"Thank you!"

After Monty had gone a short distance, Katie pointed to a building with a purplish-red and white painted exterior. "That's McGurk's," she said. "Got bombed. Fifteen people died."

"When was that?"

"Years ago. Long before I was born. The peelers and the Brits told everyone it was a Republican own-goal, but it wasn't."

"You mean they claimed Republicans did it but . . ."

"Yeah. They put out the story that it was the 'RA. That it was IRA fellas in the pub, that they set a bomb and killed their own people. But it was Loyalists, and the Brits and the police knew it all along and lied about it."

This was the sort of knowledge that formed the life of a young person growing up in Belfast.

"There it is! McCully's." Katie directed his attention to a tiny, dark little bar up the street a ways on the other side. It sported a Guinness sign and a tattered tricolour flag above the door.

"Let's see if we can find a parking spot."

"No, you just stop out here. I'll go in and get him."

She hopped out and went into the bar. Two minutes later she reappeared with Hughie Malone, who was wiping his mouth with the back of his hand. "You get in the front, Hughie. You'll be able to show him how to get there."

"'Bout ye, Mr. Collins?"

"Fine and dandy, Mr. Malone. Yourself?"

"I'm stickin' out, thank you. Now you'll be wanting to turn around. We'll go through the Falls." He directed Monty southward and then west. They drove into Divis Street, which became the Falls Road. A Republican heartland in west Belfast, with the murals to prove it.

"I don't imagine many Loyalists venture into this area," Monty said.

"We've a fence up to discourage them. And to discourage our own lads from venturing into Loyalist territory. We'll take a detour for a minute. Turn right at the next corner."

Monty followed Malone's directions until they were on Bombay Street. "There's one of our 'peace' lines. We've dozens of them all over the city. In Derry and other places, too. Comical name for it, wouldn't you say?" It was a massive wall of concrete, with a steel mesh fence along the top and a layer of metal in the middle. "It's supposed to keep the Taigs from getting at the Prods, and the Prods from getting at the Taigs. Catholics and Protestants. But you'll also see a kind of back porch on the houses on this side of the street. Get out and have a gander over there. You'll see it's not a porch where you'd want to sit out on a fine, warm evening." Monty got out of the car and went to take a look. The porch was in fact a cage enclosing the rear of the house. When Monty was behind the wheel again, Malone stated the obvious: "They're to protect the houses from whatever gets lobbed over the wall from the Shankill side."

Monty drove back to the Falls Road, and Malone continued his reporting from the war zone. "See the road to the right, Whiterock Road. That's where the Kelly's bar bombing was. Brits announced it was the 'RA that set the bomb, but the truth came out later. It was Loyalists. My brother and his pals were in there having a jar. Got out just in time. Well, in time for the UVF to fire on the survivors being pulled out. But my fellas managed to get away. Three others eventually died, and more than sixty were injured."

Monty wondered what on earth it would be like to bring up a family here, with these dreadful stories on everyone's lips. He returned to the conversation with Hughie Malone, who was cataloguing more of the atrocities visited upon the residents of the Falls.

"And if we'd taken another route," he said to Hughie, "we'd be seeing Loyalist places the IRA had blown up, I assume."

"No denying it," Hughie replied. "There does be guilt on all sides here. We'll come back via the Shankill. That's where the Prods are, so you'll see where the 'RA attacked bars and other establishments there. We could have gone out on the motorway but I'm taking you on the scenic route now."

"The Via Dolorosa, you mean."

"Aye, plenty of sorrows to go round in this place. Keep to the left here, Mr. Collins."

"Monty."

"Left here, Monty. We're going to take the Andersonstown Road and then we'll go a long way on the Stewartstown Road . . ." Hughie continued to give directions until they were out even beyond suburbia. After many twists and turns, Monty was not sure he would have any idea how to get back on the main routes. They finally turned into a narrow road, and Hughie announced, "This is it, the Ammon Road."

"What brought Mr. Flanagan way out here?" This might be a delicate question but one relevant to the events of November 14, 1992.

"Eamon grew up in this area, moved into the city for work when he left school. He still knows . . . he still knew some of the fellas he grew up with, and he'd come out here once in a while to have a pint with them. There's the place there, O'Grady's. We know he was in O'Grady's the night he was killed. We'll go in."

On a fact-finding mission or to wet the throat of their tour guide? Either way, it couldn't hurt. "Sure," Monty said and pulled in beside the old, white thatched-roof cottage that was now O'Grady's bar. There was only one other vehicle, a passenger van with a good few years on it. But when they went inside, there were a dozen or so drinkers, all men, sitting or standing at the bar. They all eyed the newcomers, and a few of the eyes rested on young Katie Flanagan, but none of the stares were unfriendly. Or creepy. The barman and a couple of the regulars recognized Hughie Malone and greeted him. There was nobody at the tables, so Monty headed for the one in the front window. When Hughie and Katie were seated, Monty offered to get the drinks. Katie asked for a mineral; she wasn't particular about what kind, so he got her a sparkling lemon and lime. Hughie requested a Guinness and a shot of Bushmills. "Crossing the sectarian boundary with that," he said, pointing to the Bushmills bottle, and two fellows at the bar had a chuckle. Monty took a Guinness for himself as well.

When they all had their glasses in front of them, and all had taken their first sips, Monty asked, "Do these people live nearby? There's only one car out there."

"Well, some live nearby and others not so near, but O'Grady's young fella gives them a spin home at closing time. You could say their policy is *slán abhaile*. Safe home."

"Very good. Now, where are we in relation to the bridge where Mr. Flanagan . . . had his accident?"

"Look out the window there and to your left. About a half a mile down that way is the bridge."

"So Mr. Flanagan would have been here in the bar and then presumably he departed on foot and walked to the bridge. Where would he have been going at that time of night?"

"Most likely heading to Assumpta's place to stop for the night."

"Who is that?"

"She's his aunt. Not my side of the family, not a Malone. Flanagan side."

Monty turned to Katie. "Would your dad do that once in a while, stay out overnight? Or was this unusual for him?"

"He did it sometimes. Not very often. But Mam would tell us he was at Auntie Assumpta's."

After spending a good part of the evening here in O'Grady's, Monty imagined. "How would he get out here, without a car of his own?"

"It was someone from his work, as far as I remember," Katie replied. "A man who lived out here somewhere and went back and forth by car. Sometimes Da would get a lift with him."

"Come here to me," Hughie said to the elderly barman. "This man is looking into Eamon Flanagan's death. And this is Eamon's wee girl, Katie."

"Oh, aye?" The barman gave Katie a nod and a look of sympathy.

"Could you tell us of any man who was here that night? It was the night of the shooting up the road."

"I was right here behind the bar and I didn't see or hear anything of note. Too busy with my bottles and taps."

There was some murmuring around the bar. Then one man in his thirties spoke up. "I was here myself." He twisted around to address an older fellow a few barstools away. "You remember it, Fergus."

"I do."

"We were both here, and we didn't — well, speaking for myself — I didn't hear a thing. No sound from the bridge down there." He pointed in the general direction. "And I didn't hear any shooting from up there." The other direction. "It'd be too far away, for the sound to carry. You, Fergus?"

Fergus just shrugged and got busy with his pint.

Katie looked downhearted, and Hughie restless. They finished their drinks, said thank you to the barman and the others for trying to help, and made to leave the bar. Monty was the last out and he closed the door. He heard it open behind him and a man say, "Bloody fags. I've got to give them up. They'll have me bankrupted."

Monty turned and saw that it was the older man, Fergus. He had taken a cigarette out of its pack and was heading outside for a smoke. "Hold up there," he said, so low that Monty could barely hear him. Katie and Hughie kept walking, but Monty hung back. The man lit up his cigarette, then spoke again. "There was a young lad. Him and his lady friend, out on a walk that night and looking for a bit of privacy. I didn't hear about this till, I don't know, a few months ago. The lad came of age, old enough for the drink, and in he came to O'Grady's. Had a few pints and wasn't accustomed to it. Made him talkative, I suppose. I heard him whispering to a pal of his, saying he'd been in some kind of confrontation with a fellow in a car. It was 'the night they shot Fritzy.' Lad's first name was Vincent. That's all I know."

And with that he walked away, to stand in front of the windows of O'Grady's and enjoy his smoke and be seen not talking to anyone who had been asking questions.

Monty met Katie and Hughie at the car, and they all got in. Monty recounted the story Fergus had told. Katie made no reply, but Hughie took up the slack. "A confrontation, a fella in a car, the night Fritzy O'Dwyer had the head blown off of him."

"Who's O'Dwyer?"

"Nobody now. He was a Provo. Lived in the Short Strand, when he wasn't living on the outskirts of Lisburn, if you know what I mean."

"That's where the prison is."

"Aye, the Kesh. Now, the lad who told the story in O'Grady's was named Vincent. Who would that be now?"

"Well, chances are he's local if he drinks at O'Grady's and was out with his girlfriend in this area. Would your Auntie Assumpta know, I'm wondering?" Monty asked Katie.

"She's lived here her entire life. She probably knows everybody."

"Any chance she would welcome an impromptu visit?"

"Sure, she loves company, only . . ."

"Only what, Katie?" Monty asked.

"I haven't been out to see her in months, maybe a year. And now I just turn up on her doorstep."

"How would you have got out here? She probably knows you don't have a limousine at your service."

"She'll be thinking I do, when she sees me pull up in a car."

"That's what you'll tell her. 'Hello, Auntie. I was touring the countryside and I thought I'd pop in for a cup of tea. Oh, don't mind old Monty here. He's only my driver, don't you know.'"

"Ha, ha. She'll not likely fall for that. See along there, a road to the left? Turn up there, and it's not long before you'll see the old farm."

A minute or two after making the turn, Monty saw a white house with a black slate roof and smoke coming out of the chimney.

"Would you look at thon place now," said Hughie. "It's not a patch on what it was."

There were a number of farm buildings, some ancient and made of crumbling stone. Like the green fields all over Ireland, these fields were squared off by stone walls. But the walls, like the buildings, were in need of repair. A black-and-white sheepdog came bounding towards the car.

"There's Lulu!" The instant Monty came to a halt in front of the house, Katie was out of the car and hugging the animal. The dog wagged her tail and barked excitedly. It was obvious they were old pals.

Monty stood in the darkness and breathed in the cool February air, pungent with the distinctive aroma of a turf fire. He didn't see any animals other than Lulu and a few birds pecking at the ground.

The front door opened, and a tall woman with shoulder-length white hair emerged and called out to her visitors. "Katie Flanagan, *a leanbh mo chroí*, how lovely to see you! Come in, come in." She gave Katie a kiss and a hug, then spotted Malone. "Hughie Malone! Out on good behaviour, is it? Or on compassionate grounds?"

"Sure, they declared me harmless. I took umbrage at that! But nobody was interested; they let me go and turned to more urgent matters."

Just a bit of banter or a history with the criminal justice system?

With Lulu at her heels, Katie started in to the house, then turned to Monty and said, "This is Mr. Collins. Monty. I'll explain him when we're inside."

"No need, *a stór*, no need. Come in, all of you. How's your mother?"

"Ah, she's not very well," Katie replied. Hughie gave Monty a look that suggested he held a second opinion about the diagnosis.

Assumpta brought them into a sitting room where she had obviously been reading by the fire; a book and a pair of glasses sat on the arm of a big leather chair. "Pull up those chairs, and I'll wet the tea."

"Let me help you, Auntie Assumpta." Katie got up and followed the older woman into the kitchen.

"Where d'you get your turf, Assumpta?" Hughie called out.

"Now you know better than to ask me that, Hughie!"

"Right, right. I withdraw the question."

"Good man."

"How much do you burn in the run of a week?"

"The pensioner's dilemma, Hughie. I have to get by on a few quid a week but, because I'm not out of the house working, I need the fire to keep me warm all day. But I'm well fixed for fuel. That pile on the left there will do me for two days." There were bricks of turf, roughly cut from the land, stacked up beside the fireplace.

"Have you enough for the rest of the winter?"

Assumpta poked her head around the corner and said, "Did you see the turf shed at the end of the drive? It's full to the rafters. That ought to do me, with a bit left for next year, God willing."

"Things are crumbling away out there, Assumpta. You need a man about the house."

"Are you offering up yourself to me, Hugh?"

"Ah now, don't be putting notions into an oul fella's head."

"You're incorrigible, Hughie Malone."

"That's what my teachers all said in school."

"If only they could see you now." She shook her head and went back into the kitchen.

Hughie got up and roamed about the room, pulling books out of Assumpta's shelves. Monty could hear the young woman and the old chatting in the kitchen, and then there was the whistling of the kettle. A few minutes later, Katie came in carrying a tea tray, and Assumpta came in behind her with a plate of sweets.

Monty stood and said, "I didn't introduce myself properly, Mrs. Flanagan. My name is Monty Collins."

"You're helping wee Katie find out what happened to poor Eamon, she tells me. She is grateful to you, and so am I."

"I'm not sure I'll be able to get to the bottom of it. I wish I could offer you some assurance but I just can't."

"Sure you'll do your best. Nobody can ask more than that."

"Now the latest piece of information we have is that, on the night

Eamon died, there was a man in a car out here somewhere, and he had a confrontation of some kind with a young guy who was with his girlfriend. Sounds as if the young couple had been enjoying a bit of privacy . . ."

"Aye, and a rub of the relic!" Hughie laughed.

The young woman caught the eye of the old, and they both shook their heads as if to say, from long, weary years of experience, *Boys will be boys, even when they're past seventy years of age.*

"Yes, Mr. Collins, you were saying? Before this oul *baste* spoke out of turn."

"The first anyone — anyone in O'Grady's at least — heard about this was when Vincent came into the bar just after reaching the legal drinking age a few months back."

"Lad was more interested in his mot than in the drink, by the sound of it," said Hughie, "and wasn't used to the stuff. So on his first day in O'Grady's he had a few too many and started blethering to a mate of his about this incident with the car."

Monty said, "I have to admit, Assumpta, all this sounds pretty thin. A car on the Ammon Road the same night as Mr. Flanagan's death."

"And the same night as the shooting," Hughie put in.

"Right. So that's all we have to go on, that and the young guy's first name. Vincent."

"From around here?"

"Seems likely."

"Well, it wouldn't be Vincent McDonnell. He has a lady friend, yes, because he was widowed some years back. But he's not young at all. It would have to be Vincent McKeever. Couple of years older than you, Katie. Well, eighteen, if he reached drinking age this year. And there wouldn't be much privacy in his house, with seven children, the parents and the old gran all living there."

"Thank you, Assumpta. What would be the best way to get in touch with him, do you think?"

There was no need to state the obvious, that a knock on the door of his family home would not likely induce the young man to speak freely if he had been a witness to a questionable incident, or had been in a confrontation with those who may have been involved.

"Leave it with me. He does some work for the farmer up the hill there, and he walks by here quite often. I'll find a way to approach him without causing him any undue alarm."

"Perfect. I really appreciate your help with this, Assumpta."

They stayed on and chatted for a while beside the fire, then took their leave.

Assumpta put her arms around the young girl and said, "Call up to me again soon, Katie. It does my heart good to see you."

"I will, I promise. I'm so happy that I got to see you today."

"And tell your mam I have her in my prayers."

"I will."

"Mind yourself, Hughie."

"I will."

From there, they drove out the Ammon Road to the spot where Eamon had died, a narrow bridge over a deep gully. The river was more like a brook, with jagged rocks lining its banks. Monty estimated the height of the bridge over the rocks as thirty feet or so. It was not surprising that anyone falling, jumping, or being thrown from the bridge would sustain fatal injuries. There were good straight stretches of road at both ends of the bridge so, presumably, a pedestrian would have been able to see the headlights of a car approaching from either direction. And an attentive driver should have been able to see a person standing there, depending on how dark his clothing was. One thing was certain: if you were the driver and you hit someone, you'd sure as hell feel it and hear it, even if you hadn't seen the person until it was too late. Did the car keep on going after Flanagan was hit, if indeed he was hit that night?

Chapter VI

Brennan

When Brennan got off the bus in Andytown on Thursday after his day at Holy Cross, he walked to Ronan's place and nodded to the two security men in their car. He let himself in with his key. There wasn't a sound in the house, but Ronan must have been home or the bodyguards would not be there. Or maybe they would, to make sure nobody got into the house in Ronan's absence. Brennan went up to his room to change his clothes, and he heard a sliding sound from the floor below, followed by the sound of a door or a drawer being closed. Then, "Gráinne?"

"It's Brennan," he replied and headed down the stairs.

Ronan emerged from a room that Brennan had never seen open; he'd thought, to the extent that he'd considered it at all, that the door led to a closet. "What are you up to now, Brennan?"

"Not a thing. Just came from Holy Cross."

"Get something to wet your throat."

"I think I'll do that." He went to the drinks cabinet and poured himself a generous helping of John Jameson. "Do you miss the drink?" he asked Ronan.

Ronan gave him a shrewd look. "Wouldn't you?"

"I would." Brennan peered behind his cousin and saw what was a small office with a desk, chair, and filing cabinet. "Well, I'll let you get back to whatever you're doing, Ronan."

"Step inside, Brennan. The headquarters of a one-man investigation unit. Or perhaps reparations unit." Brennan raised his eyebrows and waited for enlightenment. "I'll explain. Go to the kitchen and get yourself a chair. I've never had the need for more than one."

Brennan grabbed a kitchen chair and set it down opposite Ronan at his desk. Ronan looked at him, took a deep breath, and said, "I'm speaking to you in confidence now, Father Burke."

Brennan imagined there were many, many aspects of Ronan's life that were confidential in nature. He said, "You needn't have any concerns, Ronan. Anything you tell me stays between you and me. *Sinn féin*, so to speak."

Ronan gave a little laugh. The words simply meant "we ourselves."

"Thank you, Brennan. As you know, I've been working for an end to the conflict. And, if you'll forgive a bit of ego, I'm hoping to take a leading role in whatever kind of peace process we can achieve."

"No forgiveness required, Ronan. You have the ability, the dedication, and the personality to get along with others, including some who will be terribly difficult to deal with." He did not add *and you're courageous enough to take the inevitable risks.*

"*Go raibh maith agat* again, Brennan. So I have this little office where I keep records of some old matters I would dearly love to see put to right. For now, I'll just burden you with one of these matters."

He opened a drawer and drew out a file folder stuffed with papers. He took out several pages and smoothed them out on the desk. Brennan saw rows of grainy photographs with handwritten notes beneath each of the pictures.

"Dublin and Monaghan," Ronan said.

"Oh, God."

"Nobody has ever been arrested for it. Not one single soul. Even though they know who did it."

Brennan was painfully familiar with the atrocity. In 1974 three car bombs went off in Dublin city centre and one in Monaghan. It was the worst atrocity — in terms of body count — of the Troubles. So far. Thirty-three people were killed, nearly three hundred injured. Women, children, men, including a young husband and wife and their two little girls. The entire family. Another casualty was an unborn, full-term baby. So, thirty-four dead.

"I was in Dublin a couple of weeks after that," Brennan said, "a long-scheduled visit. The images I saw, and the first-hand accounts I heard, still feature prominently in my nightmares. One of my closest boyhood friends was killed in Talbot Street, a lad on my Gaelic football team. Paddy Healey. I was dark of hair and eye, and Paddy was a little blondy fella, so we were known on the team as chocolate and vanilla. When we were grown, I'd still drop in and see him whenever I was in Dublin. And one of my cousins, on my mother's side, walked away from the Parnell Street bombing with minor injuries. Minor physical injuries, major psychological damage."

"An old love of mine was killed in Talbot Street," Ronan said, "and I knew several of the injured in the other two streets. A fella I know, a fireman on the scene, still to this day can't walk down a street past a line of parked cars without getting a case of the nerves. Imagine how many people are like that." Ronan stabbed his finger at the gallery of photos. "Everybody knows somebody who was killed or wounded. And everybody knows these are the bastards who did it. There were eyewitnesses who saw the cars before the explosions and were able to identify the men in the cars. The Garda Síochána —" the police force in the Republic of Ireland "— have the information, had it straight away. They brought the evidence up here to the North, because of course all the killers were operating out of the North. So the Gardaí brought the evidence here, handed it over to the RUC, and nothing was ever fucking done about it. The UVF finally claimed responsibility for it two years ago."

"The police here have evidence against several known mass murderers and have not seen fit to arrest them."

"Doesn't sound like the renowned British system of justice, does it? And then there is the matter of the timing and the technical sophistication of the bombs themselves. All of which, according to the experts, including British experts, was way beyond the capability of the Loyalist paramilitaries in 1974."

"Which tells us they weren't operating on their own."

"It's widely believed that elements of the British security forces were involved in it. There are all these shadowy units of the military, which had members of the Loyalist paras under their direction. Sabotage, assassination . . ."

"Sounds like the plot of a bad Hollywood film."

"I wish that's all it was. And these organizations, and their agents, weren't shy about crossing the border and carrying out some of their missions in the South. I've heard it said that the intention of the plotters was to unleash a civil war involving the South."

"God help us."

"And if they got it started, they were confident that they could crush the other side."

"Our side."

"Crush us all, yes."

"I can't even think about it. And I can't bear to think about Paddy Healey's family, and the families of all the other people killed and injured, waiting for justice after more than twenty years."

Ronan gave a bitter laugh. "They'll be waiting till the Second Coming."

"Will the peace process help or hinder their cause?"

"There was a peace process in the works at the time of these attacks, if you recall. The Sunningdale Agreement. Power-sharing and a role for Dublin at the table for the first time. The Loyalists couldn't have that. Ian Paisley didn't think much of this 'hands across the border' business. He memorably said, 'If they don't behave themselves in the South, it will be *shots* across the border.' Well, it was bombs across the border. And of course the agreement was part of the death toll of the bombings. It died along with all the human victims."

Brennan gestured towards the papers on the desk. "So, Ronan, what's all this in aid of?"

Ronan tapped his finger on the photo of one of the suspects. "Blown up by his own bomb in 1975." The next photo: "Shot to death by his fellow Loyalists in 1975." Two others had been "taken out by our lads." Another had died in 1989. Someone else was in prison for another murder. "And then there's this individual." The picture was a colour snapshot, cropped to show only the man's face. From the brightness of the image, it was clear that the photo had been taken outdoors. Ronan glared at the slitty-eyed slab of a man and said, "He has been living in Scotland, a long self-imposed exile. Uses another name over there, apparently. But rumour has it he's back in town."

"Marked to be taken out by our lads, I wonder?"

"I'm a man of peace now, Brennan. What I want is this fucker arrested by the forces of law and order and prosecuted in a blaze of publicity."

"Who is he?"

"His name is Brody MacAllan. I've been digging into this for some time, talking to people here and in the South, and I have a witness who got a good look at a man in one of the bomb cars that day. He couldn't put a name to him and never saw him again until a couple of years ago. My witness, Liam, works at the ferry terminal at Larne. I know him through our shared interest in Republican politics and . . . related activities. So, two years ago, he's on the job at Larne, and he sees a man in a car boarding the ferry for Scotland, and the man looks familiar but Liam can't place him. By the time he realizes where he saw him before, the ferry is pulling away from the dock. But he talks to a co-worker and looks into the boarding information and, with one thing and another, comes up with MacAllan's name. My research tells me that nobody by that name has been lingering here in Belfast for the last twenty-one years, so I'm thinking he bolted across the sea after the bombings and made the odd surreptitious re-entry into this country. Liam caught him out returning to Scotland. Anyway, Liam passes the information on to me, and I get in touch with one of our lads who is waiting things out in Glasgow."

Like MacAllan, Brennan said to himself, on the run in Scotland.

"I asked him to keep an eye out for this fucker." He stabbed at the photo again. "Nothing for two years, but my man in Glasgow sent word last month that a fellow he believes to be MacAllan recently left Scotland to come home to Belfast. So I've got someone taking a look around east Belfast and the Shankill and the other Loyalist areas, to see if he spots our quarry."

"And if our quarry is in sight?"

"I'll take him to law. Or I hope to. I've passed all this information to a person who is well known to me back home in Dublin, a member of the main opposition party in Leinster House, a man not afraid to raise dust. Or hackles. You can see a dirty cloud descend over his head any time the Dublin and Monaghan bombings are mentioned. With the Dublin government now involved in the peace process here in the Six Counties, I'm hoping he will apply pressure to get MacAllan charged with the murders. If that happens, MacAllan will attempt to get a deal for himself almost certainly, by grassing on his fellow bombers — informing on those who are still alive. So we may see some of them arrested and put on trial. Twenty-one years after the fact."

"Should go smoothly, given the history so far."

Chapter VII

Monty

On the following Monday, Monty hooked off work to go on a road trip to Dublin with Brennan and Ronan Burke. They had taken him into a little office Ronan had set up in his house and filled him in on a plan they had relating to four car bomb attacks back in 1974, in Dublin and Monaghan. Ronan wound up by saying, "You can see why this is so, well, hush-hush. Although I have done nothing wrong, and intend to follow the path of law and order, this could blow up in all our faces — pardon the expression — if word got around."

"Word never gets around from this confessor," Father Burke assured him.

"No, I've never taken you for a talker, Brennan."

"You have nothing to fear from me either, Ronan," Monty said. "We'll file it under solicitor-client privilege."

"Good man."

The Burkes had arranged to meet a politician by the name of Dinny Cagney in Dublin. Ronan was hoping that Cagney would use his connections to get the matter on the agenda once again. Ronan intimated that he did not want to be hampered by the presence of his bodyguards for the trip, so there was a bit of a to-do about the best way to travel. To Monty, the solution was simple: they would take Monty's leased car — leased from Burke Transport, southern division — and he would be the wheelman. They were staying overnight, which meant there would be plenty of time for a visit with Maura and the kids. So Monty pulled up in front of Ronan's house in the middle of the morning and waited while Ronan had a word with his security detail. One of the men opened the trunk of the security car, drew out a sports bag, and handed it to Ronan. Ronan walked to Monty's Renault and said, "Could you open the boot for me there, Monty?"

"Sure." He didn't ask what Ronan was putting in there, just waited until he climbed into the rear seat behind Monty, and Brennan got into the front, and then they headed off. Monty noticed from time to time when he looked in his rear-view mirror that Ronan was angling himself to look in it, too. Well, it was not beyond the realm of possibility that someone was watching Ronan Burke's movements and might pull in behind. The annals of this country were filled with accounts of people who had come to grief after letting down their guard.

"Thank you, Monty, for your services today."

"My pleasure, Ronan. Nobody has to twist my arm to get me to Dublin, and I love to drive. So just tell me where we're going, and I'll go there."

"Our destination is Leinster House, right in the city centre, where we'll be meeting Dinny Cagney."

Brennan said, "Yer man is a *Teachta Dála*, Ronan, so you may as well acknowledge the existence of the Dáil."

That went over Monty's head until Brennan explained. "As you may be aware, Monty, the Dáil is the Irish parliament."

"That much I know."

"This fellow's name is Montague *Michael Collins*, Ronan, and yet, sad to say, he needs instruction from time to time in the history and institutions of the land of his Collins forebears."

"And Father Burke here never lets me forget it, Ronan."

"Correct. And your lesson today is that Dinny Cagney is a member of parliament. The Dáil. Are you with me so far?"

"Yes, Father."

"And the parliament sits in Leinster House in Dublin. Some people close to our hearts, members of the Republican movement, refuse to use the word Dáil."

"Because they can't make out whether it sounds like *Doyle* or *Dall*?"

"Em, no, that's not the reason. The reason is that they do not acknowledge any parliament that came into being after the Second Dáil of 1921, elected by the people of the entire island. All parliaments after that have been partitionist constructs in a partitionist state. Amn't I right, Ronan?"

"You are infallible, Father."

"I won't go into the splits in the movement that arose in relation to this, Montague. Don't want to burden you any further with the weight of history."

"I shall be content to take instruction where and when you see fit to offer it, Father."

"Good man."

The road to Dublin took them past gently sloping pastures of brilliant green, marked off by hedges and stone walls. Ronan offered a commentary on the towns they saw as they drew close to the border with the South.

Newry. "Troubles there."

"That would hardly make it unique, I guess, Ronan."

"Indeed not. As a lawyer, you may want to see the courthouse there sometime. If you can find it."

"Small and out of the way?"

"No. Big and right in the city centre. But surrounded by high walls; you'd walk all the way around it and not know what was in there. Lovely city, though."

Then, south of the border, Dundalk. "Lots of fellas on the run there."

"On the run from?"

"The British Army, the Royal Ulster Constabulary, you name it."

"IRA fellas."

"You didn't hear it from me."

Drogheda. "Beautiful, isn't it? The River Boyne, the towers, the church spires."

"But," said Monty, knowing the catch here, "thousands of people in the city were massacred by Cromwell."

"There you go, Brennan. Monty knows what's what."

A few minutes later, when Monty looked in the rear-view mirror at Ronan to make a comment about the scenery, he saw him raise his right hand and make the sign of the cross. A glance to the side showed Father Burke doing the same. Monty realized that he had been hearing bells for the last few seconds and that they were coming from the radio. He remembered then that RTE, the Irish broadcaster, played the Angelus bells every day at noon and six o'clock in the evening. Ronan seemed to be lost in reflection, so Monty did not interrupt the mood.

†

When they arrived in Dublin, Ronan said, "Now I'm going to give you directions to the Gravedigger's. We'll pay our respects there. And you lads can enjoy a pint whilst I sit there with my tongue hanging out."

Monty wasn't sure what the connections were there, but he followed Ronan's directions to the Glasnevin area of Dublin and found a parking spot. Ronan said he wanted to visit the grave of a young woman he used to go with, a woman who died in the Talbot Street bombing at the age of twenty-three and was now lying in Glasnevin Cemetery. Brennan said he would do the same for his childhood friend. Monty followed them into the graveyard but, not wanting to intrude on their privacy, he spent his time reading the inscriptions on the monuments to such luminaries as Michael Collins, Eamon de Valera, the Jesuit poet Gerard Manley Hopkins, and the man who had described himself, memorably, as "a drinker with a writing problem," Brendan Behan.

When the others rejoined him, they walked to the pub next door, which was identified on the sign as Kavanagh's but was known to one and all as the Gravedigger's. It was a classic Dublin pub with lots of dark wood and sparkling bottles, and the barman poured a lovely, creamy pint. Monty availed himself of a glass, as did Brennan. Ronan had a soft drink and rolled his eyes as he put it to his lips. The appointment with the politician was not until mid-afternoon, so they lingered in the pub, savouring their refreshments and chatting with the locals.

"There's a wealth of lore surrounding this place," Ronan said. "Fellows digging the graves used to order their drinks by knocking on the wall between here and the graveyard. The barmen would know what to pour by the sound of the different knocks. Whiskey, porter, whatever they signalled. The barmen would take the drinks out to the gravediggers."

"And there's a ghost!" This came from an elderly woman on her way out of the bar. "He's been seen on more than one occasion and described in the very same way by people who didn't even know each other. They say he wears a butterfly collar and a waistcoat with a watch chain. Keep your eyes open, lads!"

When Monty caught sight of Leinster House, formerly the palace of James FitzGerald, the Duke of Leinster, and now the seat of the Irish parliament, Monty wished he himself was wearing a waistcoat and butterfly collar. The splendid neoclassical building made him feel small and grubby in his jeans and shirt with no tie. They had found a parking spot in a short street called Ely Place, just off Baggot Street Lower, and walked to the great building on Kildare Street.

"Remind you of the White House?" Brennan asked.

"You're right. It does."

"No coincidence there. The White House was designed by an Irishman. And this was the inspiration."

It was just as grand inside, with its elaborate mouldings and chandeliers, and Monty took it all in as they waited for Ronan's friend to appear. Dinny Cagney, Monty was told, belonged not to the governing party but to the opposition, *Fianna Fáil*. He looked less like a politician than did his friend Ronan. Cagney had unruly red hair, a youthful freckled face, and an expression that seemed to say he found the world endlessly amusing.

The two men greeted each other in Irish, and everyone was introduced. Cagney led them to a private office where they could have their talk. When everyone was seated, Ronan said, "You know why I'm here, Dinny."

"Yes, for an episode in our history I remember all too well." He turned to Brennan and Monty. "I was in Cork that day on business. Started out on the trip back home to Dublin and met up with a garda. He asked me where I was going, and I said Dublin. The garda said to me, 'Don't go. They've blown the fuck out of it.' I could not believe my eyes when I saw what had happened here. And I know we all feel the same way."

"We do, *go deimhin*," Ronan said. "I gave you the statement of the witness."

"Who says he saw this MacAllan in one of the bomb cars that day."

"Yes. So I want him added to the long list of 'known' suspects. With a difference. This time I want something done about it."

"We both do."

"Now, you told me you'd be talking to one of your contacts in the Garda Síochána. And now that MacAllan has apparently surfaced again, I hope you'll be raising holy hell in the . . . the Dáil, so this atrocity will be back in the public and political sphere where it should have been all along."

"You don't have to tell me, Ronan. I'm with you all the way. In fact, I'm ahead of you."

Ronan's face lit up. "Is that so?"

Cagney raised a warning hand. "You'll not be happy when you hear what I've discovered."

"And what is that?"

"I gave Sullivan — he's my contact in the Gardaí — I gave him the name of the suspect. And he looked into it and found out that Brody MacAllan is on record as being out of the country on the day of the bombing. And has the papers to prove it."

Ronan looked as if the sky had fallen on him, and all belonging to him.

"I know, Ronan, I know. Your witness had the best of intentions. I don't doubt it for a minute. But he was obviously mistaken."

"Liam is sure of what he saw, Dinny. And once I had the name, I did some research in Belfast and found a colour photo of Brody MacAllan playing a lambeg drum back in the day. I trimmed the picture to get just his face and I put together a handful of photographs of other faces, all in colour. That's when I played the part of a peeler and showed the pack of photos to Liam. He picked MacAllan out. Didn't hesitate."

"But, Ronan, the garda I had looking into it, he was there on the seventeenth of May, immediately after it happened. It was Sullivan's first month on the job with the Gardaí. He saw the bodies. Mangled, limbs blown off. Little children . . . He wants to fucking bury the bastards who did this. All those suspects the guards identified to the authorities in the North, in the expectation that they'd track them down and arrest them. Nothing was done. And it wasn't just the North, was it? The authorities up there, and the Brits, did pass on *some* information — early on — and it was not followed up here in the South. The government of the day was unaccountably lax about this slaughter of its citizens. And the Gardaí failed to pursue the leads they had. So now we have several of the perpetrators still alive and well north of the border, and the police and security forces up there turning a blind eye. Well, we all know about the 'close working relationship' between some of the Loyalist paramilitaries and the forces of law and order! So anything we do will likely be blocked by the authorities in Belfast all over again. History has a way of repeating itself here, doesn't it?"

"It does," Ronan conceded. "But with everybody trying to look good for the cameras during these peace talks, I'm thinking maybe somebody in Belfast might nudge the police in the direction of doing the right thing. 'We are always open to looking at new evidence' — some sort of face-saving line like that."

"Wouldn't want to bet the farm on the goodwill of that crowd in the Six Counties, Ronan. But, anyway, MacAllan wasn't here. He was over in America. He flew out of Belfast on May the eleventh, flew back on the eighteenth, and landed in Belfast the morning of the nineteenth."

"Who provided this information to Sullivan?"

"He saw the documents himself."

That was as good a time as any for Brennan and Monty to take their leave. They knew Ronan had other things to discuss at his meeting with Dinny Cagney, so they agreed to meet an hour later at the School of Economics. Monty didn't know where that was, presumably at Trinity College, just a short walk to the north of them. More architectural splendour. But Brennan headed in the opposite direction and took a left. They walked along Merrion Row, which became Baggot Street, and they stopped in front of Doheny & Nesbitt's pub. Brennan went in and Monty followed. He looked around him and admired yet another classic old Dublin drinking establishment. Monty figured a second pint would not put his driving skills in jeopardy, so he and

Brennan got their drinks and sat at one of the tables. Brennan, not being constrained by concerns about the legal or neurological effects of alcohol that day, consumed a couple more pints as they enjoyed a leisurely conversation. After they'd been there awhile, Monty looked at his watch. It had been well over an hour since they'd left Ronan at Leinster House. "We'd better get over to the School of Economics. Don't want Ronan to think we've abandoned him."

"No need to remove ourselves, Monty. This is the School of Economics."

"Eh?"

"This place is known as the Doheny & Nesbitt School of Economics, after the kinds of conversations heard in here. It's a hangout for government people and journalists."

"Makes sense."

"Makes perfect sense. And a perfect way to ease into an evening in Dublin." He drained his latest pint and went for another.

A few minutes later, Ronan walked in, nodded in their direction, and went to the bar. And ordered a pint of Guinness. Brennan halted the lifting of his own glass when he saw what his cousin had done. Ronan Burke's drinking had lost him his wife and children in the past. He had been off the stuff for years. Long, long years, Monty imagined they were. Ronan Burke's lips touching the dark, forbidden nectar of the Guinness would be like the feet of Gaius Julius Caesar touching the waters of the Rubicon. Monty could see the tension in Brennan as he watched his cousin with his glass. But he didn't say a word when Ronan arrived at the table. Brennan no doubt figured he was the last man on earth who should preach to another about the drink. Ronan lifted the glass to his lips, held it there, inhaled the rich aroma, released a sigh of longing, and put the glass down without so much as a flick of his tongue at its contents. He passed the pint to Brennan without a word. Then he got up and went to the bar and returned with something pale and fizzy. He took a sip, made a face, and spoke of the events of the day. "The fact remains that my witness saw Brody MacAllan heading south in one of the cars used in the Dublin bombings. The other cars were spotted and remembered, too."

"What makes your witness so sure it was MacAllan?" Brennan asked.

"He recognized the car because it had been behind him on his way into Dublin, and it passed him on the road about twenty miles north of the city. He was asking himself why the fellow was in such a hurry. He was a little annoyed with the driver, which is likely why he turned to glare at the car when it went by. MacAllan was in the back seat, passenger side, and our man got a good look at his face. And he had no trouble recognizing that face when he saw it again."

"But Garda Sullivan says MacAllan was out of the country at the time."

"In America with his wife, attending some big hooley or revival meeting. Television preacher. Hiram somebody."

"That would be Hiram B. Stockwell. He's a celebrity over there."

"That's it."

"And the records show he entered the U.S. well before the bombing and was not back on Irish soil until two days after it. You're not saying he was just one of the organizers of the attack; he was delivering one of the car bombs."

"I believe my man who made the sighting."

"But, Ronan, papers would tend to be more conclusive than an eyewitness."

Monty agreed but said nothing. Long experience in the courts of law had taught him about the vagaries of eyewitness testimony. And even when it wasn't vague or unreliable, he could convince a jury that it was.

"I believe the papers were forged by the authorities in Belfast to give him an alibi. Don't be giving me that look, Brennan. It's well known that a lot of these UVF and UDA types were being run as agents and informers by British security forces, military intelligence, the RUC . . . there's no room for doubt on the question of collusion in that bloody place."

"Sure you could sing it. I know. But how are you going to prove MacAllan wasn't at the Stockwell rally?"

Ronan stared into the stagnant waters in his glass and said nothing.

There was nothing to be gained by piling it on for Ronan about the difficulties of proving his case, so Monty decided to change the subject. Slightly, anyway. "How long ago did you leave Dublin, Ronan?" He looked around at the grand old pub and the convivial company within its walls. "Why, if you don't mind my asking, would you want to leave here for the war-torn North of Ireland?"

"I left in the summer of 1970. Heard the news about the Battle of Saint Matthew's. You know, the church where Tomás was married. The Provisionals' first major battle of the current war. That was the turning point for me, after sitting on my arse here in Dublin while our brothers and sisters in Belfast and Derry were being burnt out of their houses and batonned by police when they held peaceful demonstrations. They had long been denied housing, employment, and equal voting rights. And what had I been doing? Drinking and chasing women and mitching off my classes at the university. So when news came of the boys defending the church and the wee nationalist enclave of the Short Strand, I packed my bags, promised my ma I'd write, and I hitched a lift to Belfast."

"Much drinking and chasing women up there?"

"*Cinnte.* That, and fighting a war for the last twenty-five years."

"And now you're trying to bring that war to a conclusion."

"If it can be brought to an honourable conclusion."

"Retreat with honour?"

"Not a retreat." Monty could hear steel in his voice now. "We could keep fighting into the long, dark, indefinite future. The Brits can't defeat us. They never will."

"Yet, they're still there."

"Our hope has always been that if we caused enough damage to their military installations and their commercial interests, the pain of that would become greater than any advantage they would have in staying on. A war of attrition."

"But they haven't reached that point yet."

"Surprising, the amount of death and destruction they're willing to accept to keep their Unionist lackeys happy."

"Or to keep them safe."

"The Unionists have nothing to fear from a united Ireland."

"I doubt they see it that way."

"Well, in my clandestine talks with some of their representatives, some of the Loyalist spokesmen and paramilitary leaders, I'm trying to convince them of exactly that."

"How's that going for you?"

"What do they say in diplomatic circles? We've had a 'full and frank exchange of views.'"

"I see. How are your fellow, um, Republican activists taking it?"

"We have a saying in the North, about our strategy. A ballot box in one hand and an Armalite in the other. That's not the exact quote, but that's the most familiar version. You get the picture."

"That sets it out very neatly."

Darkness had fallen by this time, and Brennan said he wouldn't mind lining his stomach with something solid, a process known to others as having an evening meal. He was a little past the lining stage. Be that as it may, they left Doheny & Nesbitt's and stood outside on Baggot Street, trying to decide what they wanted to eat. They started to cross the street but a car that had been idling at the curb moved ahead. It then stopped to let them cross. Monty saw Ronan looking at the car. There were three young men inside. After they had crossed, the car moved off slowly.

"North of Ireland registration," Ronan said.

Well, whoever they were, they drove off out of sight, and Monty thought no more about them.

Ronan suggested that a cup of Bewley's coffee would be just the thing, so they made for Grafton Street. They had a fine scoff at Bewley's and then started back to the car. Brennan stopped to light up a smoke, and so did Ronan. Monty kept going and turned into Ely Place. Then he heard rapid footsteps behind him. He turned around just in time to see two men reach Ronan and Brennan and try to pull them down. Monty took off towards them at a run. By the time Monty reached them, the two Burkes had the two young attackers on the ground. Ronan had his assailant face down with both arms wrenched behind his back. Brennan's man was lying on his side with one hand clutching his stomach in pain, the other hand gripping a knife but motionless under Brennan's foot.

"Who the fuck are you, you shower of shites?" Ronan demanded. The dark blue eyes glared down at the young thugs.

"We only . . ."

"You only what?"

"We only wanted to get a few quid for a drink. Or some fags, like. We weren't going to hurt youse."

"Well, now," responded the former IRA gunman, "*we* have to decide whether we're going to hurt *youse*. And if so, how badly."

"No, please! We're sorry!"

"All right. Get up and get the hell out of here. And don't be acting the maggot with anybody else on these streets."

Ronan and Brennan released their captives, who hightailed it down the street and out of sight. Brennan kicked the knife away. His expression was one of disgust, Ronan's one of relief. Not an assassination squad out of Belfast.

Brennan spoke up then, in the tones of Winston Churchill, "Nevah, in the field of human conflict, have two young gurriers been so fortunate to have northside Dublin accents."

✝

They arrived back at the car and Ronan said, "You wouldn't mind opening the boot, would you, Monty?"

"Not at all." He stuck the key in the trunk and pulled up the lid. Ronan reached in and took out the sports bag. He opened it to reveal a device with a black rod and a grip. He pulled on the retractable rod until it was around three-and-a-half-feet long, then took it to the side of the car. Monty saw a round mirror at the end of the pole. Ronan swept it under the car and angled it so he could see.

"Not the best light, but I think we're grand here." He shortened the thing again and put it away. "A little extreme perhaps but you can't be too careful. Sinister cars have been known to travel here from north of the border, as we know all too well. Now I can tell my minders I used this yoke, and they'll be relieved." Satisfied that there was no bomb under the car, Ronan directed Monty to the flat in the working-class Liberties district where the Burkes were staying with a relative. They got out and gave Monty directions to Maura's place on the north side of the city, and he nodded as if it was perfectly clear.

In fact he took a few wrong turns, but he successfully negotiated his way to St. Brigid's Road Lower in Drumcondra, where his family had settled in. It was a nice little house with a bright blue door recessed inside an archway, which created a little porch. Dominic had immediately declared the porch his castle. It was only a short walk to the Royal Canal, and the kids were determined to assemble a fleet of paper boats to deploy in its waters.

He and Maura spent the night in her tiny but comfortable room in the house. He got to enjoy a bit of morning time with Normie before she went off to school. She was at an age when you'd be a little apprehensive about starting in a new school, so Monty was anxious to see how it was going. Back home in Halifax, she was a student at Father Burke's choir school, and he had found her a place in a similar establishment only a few blocks from the house they had rented.

"How is it?" he asked her now.

"Great! I've got a couple of really good friends and we do good music and I like the uniform. Do you like it?"

The uniform was a bright red sweater over a white shirt and a dark-coloured tartan kilt.

"Love it. You look wonderful in red. I'm glad it's all going well for you, sweetheart."

Once she was off to school, Monty had some fun playing with little Dominic and his emerging fleet of paper boats and planes. Then the nanny, Orla Farrell, arrived and the little fellow squealed, "Orla!" He pointed out the young woman to his dad, in case he had no idea who had just walked in the door. Dominic went over and gave her a proprietary hug. He was a boy in love, and he was not (yet) too afflicted with manly sangfroid to express it.

All this of course brought home to Monty how lonesome he would be for his family when he returned to Belfast. But the idea of Maura and the children living in a city where bombs had been going off and bullets flying only months before was just not on. The university district where Monty was living had been fairly safe, but he would not be at ease with his wife and kids out and about in the troubled city, ceasefire or no ceasefire. Maura, by no means a nervous type, readily agreed that Dublin would be best for Normie and Dominic.

Monty drove Maura to the law school on the south side of the city. From there he went to the Liberties to pick up Brennan and Ronan.

They drove out of the city and headed north. Just past Dundalk, Monty saw a British Army checkpoint ahead. "This again," muttered Ronan in the back seat. The soldiers of course knew immediately who he was, and they made the best of it, calling over a couple of RUC cops, who conducted a thorough and leisurely search of the car, not saying a word and not paying any heed to the long line of traffic stopped behind them on the road. Ronan was seething, as was Brennan, but they kept their cool. When they were finally released, they travelled for a couple of miles in absolute silence. Finally, Ronan said, "Almost enough to make me renounce my renunciation of the physical force tradition!"

"I can understand that."

"I must tell you about my experience here a few years ago. Well, not a few years. Mid-1970s. It's comical, looking back on it. Not so funny at the time."

Monty tuned in to the story.

"I got lifted with a couple of other lads and thrown in the Kesh. I'll spare you the details of the prolonged and ferocious beatings we endured following our capture." He fell silent then, and Monty didn't push him. Eventually Ronan resumed his tale in a lighter tone of voice. "From day one, I was planning my escape. After eight months in the cage, I got my chance. If they ever make the film, you'll see me as the dashing hero, scaling the walls, running to freedom in my clean and nicely pressed clothing, my shining locks of hair ruffled by the breeze, running into the arms of my one true love. Except that she was at home with our three children, aged one to three. And as if Gráinne didn't have her hands full with them, she was taking in other people's washing and sewing to earn a few quid to put food on the table — and her with a university degree in chemistry. But anyway, in my film I will be the handsome hero home from the wars."

"But the film will have romanticized the scene a bit?"

"A wee bit, sure. I in fact made my escape in a bin lorry. I seized the moment and leapt up into the lorry and hid by covering myself with rubbish, much of it wet rubbish, and I waited in the filth and the stink until the lorry driver returned to the vehicle and started it up and took forever to get away from the grounds of the prison. And if that wasn't enough to take the shine off my big moment, it had been a hot, humid week and there were clouds of midges outside, and a swarm of them had got into the lorry and found me amidst the rubbish and converged on me and were biting every inch of my flesh, and I could barely move of course; couldn't risk attracting the notice of the driver.

Have I mentioned that I have a particularly strong immune reaction to insect bites? So I knew my eyes and my mouth — my mouth! — were getting all puffed up. And I nearly went mental with the urge to scratch myself." He did a comic turn as a bug-ridden man twitching and scratching and going mad.

Monty couldn't help but laugh. "That's the film you should make, Ronan. A comedy perhaps instead of a war adventure, but every single person in the audience will be feeling your pain, feeling that itch. This may be just the propaganda tool you need to bring people onboard for the peace initiative."

"The lorry made a stop out on the motorway, and I decided to bail. Shook off the rotting fish and vegetables and leapt out onto the side of the road. Then I had to entice someone going by to take a chance on me and give me a lift."

Monty was about to sing some lines of the Doors' song about a killer out there on the road. Before he opened his mouth, he realized it might be a little too close to the truth. He settled for "Warning: do not give this man a lift. He could be armed and dangerous. Or, well, infectious."

"And bloody well looked it. A slew of cars went by, some slowing down so the drivers could take a good look at me, which made me even more of a nervous wreck because of course the news would be out about the peelers on the lookout, et cetera. One car stopped, and I looked inside and I could tell straight away it was a pair of Loyalist paramilitaries. So I doubled over and started retching. Made them think I would be boaking all over their car seats if they let me in. They drove off in disgust. A few minutes later, unbelievably, a woman stopped for me. Lady in her fifties. Must have been the motherly instinct in her. When I got in, I thanked her for stopping, and she said, 'You're the saddest wee thing I've ever seen. Can't leave you out here or a pack of dogs will eat you. And the flies will take what the dogs won't touch. What happened to your face?' I looked at myself in the side mirror. My face was a mass of lumps and blotches. My eyes were red and swollen and nearly shut. I barely looked human. 'You smell like a rubbish tip,' she said. 'You know that, do you?'"

"'Sure, I'm always like this,' I said to her, and she gave me a sideways look. Probably heard Dublin in my speech. Then she asked me, 'Where would you like me to . . . dispose of you?' I said, 'I don't suppose you're going to Newry today?' And she told me the last thing on her mind on any day of the week was to go to Newry. But she looked over at me, and it was clear to me that she found me absolutely pathetic and in need of charity. At that point she turned on the radio and fiddled with the dial. 'There will be all kinds of talk about the football,' she said. 'Do you follow the football?' I knew what she was getting at. The All-Ireland GAA match at Croke Park. She was signalling to me that she was a Catholic, a Nationalist, which she figured I was from the way I talk. I answered her, said something about Jimmy Barrett's winning goal. I said it in Irish, and she turned and smiled at me. I said, 'Dundalk?' and she nodded. She was going to take me across the border."

Monty looked at the handsome, well-turned-out Ronan Burke of 1995, and tried to picture the spotty, smelly young man who had made his undignified exit from Long Kesh in a heap of garbage.

"So then we chatted about football, about the war a bit, about her grownup sons and daughter, till we got close to Newry, and I got nerved up all over again. The news would have got out and the road to Dundalk was a typical escape route, and there would be Brit soldiers out on patrols. A bit of a no man's land between Newry and Dundalk. She knew why I was going quiet on her, and she said, 'Let me do the talking.' Not much more than a minute later, two British Army Jeeps came up behind us. One of them passed and motioned for us to pull over. Oh, Jesus, Mary and Joseph, I prayed, don't let this happen. Back in the Kesh, beaten and abused again. No choice of course except to pull off the road and wait for doom to fall.

"Two squaddies get out of the first Jeep and come to our window. One of them has a rifle trained on us; the other asks us to identify ourselves and to say where we're going. And my lady says, 'We're on our way to Dublin. And I'll ask you not to hold us up.' She jerked her head towards me in the seat and went on, 'Have to get this wee lad to hospital.'

"So I put a sick-man expression on my face, not that I needed it with all the swelling and red blotches.

"'There's hospitals here in Ulster,' one of the squaddies says. 'What's his trouble, that he has to go all the way to Dublin?'

"'He has to see an immune system specialist there, allergies and all that.' They don't look convinced. Then she leans towards the men at the window and whispers, though I can hear it, '*Saint Patrick's.*' The mental hospital in Dublin. They look me over and obviously find it credible that I'm in need of psychiatric treatment. At the very least, I'm clearly harmless. They let us go. They have more urgent business after all. You never know when an armed and dangerous escaped IRA man might come barrelling down the motorway."

"Jesus, Ronan, the life you've lived!"

"You have no idea."

"Did you ever get the treatment you needed?"

"I got exactly what I needed. Checked myself in to the nearest facility in Dundalk. A pub with which I was well familiar. Had a wash. Even washed my clothes while they were still on me. Then proceeded to get rat-arse drunk. There was a television set in the bar and, inevitably, the news came on and one of the stories was about a prisoner who had escaped from the Kesh. They showed a photo of what I looked like on better days. Most of the punters made no connection between the skinny, scrofulous gobshite sitting in Phelim's bar in Dundalk and the able-bodied soldier of the bold IRA as was shown on the telly. One fellow made me, though, gave me the eye across the room and raised his glass to me. I figured he was on the run, too. Later, on his way out, he stopped beside me and wished me *ádh mór*. Good luck."

"And after that? You got back in the saddle, so to speak?"

"Not for long. They caught up with me the next year, so I was back in the Kesh where I did my time and was released. Fought again. Saw friends die, saw enemies die, saw families devastated . . . on both sides of the conflict."

He wound down and seemed to turn inward. He would have quite a reel of past adventures, Monty imagined.

After a minute or so, Ronan got back to the conversation. "I will go to my grave believing the Republican cause was, and is, a just cause. That does not mean it was always fought in a just manner, as we all know. Some of the atrocities committed in the course of this war are and always will be indefensible. Unforgivable. And of course this includes acts committed by my own people as well as those committed by our enemies. But even allowing for the rightness of our cause in redressing a longstanding oppression of our people, even given all of that, I figure the people have had enough. Enough? There's a bit of British-style understatement for you, Monty! Too many lives lost, too many limbs lost, too much destruction, too much hatred, on all sides. This was all going full bore up until the ceasefire five months ago. So with a few like-minded individuals, I'm trying to bring an end to it."

The ironic tone in which Ronan had recounted the story of his harrowing prison break had given way to agitation, as he returned to the tensions of the present day.

Monty said, "You are trying to bring the war to an end, but others are not ready to relinquish those Armalite rifles."

"You said a mouthful there."

"So do you think maybe your own security . . ."

"Is at risk from the Loyalists, the Brits, and my own people?"

"Right. Do you think it is?"

Ronan caught Monty's eye in the mirror. "I know it is."

Chapter VIII

Monty

On Sunday, February 12, Maura came to Belfast with a group of professors and students from the University College of Dublin law school. They would be meeting up with their counterparts from the law school at Queen's. February 12, 1995, was the sixth anniversary of the death of Pat Finucane, a well-known Belfast solicitor. Finucane was murdered at the age of thirty-nine by a Loyalist paramilitary group, and a demonstration was planned in front of Belfast City Hall, calling for a full public inquiry into the murder. It was not a city government matter, but this was a highly visible place in the centre of town. Monty and Maura had decided to take part, and they arranged to meet up with Father Burke after he said his noon Mass at Holy Cross. Monty found a parking spot a few blocks away from the checkpoints where "civilian search units" searched all vehicles entering the city centre. He and Maura walked to Donegall Square, which was dominated by the City Hall, an enormous Baroque revival building in light-grey Portland stone with columns, carvings, cupolas at the corners, and a large central dome in green copper. Brennan was waiting for them on the front lawn.

"I can see why they call this an 'Edwardian wedding cake,'" Monty said, looking at the building.

"That's a fair description of it," Brennan agreed. He turned then to Maura. "How are things at the law school, Professor MacNeil?"

"Wonderful, Father Burke. The students are keen to learn the law so they can get out and make a difference in the world, give a voice to the disadvantaged and the unpopular client who would otherwise go unheard."

"God bless you, my dear. Even the unpopular defendant is entitled to a defence. The international corporations, the offshore banks. As unpopular as they are, they must be grateful to have you at their side."

"You haven't been listening, Brennan. A common failing in certain members of the opposite sex, I find. It is clear that you haven't heard a word I have said in all the five long years I have known you. My formative legal years were spent with the Dal Liberation Army. You may know it better as Dalhousie Legal Aid in Halifax. I would rather eat warm, raw, three-weeks-past-its-best-before-date haggis and die a horrible death with you looking on, pale and faint, than represent the offshore banks and their co-conspirators in corporate greed."

"Ah."

Nobody who had been in the presence of the MacNeil for more than five minutes, let alone five years, could be left in any doubt about what end of the political spectrum she was on. But Brennan enjoyed winding her up.

"This excursion to City Hall is not about me, though, is it?" she said. "One of my students has a sign for me. I'll see if I can spot her."

They approached the elaborately styled building, its light-grey stone dazzling in the afternoon sun. There were several hundred people, and the organizers shepherded them into formation, four abreast, for the march along the street in front of the hall. People carried signs featuring the handsome face of the lawyer, who had been gunned down in his home in front of his wife and children. Finucane had represented Irish Republican defendants in some high-profile cases. Several of the signs accused the Royal Ulster Constabulary, the British Army, and the intelligence services of collusion in the lawyer's death.

"What do you think, Brennan? Is there anything to that accusation?"

"Without question."

"Really!" Monty was surprised, not so much by the fact that, in the dirty war in the North here, such a thing might be true, but by Brennan's unequivocal reply. Monty knew there was a long-running conflict in the soul of the priest when it came to the troubled history of his homeland. He came from a staunch Republican family and he shared their view that Britain should be out and the partition between North and South should be ended, but he spent many a sleepless night wrestling with his conscience about what methods were or were not just in that struggle. Monty knew the bombings committed by the Republican side disturbed him as much as those committed by the other. And Brennan often weighed his words before speaking them. Not on this occasion.

"It's a well-known fact here," Brennan said. "Certain units of the army and the spooks and certain elements in the police force are in cahoots with Loyalist paramilitaries. Everybody here knows what side they're on. You must have heard about the Miami Showband massacre."

"Sounds like the title of a very bad movie."

"It does. But it was real. In 1975, the band was returning home to Dublin after a gig in County Down. But they had reckoned without several members of the UVF, one of the Loyalist paramilitaries, setting up a fake checkpoint and stopping the band on a pretext. Some of these UVF men were also members of a locally recruited regiment of the British Army, that being the Ulster Defence Regiment. They shot and killed three members of the band and wounded two others. So you're no safer as a musician here than you are as a lawyer, Collins."

"My God!" said Maura.

"The guys who killed the band members were soldiers?" Monty asked.

"Some of them were, yeah. As for Pat Finucane, everyone knew Pat was under threat from the Loyalists. For years. Threatened with death. Word is the security forces let it happen. People go farther than that: they say the security forces were in on it from the start."

"Jesus."

"Imagine yourself back home in Canada, and the police decide you have to be disposed of, because you represent killers and sex offenders."

"The police don't like it, but they know that's the justice system, that's my job. It's a well-known principle that lawyers are not supposed to be identified with their clients' actions just because the lawyers provide the representation to which the clients are entitled!"

"Well said, counsellor. But that didn't help Pat Finucane. Not here."

"There's Andrea!" Maura said and moved towards a young dark-haired woman struggling with three signs.

"Hi, Maura. I brought one for you and one for —" she looked at Brennan in his collar and settled on Monty "— your husband? I don't have one for you, Father."

"That's all right. I'll walk with youse anyway."

So the three of them joined the chanting protesters marching back and forth along the busy thoroughfare. There were two television crews on hand and a small group of other reporters. One man was treating the news media to a diatribe about collusion between the state and the Loyalist paramilitaries, and the media's apparent failure to keep the matter in the headlines.

People walked by and expressed their support; drivers beeped their horns and waved, joining in the chorus: "Justice for Pat!" "Executed by the state!" "Full inquiry now!" But the mood changed abruptly. The demonstrators turned to the sound of marching feet and angry voices in the street outside City Hall. A crowd bore down on the Finucane protesters, bellowing at them and waving Union Jack flags.

Police materialized as if out of nowhere, some in caps and bulletproof vests, another unit minutes later in full riot gear with helmets, shields, and batons. But no heads were cracked on this occasion. The police showed restraint, merely standing in rows between the two rival groups, keeping them apart. The Loyalists got their message out none-theless, as red-faced men shouted that the demonstrators were "dirty fuckin' Fenians" and that "the fuckin' IRA lawyer deserved every one of those fourteen bullets!" Then one of the Loyalists caught sight of Father Burke in his collar. "Fuck the Pope, you fuckin' papish!" The priest's black eyes fastened on the man with a look that consigned him to the flames of hell for all eternity.

The protest marshals urged everyone to stay focused on Pat Finucane and his family and not let the event be hijacked by the kinds of individuals who revelled in his death.

Walking away from City Hall after it was over, Brennan remarked, "I believe it was Newton who said, 'For every action, there is an equal and opposite reaction.'"

"Looked to me more like matter and anti-matter," Maura replied.

"All too predictable, but still it was a good idea to have the demonstration here in the city centre instead of keeping to the Falls Road. Disruption, yes, but also more publicity. So," he looked around, "where are you parked? Outside the restricted areas, obviously."

"Yeah, just a few blocks down from here. So, how are things with you, Brennan? I've been so busy with my tractors, I've neglected my social obligations."

"I thought you'd never ask, Montague. I got a call from head office."

"Oh?"

"Head office for you, Father, would be . . ." The MacNeil looked to the heavens.

"Close enough. I snagged the job in Rome. I start in September."

"You *what*?!" She stopped in her tracks and stared at him. Monty had not mentioned to her the possibility of Brennan's appointment to the Roman church because, well, there was no point in bringing it up if it wasn't going to happen.

"I've been appointed choirmaster at Sancta Maria Regina Coeli in Rome, where they do all the wonderful old music. Palestrina, Victoria, Gregorian chant. The music of the spheres."

"Oh my God!"

"Ah, now, there's no need of that. I'll still answer to 'Father.'"

"When did this come up?"

Brennan looked at Monty. "When was it I first mentioned it? Just after Christmas?"

Maura gave Monty a look he could interpret from long years of experience. It said, *You knew about this and didn't tell me?*

"So," Brennan asked, "are youse going to miss me?"

"Your absence will be noted," Monty acknowledged.

"Men! Of course we're going to miss you." She didn't hide the fact that she meant it. Brennan Burke had become a fundamental part of their lives since they had met in Halifax five years before. They had been through agony and ecstasy together, and he had become such a close friend he was more like family. The stars would be dimmed, the music would be in a distinctly minor key, without him. But Monty would rather be flayed alive than say so.

Maura had no such inhibitions. "How long . . . does this mean you're finished in Halifax?" The look on her face was one of consternation.

"Not at all. A one-year term while the present choirmaster is serving in Munich. I spend one year lording it over the quaking choristers at Saint Mary Queen of Heaven and then I return to Halifax, the Roman coming home in triumph."

"That sounds more like it. And like you."

"Looking forward to it, I imagine," said Monty.

"I am. But I'm also looking forward to my time here in the old country. I hadn't planned on two spells away, but Dennis Cronin has been most accommodating." That was the archbishop back home in Halifax. "And he promised not to bring in a banjo-playing, hootenanny type of choir director to fill in for me at the church or at the choir school."

"Well, you've got it all under control," Monty said. "And if you need someone to help you out in Rome with 'Ag Críost an Síol,' give me a call and I'll be on the next flight out."

"I'll do that, though there must be some Irish lads loitering around in Rome. There's an Irish-language confessional in Saint John Lateran Basilica, so that suggests Irish-speaking sinners in the eternal city."

"With one more on his way. Congratulations, Brennan!" Maura leaned over and kissed him on the cheek. He put his arm around her and gave her a hug, looking as if he could already hear the ethereal sounds of Palestrina soaring to the Roman skies.

†

Near the end of the following week, after three days of tedious paperwork and interviews out at the Canadian Earth Equipment plant, Monty found the pot of gold at the end of the rainbow. Well, some would call it a brass pot at best; some would call it a pot of a different kind and colour altogether. But to Monty it was pure Au, atomic number 79, one of the few atomic numbers that had stayed in his mind after high school chemistry. And it all came about because of Emmet Crowley, the sole criminal lawyer at Ellison Whiteside. When Monty arrived at the office on Thursday morning, he found the place abuzz with the news that Crowley had disappeared. Monty recalled his attempt to strike up a collegial relationship with Crowley, his offer to assist the criminal lawyer with some of his cases. But Crowley had never taken him up on the offer. Monty remembered him looking distracted, busy, harassed. Now, it seemed, there was a reason why the lawyer had been frazzled. Monty's colleagues today revealed that Crowley had run afoul of the Law Society of Northern Ireland and was facing disciplinary action. Now he was gone. Rumour had it he had fled to New Zealand, with funds belonging to a client.

It was clear from the talk around the office, and not just the talk today, that the firm frowned upon criminal matters, and that the partners had been putting some pressure on Emmet Crowley to stop taking criminal clients and to limit his practice to corporate law and civil litigation. Now the criminal lawyer had left, but the criminal files were still on his desk.

Later that day, Muriel Whiteside rapped on Monty's door. "Good afternoon, Monty."

"Hello, Muriel." She was a stylishly dressed woman in her late forties, one of the founding partners of the firm.

"You've heard the news, I expect, that Emmet Crowley is no longer with us."

"Yes, I heard."

Monty waited to see if she would elaborate on the reasons for his departure, but she merely kept calm and carried on. "As you probably know, his preferred area of practice was criminal law." Her good, respectable Ulster face said it all when she pronounced the words "criminal law."

"Right, I knew that."

"Well, not surprisingly, given his hasty departure, he left a few files unfinished. Cases that have not yet run their course."

"I see."

"A couple of them will be going to court quite soon and, from what we understand of the complaints lodged with the Law Society, he never briefed a barrister about these upcoming court matters. Actually, what I think happened is that he had a barrister lined up for one or more of the cases and then there was a dispute. Whatever the situation, the files need to be dealt with straight away. All this is by way of asking whether you would be interested in taking them over."

Is the Pope a papist? "I would be very interested, Muriel, thank you."

"I thought you would. We here at Ellison Whiteside are moving away from that line of work. We won't be taking on any more criminal cases, but we will honour the clients to whom we have already committed ourselves. A couple of these involve petty crimes, theft and a bar brawl." She rolled her eyes.

"Bring 'em on. I've done lots of those in between the murders and the sex crimes."

"Yes, I can imagine. Now among these files there are three of a different order altogether."

"Yes?"

"Terrorist offences."

Old Monty had hit the big time in Belfast.

"Would you like to come with me to Emmet's old office? You'll see what's there."

He got up and followed Muriel through the corridors of Ellison Whiteside. She turned and said to him, "We'll be glad to have these dealt with and off our docket."

Monty looked around him at the posh furnishings, the portraits of former solicitors on the walls — prosperous-looking personages, fusty even, like late Victorians. There were photographs of some of the members of the firm with government figures at Whitehall in London and at the Parliament of Northern Ireland at Stormont, which had been suspended early in the Troubles, revived, and suspended again, leaving Northern Ireland under direct rule from London. Wherever power was centred, Ellison Whiteside lawyers were there, shaking hands. It was, proudly, the Establishment. A bastion of Unionist privilege. None of the august men or the few women now on the wall had a whiff of Republicanism about their person, or their names. To be fair, none of them, past or present, looked as if they'd be any more at home with Loyalist paramilitaries than with members of the Provisional IRA. *Not our sort, don't you know.* Monty knew he was generalizing, stereotyping, committing the very sin he condemned in others, the sin of identifying lawyers with their clients. He also knew he was right. But somebody had taken on the occasional paramilitary case in the past: Emmet Crowley. He was "no longer with us." Was he ever *with us*? Monty wondered.

There were no longer any personal touches, if there had been any, in the office that had been occupied by Emmet Crowley. There was nothing but three thick file folders on the desk and three stacks of boxes on the floor.

"The minor offences can wait for now. These are the Prevention of Terrorism Act files. Two involve Loyalist paramilitaries, and the third —" Muriel raised her eyebrows at Monty "— the third involves the IRA."

"Right."

"So, we'll have these put on a trolley and brought into your office."

"I'll get the trolley."

"Are you sure?"

"Quite."

"Thank you, Monty."

"You're more than welcome, Muriel."

Monty was keen to tell Maura about his good fortune, that is, the misfortune of certain of his firm's clients, which would redound to the benefit of Monty himself. He would now have something interesting to do. So he called his wife at her office at the UCD law school. She agreed that this sounded more fulfilling than reading carton-loads of documents about metal fatigue and fractured disc harrow blades for his farm equipment case. Even though that case was putting coin in the coffers of his Halifax firm.

"I'm going to work overtime on these criminal files, do what has to be done on my end and then, since Montague Michael Collins, QC, Barrister and Solicitor, is not a barrister over here, I'll round up a barrister to take the matters to court. Court dates are coming up soon."

They exchanged other bits of news, and Maura said she had no lectures scheduled for tomorrow, Friday, and they decided no harm would be done by giving Normie a day off school, so they would be taking the train up to Belfast for the weekend.

Chapter IX

Monty

Monty met his family at the train station Friday afternoon and, after a round of hugs and kisses, he noticed that Orla Farrell was with them. She said she had decided to come and visit some of her relations in Belfast, and a cousin would be meeting her, and there he was now. So she said her goodbyes and promised to see the kids again soon. Dominic put his arms around her; then, a gentleman at heart, he reluctantly let her go.

"What would you like to see in Belfast city today?"

"Well, I have a small errand to perform," said Maura. "I promised one of my colleagues in Dublin that I would deliver a book to a prof at the law school here, so I should drop that off."

"Sure. Let's head there now. It's a short walk from my flat."

They drove to his place and dropped off the bags, then set out on foot for Queen's University Belfast. When they crossed the street to the main campus, they stood gazing in awe at the splendour before them.

"A castle!" Dominic exclaimed.

"It looks like one, doesn't it?" his sister replied. "Or like a great big old church, except that it's wide instead of long!"

They were looking upon the magnificent Lanyon Building, a Tudor Gothic edifice of warm-red brick and honey-toned sandstone. The building had big leaded-glass windows and three towers with crenellations; the central tower was topped by pinnacles at each of its four corners. But most pleasing to the children were the two angels guarding the entrance.

"Is that the law school?" Normie asked. "The angels are watching out for everybody there."

"No, it's not the law school," Monty told her. "That's in another part of the university."

"Not many angels *there*, I'll bet," his wife declared. "Bunch of lawyers and future lawyers."

"But lawyers are good! They help people get out of trouble."

"God love you, Normie. You're right. Most of them are on the side of the angels."

"Except sometimes when they're on the side of the bad guys. Like you, Daddy, when you work for killers and bank robbers."

"Now, sweetheart, the bad guys need protection, too. Because sometimes they didn't do it."

"Yeah, I know. If it wasn't for guys like you, the police could throw anybody they didn't like into prison."

"And that's exactly what happens in some places in the world."

"Not here, though, right?"

"No, of course not, sweetie." He and Maura exchanged glances over their little girl's head.

"The law school is nice, too," Normie said. And it was. They had made the short walk to the School of Law, which was located in a beautiful terrace of houses on University Square. The law school occupied several of the buildings.

"I love those red-brick places! Like yours, Daddy," said Normie. "We should have streets full of brick buildings like this at home."

"That would be lovely, wouldn't it?" Maura agreed. "There aren't many in Halifax. A few near the law school, though, coincidentally."

"Yeah, those are really nice. We should buy one of them when we get home."

"Talk to your father."

"Ha ha. You always say that when the answer is no." Then she pointed to the last house in the row. "The corner house is made of different stuff. It looks like little brown stones."

"That's right. It's called pebbledash."

Normie's eyes widened with delight. "Pebbledash! What a cool word!"

Ah, for the days when the sound of a simple word was enough to bring joy to the heart.

✝

After she had made her delivery, Maura expressed an interest in taking a bus tour around the city. And Dominic concurred. "Bus!" But Normie had always liked visiting Monty's office at home, so she decided that's what she would do today. When mother and son headed off to find a tour bus, father and daughter went to work.

Monty wanted to spend some time reading through his new files. Normie was happy to spend her time writing a story on his computer while he worked. His secretary, Laura, poked her head in, greeted Normie, and said, "Monty, you didn't forget the call from Miss Flanagan, did you? She called again when you were out."

"Oh! I'm sorry, Laura. I meant to call Katie. I'll do it right now."

He picked up the phone, reached Katie Flanagan, and apologized for not calling sooner.

"That's all right, Mr. Collins."

"You can call me Monty."

"Um, Monty, my mam's in the hospital."

"Oh, I'm sorry to hear that." As if Katie and the other kids didn't have enough to deal with. "What happened?"

"Oh, it's just her nerves going on her. It happens sometimes. But what I wanted to tell you was that Auntie Assumpta is coming in a little later to see Mam. It's close by. Musgrave Park Hospital. And she says she has some information for us, Assumpta does."

"Oh, good. She's going to stop in at your house?"

"Aye. So I'll let you know whatever she says."

"Better still, why don't I take a drive out and see what she has to say?"

"Good. I'll see you soon."

He looked at Normie, absorbed in her work. He had learned never to interfere with the creative process by asking her what she was writing; when she was ready, she would tell her parents or not, as she saw fit. He considered leaving her here in the office to write, but then thought she might like to go for a drive out to the suburbs. In the usual course of things, he would never, ever bring his children anywhere within the orbit of his clientele because, in the usual course of things, his clients were people charged with murder, assault, armed robbery, sexual offences, and/or any number of other things that made necessary an impregnable wall between his life at work and his life at home. But Katie Flanagan was not in that league. No reason Normie couldn't come along for the trip. He told her he had a young client named Katie, and they were going to see her.

"How old is she?"

"Sixteen."

"That means she's a young offender, right?"

"No, no. Sorry, sweetheart, I should have explained right away. She's not charged with an offence."

"So how come she's one of your clients?"

"Her dad died in an accident. He fell, and it may be because he was hit by a car."

"That's awful!" Normie's hazel eyes were huge with concern behind the lenses of her wire-framed glasses. "I wouldn't be able to stand it if that happened to you!"

"And there are four younger kids."

"This is terrible. What are you going to do?"

"I'm hoping we'll be able to find the guy who was driving the car that hit Katie's dad, if that's what happened, and sue him for money for Katie and her family."

"I hope so! Why can't you find him?"

"Sometimes people leave the scene of an accident."

"They shouldn't be allowed to do that! They should stay and help the person or get the ambulance."

"That's what they're supposed to do."

"Some people are rotten!"

You said a mouthful there, little one.

They drove through the city towards the Flanagan residence, and Monty did not point out the sites of bombings and other attacks that had been pointed out to him on his travels with Katie Flanagan and Hughie Malone. When they got to the Musgrave Park neighbourhood, he found a parking space a few doors away from the Flanagan house.

"These places look newer than the ones we always see in town," Normie remarked.

"I suppose they are. And that one is Katie's."

They walked to the house with the light brown bricks and knocked on the door. Katie opened it and invited Monty in. "'Bout ye, Mr. Collins? Monty, I mean." Then she spotted the young red-haired girl at his side. "Oh! Who's this now?"

"Hi. I'm Normie." She pointed to Monty. "He's my dad, and I was in his office, and he said I could come."

"I'm Katie. You're welcome to come inside."

They followed her into the house. All the furniture in the living room was covered with children's clothes. "I did the washing and hung it on the line outside but then it started to rain, so . . ."

"That must happen a lot," Normie said. "You get quite a bit of rain here."

"We do."

"But it's nice again now, so do you want me to help you hang the clothes up again?"

"No, I couldn't be arsed to do it all again. But thank you, Normie."

"So, Katie," Monty said, "how are you doing these days?"

"Good."

"Where are your sister and brothers today?"

"Darren and Dermot and Clare are with their school. There's a field trip to the Giant's Causeway."

"Oh, I'd love to see that!" said Normie. "I saw a picture of it in a book."

"I'm sorry to hear about your mother," Monty said again.

"Yeah, it's just . . . she has to go in sometimes. She gets depressed and upset."

"Yes, I'm sure she does."

"I got invited to debating club today."

"Oh? Where's that?"

"At Saint Columba's, my old school. Even though I don't go there anymore, Mrs. Donnelly rang and invited me."

"Wonderful," Monty said. "I'll bet you make a very good debater."

"I really liked it when I was in it at school. I won a prize. And Father McMullan came up to me after and said, 'Miss Flanagan, you'll be prime minister someday, the first Catholic prime minister of the U.K.! You can count on my vote!' I loved him saying that. And then he went on, 'Best thing to do is start out as a solicitor, and then simply move up to Number Ten! You'll make some much-needed changes around here when you're in the top job.' I'm sorry, I shouldn't boast about it. But I really love debating, writing up the arguments, taking apart what the person says on the other side. Anyway," she looked down then, embarrassed, "I liked it."

"Good for you, Katie. You must really have a talent for it. So, did you go today? Or you haven't gone yet?"

"Ach, I can't go to it. But it's nice to be invited."

"Why can't you go?"

"Timmy's here."

Monty looked around for the little boy he had met last time. "Timmy is Katie's brother," he explained to Normie.

"Where is he?" Normie asked.

"Not here in the house. He's outside with the lads playing football, but I have to mind him. I can't keep annoying Mrs. Hamill to watch out for the kids. That's my job. And besides, she works at a newsagent's and isn't home that often."

Monty thought about it. "What time is debating club?"

"Half four, and it goes for an hour and a half, so . . ."

"Is it a regular event?"

"This is the second time. They're going to have it every Wednesday and Friday. Anyway, Auntie Assumpta will be here soon. She can't stay. She's coming with a friend who has a car, and she's going to visit Mam, but she'll give me — give us — the information she found."

Monty felt a little sharp elbow nudging him. He looked down and Normie was giving him a significant look. "Ahem," she said. He knew what she was thinking. He smiled down at her and told Katie, "We'll wait for Assumpta, and then we'll watch Timmy's game, and you can go to your club."

"Ach, youse couldn't do that. I told Mrs. Donnelly I wouldn't be able to join it. She understands."

"Katie, go!" That was Normie. "I love to watch little kids playing. We have Gaelic football matches at my school sometimes, back in Nova Scotia I mean, because Father Burke used to play it when he was little here in Ireland and he misses it so he started up a league. Is it Gaelic football your brother is playing?"

"No, it's Association football. You know, Celtics, Rangers type of football."

"Soccer," Monty explained to Normie.

"Oh, right, we have that at home, too. But you better hurry. It's after four o'clock, and you might be late."

"Are you sure?"

"Absolutely," Monty assured her. "Get yourself ready and take us over to Timmy when you're set to go. I'll keep an eye out for your aunt."

"Lovely! The debate today is *Medical experiments on animals are justified, yes or no.*"

"And what side are you taking on that question?"

"I won't know till I get there, because I missed the session on Wednesday, but that's all right. So I have to consider what status animals have in the whole of existence. Are humans entitled to greater rights? If so, on what grounds?"

Getting right to first principles. Monty liked that.

The young girl continued, "I remember learning that Aristotle said we humans are rational animals. But if some animals are not rational, is that their fault at all? Do we have the right to use that against them? What about more intelligent versus less intelligent animals, even though it's not the fault of, say, a slug in the garden if he hasn't evolved very far and he's never had an intelligent thought in his poor little life. And what if you're the mother of a baby who might die if the right kind of drug can't be found, and experiments have been forbidden because the 'no' side of the animal debate won the day? Oh! I have to change my clothes and wash my face. Or wash first, and then . . ." Her face was flushed with excitement. It was the most animated Monty had ever seen her.

Five minutes later she bounded down the stairs, wearing a little bit of makeup, a dark tartan skirt, a bright blue sweater, and a great big smile. Monty and Normie followed her from the house and down the street. They came to a big empty lot where a bunch of little boys in pint-size Celtic FC green-and-white-striped jerseys had set up two goals and were playing a spirited game of soccer. A few of them looked over at the new arrivals, and Katie gave them a timeout sign. "Timmy!"

"What?"

"Come talk to me."

"Aw!"

"Only for a minute."

He ran over and looked at his sister and then at Normie. "Who are you?"

"I'm Normie. I'm going to watch the match. Katie's going to debating club."

"Do they have chocky biscuits there?"

"They do not!" His sister laughed and ruffled his short golden curls. "It's serious business we do. Debate the great questions of the day."

"I want to play football."

"And you will. Normie and Mr. Collins are going to mind you while I'm gone."

He looked up at Normie again and said, "Watch this!" He tore off towards the centre of the field, took his teammates and opponents by surprise, and grabbed the ball. He held it under his left arm, kept his right out to fend off the defenders, and ran to the net, hip-checked the goal keeper and then put the ball down and booted it into the net. He raised his arms and did a dance of triumph. He was met with a chorus of "That doesn't count, ya bollocks!" He laughed, and then they resumed the game according to Association rules.

Katie turned to Monty and Normie and said, "Are youse sure you want to stay with that wee sprog?"

"Yeah, it'll be fun!" Normie assured her.

So she left for Saint Columba's school, fairly skipping as she went.

Monty watched from the street, so he could see Assumpta when she arrived. It was a high-scoring football match, played with great exuberance, until one of the mothers on the street called the boys in for their tea.

"That's Barry's ma. She makes a lovely tea," Timmy told Normie when the boys came off the field. "She makes gingerbread and cherry cake and lemon bread and she always has the digestive biscuits with the chocolate slathered on the top of them. Dead on! She's fuckin' brilliant, she is!"

"We all are!" boasted a boy of Timmy's age, with cropped hair almost the same colour as Tim's and sparkling green eyes.

"This is Barry himself," Timmy explained. He leaned forward and whispered to Normie, "Me and Barry are best mates." Raising his volume, he declared, "We're going to go to Glasgow and play for Celtic and kick those Rangers' bums!" He reached out and pounded his best mate on the shoulder, and Barry got him in a headlock. They fell to the ground in a joyful heap, then rose and bounded towards Barry's house, each attempting to shove the other out of the way in the race to the door.

Monty and Normie went back to the Flanagan house. About ten minutes later, a car pulled up and Assumpta Flanagan got out.

"Hello, Assumpta! Katie's gone to her debating club and she's left me in charge."

"That's grand, Mr. Collins. I'm so happy she's stayed with the club. She's marvellous at it; everyone says so. She has a brilliant future ahead of her. If, well, if she has a future! And I told her I couldn't stay and visit, so this works out well. I'm off to see Winnie in the hospital. I know she's having a rough time of it. She's not a strong woman. But I'm hoping I can encourage her to —" her lips tightened and she searched for the appropriate words "— well, participate a little more."

Monty introduced her to Normie, and they exchanged greetings. Then Assumpta handed Monty an envelope.

"It was Vincent McKeever who saw the car that night just off the Ammon Road. I knew I'd see him walking by on his way to work at the farm. I asked him about it, and he was jittery about it, let me tell you. But I told him that it was my nephew who died that night, leaving a wife and five children, and that any information might help them. He got the picture, and he's agreed to meet with you. I reassured him that you are not from this area." Not affiliated with any of the factions here. "You're to come alone. And he doesn't want to be seen talking with you anywhere near home, so here's a map of where he will be — at the edge of the wood! — at two o'clock on Sunday."

She pointed to the woman driving the car that had brought her. "Time for our hospital rounds. Best of luck with the investigation."

"Thank you very much for your own investigative work, Assumpta."

"Think nothing of it."

Chapter X

Brennan

"We have to find out whether he's in the city." Ronan was talking about Brody MacAllan, the man Ronan believed had planted one of the car bombs in Dublin in 1974, the man who had the papers to show he was in the United States at the time of the attacks. Brennan was sitting opposite his cousin in the house in Andersonstown. "The lad I put on the case thinks he spotted MacAllan going into a bar across the river. The Iron Will. But our lad can't go into the bar or loiter outside it — he might be recognized — so he can't get close enough to make the identification. And it's far from a sure thing; MacAllan, like the rest of us, is twenty years older now."

"Was this just one sighting by your man in east Belfast?"

"He caught sight of him and then made a point of watching the bar at certain times of the day, from his vantage point in a second-floor flat nearby. Seems MacAllan, if it's him, drinks in this bar on weekends, arrives early in the evening. Don't know where he drinks on the other nights."

Brennan offered no comment on the assumption that a man drinks somewhere every night of the week. Who was Brennan to talk? All he said was "You'll have to equip your agent with the proper spy gear."

"Ha, should have thought of that. Rob some gear off the Brits. We did spring for a pair of binoculars. But he still couldn't be sure. And we had to pull him out for other reasons. There's nobody we can send into the bar. MacAllan sure as hell wouldn't fall for one of our lads from the Falls tracking him down in east Belfast and chatting him up about a come-to-Jesus meeting in Kentucky or Texas or Tennessee or wherever it was. I'd recruit you for the mission, Father, but somehow I don't think a papish priest born in Dublin and educated in Rome — and soon to be back in Rome as a choirmaster — would succeed in getting a confession out of a militant Protestant Loyalist paramilitary who's trying to cover up his role in a massacre in the Republic of Ireland."

"O ye of little faith." Brennan raised his arms and his voice, which was now the voice of a preacher from the American South. "Praise the Lord! Praise Him! Mabel, honey, why don't you fry up a mess o' grits for the Sunday picnic!"

Ronan laughed. "You'd better hope you're what you claim to be, a representative of the One True Church. Because if you're not, and the evangelical Protestants are the ones at the right hand of our Lord, and you have mocked those who bear His word, you have just consigned yourself to the smoke and flames of eternal damnation."

Brennan gave an exaggerated shrug. "We'll see in the end, won't we?" Then he asked, "Where was this evangelical event, though, do you know?"

"Somewhere in the American South. Hold on, while I look it up." Ronan flipped through his notes and said, "Right, it was Tennessee. That's the South, isn't it?"

"It is."

"Ever been there?"

"Nope."

"Pity. I could send you in to MacAllan's local to talk Tennessee with him if you knew the territory. You'd be a local preacher, over here to catch a fire-and-brimstone sermon or two by the Reverend Doctor Ian Paisley."

"Might create a bit of suspicion if a God-fearing, clean-living American minister showed up in a drinking hole."

"You're saying some of them wouldn't have our taste for whiskey and porter?"

"Some of them are teetotallers, Ronan. There are churches in the United States, and even in Canada, where they serve grape juice or even the children's drink, Kool-Aid, instead of wine at communion!"

Ronan, who no doubt thought he had seen and heard it all in the streets and prisons of troubled Ireland, gaped at his cousin, unbelieving. "You're havin' me on, Brennan!"

"I'm not. There are sects over there that are death on drink."

"But Jesus Christ Himself, bless His Holy Name, lifted the cup, as we know. Turned water into wine!"

"Don't ask me to explain it, Ronan. I'm as perplexed as you are yourself. Anyway, it might not be all that credible, a southern U.S. minister cozying up to MacAllan on a barstool."

"I know, I know. I wouldn't try to infiltrate you into enemy territory in circumstances like that."

"An American tourist could stumble in to the Iron Will, though, looking for a beer and a bit of local colour. Show me his photo again."

"Here he is."

Brennan studied the narrowed dark eyes, the uncombed dark hair resting on the man's collar, the flat, uncompromising face. It was a face he would not soon forget.

†

Brennan had made plans to meet Monty and the MacNeil, she being Maura MacNeil, on Royal Avenue Friday evening, so he said goodbye to Ronan, went out, and hailed one of the black taxis that served the people of west Belfast. The old London cab already had three passengers but they made room for Brennan, and he squeezed himself in. When the taxi got to the Falls Road, Brennan saw two grey-green armoured vehicles pull out of a side street and rumble off in the direction of Andersonstown. British Army, still here after more than twenty-five years. His fellow passengers barely accorded them a glance. A few blocks later, he watched as a squad of British soldiers moved along the pavement in a sort of diamond formation. They wore camouflage fatigues and berets and carried assault rifles. The residents of the Falls ignored them.

Brennan's friends were waiting in front of the CastleCourt Shopping Centre when he arrived. Orla Farrell was looking after their two children, they said, and it looked as though the kids would have reason to be pleased when their parents returned home. Maura had a shopping bag that was overflowing, and Brennan could see the nose of a toy airplane, which their little boy Dominic would love, and when he peered into the bag he spotted a xylophone, which would be for Normie.

"You're the fearless wee colleen, aren't you now?" he said, eyeing the big new glass and steel shopping emporium.

"What do you mean?" Maura asked him.

He gestured to their surroundings. "Going into a glass building in Belfast."

"Oh, Christ," Maura replied.

"Don't be concerned, my dear. I don't believe it's been bombed lately."

"But it has been . . ."

"Several times. Prime target for what is sometimes referred to by Republicans here as a 'routine commercial bombing.'"

"Imagine getting to the point where something like that is *routine*!"

"Oh, it got to that point a long, long time ago. Just as everyone got used to the 'Ring of Steel,' those massive security gates surrounding the city centre here. All just part of everyday life in Belfast."

"Makes me want to scurry back to the safety of a university campus. After all, universities are often mocked for not being part of the real world. That may not be a bad thing after all."

"Just don't look for refuge in the Celtic department at Queen's here."

"What do you mean?"

"The Irish language — the *native* language — to some of the Loyalist paramilitaries is like a full moon to a rabid wolf. They attacked the department several times in the 1970s, so there's no neon sign advertising the department now. But let's not dwell on any of that." He regretted making light of the tensions in the city, the atrocities committed by all sides, and he reflected on the fact that you didn't have to be in Belfast very long before you got accustomed to the situation and began making quips about it. "We'll have a quick meal, and go around the corner to Madden's."

So they ate at a nearby restaurant and then walked behind the shopping centre to Madden's bar. Brennan felt as if he had died and ascended into heaven, the way he always felt when he entered the establishment on Berry Street. The staff greeted him by name, and he saluted them. To walk into Madden's was to enter a world of Gaelic culture with signs in the Irish language all over the place, tributes to various Republican heroes and organizations, and notices of frequent sessions of traditional music. And Madden's poured you a decent pint and a fine glass of whiskey.

"I may not see youse for a while," Brennan announced when the first pints had been poured and sipped.

"Why not?" Maura asked. "Are you going to Rome sooner than planned?"

"No, no, not at all. I'll be about as far from Rome as you can get."

"Where now?"

He leaned towards her. "I'm going undercover."

"Undercover as what, for Christ's sake? Where?"

"As an American tourist in east Belfast."

"I believe you made the point at Tom Burke's wedding that you and your kind are not welcome on the east side of town. But that's as far as I can follow your logic, Brennan."

"Good, darlin'. Maybe my target won't follow it either."

"And your target is?"

"A suspect in the bombing of Dublin in 1974."

"Brennan, what in the hell are you talking about?"

"My dear, it's very hush-hush."

"My lips are sealed. Now, get on with it."

"You know there were car bomb attacks in May of 1974 in Dublin and Monaghan." This met with wary nods from both of them. "One of the victims was a childhood friend of mine. Paddy Healey. The police on both sides of the border have had a list of suspects almost from the beginning. The Ulster Volunteer Force claimed responsibility in 1993, but nobody has ever been charged."

"Why the hell not?" Maura demanded.

"Because of the way things work in this place. Because the people who did it have strong ties to the police and security forces here."

"That's outrageous!"

"Welcome to Belfast justice, Professor MacNeil."

"I know. I've received an earful about this sort of thing from my colleagues at UCD. But that doesn't soften the blow every time I hear about it all over again."

"So," said Monty, "after twenty-one years of inaction, and the forces of the law and secret intelligence and the military arrayed against you, you are somehow going to solve this crime. And your plan requires you to be in costume as a Yankee tourist . . . Help me here, Brennan."

"Not a Yank, strictly speaking. Good ole boys from the American South would take umbrage at being called Yankees. Yankees is northerners. But other than that, you're on the right track. One of the suspects claims to have been in the state of Tennessee attending a religious event at the time of the bombings. I'm going to try and open him up a bit about that experience."

"Did he participate in a monastic retreat?" Maura asked. "A seminar on the Virgin Mary? A Knights of Columbus piss-up and devotional weekend?"

"Em, no."

"Didn't think so. Not a Catholic event. So you, as a papist, are going to get to the bottom of this and then convince the authorities, after all these years, to take this man in and charge him with the bombings."

"I am, yeah." Brennan sank the rest of his pint and said, "But I won't be a papist when I darken the doorway of the Iron Will bar. I'll be a staunchly Protestant tourist from — not Tennessee, that would be too obvious — Kentucky maybe."

"Oh. Why didn't you say so? It all makes sense now."

"Right."

"Brennan, you have the look of a Roman choirmaster. Or a cardinal. You do not have the look of a good ole boy from south of the Mason-Dixon line. I don't mean that in a bad way, as Normie would say. You could take it as a compliment."

"I will look the part by the time I go in undercover. I'll put a Stetson or a ball cap on and a plaid shirt. Hell, I don't know. I'll get it sorted."

"And then," Monty said, "you'll sidle up to this guy in the bar, and he's going to start blabbing to you, a man he's never seen before, who just happened to wander in to his local."

"It does need work, I admit. Though my only real assignment is to verify that he is there. The man we have in mind drinks there on the weekends, goes in early in the evening."

"It never ceases to amaze me," Maura said, "that everybody in this country seems to know where everybody else drinks, and when, and how much."

"That's why we have the phrase 'yer man's a regular' at such and such a pub, *acushla*. Anyway, if I can spot him, I've fulfilled my mission. If I can get him talking, all the better."

"I can think of one thing that would make you look less suspicious and more like a tourist," said Maura.

"What's that?"

"A wife."

"Don't even think about it," Monty warned. The humour had gone out of him.

His wife ignored him.

†

The following afternoon, Saturday, Brennan made a call to an evangelical pastor he knew in New York and asked him if he could think of someone Brennan could talk to about a rally featuring Hiram B. Stockwell back in the 1970s. The man suggested a couple of people who had probably attended, and one was a Baptist minister from Ohio whom Brennan had met at an ecumenical conference a few years ago, Harold Tait. The Reverend Mr. Tait was more than happy to assist. Brennan had to be cagey about why he was making the inquiry, but he said he had to know whether a certain man had been in the United States when he claimed to have been there. He said it was in relation to the "political situation here." Tait didn't ask for details. After the preliminaries were over, Brennan asked about the Stockwell rally in Tennessee in May of 1974. Tait said he would look over his notes and call him back.

"Oh, it was a huge event," Tait told him later that day. "Sixty thousand people, and it went on over the course of five days. Or the conference did. Hiram Stockwell wasn't on the stage every day and night, of course. There were other speakers. But Stockwell was the main attraction."

"It ran from when to when?"

"May the thirteenth through the seventeenth."

"Now, here's the hard part, and I'm sorry for keeping you on the line about it. But can you give me a few details I should look out for when —" Brennan didn't say *if* "— I talk to the man here? Things that I'd expect to hear if he was really there?"

Tait gave a quick rundown of the schedule as he remembered it, the size of the crowds, the subjects of the talks, the session with a faith healer. His notes recorded how bad the weather was, muggy and cloudy, with showers and a few real downpours. And the events with Stockwell were outdoors. There was a big marquee where the merchandise was being sold, eight-track tape recordings of his sermons and such. And other tents and marquees but not nearly enough of them to cover the entire congregation. One day, Tait recalled, the sun broke through, and the folks roared their delight. Stockwell had a bit of fun with that, joking that the Lord was showing his approval but didn't want anyone to get too overconfident, so everybody should expect the clouds to return.

'Twas great *craic* altogether taking on the dramatic personae of Duane and Ruby Jean ("Don't call me Rube!") from Paducah, Kentucky. The MacNeil was having the time of her life working on her dialect and outfitting Brennan as a southern redneck, with herself as his down-market southern belle. She had been to a couple of charity shops earlier in the day, and the costuming was being done at the Collins residence in south Belfast. The two children, Normie and Dominic, were enjoying the spectacle. They had been told their mother and Father Burke were going to a costume party.

While the kids were occupied with the kitsch their mother had procured, Brennan filled her in on everything he'd been told about MacAllan and the Stockwell event in Tennessee. She took it all in, then got back to the comedy.

"How 'bout Huckabee as our last name?" the MacNeil asked him.

"Not believable. Particularly when you sound as if you're choking to death on that first syllable."

"There are Huckabees in Amurrica."

"Where the hell else would there be Huckabees?"

"All right. A plain, no-nonsense name."

This went on for a while and then they settled on Ballard. Maura had found a surprisingly real-looking wig that gave Brennan long, straggly salt and pepper hair. Knowing him well, she had shampooed it and dried it before bringing it into the room with him. He had gone without shaving, so there was a bit of dark scruff on his face. She had found a ball cap with the Dallas Cowboys logo on it, and he pulled that down over the wig. She had resisted the temptation to rig him out in a Hawaiian shirt and settled on plaid with a pair of jeans. There was a plain denim jacket and another with a longhorn steer on the back, his choice. But the garish white and green track shoes were obligatory. After he'd got himself kitted out with the longhorn jacket and all the rest of the clobber, she slung a big camera on a strap around his neck, stood back, and then decided that was overdoing it. She would bring her own little camera. She did insist, however, on what she called a "fanny pack," a nylon money pouch that was tied around one's waist with a belt. It looked ridiculous.

"American tourists always have these. You're going to wear yours in front. I'll put mine over my fanny."

"Don't be using that word around here, darlin'. Trust me."

"How come?"

"Let's just say it applies only to women and it doesn't refer to your arse, and we'll leave it at that."

The MacNeil had outdone herself with a big bouffant hairdo, gobs of makeup on her eyes, and bright pink lipstick. She wore a fluffy pink sweater with little puffs of wool all over it and skin-tight leggings of a darker pink satin. She, too, had oversized, boat-like track shoes on her feet. She acknowledged the February weather with a white fake-leather jacket.

She hauled him over to a mirror, and he could hardly believe his eyes. He would not have recognized either of them.

"All right, now, hon," she said, "let's work on our dialect. Do I sound like the li'l southern lady you've always dreamed of?"

"You sure do, sugar. Let's git out there in the pickup and scrape up some roadkill fer supper."

"When we greet folks in the saloon, should we say 'howdy' or would that be too much?"

"I'd leave it out."

"Okay."

They carried on with the foolishness for a few more minutes, until Monty came in from a Saturday stint at the office. He did the best, completely genuine, double take Brennan had ever seen. "Jesus Christ, you two! This is unbelievable."

"What are you lookin' at, stranger?" Brennan challenged him.

"Have we gone too far over the top?" Maura asked.

"We've all travelled, and we've all seen worse. But . . ."

"I know," said Brennan. "Over the top doesn't begin to describe it. Gotta tone it down, darlin'."

"Yeah, but it sure was a load of fun while it lasted."

In the end, Brennan jettisoned the wig but kept the ball cap, pulled down low, and the plain denim jacket over the plaid shirt. Maura brought her hair down from humongous to merely big, wiped off the pink lipstick and some of the eye makeup, and put on a generic pair of dark trousers with a white shirt and the white leather jacket.

"One more thing, Brennan," she said. "We should have wads of gum in our mouths. Americans are always chewing on something."

"No need to go that far."

"Right. We wouldn't want to be tacky."

"Only thing going in my mouth, sugar, is moonshine."

"Speaking of mouths, did you ever notice that tourists often have their mouths gaping open when they gawk around them, blocking everyone else on the sidewalk?"

"I'll have to remember that."

Monty turned serious then. "You know what I think of this scheme. This isn't theatre. This is a hard-core Loyalist bar where you're going to be meeting a killer. And others like him. There will be nobody there to pull you out if it gets dangerous."

He was right. For all the fun of dressing up and carrying on, the actual performance was fraught with risk. Going back into character, Duane said, "I'm goin' in alone."

He could have predicted the MacNeil's reaction. "You're *what?*"

"I'll do this. There's no need for —"

"No need for the little woman, is that it?"

"That's it," Monty chimed in and received a black stare from his life's companion.

"Let me spell things out for you two gallant swains," she said. "Nobody knows me here; hence, there is nobody who can recognize me. No member of the Burke Battalion of the Bold IRA drinks in the bars of east Belfast. Am I correct in that, boys?"

Brennan conceded the point with a reluctant nod.

"The possibility of recognition is remote for a member of the Burke family who, as far as we know, is not a member of said organization or any other paramilitary outfit and who is not even a resident of this island, let alone the city of Belfast. How am I doing so far?"

"MacNeil, why don't I just —"

"Why don't you just give your gob a rest and listen."

"The arse is out of 'er now, b'y," said Monty in an imitation of his wife's Cape Breton accent.

"There is no way we can be recognized. Is there a way we could be spotted as fake Kentuckians? Possibly, if there happen to be other southern Americans in the Iron Will bar at the same time as us. How likely is that? All we're going to do is wait and see if this MacAllan character shows his face in the bar. If we get to hear him called by name, that will be a bonus. If we are able to make the identification, we polish off our mint juleps and walk out. Take ourselves a fair distance from the bar and hop in a cab. The worst-case scenario is we come off as a pair of clowns."

Everything she said made sense, but Brennan still didn't like it. Didn't like taking even a minimal risk with Maura beside him. "How about this? We both go as far as the door, then you say goodbye and warn me not to drink too much. And maybe I get a wee kiss goodbye, all in the cause, of course, and —"

"Maybe you get a wee kick in the arse."

"Oh. Well, there's always that risk."

But it came to him then; he had a plan. "All right, let's put our game faces on, y'all, and git movin'. We'll be careful," he promised in his real voice.

"Yeah, right," said Monty. "What could go wrong?"

Monty looked understandably tense as he drove the two impersonators along the Newtownards Road with its Loyalist graffiti and murals. Brennan could see him trying to rally and get into the spirit of things, but he couldn't quite manage it. Brennan, though, was about to put his friend's mind at ease. He knew the cross street was coming up, the street where the bar was located. When Monty stopped for a red light, Brennan made his move. He reached over, wrenched his door open, and jumped out into the semi-darkness of the street. He looked through the windscreen at Monty and said, "Go!" Then he turned and walked away, in the direction of the Iron Will.

But it wasn't just an east Belfast bar owner who had a will of iron. He heard the clatter of footsteps behind him. He didn't even have to turn around. "Hell hath no fury," he said.

"You got that right, hon. No sugar for you tonight. There's more I could say . . ."

"No doubt about that."

"But the show must go on." She took Brennan's hand in hers and got into character, giving him a big corny smile and praising the Lord for giving them such a fun trip to Belfast. He knew it was time to rise to the occasion. There was a cold, damp wind blowing, and they made comments about how warm it must be back home. They walked along the east Belfast thoroughfare, past all the Union Jacks and Ulster Red Hand flags and the Loyalist "No Surrender — No Pope Here — Death to the IRA" graffiti. They posed as starry-eyed tourists, poking their heads into shops and bars along the way, stopping every once in a while to snap pictures of each other. Then they arrived at their destination. "Ah could do with a nice cold beer, Ruby Jean. Just the one. Honest."

"Oh, that's okay, hon. We're on vacation! It will be fun to go into a pub! Let's go!"

And they walked from the twilight into the dark heart of the Iron Will bar. It was the mirror opposite of the Republican bars Brennan knew so well. There were flags and photos and memorabilia. Here, the flags were red, white, and blue. A huge painting of King William III on his white horse took up nearly an entire wall of the pub. Photos showed Orangemen marching through the city with their sashes and lambeg drums; other pictures showed gunmen attending Loyalist funerals or crouching beside armoured vehicles. Looking around him at the clientele, Brennan had no trouble imagining many of these punters carrying guns and aiming them at members of Brennan's family on the other side of town. It was a hard-looking crowd that did their drinking in the Iron Will.

Duane Ballard put on a look of keen touristic interest as he gawked around the place. "Look at that, hon. That's King William on that horse."

"And there's a table right by the horse's hooves. Let's sit there."

"Nah, there's a seat right up at the bar. You take that, and I'll stand."

"Typical man, wants to belly right up to the bar!"

The typical man wanted the bar because the place was fairly packed and most likely that's where Brody MacAllan would end up. So Ruby Jean plunked herself down on a barstool, and Duane stood beside her and asked her what she wanted to drink. There was a big song and dance about what to choose, until she settled on a Singapore sling. Duane took a Budweiser. They babbled away about their vacation, and what the folks back home would say when they saw the holiday snapshots, and on and on. Brennan noticed that people were casting glances in their direction. Little wonder, with the foreign accents and behaviour; now that they'd been noticed, there was all the more reason to stick to the script.

Just when Brennan thought they might not be able to keep the crazy talk flowing, in walked a man who was almost a perfect match for the photo Brennan had seen of Brody MacAllan. The dark hair was shorter, the face older and mellowed by drink, but Brennan recognized him. There was no doubt it was MacAllan. Duane moved over to make room for him. One man managed to get in between them, but Duane was not deterred. Just talked louder.

He engaged in a lot of mindless, voluble chatter with his wife about where else they hoped to go on their short visit to Ulster, and then threw in a bit of speculation about what the folks were up to back home.

Finally, MacAllan took the bait and leaned across the other man. "What part of America are youse from?"

"We're from Kentucky!" Ruby Jean declared. "We're a long way from home, but we're havin' a real good time here in Belfast!"

"Kentucky. What's that close to?" MacAllan had one of the harshest Belfast accents Brennan had ever heard.

"Well," Ruby Jean answered, "it's right next to Ohio, and to Missouri and Tennessee and West Virginia. It borders on a lot of states. And — folks over here like horses, don't they?"

"Aye, they do, unless they lost their pay packet at the races over the weekend."

"Sure, of course, it's not always good. I was going to say we have the Kentucky Derby, which is really good. Unless, like you say . . ."

"No, no, I like the horses myself, and I'd like to go to the Kentucky Derby someday."

"Oh, you should! Pack up the kids and take them over to America! If y'all have as much fun as me and Duane are having here in Northern Ireland, it will be just wonderful! I'm Ruby Jean by the way. And he's Duane."

MacAllan didn't introduce himself but nodded to her and Duane, then ordered a Bushmills. It was obvious to Brennan that MacAllan had been lifting a few prior to arriving at the Iron Will. MacAllan got his drink and exchanged a few words with the man in between them.

Duane had completed the critical part of his mission, which was to verify the presence of MacAllan in the bar; if he could get the fellow talking, all the better. But he didn't want to push things, so he babbled away to Ruby for a while longer. The man who stood between them polished off his drink and made to leave. MacAllan gulped down his whiskey and it looked as if he was about to follow the other man, but he stayed put and eyed the bottles behind the bar. Duane took advantage of the situation to say, "Could we treat you to a drink of your choice?"

"Wouldn't say no to a Bushmills."

So Duane ordered the Bush for MacAllan, another Bud for himself, and a sling for Ruby. "My wife is real taken with sweet drinks like a Singapore sling. Girly stuff!"

"I like drinks that taste just like dessert!" she said. "Anyway, like I was saying, you should come visit America. I know people think we're always bragging up our country, but there really is a lot to see and do."

"I've been to America," MacAllan said then.

"Oh! Whereabouts?" Ruby Jean was on the case again. "Let me guess now. New York! That's where most people go when they come to our country."

"No, Tennessee. Not far from you, if I heard you right."

"Just next door. What brought you there?"

"Went to hear a minister, years ago. One of those big revival meetings. Went on for days." Reiterating his alibi, all these years later.

"Is that right?" Duane asked. "Who was the preacher, if you don't mind me askin'? We love to hear the Word from a man who knows his bible."

"His name was Stockwell."

The drinks arrived then, and MacAllan looked grateful to have a jar in front of him. He raised his glass to them and took a long swallow. Duane Ballard was grateful that the man was on the drink and talkative with it.

Duane took a sip of his beer, then said, "Hiram Stockwell!" He took his wife's hand and squeezed it. "Me and Ruby Jean have heard the Reverend Stockwell preach in Mississippi and over in Arkansas. We've heard Billy Graham, too, and I have to tell you, Hiram Stockwell is every bit as good as Mr. Graham. Both men of the Lord and they do Him credit."

"We didn't get to hear Billy Graham, but I agree with youse about Stockwell. Well worth the trip." MacAllan took a good generous gulp of his whiskey and went on, "Too much of a gentleman, though."

"How d'ya mean?" asked Duane.

"There were a few times when he should have let loose and told the people what he really thought. A barmy crowd of geezers with long beards and raggedy clothes were up near the stage and kept telling Reverend Stockwell that the end times were near and he should let them up on the stage to give the people detailed instructions about where to go and what to do. He just smiled and went on with his talk. And another bloke elbowed his way through the mob and waved a piece of paper at Stockwell and shouted out about some new Roman Catholic churches that had been built, saying the papists were taking over the country."

Ruby Jean put her hand over her mouth to stifle a giggle, her eyes gleaming at MacAllan.

Encouraged, he embellished the tale. "I felt like saying, 'Take a trip across the sea to my wee country if you think you've got a problem with them here!' But all Stockwell did was make a bunch of gooey statements about the United States welcoming all kinds and living in peace, and all that guff."

"Same problem everywhere," Duane drawled. "They breed like goldarn rabbits, the RCs." Brennan Burke, Father Burke, Roman PhD recipient and choirmaster, knew papists were a minority in the United States, always had been, but Duane Ballard kept that to himself.

"Aye, that's what Ian Paisley said. 'They breed like rabbits and multiply like vermin.' Doctor Paisley was dead on," MacAllan affirmed and took a quick, hard drink of his whiskey. "Hiram Stockwell, now, he was the best preacher I ever heard. The wife bought all these eight-tracks of him preaching. We're on our way off the grounds, day's turning to night, and we have to catch our plane, and she's there, loading up on tapes. Still listens to them, as far as I know."

So the wife wasn't living with MacAllan now? Maybe she was still in Scotland where he had gone after the bombing. Duane said, "The women are all in love with him!" And he directed a pointed look at Ruby.

"Don't look at me like that! I just respect him as a man of God. But I have to say he is pleasing to the eye!"

"That must be why she made me lug a big fuckin' poster of him home on the plane, the wife. Made me buy it for her, frame and all, and we didn't even have time to get it crated for the flight. The glass cracked. I told her that would happen. She's still got it up on the wall of her flat."

After a minute or so of quiet drinking, Ruby asked, "How'd you like the South? Can't beat it for the weather, for sure. Everybody must have been jealous of you coming back to Belfast with a real American suntan!"

"Suntan? That's what we were expecting when we signed up. Sun, sun, sun. But, no, we had to go out and buy raincoats."

"Well, aside from that," said Ruby, "were you sorry to be leaving the United States? It's a big country. Too bad you didn't get to see more of it."

"Aye, we wished we'd had more time there. I wanted to see the Grand Canyon, and my wife wanted to see New York. But we were a long way from those places."

"Next time," Ruby assured him.

"Mmm."

The door opened then, and the conversation in the bar fell to a murmur. Glasses were held in mid-air as everyone eyed the man who had just walked in. Brennan could feel the tension even though he had no idea who the fellow was. His hair was buzzed to his scalp and his eyes looked like slivers of pale blue ice; he had so much bulk under his plain black windbreaker that Brennan wondered whether he had on a bulletproof vest. The chilling eyes fixed on Brennan, and then on Maura. Was this lethal individual on to them? Brennan made an effort to show no interest; he let his eyes light upon the new arrival and then move on to others in the Iron Will. He sipped his beer as if he hadn't noticed who was in the room and who was not.

MacAllan was summoned to attend the newcomer. He left his drink on the bar, excused himself, and walked over to the man. Brennan watched the two exchange some kind of silent communication and move off to a quiet corner of the pub. For the first time since beginning this charade, Brennan allowed thoughts of the Dublin bombing to come into his mind. As he eyed Brody MacAllan across the room, he pictured the man sitting in a car laden with explosives as it drove into Talbot Street just before rush hour, when it would do the most horrendous damage and cause the most deaths and grievous injuries. Brennan saw in his mind the images of the bombed-out street, the rubble, the terrified and injured people, the mangled corpses. Including that of his friend and teammate, Paddy Healey. He pictured Paddy, his fair hair flying in the wind as he ran down the pitch and tried for a goal. Brennan willed himself to stay in character, to see out the whole foolish pantomime until the end. He sent up a silent prayer that he would not fail in his endeavour, and that he would get Maura safely out of the Iron Will and out of east Belfast before things went, well, south.

He leaned over and whispered in her ear. "Get up and walk out now. I'll follow after I finish my beer. To make it look real, I mean."

For once, she didn't give out to him about being gallant; that said it all about the atmosphere in the place. All she said was "Getting up will draw too much attention. We'll wait it out."

MacAllan and the sinister looking newcomer remained in intense conversation for several long minutes, then the cold-eyed man gave him a terse nod, scanned the personnel in the bar once more, and walked out. MacAllan returned to the bar, and Brennan as Duane offered to buy a round again.

"Same for you, sir?"

"Aye. Thank you."

"Ruby?"

"Nothing for me, hon. Two was plenty. And I think maybe you've had enough yourself, don't you? I mean, you're not used to it, darlin'."

Duane winked at MacAllan, who smirked back at him, man to man. Let the little woman think Duane Ballard hardly ever touches the stuff; good way to maintain family harmony. Then Ruby Jean suggested that it was time they said goodbye and returned to the hotel. Have an early night. Big day tomorrow, bus leaving early for a trip to — bless her, she remembered to use the Loyalist name for it — "Londonderry."

Duane clapped his new friend on the back, said how pleased he and Ruby Jean were to meet him, and expressed the hope that he would make it back to America again before too long. He went up to the bar and paid for MacAllan's drink, pretending to fumble with the unfamiliar currency, and then the outlandish couple left the bar. They were careful to stay in character when they got outside and exclaimed about all the sights in southern cornball dialect.

Then they hoofed it out of east Belfast to the city centre. "I suppose you'll want to go home and change into a soutane or vestments for Mass, Father, as an antidote to your Catholic-hatin', redneck persona tonight."

"It's either that or my drinking clothes."

"What tiny, particular subset of your wardrobe is reserved for those rare, exceptional occasions when you go drinking, Brennan?"

He raised his eyes to a cold, uncaring heaven. "She does my head in, this one."

"You're well able to handle it, Burke. The verbal abuse, I mean, if not the liquor. Let's get back to the flat and ditch these outfits before somebody sees us and has us deported."

They hailed a taxi, and Duane asked to be taken to the campus of Queen's University. Brennan didn't want anyone making a connection between the two gaudy tourists and Monty's address in south Belfast. They found nobody in residence when they arrived at the flat. Monty had the children out somewhere. They shed their costumes for normal attire, Brennan had a shave, and they set out on foot to find a place to lift a glass. Not that there was any shortage of bars. They decided to keep walking till they got to Morrisons, found a table, and settled in for a pint. Or two. They chatted about inconsequential things, and Brennan had a couple of shots of whiskey to complement the Guinness. He felt the tension ebbing away. It wasn't long before they were reminiscing about the time they travelled together all the way from Kentucky to Norn Iron. "I'm thinking our adventure should be immortalized in song," he said.

"You're too right, Father. Should it be in the classical tradition or more of a Gregorian chant?"

"A hurtin' tune, country style. 'The Ballad of Duane and Ruby Jean.' You start."

She thought for a bit and then resumed her Kentuckian voice:

> I seen you settin' on that bar stool
> Far from Kentucky, lookin' like a fool.

While a gun-totin' stranger looked you in the eye
And you lookin' back and sayin' do or die.

Brennan polished off his latest drink and added to the composition:

I ain't a-feared a no gun-totin' man.
He's only a varmint that I'm better than.
My trigger finger's got a awful itch;
I jes might plug that son of a bitch.

Mercifully a session of real music started up, and the two com-
posers had to postpone completion of their corn-pone opera. "You
know," Maura said, "'The Ballad of Duane and Ruby Jean' is so far
from what I hear you sing in Mass, Father, so far from the repertoire
of your heavenly choirs, that I'm a-feared you might be possessed by
the devil."

"When I'm possessed by the devil, you'll know it, you little rip."

"Wouldn't know whether to take that as a threat or a promise,"
said a young woman, who plopped down at the table next to them.
Her boyfriend tripped over the table leg before finding his place on
the chair. The pair of them were well on, but there was more to come.
A companion managed to handle three shot glasses and three pints
and land them safely on the table. The female of the group returned
to her earlier observation. "I wouldn't mind a bit of deviltry coming
my way from *him*," she said, pointing her pint glass at Brennan.

"Pay her no mind," her boyfriend said, "whether it's you or any
other bloke that walks into this place. She'd get up on a stiff breeze."

"Whoa!" said Maura. She leaned across the table towards Brennan,
so they could talk without their every word being made scandalous by
the crowd beside them. Seeing her lean towards him gave rise to scandalous thoughts in his own mind, and he made a determined effort to
banish them, to concentrate on what she was saying as she spoke ani-
matedly of the wonderful time the children, Normie and Dominic,

were having in Dublin. She'd been talking to the oldest son, Tommy Douglas, in Halifax, and his band had a gig coming up at a university dance. Against his will, Brennan pictured himself walking at her side through the streets of Dublin, or Belfast, or Halifax, pictured himself as the father of her children. Stopped before anything more graphic came into his sozzled brain.

He got up for another round of drinks, gulped one shot of whiskey while waiting for the two-part pour of his Guinness, and added another shot to his order. He knew he'd had enough but, well, he wanted more. He also needed a smoke. He lit one up, took a few long drags, and received a much-needed hit of nicotine, then squashed the rest of it out in an ashtray and returned to the table. He sat across from her, an attentive audience, as she regaled him with comical tales of Monty and the unpleasant surprises that had sandbagged him in the courtroom. Monty. His best friend.

One of the fellows at the next table leaned over and whispered to him. He turned from the MacNeil to listen to the interloper. "What's her name, the one you can't tear your eyes away from? What's her name?"

Brennan tried not to react to the insinuation. He came up with an answer in Irish, "*Ar Éirinn ní neosainn cé hí.*"

"Spoken like a true gentleman," the fellow said. Apparently he was not quite as thick as Brennan had thought. "Lads!" the fellow called out then to the band, who had just come back from a break. "Give us '*Ar Éirinn Ní Neosainn Cé Hí.*' We'll all have a dance."

The band did the old, traditional ballad and did it well. Everyone who wasn't legless got up to dance and that included Brennan, who still had legs under him, though he didn't know how long he would. He took the MacNeil in his arms, cautioning himself not to hold her too close, and they waltzed to the beautiful song. As always, he couldn't stop himself from singing along.

> *Aréir is mé ag téarnamh um neoin*
> *Ar an taobh thall den teora 'na mbím,*

Do théarnaigh an spéirbhean im' chomhair
D'fhág taomanach breoite lag sinn.
Do ghéilleas dá méin is dá cló,
Dá béal tanaí beo milis binn,
Do léimeas fá dhéin dul 'na comhair,
Is ar Éirinn ní neosainn cé hí.

When the dance was over and he relinquished his hold on her, she said, "I have to say you sang that more beautifully than you did 'The Ballad of Duane and Ruby Jean.' What do the words mean?"

Last night as I strolled abroad
On the far side of my farm
I was approached by a beautiful woman
Who left me distraught and weak.

He skipped a few of the more romantic passages and ended with the last line, "For Ireland I'd not tell her name."

Chapter XI

Monty

Vincent McKeever had agreed, with obvious reluctance, to meet Monty on Sunday afternoon. The rendezvous point was a wooded area off the Colinglen Road southwest of the city. Monty had no trouble finding the road but it took a few minutes of driving before a young man popped out and signalled him to stop. He parked and they walked into the shelter of the trees. Vincent McKeever was of medium height, wiry, and sandy-haired. He looked nervous, with one leg jiggling as he leaned with his back against a tree, his eyes constantly scanning the area around him. As if anyone would spot him out here.

"What are you worried about, Vincent?"

"What do you think?"

"Who do you think was in the car you saw that night?"

"I don't have a bloody clue. But whoever it was, he pulled a knife on me. And you're asking why I'm worried?"

"A knife?"

"You heard me."

"All right. This won't take long. Tell me what you saw that night."

"Me and my girlfriend were . . . out for a walk, and the car comes flying in."

"And this was on the Ammon Road where O'Grady's is, and the bridge."

"Yeah, I heard it come squealing off the road and into the . . . it's a wee wooded area just off the road. It was a fine, warm night. Me and my girlfriend were in there."

"Right, so you heard the car, and then what happened?"

"I heard it, so I got up . . . I walked out from the trees where we were, and there it was in kind of a clearing with bushes around. I was going to give out to the man about tearing around the countryside and maybe running people down. I went up to his door, the driver's door, and yer man gets out and has a knife in his hand. One of those flick knives, or switchblades, whatever you call them. I backed away 'cause I didn't want that going into my gut."

"What did the man look like?"

"I had my eyes on the blade, for fucksake, not on the colour of the fella's eyes, or what kind of shirt he had on that day."

"Fair enough. But you could tell whether he was tall or not."

"A short wee get."

"Shorter than you."

"Aye."

"Did he say anything?"

"Fuck off is what he said."

"What did he sound like?"

"What do you think? He sounded like a fella telling someone to fuck off. So I did."

"Was he alone in the car?"

"Yeah. The light went on when he opened his door. Nobody else in there."

"What did you see of the car?"

"A Ford Orion, only a few years old. I only saw the arse end of it before I fucked off."

"So what did you notice?"

"I didn't take the time to read the number off the tag, if that's what you're asking. The car was black or dark blue. I saw a couple of bullet holes in the bumper. And the shots fired were only a short time before that, so you can draw your own conclusions. I don't know any more than that, and I don't want to know. Nothing else I can tell you. I have to be somewhere."

"Hold on a second, hold on. You heard shots fired?" He looked even more wary then, aware that he had blurted out new information. "Tell me."

"Yeah, I heard them."

"Shots where?"

"Back along the road."

"In what direction?"

"I don't know. Way down past the bridge, I guess."

"So the bridge was between where you were and where the shots were fired."

"Yeah." He made the sound of several shots in rapid succession.

"How many shots did you hear?"

"I didn't fucking count them, man. Seemed like a lot. A burst of gunfire and then, a few seconds later, some more. I looked at my girlfriend and she looked at me, and we were thinking we were going to get out of there, and then I heard the car coming."

"And you saw how many bullet holes in the back of the car?"

"I think it was two."

"What time of the night was this?"

He shrugged and then said, "One o'clock, maybe, in the morning. Something like that."

"How were you able to see, if it was nighttime?"

"What? Now you're saying I didn't see anything? That suits me fine. Can I get you in as a witness if the wee bastard tracks me down? You can tell him, 'Forget it. Don't worry about this eejit. He didn't see a thing.'"

"I know you saw the man, the car, and the bullet holes."

"There was a bit of a moon out, all right?"

"All right. Thank you, Vincent. The Flanagan family will be most grateful."

"Right. They can make a fine speech over my grave."

†

Monty wanted to keep his research under the radar as much as possible, though he could not have said why, given that the shooting in the small hours of the morning of November 14, 1992, was a matter of public knowledge, and asking about it would not necessarily raise suspicion. About anything, really. But he was representing the Flanagan family, and he did not know what had happened to their father; if it was connected to the shooting, it would obviously be a sensitive matter. So he decided to take a walk to the city library and look through the newspapers, in whatever form they were available, for the days immediately after November 14. It didn't take long for him to find a series of stories about the shooting of Francis "Fritzy" O'Dwyer, who was known to be a member of the Provisional IRA. O'Dwyer was described by unnamed sources as "one of the hard men from the Short Strand." His body was found "riddled with bullets" by the side of the Ammon Road after the Royal Ulster Constabulary received an anonymous phone tip from someone who had heard shots just before one o'clock that morning. There had been no arrests; Monty knew the murder had never been solved.

He didn't have much of a foundation on which to build a case. A dead man in the water. A car that may have been involved, or not. A driver who, what? If he had a gun, he wouldn't have settled for pulling a switchblade on McKeever. But he did have bullet holes in the back of his car. Was he a witness to the shooting? It didn't stretch the imagination to conclude that a car happening by the scene of the crime might get fired upon. And McKeever heard two bursts of gunfire. The police had found nothing to suggest a hit and run. But what else might they have that could further Monty's investigation? Would they share any of their information with him? Only one way to find out.

It took a few exasperating phone calls on Monday morning, and a few instances of being placed on hold, but he finally secured an afternoon appointment with the lead investigator into the death of Eamon Flanagan.

The Royal Ulster Constabulary barracks was surrounded by an enormous blast wall and not without reason, in the land where the car bomb had become a weapon of choice during the Troubles. Monty went through the formalities of being vetted and admitted and sat down to wait for Sergeant Garth Brown to arrive. It wasn't going to be a long meeting. Brown, a tall, burly man of about fifty with a pugnacious red face and a ginger moustache, didn't invite Monty into an office or even an interview room. Whatever Monty had to ask, and whatever reply might be forthcoming, would be dealt with over against the wall out of earshot of the cop on the desk.

But Monty opened with a courtesy nonetheless. "Thank you for seeing me, Sergeant. I appreciate that you're busy here."

"Buzzy doesn't begin to describe it. Now what do you think I can do for you?"

"As I indicated on the phone, it's about the death of Eamon Flanagan on the fourteenth of November, 1992. I have been retained by his family to see what compensation might be available to them as the result of their father's death. I have seen the autopsy report —"

"Then you know as much as we do about what happened."

"Well, I'm hoping that's not the case, actually. I'm hoping there is something else you can tell me —"

"I reviewed the file. Nowt I can tell you. The man drowned."

"No, he died of his fractures."

The cop ignored that. "I don't know how you expect to get any payment for his wee bairns out of that, sad as it is for me to say it." He didn't look overly sorrowful over the fate of the Flanagan children. Monty could not imagine his face arranging itself into an expression of mourning for a widow or a houseful of orphans or any other victims of misfortune. But perhaps that was to be expected from someone on the front lines of a bombing and shooting campaign that had taken more than three thousand lives.

"But, Sergeant, bear with me for a second if you will. Have you any idea what time he fell?"

"We know he left O'Grady's bar at ten minutes to one in the morning of Saturday, fourteenth November. The bridge is only a few minutes' walk from the bar."

"I noted in the autopsy report that Mr. Flanagan had a fracture to the front bone of his leg."

"Nothing surprising about that, since he'd been on the rattle since arriving at O'Grady's right after finishing work on the Friday afternoon, and he plunged thirty-five feet down onto the rocks beneath the Ammon Road Bridge."

"All the other bony injuries were to the back of his head and body."

"You're looking for somebody who knocked him off the bridge, but that didn't happen. Only other recourse I see for his wife and his weans is the social services or whatever it's called now. State assistance."

"Eamon Flanagan wasn't the only person who came to grief that night." Sergeant Brown stood over Monty like a pillar of stone: silent, expressionless. But Monty persevered. "A man was shot not far from that bridge, and not long before the estimated time of death for Mr. Flanagan. You're well aware of that, of course."

"Aye. We are. How does that play into your accident case, Mr. . . . ?"

"Collins."

"Collins, right."

"There are reports of a car in the area."

"A car. It's a public road. Why would there not be a car? Or cars?"

Monty reminded himself, as he had done so often during his career questioning police officers and other reluctant witnesses, to remain patient and friendly. There was nothing to be gained, and everything to lose, by becoming surly and aggressive. And he was not going to tip his hand about the information he himself possessed, about the Ford Orion with two bullet holes in the back. He was here to obtain information, not give it away.

"I think Flanagan was the victim of a hit and run."

"There's no evidence of that."

"And if there was, you would have looked into it."

"Are we funnushed nye, Mr. Collins?"

"Apparently so."

The sergeant gave him a brisk nod and walked away.

Monty returned to his office. He needed more information about that car. Where to turn now? To somebody right here in the office, one of his fellow solicitors. He went to the open door of Muriel Whiteside and asked if he could have a word. She smiled and invited him in, and he sat down. Monty knew she had a sizeable insurance defence practice.

"You may be able to help me, Muriel. I'm hoping to trace an unidentified motor vehicle, which may or may not have been involved in an accident over two years ago."

"I don't see any difficulties there. Just let me go down my list of unidentified cars waiting to be identified with accidents that happened in years past."

"Yeah, I know. Hopeless, I'm sure."

"Anything else you can tell me, or was that it?"

"No, that was it. Thanks for your time." He made to get up off his chair, and she laughed.

"So. What else do you have?"

"Date, November fourteenth, 1992. Place, the Ammon Road Bridge."

"Eamon Flanagan."

"Right. I went out there with a Mr. Malone."

"Hughie." She rolled her eyes. "Living proof that porter is a preservative."

"He does seem to enjoy a drink. Anyway he took me to a pub out there on the road, and one of the locals had a story about a young fellow who had —"

"So I'm hearing third-hand information."

"Second-hand. I've since met with the young fellow himself."

"All right. Go on."

"This kid was with his girlfriend out in the country in a private spot. They were sharing their love presumably, and a car came speeding into the clearing near them. The young fellow got up to have a look and saw the car. It had been driven way off the road in amongst some trees and bushes. This was the night Eamon Flanagan died."

"In the river bed. So why the interest in a car?"

"Again, it's a long shot. But Mr. Flanagan had a bunch of fractures to the back of his head and body, and only one in the front. Fractured left tibia. Fragments going inwards. I've seen that type of break in pedestrians who've been hit by a car."

"Yes, I have, too."

"So I'm proceeding for now on the notion that it was a hit and run."

"If that had been established, the MIB would have paid compensation to the family. The Motor Insurers' Bureau. Well, you're likely aware of the Untraced Drivers Agreement, which provides compensation when someone has been struck by an unidentified vehicle."

"Yes, but this was deemed to be nothing but a fall from a bridge. Pure accident. The evidence of a car is new. I spoke to the RUC sergeant in charge of the investigation. Didn't get anywhere with him."

"He had no information for you."

"For me, no. Whether he had information he wasn't sharing is another question."

"One for which you'll not be likely to find the answer."

"Why would the police not look into a possible connection between the shooting that night, and the possible commotion arising out of that, and the death a few minutes later of a man in the same area?"

"I think you can answer that for yourself, Monty. One, they think there is no connection. Or, two, they think there may very well be a connection and they don't want to talk about it."

"If it's the second option, I can't help wondering why."

"Get used to it."

That was the kind of thing he had heard from his Republican acquaintances here in Belfast. He had not expected to hear it from Muriel Whiteside in this bastion of the Northern Irish establishment.

"So," he said, "this lover's lane story is the only lead I have. The Ammon Road isn't the M1 motorway. It's pretty quiet out there, so it's not as if there are hundreds of cars. All the young fellow saw was the rear and side of the car. He recognized it as a Ford Orion, black or dark blue, a few years old. Didn't take any notice of the tag number. He wasn't in a position where he could see the front, let alone examine the front bumper for a mark or indentation."

"This case isn't going to fund your retirement, Monty."

"No, I'm going to have to take on a second job if things don't get any better than this. Bartender, parade marshal for the Orange Lodge, handler of a bomb-sniffing dog."

"Well, we'll see if we can help you avoid those career choices. I have a number of insurance people I deal with. Adjusters, claims people. If someone brought a Ford Orion in for repair around that time . . ." She turned and withdrew a couple of file folders from a shelf behind her and put them on the desk. "I could try some of the people listed here."

"Something that might stand out in their minds: there were bullet holes in the back end of the car."

She pulled the files back towards her. "Bullet holes."

"Yeah. And there's something else."

She looked at Monty the way a schoolteacher would look at a particularly exasperating young student. "What else?"

"Driver pulled a knife on the young fellow and told him to fuck off out of there. And the young fellow did. Makes me think the driver was a little touchy about something. Worried, maybe."

"I see."

"You're going to tell me that this additional information . . ."

"Bullet holes, a knife."

"That those additional facts will make it less likely that the owner or operator of said motor vehicle would have gone to his insurance company and made a claim for the repairs."

She surprised him then. "Not necessarily. A car with bullet holes and possibly damage to the front end is not something you'd want to be seen with in public. Particularly after a well-publicized shooting. All the more reason to have the damage repaired. But, as you say, perhaps not through official channels such as one's insurance company. That might tend to attract attention, and raise the amount of future premiums. More likely he'd ask a pal to do the work for cash, somebody in the auto repair business."

"What are my chances of tracking down something like that?"

She laughed.

He'd have to leave it at that, for now.

Chapter XII

Brennan

Brennan wanted to do some fact checking with his evangelical contact in the United States. It was mid-afternoon on Tuesday in Belfast, morning in the eastern U.S.A. He had just picked up the phone when Ronan came in from a half day's work at Burke Transport.

"I'm calling the Reverend Tait in America. Want to check something Brody MacAllan said."

"Good. I'll wait to see what the rev has to tell us. And then I'll be off to the monastery."

"Oh? Are you retreating from the world to take up a life of contemplation and Gregorian chant?"

"It's tempting, but no. I'm going to see Father Alec. You must know who I mean, Alec Reid."

"Of course."

"Why don't you come along with me? I'll introduce you."

"Great. I'd love to meet him. I've only seen him saying Mass. Well, took Communion from him. Hold on a sec while I consult Harold here."

He pressed the number and Harold Tait came on the line. They greeted one another, then Brennan said, "There was one thing our man here said about the rally in Tennessee, an incident he recounted, and I wanted to check it with you. He said a fellow in the crowd interrupted Hiram Stockwell at one point and shouted out a complaint about the numbers of Catholics increasing in the United States. Stockwell asked what he meant, and the man expressed alarm at the figures supposedly showing creeping Catholicism in the nation. Not true, of course, but when did that ever matter? And Stockwell came up with a bland reply, trying to smooth the fellow's feathers and get on with the show."

"I don't know. I certainly don't remember hearing about it. But it was a long time ago. A minor interruption like that wouldn't make the news, so I'll have to ask around."

"Great. Thanks, Harold." Brennan ended the call and turned to Ronan. "Is jacket and tie *de rigueur* where we're going, Ronan?"

"Not at all. You are quite presentable in a shirt and jumper. I only wish I'd seen you in your cowboy get-up or whatever you wore when you met MacAllan in the bar."

"It's as well you missed it. You'd never look at me the same way again."

Just as they left the house, it started bucketing rain. Ronan made a beeline for the car, Brennan on his heels. They got in with the driver and another security man, tried to shake some of the water off themselves, and were chauffeured to the meeting.

"So, what's the story?" Brennan asked.

"Father Alec has been the honest broker between me and a couple of other Republicans on the one hand and constitutional Nationalists on the other. The physical force tradition versus the political tradition, you might say. I'm going to have a quick chat with him. Good chance for you to meet a man who will be honoured in the history books in the ages to come."

"I appreciate it."

Brennan gazed out the window as the car passed the Milltown Cemetery on the right and, farther ahead, the Belfast Cemetery on the left. People scurried past the shopfronts on the Falls Road, obscured by black umbrellas. Running off the Falls were side streets lined with brick row houses. Republican murals adorned the gable walls of many of the buildings.

All was quiet in the car until the driver switched on the radio and a familiar, grating voice blared out at them.

"Old Saint Nick," Ronan muttered. "Oh, and he's got John the Baptist with him."

"Saints, is it? Should I fall to my knees?"

"That won't be necessary, Father. The pair of them dig with the other foot and wouldn't appreciate our Romish rituals."

"I take it this is the Old Saint Nick I've been reading about for years in connection with the conflict here?"

"It is. Real name, Gideon Sproule."

"I'd much rather be known as Old Saint Nick."

Anyone who had been following the news coming out of the North of Ireland over the past number of years would recognize the pugnacious white-haired firebrand. Fire and brimstone preacher, fierce Loyalist, staunch Orangeman. This was a man who recited "No surrender" as often and as piously as Brennan recited the "Ave Maria."

"And the other fellow?" Brennan asked.

"John the Baptist is John Archibald Geddes, another minister of the Word who has close ties, shall we say, to the Loyalist paramilitaries."

"Right. Geddes. I've seen him in the papers, too." He pictured the man, late forties with bushy dark hair and an intense demeanour.

"Practically speaking, nothing in the way of a peace agreement, let alone a power-sharing agreement, will see the light of day without the imprimatur of those two."

"Just as nothing will be approved on the Republican side without the approval of Gerry Adams and Martin McGuinness."

"Something like that, yeah."

Now, on the radio, Old Saint Nick was ranting about, what? Road works? That couldn't be it. Brennan tuned in to the strident voice, the thick northern accent. "They tell us these works are going to be carried out in the high summer. Why weren't our people consulted? We don't want to be marching through potholes and over barricades, but you mark my words: march we will! Nothing will stop our people from taking their rightful place on the streets on the twelfth of July!"

"What's this?" Brennan asked. "They're fretting about street repairs that are scheduled for the summer? They've got their knickers in a twist about this in February?"

"Welcome to my world, Brennan."

The preacher was still going on. "And that goes for Donegall Street, too! Major works planned there. The street looked fine to me last time I saw it. That makes me wonder if there's another agenda here!"

"What's he on about now?"

"Saint Patrick's church is on Donegall Street."

"What does Saint Patrick's Roman Catholic church have to do with an Orangemen's march?"

"Maybe the street repair plan is a giant popish conspiracy. The church is on the Orangemen's parade route. They march by our church, banging their drums and belting out their songs. If the street is torn up, Saint Nick and his followers may miss out on that moment of inter-faith dialogue."

"That moment of rubbing Catholics' noses in their defeat at the Battle of the Boyne three hundred years ago."

"Methinks you've caught the spirit of things here, Father Burke."

Brennan shook his head and raised a hand to ward off any more lunacy. He'd heard enough.

The car pulled up beside Clonard Monastery. Brennan had been in the twin-spired church but never in the monastery itself. It was a four-storey building done in red brick with a mansard roof and dormers. The two bodyguards got out first, seemingly oblivious to the rain, and surveyed the area. They nodded to Ronan, who got out and headed into the building, followed by Brennan. They stood together inside the door and were joined by a slight, white-haired priest whom Brennan recognized as Father Alec Reid. Ronan introduced them, and Brennan said he was honoured to meet the man who was putting heart and soul into bringing about a solution to the conflict. Father Alec gave them a friendly greeting in the accent of County Tipperary where he had been raised. He asked about Brennan, his family, and home parish, and said he'd be back in a tick to sit down with Ronan and hear what he had to say.

A couple of minutes later, Father Alec returned with another man by his side. The fellow appeared to be in his early forties, with thinning light brown hair and wire-rimmed glasses. He had the look of a scholar. He was introduced as a Methodist minister by the name of Clark Rayburn. "Clark and I have had our chat," Father Alec said. "Your turn now, Ronan."

Ronan said, "Give us half an hour, Brennan?"

"Take all the time you need."

He turned to the Reverend Rayburn and made a bit of small talk till the minister said, "I've a taxi coming for me at four o'clock. Thought I'd step out for a bit of refreshment first. Would you care to join me, Father?"

"I'd be happy to. Please call me Brennan."

"Clark," the other man said, and they got up and ventured out into the rain.

"We'd best duck into the first place we see," Brennan suggested, and it didn't take long before he spotted a bar on the Falls Road and started for the door.

"Ach, I was thinking of something more in the line of a cup of tea," said Clark, almost apologetically.

"Right. Sounds good," Brennan hastened to say.

They found a café a few doors down and went inside, shaking off the raindrops. They sat at a table, ordered tea and a plate of biscuits, and enjoyed a friendly chat about their respective vocations. Clark Rayburn had entered the ministry after completing a master's degree in biology. He had considered going into medicine but "I'm too queasy in the presence of sickness and blood! I'm much more effective ministering to people with no open wounds."

"I hear you, brother," said Brennan, who was the same way himself.

"Open minds and open hearts are what I look for in people. Not everyone has those gifts!" He cast a rueful eye to the television in the corner of the café, where Old Saint Nick filled the screen, his face nearly purple.

"We've got close-minded, hard-hearted bas . . . people on our side of the line, too," Brennan allowed. "But I'm not telling a Belfast man anything he doesn't already know!"

"You've got your gunmen and bombers, and we have ours," said Rayburn. "You've got your sectarian killers and we have ours. We had the Shankill Butchers!"

Brennan knew about them, a gang who patrolled Catholic neighbourhoods in a taxi and picked victims off the street to be slashed with knives and murdered.

"I was about to say, Brennan, that I condemn them all equally, killers from both sides, forgetting for a moment that I'm a minister of the Word. I'm supposed to say 'forgive,' not 'condemn'! What happened to all my years of bible study?"

"I've a bit of trouble with that part of the Lord's message myself. Whenever I hear of civilians being killed, whether by Republicans or Loyalists, I find myself in a far from forgiving frame of mind. And I've never been clear in my own conscience about what I would do if I received a terrorist in the confessional, someone who had killed or injured civilians. Would I be able to grant genuine absolution, or would I only mouth the words while secretly hoping the killer would be damned for all time?"

Rayburn laughed. "You've thought about this, I see, Brennan."

"I have, much to the detriment of my sleep, I'm afraid."

The minister glanced up at the television. It was obvious that Old Saint Nick was in high dudgeon about something, but the TV's sound was mercifully muted. "He's no Alec Reid!"

Brennan searched for a reply that would not sound sectarian and settled on, "How many of us are?"

"Alec is a modern-day saint." Clark said. "You'll have seen the photograph."

Brennan nodded. There was no need to ask which photograph. It was an image that had flashed around the world, illustrating the horrors of the war in the North of Ireland. Two British Army corporals in civilian dress had driven — unwittingly, it was said — into a Republican funeral procession. This was on March 19, 1988, three days after the murder of the three mourners at the funeral in Milltown Cemetery. The March 19 funeral was for one of the victims of the Milltown massacre, Kevin Brady, an IRA man. Feelings were running high, and people were afraid of another Loyalist attack, so Sinn Féin had stewards on hand, checking cars. When a steward directed the soldiers to turn around, they tried to find an exit, reversed at speed, and ended up scattering the mourners. The crowd set upon the car and tried to get into it. One of the soldiers drew his gun and fired a warning shot into the air. This of course intensified the fears of another attack. The crowd eventually managed to drag the two men out of their car and proceeded to beat them. It was a horrific incident. Then the two were taken to another location nearby.

At that point Father Reid, risking his own life, tried to save the two men from further harm. But the IRA shot them. Afterwards, the priest walked to where the two men were lying on the ground. Believing one was still alive, he tried to breathe air into him. He then knelt and anointed them both. A photographer had left the funeral procession and managed to record for all time the image of the priest and the slain soldiers in that desolate field.

Priest and minister were silent for a few long seconds after that. Then they finished their tea, paid up, and returned to Clonard.

Ronan and Father Reid were waiting when they arrived.

"Sorry to keep you waiting," Clark said.

"Not at all," Father Reid assured him. "We just finished solving all the North's problems seconds before you came in the door."

"That's all it took, you two gentlemen having a wee gab by yourselves?"

"Simple really."

They all laughed. The complications involved in any attempt at détente were clear to everyone in the room.

Ronan and Brennan took their leave after expressing their appreciation to Father Reid and the Reverend Mr. Rayburn. When they were in the car on the way back to Andersonstown, Ronan said quietly, "There's something in the works. Stay tuned to the news over the next day or so. That's all I'll say for now."

"Fair enough." Then, "Clark Rayburn is a fine fellow."

"He is."

"We talked about Father Alec and the two soldiers."

"Did you know what Father Alec had in his pocket that day?" Ronan asked. Brennan shook his head. "He had a letter from Sinn Féin, setting out the party's position on a solution to the conflict, a letter he took later that day to the Social Democratic and Labour Party in Derry. It was all part of his attempt to get the two Nationalist groups onside with one another for a possible agreement for peace. As he bent to assist the soldiers, blood got on his face and on the envelope holding the papers. How's that for symbolism?

"It was an English photographer who captured the image of the priest with the blood on his face, Alec on his knees by the battered and nearly naked body of one of the soldiers. Will I ever forget the anguished look on Alec's face as he knelt there?"

Brennan had never forgotten it either.

†

Back at Ronan's place, Gráinne told Brennan that a Mr. Tait had rung from America. Brennan called the number and spoke again to Harold Tait.

"That little disruption you mentioned, Brennan. Some guy who questioned Hiram Stockwell on the clear and present danger of Catholicism infecting the good Protestant nation of America."

"Right."

"Well, a colleague of mine was there when that happened. The incident stuck in his mind because he's keen on the ecumenical movement. Why can't we all get along, that kind of thing. He recalled Stockwell being very polite to the questioner. He made an attempt to smooth things over by quoting from the Statue of Liberty, 'Give me your poor, your tired, your huddled masses yearning to breathe free.' And apparently somebody hollered out, 'Yeah, and your wretched refuse!' But Stockwell talked about the principles on which the United States was founded, and how its protections and freedoms are for everyone who comes to our shores. And that was the end of it."

"And that wasn't reported."

"No, things like that go on all the time. Not newsworthy."

"Thank you again, Harold."

That and the deluge from the sky, which Tait and MacAllan both mentioned, everyone running for rain gear. MacAllan was telling the truth. He really had been in the United States when the bombing of Dublin and Monaghan took place. Brennan sank down into his chair, deflated. He could say goodbye to the only promising opportunity to seek justice for Paddy Healey and all the other victims after twenty-one years.

†

Ireland made headlines around the world the following day, Wednesday, February 22. The governments of Britain and the Irish Republic released a "New Framework for Agreement." Brennan sat at the dining table and read all about it in the papers. There would be new institutions. Any new political arrangements were to be based on "full respect for, and protection and expression of, the rights and identities of both traditions in Ireland and would even-handedly afford both communities in Northern Ireland parity of esteem and treatment, including equality of opportunity and advantage." The British government stated that it "is for the people of Ireland alone . . . to exercise their right of self-determination on the basis of consent, freely and concurrently given, North and South, to bring about a united Ireland, if that is their wish." But, hold on: "the Irish Government accept that the democratic right of self-determination by the people of Ireland as a whole must be achieved and exercised with and subject to the agreement and consent of a majority of the people of Northern Ireland." Nationalists and Republicans would see this as the same old Unionist veto. One of the most interesting statements in the proposal was the British government's declaration that it had "no selfish strategic or economic interest in Northern Ireland." The Irish government pledged to amend its constitution to give up any "territorial claim of right" to the entire island. But it would continue to be the case that every person born anywhere on the island had the right to be part of the Irish nation.

When Ronan came in the door, Brennan said, "What's new, Ronan? Anything at all?"

"It's been a long and eventful few days."

"So I see."

Gráinne came downstairs and gave her husband a hug and kiss. "Home from the field, good soldier that you are."

"Soldier? Good *diplomat*, my love."

"Ronan, you could charm the birds off the trees and the Paisley family up the hill of Croagh Patrick, with beads a-rattling."

"I only wish. All this," he said, pointing to the newspapers, "is only the beginning. All the good feeling and fine intentions have been committed to paper. Now we have to find a way to make it work."

"You mean 'we' in the particular sense and not just the general sense, I'm thinking."

"Well, you're right, there, Brennan. I hope to be able to contribute."

Gráinne said, "If there really is any sharing of power — and I'll believe that when I can see, smell, and touch it — Ronan here will have a new life as an elected politician. We'll have to make sure he doesn't become too grand to remember all us wee folk here in Andytown."

"Ach, we have enough memorable characters here not to be forgotten."

They shared a laugh but Gráinne turned to Brennan and mouthed the words, "He really will be voted in."

Chapter XIII

Brennan

Brennan worked from early morning to noon on Thursday at Holy Cross church, then slipped off his collar, grabbed a sandwich at a convenience store, and planted himself on a barstool at Madden's. He had a few scoops and enjoyed some barroom banter, and he toyed with the idea of staying on for a trad music session scheduled for the early evening. But that would inevitably — why should it be inevitable, he asked himself but received no answer — inevitably entail a gargantuan quantity of Arthur Guinness's draught before the night was done. He would do the responsible thing and take a black taxi to Andersonstown.

Ronan greeted him upon arrival. "I believe you told me you do prison visits as part of your ministry over in Canada. Do I have that right, Father?"

"You do."

"So you wouldn't go weak at the knees at the sight of barbed wire and guard towers."

"Not in the least. Are you turning yourself in to the authorities?"

"No, not yet, anyway. Lorcan and I are going to visit a young prisoner, friend of the family."

"Right."

"And where you fit in is this: Lorcan thinks it would benefit this young lad to speak to a priest. Don't get me wrong now. Lorcan is not exactly an altar boy, but if his mate needs a *sagart,* he should have one. So, fancy a trip to the Kesh?"

"I'm ready when you are." *And I'm relieved that this* sagart *didn't linger any longer in Madden's, skulling pints and killing off brain cells.* "Should I don my priestly garb?"

"No need, Father. Your sanctity shines through, no matter how you are attired."

Ten minutes later Brennan, Ronan, Lorcan, and the bodyguards were driving along the M1 motorway. They saw a sign for Lisburn, and Brennan said, "Now that the peace framework is in place, does that mean we can stop in at HQ for tea?"

"We're not quite at that point yet, Brennan."

"No, I suppose not." Lisburn was home to the headquarters of the British Army in the North of Ireland. Long Kesh prison, widely known now as the H Blocks and officially named Her Majesty's Prison Maze, was just outside the town.

"The H Blocks are not unknown to you, Ronan."

"They are not, *go deimhin.* I was there at the time of the hunger strikes."

The Republican prisoners had refused to wear prison clothing and do prison work because they considered themselves political prisoners, not criminal prisoners. Paramilitary inmates had enjoyed special status for several years in the early 1970s, organizing themselves like prisoners of war, answering to their own officers, wearing their own clothes. Their logic was that they were fighting a war against the British Army and that their actions were considered criminal while the actions of the British soldiers and their commanders were not.

But those privileges were taken away in 1976, and the protests began. The government of Margaret Thatcher refused to make concessions, and ten young men died on hunger strike.

"I knew all those lads," Ronan said, "and saw what they went through as they starved. Their suffering was horrific. No matter where you stand politically, there's no denying the courage and dedication of people who gave up their very lives. And of course there were the routine beatings our fellas endured till the blood flowed, perpetrated by the soldiers of the empire. Pretty well every month, there were prisoners who were made to walk a gauntlet past the soldiers and their dogs, and sometimes the dogs attacked the boys, too. It was a savage place."

"Dogs!"

"Stick around this part of the country for a while, Brennan, and nothing will surprise you. I was so enraged by what our boys were putting up with — the rest of us were abused, too, of course — I was so enraged that all I wanted to do was get out of there. For selfish reasons, yes. But also to resume the fight, to bring the war to those savages."

Brennan could hear the rage in the voice of his normally cool and affable cousin, all these years later.

"Well, the war was brought home to some of them," Brennan recalled. "A number of prison officers were shot to death during those times."

"They were."

"Served the fuckers right," Lorcan muttered.

Brennan said nothing but reflected on the fact that they were not the first or last people in this conflict who were shot before or after committing acts of violence. Shot instead of arrested and brought to trial. But he knew that the chances of prison officials being arrested and tried for brutality was as unlikely as a statue being raised to Margaret Thatcher on the Falls Road in Belfast.

Their driver approached the compound, and Brennan saw the watchtowers, the barbed wire, the cameras. "It's a gruesome sight from the outside, Ronan. I'm sure I'd lose the will to live if I were confined inside it."

"Not easy to do your whack without complaint in a place like this. Suicides, alcoholism — places like this take their toll."

"Inevitably."

"I wanted to top myself after only three weeks in there." That was Lorcan. So, two members of the family — at least two — had served time in Her Majesty's prison. Brennan didn't ask for details.

"Now, it'll take a bit of time before we see Jonno, as you might expect," said Ronan.

It did indeed take some time to get through the screening process, but they eventually found themselves in a crowded room where the families of the prisoners waited for their turn. When Jonno's name and number were called, the Burkes got up and were led outside where they were loaded into a van for transport to the visiting area. The windows of the vehicle were blacked out; this was no tour bus. They got out and were taken to yet another waiting area. The protests and hunger strikes of the 1980s had borne fruit to some extent; inmates were permitted to wear their own clothing. The warders were in uniform: dark trousers, a white shirt with epaulettes and a tie. Some wore peaked caps. One of the warders called Jonno's name and, once their passes were examined, the Burkes were told that the prisoner was ready to meet them. They entered a large hall and walked past rows of numbered cubicles with low dividing walls until they got to the one where Jonno was waiting. Ronan made the introductions and the three visitors sat facing the prisoner across a narrow table.

"Jaysus, you're not on hunger strike, are you, Jonno?" Lorcan exclaimed.

"Not intentionally, Lor."

Jonno was dressed in a shabby grey track suit. It was well worn. He was ginger-haired and pale, so thin you could almost see through the front of him to the back.

"Jonno, meet our cousin, Father Burke from Canada. Or most recently from Canada, anyway."

"How about ye, Father?"

"All my cousins call me Brennan. But don't be concerned about how I am, Jonno. It's you we're concerned about here. Do they not feed you?"

"They do, right enough, but I've not much of an appetite. . . . Em, I'm wondering if I could speak to youse . . ." He looked from priest to father and son.

"Separately?" Brennan asked.

"Right. I mean if . . ."

"That would be fine," Ronan assured him. "Father Burke and I will sit back there till you're ready."

They got up, signalled to a warder, and explained that they would be waiting for a few minutes before taking their turns with the prisoner. The guard directed them to a cubicle near the other end of the room. Lorcan had his visit, followed by Ronan. Ronan appeared distracted when he returned, but then he directed his attention to Brennan and said, "Go ahead now, Brennan. And don't be too worried about privacy. The warders are more concerned about smuggling than they are about conversation, so you should be able to speak freely, the two of you."

When Brennan was seated across from Jonno, there was no confession of murder or mayhem. It was a domestic matter: Jonno told Brennan that his girlfriend was pregnant, and he wondered how they'd manage to get married with Jonno in prison. It was commendable that the young man wanted to "do the right thing" by the mother of his child, but Brennan saw a coldly practical side to this question. He asked as gently as he could. "How long are you in for, Jonno?"

"Eight years! But my brief is appealing it."

Even with a child on the way, Brennan did not want to be party to an arrangement that would see a young woman tied to a man she would have to live without for eight long years. Of course, the imprisoned man might well want to see her tied, so he would not have to lie in his cell for all those years imagining her with another man. Brennan had to tread softly here.

"You could get married, but don't rush things."

"That's not what the priests used to say!"

"I'm sure you're right. But have as many visits as you can with your girlfriend, talk things over. You both may decide to wait, see how the appeal goes."

"Yeah, I know. All right, thanks, Father. I'll be seeing her two days from now."

Brennan commiserated with the poor lad, but rushing a young couple to the altar — such as it might be in a place like this — would not be in anyone's best interest, including that of the baby.

The Burkes left the mammoth prison camp after that and headed back to Belfast. Lorcan filled his father in on the prison news, in case Ronan had not been given an update.

"Danny's there, but word is he'll be released soon. After five years inside. Jimmy's still at it, trying to make a batch of *poitín* that won't have the lads boakin' up all over their cells."

Powerful stuff, the potcheen; the homemade spirit had an extremely high alcohol content. Brennan remembered hearing that it had been outlawed for three hundred years. He could well believe it could make you sick, or worse, if not properly distilled.

"Donnacha's still teaching the lads Jailic."

"You're only after leaving the Jailtacht, Brennan," said Ronan. "Likely the only Gaeltacht in the Lisburn area."

"More than likely." A Gaeltacht was a region where the Irish language was spoken by the population.

"Fiach is camp OC now," Lorcan continued. "Doing his best to fill your shoes, Da."

Brennan took that to mean that Ronan had been the officer commanding of the Republican prisoners when he himself was in the Kesh.

Lorcan kept chattering, and his father responded, but Brennan could hardly miss the troubled look on Ronan's face. They finally arrived at the house and, thinking there might be things Ronan wanted to discuss with his immediate family, Brennan took himself off for a long, leisurely stroll around Andersonstown. He returned an hour later, in time to see Tomás Burke walking away from the house. Brennan went inside and found that Lorcan had gone and Gráinne was upstairs. Ronan clearly had something on his mind when he greeted Brennan in the sitting room. "What do you say we have our supper and then head out somewhere for a bit of *craic*?"

"I'd been thinking of taking in an early session at Madden's. I'll not pretend it will be my first visit of the day."

"Sure I'm not one to be pegging stones from my house of glass. We'll both go."

So they joined Gráinne for their evening meal and talked about matters that had nothing to do with crime and punishment. Then Brennan and Ronan excused themselves, went out to the car, and asked the driver to take them to Madden's in the city centre.

When they arrived, one of the security men stayed in the car while the other accompanied the Burkes into the bar. The man squeezed into a seat against the wall, where he could keep an eye on the window, the door, and the punters inside. Ronan was greeted warmly by the bar staff and many of the clientele. One of the drinkers asked, "Can we cast our votes for you now, Ronan, and get ahead of the crowds?"

"Ah, now, I wouldn't want to get ahead of anyone. Or get ahead of myself! We've a bit of a ways to go before there will be any kind of a vote."

"Fuck that," another man said. "We'll hold the election right now, right here. How many of youse say Ronan for taoiseach? All those in favour, raise a glass!"

It looked to Brennan as if every glass in the house was raised. A chant went up then. "Taoiseach! Taoiseach!"

The word was loaded with significance. It was an ancient term referring originally to the chieftains of the old Gaelic order; it now meant the prime minister of the Republic of Ireland. The Six Counties had always been ruled by Unionists at Stormont or by the government of the United Kingdom. The word taoiseach was anathema to those who wielded power in the North of Ireland. The politically minded punters here in Madden's had, in their minds, the country reunited, with Ronan Burke as the head of government. Brennan could not imagine how far in the future it would be before such a monumental development might happen. Ronan took it all in good humour and made a courteous bow to his supporters.

There were a few men and women who asked to speak to Ronan privately, almost as if he was already their elected representative, and two fellows got up and gave Ronan their table, so he could speak with his constituents in relative privacy. The men stood by the bar, and Brennan joined them, buying each of them a pint. He took the same himself. He watched his cousin as he conducted his meetings. Brennan could see him nodding his head, laying a hand on a shoulder, writing things on cigarette packs or bar coasters, until the conferences were finished and Ronan signalled to the two fellows that their table was free again. But they were on their way out, so Brennan brought his glass and a bottle of fizzy water and sat down.

"Sorry this is all I can bring to the table for this conference, Taoiseach."

"Sure you're grand, Your Holiness. It's a bit of aggravation I brought on myself, with my overindulgence in the past." But he grimaced before taking his first sip. Brennan didn't slag him any further about it. Down through the history of Ireland there were tales told of heroic drinkers. To Brennan's mind, Ronan's successful efforts to get off and stay off the drink were truly heroic. Brennan would like to think he himself could manage it . . . but, well, there was no need really in his case, was there?

One by one the musicians had arrived for the session of traditional music; their ages ranged from twenty to seventy, one woman and the rest men. They got settled at tables at the front of the room, checked their tuning, sipped their pints, and began to play. There was a fiddle, an accordion, a bodhran, and a couple of guitars. After a few jigs and reels, it was time for some vocals. Brennan joined Ronan and others in the bar singing along with the ballads and occasional rebel songs, and he got pleasantly gilled as the night wore on. At one point the accordion player called out, "How many of youse have been in the Crum?" The Crumlin jail, more properly styled the Crumlin Road Gaol, was down the road from Brennan's local church, Holy Cross. That was as close as he'd ever want to get to the imposing Victorian prison. Others in the room had not been so fortunate, if the number of raised hands was any indication. The band duly sang their anthem, "Our Lads in Crumlin Jail."

That got an animated response so the musicians followed it up with "The Men Behind the Wire" by local man Paddy McGuigan. The song was about men who had been interned — thrown in prison — without trial during the Troubles.

Not surprisingly, the theme of the night's entertainment set Ronan brooding, maybe about his own times served in prison, or maybe about the young fellows wasting away in the H Blocks now. And, perhaps, about whatever they had done that put them there.

Brennan spoke in a quiet voice. "What was troubling you after your visit to the Kesh? Apart from the obvious, I mean, seeing a friend in there and him so young. I'm hoping I can help you, though I suspect the problem is not something within the realm of the spirit."

"Something in the realm of hard, cold physical reality. To be more precise, the classic smoking gun."

"Literally, you mean?"

"Yes."

"Ah."

"You remember when you came into the little office I have in the house, and I told you there are some things I want to see resolved before I assume what could be a leadership role in the peace process here? One of those matters is of course the 1974 bombings and the need to bring somebody to justice for that. And it hardly needs to be said that the Unionist-Loyalist side has grievances as you can imagine, which have never been addressed. Crimes against members of their community that have never been solved."

"Of course." Crimes committed by Republican paramilitaries.

"Well, another matter is even more personal, closer to home. And, again, this is a very sensitive subject."

Whatever it was would be painful, Brennan knew, judging from the troubled look in his cousin's eyes. "Again, Ronan, be assured that anything you tell me will be kept in the strictest confidence. But you know that already."

"I do." He glanced round the bar to make sure nobody could hear him. "I haven't led a blameless life, to put it mildly, as I'm sure you know. And neither have . . . some of the other people in my life." Brennan merely nodded and waited for him to continue. "I hate myself for saying this, for revealing it, but I have no choice."

"Remember, I hear confessions for a living, Ronan."

"Well, here's another one for you. There was a young man killed. Espen van der Meer. He was a tourist from the Netherlands, who'd been backpacking around Ireland, and was going to visit Scotland, Wales, and England. He'd been away from home for a couple of months." Brennan stayed silent and waited for the rest. "The person who shot him did so in self-defence. Except that . . . Well, I'll try to explain it. It's not clear how this young backpacker ended up where he was. He may have been a hostage of sorts. We're just not sure. I know this isn't making a lot of sense to you, Brennan."

Brennan remained silent as he thought about yet another in a long line of innocent victims in this long-running conflict.

"The fellow who did the killing knew what kind of a storm would blow up over this. He and another person took van der Meer's body away and buried it in a place where it would almost certainly never be discovered. The body has never been found, and his family to this day have no idea what happened to their son. It was a few weeks apparently before they raised the alarm, because the lad was travelling on his own with no planned itinerary and he wasn't in touch with home very often. The parents are of course desperate to believe, against all reason, that he is alive somewhere. That Espen was taken and will someday be returned. I'm sure they know, deep in their hearts, that that is not going to happen. But you can imagine how they cling to the thinnest skeins of hope."

Ronan looked over at the bar as if a good stiff drink, after years on the dry, might serve to ease his pain. But he tore his eyes from the tempting, glistening array of bottles and taps and returned his gaze to Brennan. He said, "The person who killed this boy and buried his body was my son Tom."

That one of Ronan's sons was implicated was not entirely unexpected, given the preamble to the story, but Brennan felt it nonetheless as a blow to his heart.

"Tom has regretted it every day of his life since. It's important to me that you understand that."

"I do."

"What I am determined to do, anonymously of course, is give that boy's family at least this much: the location of his body, so they can mourn and give him a proper burial. And I want to get a message to them somehow that it is known that he was an innocent bystander, not involved in anything illegal. And that his killing was not sanctioned by any paramilitary group. It's little enough but it's all they'll ever have. But I'm a parent, too, and there is something I have to do first. I have to protect my own. The only way I can do that is to retrieve and destroy the gun that will connect Tom to that killing. The possibility that Tom could go into the Kesh for the rest of his life, him with a new wife, and two little stepchildren — we all just call them his children — who adore him . . ."

"I understand, Ronan. It's a terrible situation all round. If there is any way I can help you, I will."

"Tom committed the crime, Brennan, even though it was done in self-defence, or so he thought . . . He deserves to be punished for it, I know. But he's my son and I'm not going to, well, pull the trigger on my own child. He'll have to live with it for the rest of his life, to employ an overused phrase."

A parent protects its young. End of story. Brennan understood that perfectly.

Ronan took a sip of his fizzy water and said, "I have to think of some way to get that gun and dispose of it."

"How would the police be able to connect the gun to Tom?"

Ronan sighed. "His fingerprints. There was no time to clean the thing off. The peelers don't actually get prints off a gun very often, but it does happen occasionally. And if we reveal the location of the buried body with the bullets in it, ballistics will connect the killing to the gun. I simply cannot take that chance."

"True enough."

"I know, I know. And, by the way, nobody else in the family is aware of Tom's involvement in that shooting. Not even Lorcan. He's the one we usually think of as the hothead in the family. Well, that's why I wanted to make sure he was kept out of all this."

"Just as well."

"So, Brennan, I have to retrieve that gun. Once I've done that, I will set the wheels in motion to inform the victim's family of the location of their son's unhallowed grave and give them that small . . . well, comfort is not the word. Partial resolution."

"You said 'retrieve,' which suggests to me you know where this gun is."

"I do now, but it's not someplace where I can just waltz in and say, 'Excuse me, lads, I'll take that pistol if you don't mind. It reflects badly on the family, you understand.'" Ronan could not quite pull off the effort to lighten the tone.

"When did you find this out?"

"Today. From Jonno. He told me but he didn't tell Lorcan. From what Jonno said, I know this is reliable information."

"I suppose I shouldn't ask where the gun is."

"You may indeed ask, Father Burke. It's in the parochial house of Saint Matthew's church in east Belfast."

"What the fuck is it doing there?"

"Your astonishment is understandable, Father."

"Do they keep a stockpile of weapons in case Saint Matthew's gets attacked again?"

"No."

Ronan drank his non-drink in silence for a few minutes, then elaborated, "It's a Browning Hi-Power nine millimetre pistol, and it was placed with the parish priest there for safekeeping. Now the priest is dead."

"Gun, dead priest. Is there by any chance a connection?"

"No, actually. Father McCarthy was seventy-six years old. He died of natural causes."

"And the gun was placed with him why?"

"You don't want to know. And you're better off not knowing."

"So nobody can come at me with a rubber truncheon and beat the truth out of me."

Ronan didn't laugh. There was nothing fanciful about it. Not here.

"What has me even more rattled is that Tom wants to go in there and get the gun himself. I rang him and got him over to the house as soon as we got back from the Kesh. Now that he knows where the gun is, he'll have nothing else on his mind till this gets resolved. If I could find any humour in this, I'd be plotting to dress myself up as a cowboy and go in there and *hunt for that there gun*."

Ronan changed the subject and they spoke of other matters and listened to the music. Brennan, though, his tongue loosened a bit by drink, again brought up the elephant in the room. The gun in the parlour.

"Whereabouts in the church is it, do you know?"

"In the cellar. I don't have anything more specific than that."

"Could someone get into that cellar and out again? What's it used for?"

"I've never seen it. Remember, we didn't have Tom's wedding party there, just the ceremony itself. And the wedding of course is another reason Tom can't be showing his face there; somebody might remember seeing the young groom going in and out of the church."

"So, Ronan, I guess walking up to the door of Saint Matthew's, greeting the parish secretary or the priest and saying, 'Say, have you got a pistol lying around and can I have it?' is just not on."

"You have shrewdly identified the problem, Brennan. I can't go knocking at the door. Anything I do, and this goes double for anything I do in east Belfast, gets noticed. And getting noticed in relation to something like this would toll the death knell for my hopes to participate in the new power-sharing institutions. If in fact those institutions get established."

"I can see that. So there'd be a new priest at Saint Matthew's now? Is there a full-time secretary?"

"Yes, and yes. And they are out of the office for the duration of the noontime Mass. So there is the better part of an hour when the place is unoccupied, but — Brennan, in case you suspect I'm going to try to use you to do my dirty work *again*, I am not."

"It doesn't sound as if it would require me to dress in outlandish garb and affect the dialect and mannerisms of a southern U.S. redneck, so that alone tempts me to offer my services."

"Brennan, I am not about to take advantage of your kindness. Or of the fact that there has been drink taken here tonight. I have fond memories of drinking myself, as you know, and not-so-fond memories of some of the decisions I made and the mornings I suffered as a result."

"This isn't the drink talking here, Ronan."

"You have worked above and beyond the call of duty in the Dublin bombing investigation. I will not prevail upon you again."

"You forget. I have a personal interest in having the Dublin bombers prosecuted, just as you have, and that accounts for the bit of bad theatre I took part in at the Iron Will bar."

"True. This, however, is something else altogether."

"It may be. But it's a parish office with a priest and his secretary. It is not a bar full of murderous Loyalist paramilitaries. I survived that; I should be able to deal with a couple of church folk."

"No, Brennan. I shall call upon my former . . ."

"Men who served with distinction with you when you were second-in-command of the Belfast Brigade of the IRA."

"They were loyal soldiers. I'm sure one of them will volunteer for the mission, though I'd never be able to reveal the reason for it."

"I, on the other hand, would look completely at home in a Catholic church or office. It could be as simple as me appearing at the office a few minutes before Mass time, with some excuse or other and then expressing an interest in attending Mass. *Oh, but could I use the phone and make a couple of calls first, before I join you for the Eucharist? I'll be there as close to twelve o'clock as I can make it.*"

"Then you'd clatter down the stairs to the cellar and set about ransacking the place looking for the weapon, hoping it's just lying around, not locked away or anything."

"That would be my hope." He got up and went to the bar for one last pint. When he returned to the table, he took up the conversation where he had left off. "Of course if there's a vault, I have no experience as a safecracker. My only experience has been a bit part as a yokel new in town and wonderin' where the country music bars are located."

"There's no safe, or so I'm told. Maybe some old filing cabinets, which of course may be locked."

"And the new priest may have got rid of the weapon by now."

"He hasn't."

"You know that?"

"He probably doesn't know it's there."

"Well, if he looked through his new workplace, surely he'd find whatever was there."

"It's hidden, and he'd have no reason to search every nook and cranny for something he doesn't know exists."

"And yet whoever you send in will be able to find it."

"Tom is bound and determined that he is going in for it. Which would be the end of him, and I've made that clear to him. He doesn't know anything about the cellar, how to get access to it, whether there is an alarm. If it's someplace fairly open and neglected, maybe he could get in and root around. But he doesn't know that, and he can hardly go into the parish house and ask."

"There could be two parts to this mission. The first, an innocent visit to Saint Matthew's, to case the joint without appearing to do so. The second depends upon the first. If the basement is seen to be easily accessible, the search is conducted, and, with a heap of luck, the gun is found and removed."

"And luck will abound, inevitably."

"O ye of little faith."

"I'm more of a Murphy's Law kind of a man, Brennan. You know, if anything can go wrong, it will. So I'm telling you what I told Tomás: stay away!"

He was almost certainly right, but Brennan refrained from saying so. Because he knew, as surely as he knew the "Pater Noster" and the "Tantum Ergo," that Tomás Burke was going to go after that weapon.

Chapter XIV

Brennan

Brennan awoke on Friday morning with a full bladder, a queasy stomach, and the unshakeable perception that the world was spinning around him. The planet was spinning, he knew, but surely with him securely on it and not at the speed of light. How had he got himself into such a fix? Again. Madden's, that was it. The music was brilliant, the *craic* was mighty, and the taps did ne'er run dry. Did Brennan have to get up? Could he just pass the day in bed, then wake up refreshed and sober and not the least hungover? But he had to have a slash. Urgently. And once he was on his feet . . . He forced himself out of the bed and into the bathroom, got himself cleaned up, and then returned to his room where he sat at the little desk, head in hands. Wasn't there something he had to do?

No, it was all that talk with Ronan about Tom and the murder of that poor young backpacker, killed somehow in self-defence. And Tom's gun was now stashed in a church basement. How did it get there? Ronan hadn't answered that question and likely never would. There was nobody home when Brennan went down for his breakfast. A relief, really. He wouldn't have to look across the table at his cousin and be faced with how worried the man was about the fate of his son.

Brennan headed out to Ardoyne to do good works at Holy Cross school and put his family's troubles out of mind for the remainder of the working day. But when he said a private Mass in the empty church before returning home, he was overwhelmed with worry and sorrow, for his own relations and for the van der Meers, the family of the young lad who had been killed, the family that had no idea where their son had gone. Brennan felt compelled to try to assist in some way, but he didn't know how. Climbing out of a cellar in east Belfast with a gun in his hand was obviously not an option.

Leaving Holy Cross church he saw the parish secretary, Mary Pat, locking the outside door to the office and preparing to leave. "Hi, Father. I'm leaving a wee bit early today. Appointment with the dentist! I hope no calls come in to the office while I'm gone, but it's the only time I could get an appointment."

"Just say three Hail Marys and a Glory Be, and your sin will be forgiven."

She laughed and said, "Thank you, Father, I'll do that."

"I could go in and answer any calls, if you like. Till when? Five?"

"Oh, no, I wouldn't want to trouble you."

"No trouble." It would just be half an hour.

"Well, if you're sure . . ."

"I'm sure. Just open up and let me in. If anyone rings, I'll take a message."

She unlocked the door and told him just to shut it tight when he left; it would lock. She thanked him and went off to her appointment.

Brennan went inside the office and sat at the desk. In fact no calls came in, and there was nothing he had to do. He stood up and looked at a display of photos of the church and the Crumlin Road in former times, including some tough times for Ardoyne at the height of the

Troubles. At five o'clock he got up and closed the door, making sure it was locked, and he walked out to the Crumlin Road to wait for his bus. On the way to Andersonstown it struck him how easy it would be to pay a friendly visit to the parish office across town at Saint Matthew's, have a chat with the parish secretary — he had been told there was just the one — and keep her attention on him while someone else had a look at the cellar, and the possible ways to achieve access thereto. And if that someone returned to the cellar at a later date and found a gun there, would anyone connect an unmemorable, innocent visit from an amiable priest and a later escapade involving a gun? If indeed anyone got caught with a gun? As long as Brennan had no contact with the pistol, and there was a gap in time between the two events, surely there would be nothing to connect him to the weapon, or at least nothing that could count as evidence against him.

He knew all too well that any plan could go awry but he couldn't think of any other way to help Ronan in his laudable effort to give the bereaved family the remains of their son, and to put out of circulation the one piece of evidence that would condemn Ronan's own son to life in the Long Kesh prison.

†

It was a painful encounter with Tomás Burke that evening which set in motion the Saint Matthew's church weapon retrieval scheme. They were sitting in Tom's car, the young man's head down and his tall frame slumped over the steering wheel. He fought back tears as Brennan told him he knew about the shooting, knew it wasn't an intentional act of murder, and knew where the gun was located. Even though Tom did not provide any details of the incident, Brennan assured him that he would treat the matter with all the confidentiality of the confessional seal. He then outlined the plan he had in mind.

"My father can't know," Tom said. "He'll kill me if he finds out what we're going to do."

"You and me both, Tom. He warned me not to get involved."

But he was involved; he and Tomás were in it together. Three days later, a few minutes before noon in the bucketing rain, Father Burke washed up at the door of Saint Matthew's parish office. Dressed in his black clerical suit and white Roman collar under a light-weight nylon jacket, he tried not to look as if he had the janglers. He was not usually a skittish type, but this was east Belfast, a serious crime had been committed, and he was conspiring to make a key piece of evidence disappear. And the whole performance would have to be improvised. He was going in on a wing and a prayer. Not that he had the gall to pray to the Man Above for assistance in this caper.

The first thing he noted was an alarm system and a keypad beside the entrance to the building. But this was the middle of the day, so he opened the door and went inside. The closest inner door bore a sign "Parish Office," so he knocked and waited. A few seconds later the door was opened a crack, and a female voice said, "Who is it?"

Giving his name as Burke was obviously out of question, and he had reasoned that giving a false name could come back to haunt him later. Why engage in deception if he was innocent of any wrong-doing? So he had decided he would lose his voice. And become one of those public sneezers and coughers who were such an annoyance in real life.

He smiled and pointed at his throat, then held his right fist up to his ear miming the use of a telephone. The door opened an inch or two more, and a pair of watery pale grey eyes looked him over. She took in his collar.

"Oh, Father! You're half-drowned!" The parish secretary was a short, stout, grey-haired woman in her late sixties. "This weather!"

He gave what he hoped was a rueful laugh and nodded in agreement.

It was precisely because of this weather that he and Tom had waited and embarked on their mission today; it meant that Tom could walk around the church property obscured in a rain jacket and hood and not raise suspicions. His task was to scope out the entrance to the building and the cellar for a later visit.

"I got soaked myself when I came in at half six. It's been going on that long!"

Now he had to get into the office and close the door so Tom could slip into the corridor behind him. Brennan turned away and sneezed a couple of times into his hand, then smiled at her again and tried to look sheepish.

"Sure you've an awful cold."

He nodded and mouthed the words, "I've lost my voice."

"Come in, Father, and get out of that rain."

He stepped in and shut the door behind him. Then he mouthed a bunch of words that he knew she couldn't catch.

"I'm sorry, Father, I can't understand you."

At that point he reached for his wallet and took out a holy card, which featured a picture of the Blessed Virgin Mary ascending into the clouds. He then made a gesture of writing, and raised his eyebrows. Oh yes, she had a pen for him. She went over to the desk and he followed at a respectful distance. She handed him the pen and he bent over and wrote on the card, "Lost my voice. Came to see the cranes. Now need taxi!"

"Oh, you wanted to look at Samson and Goliath." The nicknames for the big cranes at the Harland and Wolff shipyard, which dominated the skyline of east Belfast.

There was the sound of a door opening outside. Brennan knew Tom would have made his entrance, silently, well before now. Brennan steeled himself for a new arrival in the office. But the footsteps kept going.

"That will be himself," the secretary said, "Father Mulholland here for our noon Mass."

Good. The priests use that entrance when they come into the parochial house, or one of them does anyway. And the Mass times posted outside showed there is a Mass at seven in the morning. The sun would not be up then.

Brennan put the holy card back in his wallet. He thought of something then and directed his eyes over her head at a photo of the Pope. She turned to see what he was looking at and he took the opportunity to rub the pen all over on his wet jacket. Not that he expected his *prints* to match anything controversial in Belfast! She made a comment about the lovely picture of His Holiness and turned back to Brennan just as he was replacing the pen. He made a gesture to indicate that he had got it all wet.

"No worries," she said and laughed, and she dried it off on her skirt. "I'll ring for a taxi now, Father. Then I'll be off to Mass. Starts on the stroke of noon!"

She called the taxi and told her visitor, "He'll be here in ten minutes. They're busy today in the rain. You're welcome to stay in here till he comes. Stand over by the radiator and get some heat on you."

He mouthed a "thank you" and moved over beside the radiator. She said goodbye and left for Mass, and he made the sign of the cross over her, mouthing the words, "Bless you."

He stayed in the office for three minutes or so, praying in his unworthiness that nobody else would come in before he made his escape, and agonizing over the fact that this pantomime would likely be more memorable to the secretary than just coming in and giving a false name. With the lost-voice skit, though, he could at least later deny an intention to deceive, which he would not be able to do if he lied about his identity. By now he figured that Tom would have had plenty of time to check out the access to the cellar. Brennan got up and walked unhurriedly to the exit and submitted himself once again to what felt like forty days and forty nights of rain coming down all at once on his head. He had no intention of getting into a taxi.

Chapter XV

Monty

After work on Tuesday, the last day of February, Monty headed to the south part of the city where several of his colleagues were meeting some of the law profs and students from Queen's University. They were gathering for a regular weekly gripe session held in Laverys —no apostrophe — bar. Maybe he should open his own bar, call it the "No Apostrophe." It would be informally known as Collins. Anyway, in Laverys Monty was soon planted on a barstool and was introduced to a number of professors, law students, barristers, and solicitors, all intent on an evening of serious drinking and conversation. Like their kind everywhere, they got into a groove regaling each other with war stories from their days in the courts or with their clients. Here, of course, there really was a history of war, and some of these people had been close enough to get powder burns on their barristers' wigs. Then there was the ecstasy of victory and the agony of defeat in the Diplock courts, where juries had been abolished along with some other cherished cornerstones of the justice system. One of the profs at the law school, Bill Akerman, told Monty he had just published a paper on the subject, and Monty said he would make a point of reading it.

"Read it, sure," the lawyer said, "or go over and talk to that fellow who just walked in. The O'Reilly. He's a very experienced solicitor, a fixture in the Crumlin Road Courthouse." He nodded in the direction of a tall, distinguished-looking man with a mane of copper and silver hair, who had just arrived at the bar and was ordering a drink.

"That's the famed Reddy O'Reilly. The yellow press calls him 'the IRA lawyer' but that's just the usual slander of identifying the lawyer with his clients."

"I guess that would make me the *killers' lawyer* back home in Nova Scotia. Or, here, the *malingerers' lawyer*, for all the personal injury claims we do at Ellison Whiteside."

"Yeah, I know. I had my own practice for fifteen years before I began teaching at the law school, and I used to get the same treatment. You want to say to those people, 'Just wait till the knock comes on your own door at midnight, peelers or the army there to fit you up for a crime. See how quick you'll be to plead for my services then.'"

"Exactly."

The O'Reilly was hailed from various tables around the room as he waited for his pint. Then, glass in hand, he made the rounds, greeting people and trading quips, if the laughter was any indication. He caught sight of Bill and came over. A pair of steady hazel eyes took in the new boy in the bar. There were laugh lines around the eyes; Monty guessed he was in his late forties, like Monty himself.

"I'm Monty Collins," he said and put out his hand.

"Redmond O'Reilly," the man replied, and they shook.

"Join us?"

"Thank you." He took the stool beside Monty's and held court from there, as a succession of lawyers came in and stopped for a word. Monty and Reddy started in on their stories and stayed on the drink, and by the time Monty left Laverys, he had an experienced solicitor for his IRA client and a recommendation for the two Loyalists. "I'd never work in this town again," O'Reilly told him, "if I took on a UDA or UVF case. But I'll send you to someone who'll do a stellar job for you on those two files. And I'll give you the ins and outs of briefing a barrister when you get to that stage."

Brennan

When Tom and Brennan met up at Ronan's the day after their excursion to east Belfast, Tom reported that Ronan was still at his office at Burke Transport, northern division. Gráinne was nowhere to be seen. So Tom was able to give Brennan a rundown on the cellar of Saint Matthew's parochial house. "There's an alarm on the door to the building, as you'd have seen for yourself, but once you're inside, the door to the cellar isn't locked. It's just a regular door off the corridor. I walked in after you and went down the stairs. Doesn't look as if there's anything important down there. Statues, metal cabinets, no Vatican gold."

"Well, the alarm will be off when the parish secretary gets in. She must be the first one there. She told me she got there at half six in the morning. There's a seven o'clock Mass, so the workday starts early."

"*Is maith sin.*" That's good. "The sun doesn't come up till around half seven. Once she goes in, I go in. I search the cellar, find the fucking gun, and get out of there. I'll leave a gap of a few days so she won't connect me with you if, God forbid, she spots me there."

With that, Tom left for home, and Brennan tried to put the gun scheme out of his mind. Nor did he care to dwell on the fact that he had conspired with Tom to do something Ronan emphatically did not want his son to do, and that he was keeping Ronan in the dark about the plan.

†

But one unpromising scheme led him to brood on another. Brennan was haunted by the fact that he had not been able to help his cousin make a case against one of the many perpetrators of the 1974 atrocities. Harold Tait in the United States had given Brennan some details of the evangelical rally in Tennessee, and Brody MacAllan had confirmed, however unintentionally, that there had been a downpour on one of the days and that a man had shouted out his concerns about papists outbreeding the Protestant population of America. Hiram Stockwell had put the man down gently with a reference to America being the home of people of all faiths. Something like that. As Tait said, neither of these incidents would have made the news, so MacAllan would not have read about them. There may have been news photos of the attendees, drenched to the skin, but the local Tennessee papers would hardly be available in the Belfast library, for MacAllan to see or for Brennan to research. So Brennan had been convinced that MacAllan had been in Tennessee as he claimed. Yet Ronan's witness was absolutely certain that he saw MacAllan in one of the bomb cars. Brennan tried to work through all this in his mind. What else had Tait told him about the rally? There was merchandise on sale. MacAllan had told Duane and Ruby that his wife had stopped to buy eight-track tapes and something else when he was trying to get her away and off to the airport. A poster was the other purchase, something large and inconvenient to carry because it was enclosed in glass and a frame. And his wife still had the poster on her wall, wherever she was living now. Evidence right there of her husband's alibi. Was it possible, Brennan wondered, that she had sent away to Tennessee and ordered these things? Brennan chastised himself for persisting with this in the face of MacAllan's accurate accounting of the Stockwell event. But, with nothing else to go on, he decided to give the Reverend Tait a call again.

"Can you bear to hear my voice again, Harold?"

"Any time, Brennan."

"You told me about audiotapes and things being sold at the Stockwell rally in 1974."

"Oh, yes."

"Would someone have been able to send away and order these, have them delivered?"

"I don't think so, Brennan. Nowadays, yes, there's a bit of a mail order business, but not back then. You had to grab what you could while you were there." Tait laughed then and said, "And people did, once they noticed the *Scottish* poster. It became something of a collector's item."

"Scottish poster? What was that?"

"There was a misprint on the posters of Hiram Stockwell. Superimposed over the image of Stockwell himself, at the bottom of the poster, was a verse from Psalms. 'Be still and know that I am God. I will be exalted among the heathen, I will be exalted in the earth.'"

It was Brennan's turn to laugh. "They weren't claiming the Scots were heathens, surely not!"

"No, but the typo was in the word 'heathen.' There was an R instead of an N, so it read 'exalted among the heather.' People had some fun proclaiming that the Lord's new promised land was Scotland."

"Wonderful. I should get one for my friends in Nova Scotia where I'm based now. New Scotland. Maybe I could make copies and sell them as a fundraiser for my parish."

"Your heart's in the right place, Brennan, but they're no longer available. Stockwell was good-natured about it, made a couple of little quips, but he took them off the market that day and brought out a corrected version a week or two later. Exalted were they who managed to grab a little collector's item before they were removed from the kiosk."

"Removed them while the rally was still going on."

"Oh, yes, it was a bit of fun but one wouldn't want to prolong any mockery of sacred scripture! Anybody arriving for the last two days of the rally was out of luck. The heather posters — they were in fact the only posters — were gone."

Brennan let this sink in for a moment. "And the dates of the rally were?" Brennan knew but he wanted to hear it again from the minister who had been there. The witness.

"May the thirteenth to the seventeenth."

Brennan felt a surge of hope. "So the last day for the posters was what, the fifteenth?"

"You got it. They weren't available the last two days."

Ronan came in an hour or so later with Gráinne and Lorcan. Lorcan was carrying an acoustic guitar. "So you're a musician, Lorcan."

"Yeah. Me and Carrick have a regular gig at McCribbon's bar."

"What music do you do?"

"Traditional music, Republican songs, that kind of thing."

"You must enjoy that."

"I do, though it means I never get away from the 'office.'"

"Office?"

"I work as a barman at McCribbon's, usually in the day, sometimes at night. But it's all right. It's a good place."

"They're good, the pair of them," said Ronan. "Lots of music in our family." He gave a nod to Brennan, the choirmaster. "Our boy had a harder sound with his previous band. Tell him what you called yourselves, Lorcan."

"We were the Gobscheiss Militia."

"That's brilliant!" Brennan appreciated the Germanic twist on the familiar Irish term of abuse, gobshite. "What happened to the Gobscheiss Militia?"

"Our drummer and bass player are out of circulation right now."

"Ah."

"I'm about to wet the tea," said Gráinne. "Who'd like some?" They all would and, when it was ready, they all sat in the front room with their cups and saucers.

"I have some news," Brennan announced.

All three of them looked wary. News was something to be leery of, even during a ceasefire.

"Brody MacAllan was in Tennessee at the evangelical rally in May of 1974."

"Yeah, we know," Lorcan replied.

"And he has papers showing that he left Belfast for America on May the eleventh and had a return flight on the eighteenth, landing here the morning of the nineteenth."

They all knew that as well.

"But I just received evidence — or what will be submitted as evidence — that in fact he left the United States on May the fifteenth. He flew out that evening and would have landed here the next morning. So he would have been back here in time to commit the bombings on the seventeenth."

"No!" Gráinne exclaimed. Ronan and his son merely stared at Brennan.

"The minister I know in the States told me there was a poster on sale at the rally, but it had a typo in it, a misprint that was memorable because it was comical. When the mistake was discovered, the posters were removed from sale. The last day anyone could have bought one was the fifteenth of May. MacAllan obviously knew nothing about the posters being withdrawn; he slipped up when he told us his wife bought one of the posters and almost made them late for their flight out that same day."

"I knew it!" Ronan raised two fists in triumph. "He was in the thick of things with the bombings, and he had papers forged to back him up. I believe the word 'collusion' has come up in our conversations from time to time."

"Yeah, he clearly had help from official sources."

Lorcan looked at Brennan sharply. "Did you just say you met MacAllan?"

"I get around."

"You're getting to know your way around this wee town. Were you over to his place for tea?"

"In a manner of speaking," Brennan answered, "but it wasn't tea. It was the Iron Will."

Ronan said, "We heard that he's been spending his weekends there since he returned from Scotland. Brennan went in there, undercover, and confirmed it."

"Brilliant. Now, this bar. It's off the Newtownards Road, right?"

"Don't even think about going in there, Lorcan."

"So what are we supposed to do, Da? Let him slide into a comfortable old age?"

Brennan ignored this and said, "What happens now?"

Ronan and his son exchanged a look, and Ronan said, "We go to the peelers."

"Where our people have had so much success in the past."

"Lorcan, remember our objective here. We don't want to put a bullet in this fucker's brain and have the whole thing written off as 'another killing by the IRA.' We want MacAllan publicly identified and prosecuted as one of the Monaghan and Dublin bombers. We want this to focus the minds of the police and the public on the fact that all the bastards who planned and carried out the attacks were able to get away with it. Till now."

"I wouldn't be putting my faith in the Royal Ulster Constabulary if I were you, Da. But then, you've known them longer than I have. Which should make you even more cynical about the bastards."

"This operation is to put the police in the spotlight as much as MacAllan. Shame them into doing their jobs and arresting MacAllan and sending him south for prosecution. We go to the RUC and the Garda Síochána with the evidence. His name and photo, the witness who saw him in the car the day of the bombings, and this poster and a sworn statement from the American minister. We bring forward the flight and re-entry documents we now know were forged, and anything else we can come up with. And what's he likely to do in response? Grass on the rest of them who were in on it."

"But we have to tread carefully," Brennan warned. "You'll want a lawyer's advice before you decide how much of this to disclose to the police. Presumably you reveal just enough to get him charged, keeping the rest in reserve. You want him wedded to his story of leaving on the eighteenth. Bring your evidence out when it will do the most good. If it's handled right, you may be able to set in motion the first prosecution in the bombings of Dublin and Monaghan."

Ronan smiled, put his hands together in prayer, and looked to the skies. "Thank you, great God of mercy and truth!"

"I want to see that fucker." Lorcan was already seeing that fucker in his mind's eye, viewing him through the scope of a rifle.

"No, you don't, Lorcan," his father insisted. "And you don't want him seeing you or any of the other lads. It's going to take some careful manoeuvring to make this happen after all these years. We can't let anything tip him off. We can't do anything to blow this one chance to get justice for the families."

Chapter XVI

Monty

Monty was making progress in his Canadian Earth Equipment case, having found a number of documents that showed defects in the metals that were supplied to the company over the course of several years. This meant Monty's client was on firm ground in claiming that the fault lay not with Canadian Earth but with the metal supplier. He called his Halifax law firm and was commended for his fine work. But his contentment was short-lived. Minutes after that call, he received some disheartening news from Katie Flanagan. The bank had finally foreclosed on the family home, and Katie, her mother, and the other children had to leave. The Northern Ireland Housing Executive had found them a flat in another part of the city, far from everything and everyone they knew in Musgrave Park. Winnie Flanagan said she couldn't bear to prolong the agony. The new flat was ready, and she was going to make the move right away. Monty had immediately offered his assistance.

Monty dreaded seeing the family leave their home. And it was going to be even worse, because moving day was a Saturday and Normie was with him. She had insisted on helping with the move. Rather than pay a moving company, he had rented a cargo van and conscripted Brennan Burke to help with the heavy lifting. Brennan arrived, still in his clerical suit and collar from some priestly activities earlier in the afternoon, and the moving party was set to go. Normie climbed into the van beside Monty, Brennan got in on the other side of her, and they headed out. When they pulled up in front of the house, it was like an old-fashioned photograph of children about to be taken to an orphanage. Or a family being evicted from their home, which it was. Katie and her sister and brothers were in front of the house, each of them with a prized possession in hand. Katie was juggling a pile of books and a chipped red Pyrex mixing bowl. Clare clung to an enormous stuffed lamb with drooping ears. Dermot had a tin whistle in one hand and a train engine in the other. Darren had a hurley. Everyone was there but young Timmy. Several mothers were out in the street, arms around their children, looking on.

Monty quickly introduced Brennan to them, and they all said, "Hello, Father." Aside from that, no time was wasted on pleasantries. Monty and Brennan were obviously thinking the same way: get the children's minds off it by throwing themselves into the heavy work immediately. They went into the house and cased the place, deciding what should go out in what order, and they got to it. Mrs. Flanagan was inside, a worn-looking leather suitcase in her left hand, the right hand held out in front of her as if she could ward off whatever awaited her outside her home. She was thin and blond; she looked faded, wan. It took her a couple of seconds to register their presence and decide who was who. "Oh! You must be Mr. Collins."

"That's me. Monty," he said and put out his hand. She took it and held it as if she had no idea what to do with it.

"This is Father Burke," he said. "Mrs. Flanagan."

"How do you do, Father? I'm Winnifred, but you can call me Winnie."

"And I'm Brennan."

"Thank you very much for helping us today, and for all your legal help, Monty."

"You're more than welcome, Winnie."

"I'm sorry," she said, "that I've been so, so useless through all this. I've let the children down. My own children! It's just that I haven't been able to . . . Eamon dying like that. Someone smashing into him and knocking him off the bridge, and not staying to help him. That's the part of it I can't get past: someone did this to him, and that person is still out there, living his life, and hasn't been charged. It's not the money." She laughed at herself then. "Everybody says that, I know. It's not *only* the money. We're in need of it, no denying. But I want to see someone brought to law for what he did to my Eamon!"

"I understand, Winnie. I know. And I'll do my very best for you."

"I know you will, Monty."

His "very best" hadn't done much good for her and the family today. Most likely it never would. But he kept that to himself.

He did, however, have a question about money. "Winnie, Katie told me that for a while there you were getting sums of money from somewhere. Deposits into your account. And then —"

"And then it stopped. The money stopped coming."

"What was the source of those payments?"

"Monty, we never knew."

"How did the payments get into your account? What did the people at the bank tell you?"

A pink flush spread over her face, and she looked away from him. "I made a hames of it when I asked them. They told me a cheque had arrived, I think they said by post, from a company called Day Sure Investments. And I . . . I didn't want them to take it back or something, so I said, 'Oh, yes, Eamon told me something about investments he had.' And I didn't ask any more questions."

Monty nodded, as if this was all quite in order. Then he asked, "What amounts are we talking about?"

"Sometimes it was eight hundred pounds, sometimes a bit less. Once a month."

"I see. When did the payments stop?"

"Well, they started about three months or so after Eamon's death and stopped before the first anniversary. I think it was seven months of payments in all."

"All right. Thank you, Winnie. Let's get back to work here."

They lugged the boxes and pieces of furniture out and loaded them into the van. Monty pointed to the books and bowl in Katie's arms and said, "We can just put all the things in a box, Katie. Nothing will get lost."

"I suppose so. You're right." She handed over the books. "I'll keep this. It might get broken if it's a rough trip."

"All right." He turned to the younger children and offered to pack the lamb and other treasured items. The kids looked at him with big, sad eyes and shook their heads. He got it then. It wasn't fear of having things lost or broken. It was fear of the unknown, the desolation of leaving their home. The beloved toys and other objects would comfort them on the journey none of them wanted to make.

"Where's Tim?"

"Playing football."

"Right, okay."

Monty went back to lifting and lugging. On one trip out, while he was carrying a big stuffed chair, Monty saw two girls in the uniform of Katie's old school, telling her they would miss her in the debating club.

"I'll not be winning another round as long as I live, if you're not there to prop me up!" one of the girls said to her.

"You're the best," the other one said. "It'll never be the same without ye. Sure you're moving house, but why aren't ye staying in the club anyway?"

"It's too far. I won't be able to get there. And I have to mind this lot." She pointed to her siblings.

Monty heaved the chair into the van and came out again, to see the girls in a big group hug. The other two went off then, down the street, their arms around each other.

Katie was in the doorway, trying to stem her tears. "Mortgage is a nasty-sounding word," she said.

"It is," Monty agreed. He formed a picture in his mind of the mortgage holder of Vaudevillian times, wearing a sneer and a black top hat, twirling his moustache as the family was thrown out on the street.

Normie was doing her best to help the other children get their stuff out, reassuring them that they'd see their friends and their old neighbourhood again. She looked like someone suffering from shell shock.

When Brennan and Monty had loaded the beds, dressers, chairs, table, dishes, two trunks full of clothes, boxes of books and toys and all the other accoutrements of family life into the van, it was time to arrange transportation for the human cargo. There wasn't room for nine people in the furniture van. Monty's solution was to call for an airport-type taxi designed for multiple passengers. It was time to make the call. But one more thing . . .

Monty cleared his throat and said to Katie, "Time to get Tim."

"I know."

She turned and walked down the street. Normie, Monty, and Brennan followed along behind her. They stopped at the field where the Clarkson Terrace Celtics played their home games. There was a goalmouth scramble happening when they arrived, all the players wriggling in a heap in front of the far goal. It was a cool day and the ground was wet from a shower; the players had their team jerseys on over jackets and sweatshirts. They were covered in mud. The boys looked up and saw the faces of doom waiting at the edge of the field. All of them, to a man, looked away.

"Timmy Flanagan!" Katie called to her brother. "Come on, love!"

"Ach, no, not now!"

"Have to go."

Timmy brushed some gobs of mud from his jersey and stood

looking at his sister. Then he commenced his last, slow walk to the street. Whether planned or not, the rest of the boys formed two uneven lines, one on either side of him. A raggle-taggle guard of honour. They watched in silence as he walked, looking straight ahead. His best friend, Barry, stood at the top of the line closest to the street. When Timmy reached him, the two boys stood facing each other. Then Timmy gave a curt nod and said, "See ye."

Barry nodded back. "Yeah, see ye."

Timmy headed straight for the van. Katie reached for him, but he shook her hand away. He turned to the rest of us. "What are youse waitin' for?"

Normie looked on with anguish. She said to Monty and Brennan, "That's his best friend! He's moving away from him! If I had to say goodbye to my best friend . . . if I ever had to leave Kim, I wouldn't be able to stand it!" She could no longer hold back her tears. "How come he didn't — I don't know — he just said, 'See ye.' How come they didn't . . ." She looked Brennan and Monty square in the face and said, "It's because they're boys, isn't it?"

"Yeah," said Monty.

"Mmm," Brennan agreed.

"Men!" She pinned them with a look of disgust far beyond her years, condemned them with all the ancient authority of the wiser sex, the eternal feminine.

All the Reverend Doctor Brennan Burke and Monty Collins, QC, could do was stand there and take it.

†

They timed things so the van and the big taxi would travel together. The taxi waited while Monty went into a take-out for fish and chips for all. But that did nothing to improve the mood in the van as Monty, Brennan, and Normie followed the family to the Heatherfield Villas housing estate. When they arrived, everyone scrambled out and took a look around. Monty was not in the least surprised to find that "Heatherfield," not to mention "Villas," turned out to be a misnomer.

"A bunch of naff tower blocks!" Darren exclaimed.

"Now, Darren," his mother said.

There were several high-rise apartment buildings on the estate. Other buildings, lower to the ground, sported Republican and IRA murals with warriors wearing balaclavas and brandishing machine guns. One of the older, more scuffed-looking images shouted "Up the Third Battalion!" Unwritten, but glaringly obvious, was "Deprived Area."

"All right, let's see your new house," Monty tried.

"That one," Katie replied, pointing at one of the high-rises.

"House!" Dermot groused. "It's a fuckin' kip, so it is!"

"Now, Dermot," Winnie Flanagan said, "not everybody lives in a house. We'll make a home of this place, you wait and see."

"We will in our hole!"

"Dermot!"

Katie had picked up the key to flat 705 the day before. Everyone squashed into the elevator, which wheezed and clanked its way to the seventh floor. The elevator walls were covered with graffiti, some of it Republican, some of it just plain obscene, some of it — Monty noted Brennan's disapproving glare — misspelled. The elevator stank of smoke and weed and piss. When it clanged and shuddered to a stop, they all got out and trudged to door number 705. Katie opened the door and they entered the flat. The first thing you noticed was the acid green carpet, flecked with brown and yellow. Monty hoped the flecks were in the original design. He wanted to assume it had been cleaned, prior to the new tenants moving in, but it didn't look it. Or smell it. There were three bedrooms. There had been five beds in the family home but one had to be left behind. There was barely room for four in the new place. Space and privacy had to be sacrificed along with so much else.

"It's manky in here," Dermot complained, holding his nose.

"Why do we have to live in a rubbish tip like this?" It was Clare this time. She was crying. "I'd be scundered to have any of my friends see it."

"No worries there," replied Darren. "Our mates are too far away to find their way to this rat hole. We'll never see them again."

"Oh, God!" Clare cried out and began sobbing.

Then it was Dermot: "What will the school be like, if this is the *house*?"

"Things will get better, lads," his mother tried.

On their way in and out as they unloaded the van and moved the family's belongings inside, Monty and Brennan ran a gauntlet of hard-looking young people and kids, many of them skinny, shaven-headed, and tattooed. None of them spoke, but they watched the proceedings with a collective expression that bespoke boredom and contempt. Brennan looked ahead to the Flanagan children, scuffing along ahead with their toys. "God help them," he muttered.

On one trip in, after Monty had set up the kitchen table and chairs, Katie placed the red mixing bowl carefully on the counter. "I always have this out on display. It was my gran's favourite bowl. She made cakes and other good stuff for us in it."

They ate the fish and chips. The children left the table in near silence. Their mother stood looking at all the items they had moved in, as if finding space for them was utterly beyond her.

Brennan gazed around the kitchen and the rest of the flat, then took a gander out the window at the riffraff milling about in the dusk below. He made a furtive sign of the cross and said, *sotto voce*, "Almighty and loving God, bless this house and all who dwell within it."

Normie stood to the side, trembling.

When they were finished and had taken their leave, they headed for Andersonstown and turned into Ronan Burke's street. Monty saw a car in front of the house. In the dim light coming from the houses, he could see the silhouettes of two men inside. Both of them sat bolt upright as the cargo van approached; both of them leaned to the right at the same time. Monty could picture their right hands going for weapons.

"Let me hop out right here, Monty," said Brennan.

"Sure."

He brought the van to a gentle stop, and Brennan got out. He slowly raised a reassuring hand to the men in the car, and Monty could see their postures relax.

"Goodnight, Mr. and Miss Collins."

"Goodnight, Father," Normie replied.

"*Slán abhaile.*" Safe home.

Chapter XVII

Brennan

When Brennan returned from his shift at Holy Cross church on Tuesday, he was met at the door by the *Teachta Dála,* Dinny Cagney, just going out. The Dublin politician was all smiles, as was Ronan behind him in the doorway. Ronan reintroduced priest and politician and filled Brennan in on the purpose of the visit. Cagney had given the Dublin policeman, Sullivan, all the information Brennan had gleaned from Harold Tait in the U.S.A. The poster with "heathen" misspelled as "heather," which had been taken off the market on May 15, the apparent presence of the faulty poster in the home of Brody MacAllan's wife, and the conclusion that MacAllan had returned to Ireland before and not after the 1974 bomb attacks. And, Brennan was pleased to hear, the Reverend Tait had told Garda Sullivan that he would provide sworn evidence of all of this when the time came. God bless him. Garda Sullivan wanted to do some more work on the case file and when he had it all together, he would present it to his counterparts in the Royal Ulster Constabulary here in Belfast. Giving them the "good" news that there were now grounds to reopen the investigation.

"Sure they'll be overjoyed," said Brennan.

"They'll be dancing a merry jig all round the barracks," Cagney agreed.

"The fact that the police on both sides of the border had evidence from day one and had never acted upon it is something that I just can't . . ."

"Let's hope they'll be shamed into acting now. Anyway I'm off, lads. Back to the Republic of Ireland, such as it is at this point in history."

"Don't be rubbing our faces in it, ye messer," Ronan said.

"All right. *Slán agus ádh mór.*" Goodbye and good luck. "And," he said, looking pointedly at Ronan, "mind yourself now, Ronan."

"I'm going to make a career in politics, Dinny. Nobody ever said politicians don't take good care of themselves!"

"Who's the messer now?"

He gave Ronan a quick embrace, nodded at Brennan, and went off.

But good news doesn't come in threes in Belfast. Or even twos. While Ronan and Brennan were seated in Ronan's office, Ronan scribbling notes in his file, Tomás came flying in the door.

"Fuck!"

"What is it?" his father asked, trepidation written all over his face.

"She fucking caught me with the gun!"

"Who caught you? What's happened?"

Oh, Christ, here it comes, thought Brennan. He and Tom had embarked on a desperate scheme to retrieve the pistol, Tom got caught, and this was the way Ronan was going to hear about it for the first time.

"We . . . I went in for the gun."

"Jesus Christ! I told you to stay away from it. What in the hell were you thinking?"

It was Father Burke's turn to confess. "It wasn't just Tom, Ronan. I was in on it. More than that, I came up with the plan."

Ronan Burke stood before his son and cousin, his face grey with shock. "I don't fucking believe this."

Brennan had no choice but to describe the events of February 27, when he and Tom had gone to the church. Tom looked ready to explode with tension. His father turned to him and demanded, "Well? What happened today?"

"I waited a few days, to put time between me and Brennan, and I waited for rain. Don't have to wait long for that in Belfast. So I put on my rain jacket with the big hood over my head, and I had a scarf around my neck, in case I'd have to pull it up. I go over there well before half six, when the secretary said she comes in. It's pitch dark out. I find a wee hiding place on Bryson Street and watch. She arrives, puts in the code and turns off the alarm. I wait until I see the light come on in the office, and then I walk over. Look around. Nobody there. I try the door. It's open and I slip inside."

The young man was breathing heavily, living through it all again. His father was motionless, staring at him.

"I open the cellar door. No worries there. I go down the stairs. I'm in the basement. All well and good. It's as dark as the devil's hole, and I can't take the chance of beaming a torch about the place. So I know I have to be careful not to trip on anything. I'll have to search by touch. I start by crawling all along the floor, even though I know the gun wouldn't be lying there in plain sight. But I get to know the layout. Then I run my hands over the statues, feeling a bit like a pervert touching somebody up. No little hiding places carved into the plaster, so I move on to the obvious places. The filing cabinets. I open drawer after drawer. Nothing but papers, old books, and accounting ledgers.

"Just when I'm pawing through the last of the cabinets, there's a creaking noise. Someone walking just above me. Coming to the basement door? I freeze and try to figure out where to conceal myself if somebody turns on the light and comes down. But nobody does. I don't hear the footsteps again, so that has me spooked. But after a few minutes I start again. Nothing in the last cabinet. I look up at the ceiling, which is made of tiles, acoustic tiles. Could somebody have stashed the gun up there? There are a couple of old broken wooden chairs, so I climb up on one and poke one of the tiles out of place. A big fucking shower of dust comes down on me and I'm nearly choking on it. It's all in my eyes. But I keep on with the tiles. I move the chair from place to place, trying not to make a sound. Halfway through the room, I knock a tile out of place. Again the shower of dust. But I probe around with my hand and, *buíochas le Dia*, I feel it there. The gun. Slowly, carefully, I draw it out and get a good grip on it."

Brennan felt as if he were right there in the subterranean darkness with young Tom.

"I've got the gun in my hand and I start to climb down off the chair, and one of the fucking chair legs comes loose and the chair clatters to the floor and me with it. And of course it's the only noise in the whole silent building. I get up and run for the stairs and I'm pulling the scarf up to my eyes and I get upstairs to the corridor and it's in semi-darkness. And there in front of me is the church secretary with her eyes out on sticks, looking at the gun in my hand, petrified with fear."

"Oh, Christ," Ronan muttered.

"And the poor wee woman doesn't know what to do. She says, 'Noise down there. I called for the police. They're on their way.' She's babbling away and not making any sense. She could not have rung the peelers in that short a time. But I'm just as mindless, and I say something like, 'No police' and 'I'm not going to hurt you,' and I turn and take off at a clip and it's only a few short minutes before I hear sirens. She's gone back into the office and called the peelers and they're out looking for me!"

Would there now be police sirens approaching the house in Andersonstown?

Tom continued his sorry tale. "I'm out in the street running like a madman and I've got the gun in my pocket. My whole fucking purpose was to get the gun and take it out to the deep water of the lough, and now I haven't a hope in hell of doing that. Can't even make it to the river. Can't be caught with it. So I have to ditch it. I come upon a building site and I see one of those gigantic rubbish skips. There's rubbish lying about, including some plastic sacs from the shops. I look around me. Nobody on the site yet. I take out the gun, stick it in one of the bags with some stones, tie the bag shut, and climb up the edge of the skip, lean down and bury it. Then I fuck off out of there. I can hear the sirens getting closer. I head deeper into the Short Strand, where I figure I can ask for refuge if need be." The solid Nationalist enclave in east Belfast. "And of course the peelers come creeping in there in their cruiser. But I'm able to dodge them, running through people's back gardens. If anyone in the Strand sees a fella hiding out from the peelers, they're not likely to inform on the poor bastard. Anyway, I zigged and zagged all over the city. They didn't spot me, and here I am. Without the Browning."

"And," his father said, as if it needed saying, "with the peelers out there looking for the man who fits the secretary's description of the man with the gun."

Chapter XVIII

Monty

It was during the week of March 13, 1995, that the scales — scales Monty didn't even know he had, after more than two decades practising criminal law — fell from his eyes. This happened during the four days he spent in the Diplock court. His discussions with Reddy O'Reilly had convinced Monty that, even with all his courtroom experience in Canada, he and his clients were better off with a solicitor who was familiar with the peculiarities of the courts in Belfast. All the more so, given the short preparation time left to him. Monty was fully prepared to act as the more junior solicitor on the case, with a humbler slice of the fees payable by the clients. Ellison Whiteside had no problem with this; the firm just wanted the case file off its desk. So Monty attended court alongside O'Reilly on the IRA file he had inherited from Emmet Crowley. Three alleged members of a proscribed organization, the Provisional Irish Republican Army, were accused of bombing a bar to ruins and leaving three people dead.

Monty and Reddy had briefed a barrister, Pearse McKendrick, who would argue the case before the judge.

The Crumlin Road Courthouse was one of Ireland's neoclassical buildings. It had Corinthian columns and a triangular pediment bearing the royal court of arms. Atop the triangle stood the lofty figure of Justice. But the effect was marred by the coils of razor wire all along the fence in front. On Monty's first day on the Crumlin Road, a group of picketers marched to and fro outside the building, with signs reading "Stormont Star Chambers!"; "An End to Diplock Courts!"; "Stop Torture Now!" The torture sign had a gruesome photo of a man whose face was swollen, bruised, and cut.

The bombing at issue in the trial had occurred in 1993, before the ceasefire. It was said to have been in retaliation for a bombing at a Republican bar two weeks earlier, in which five people died. But who knows what *that* attack had been meant to avenge? Monty thought back to the discussions he had had recently about lawyers being identified with the clients they defend; he sure as hell would not want to be identified with this. But for a lawyer practising his craft, there was nothing to equal this kind of case in this kind of court. The three defendants, Whelan, Buckley, and Dolan, were young men in their early twenties, "alleged" to be members of the IRA.

Now, Monty and Redmond entered the courtroom together after being searched and scanned for weapons and explosives. They were seated with their backs to the judge, at a table facing the barristers. With this arrangement, communications could be relayed between barrister and solicitor. Their clients were farther down the length of the courtroom, in the dock. Everyone rose when the judge walked in, bewigged and stern, and the proceedings got underway. The jury box remained conspicuously empty. The rationale was that jurors could be threatened, intimidated, or improperly influenced to acquit or convict, depending on their politico-religious affiliation and that of the defendants. Never mind that judges, too, were under threat.

So now the defendants entered the courtroom without the long-held protections that the jury system offered.

Whelan and Buckley were thin, almost emaciated. Whelan had a scar running down his cheek from the left eye and another on his upper lip. He grimaced, revealing a missing front tooth. Buckley had patches of green and yellow on his face from old bruising. The barrister, McKendrick, needed no prodding from Redmond O'Reilly or Montague Collins to milk that for all it was worth. The third client, Dolan, was in better shape, but his expression was one of simmering anger.

The prosecutor opened his case with police witnesses who testified about the horrific scene at the Flute and Drum after it had been blown up by a ten-pound bomb. The officer described in detail the smouldering remains of the front of the building, the rubble of concrete and charred wood, the smell of burnt flesh, the death-stilled bodies of a twenty-three-old woman who was tending bar that night, a young man of twenty, and the mutilated body of the elderly owner of the bar.

The bereaved families of the victims, sitting in the gallery, stared at the three accused men through tears of grief and rage. All three avoided their gaze. The two defendants with battered faces showed none of the defiance of the protesters outside the courthouse, and none of the insouciance that many of Monty's clients displayed as they sat in the prisoners' dock. Dolan maintained his angry demeanour throughout the police testimony.

The police witnesses described the arrests of the three accused men, two from the Ballymurphy housing estate and one from the Markets area.

At this point, one would expect to hear evidence of an eyewitness who could place the accused men close to the Flute and Drum around the time of the explosion or who had seen the car belonging to one of them speeding away from the scene. One would expect a police witness who had noted traces of explosives or chemicals on the defendants' hands or clothing or who could testify about a phoned-in warning traced somehow to the defendants. But Monty knew the file. There was no evidence of this nature at all. The evidence against the three came from the Crown's star witness, a snitch, a tout, an informer, who had been given immunity for his role in the bombing in return for testifying against the three others who, he claimed, had been in on the bombing with him.

By the time it was over and all three men convicted, Monty had seen things he had never seen before in a court of law. Including the "helpful intervention" of His Lordship on the bench. The judge butted in several times over the course of the trial, only once during Crown counsel's questioning, but frequently during Pearse McKendrick's time with the witnesses. The evidence was inevitably shaped and altered as a result, as the Crown witnesses twigged to what they should be saying and how they should be saying it. As for the defence witnesses, His Lordship at times conducted his own cross-examinations, thus assisting Crown counsel where Crown counsel might otherwise have fallen short. And, in the course of all this, the judge made it clear that he did not consider the defence witnesses worthy of belief. It was all Monty could do to remain quiet and not jump to his feet with an objection. It wasn't his court, it wasn't his country; he felt as if it wasn't his world. Here was a judge abandoning his role as a supposedly neutral umpire and interfering with the examination of a witness, derailing the defence's case in the process.

Then there was the torture. Whelan had made a confession, which he now said he only made because he was tortured into giving it. "I would have said anything. I would have pleaded guilty to killing President Kennedy. Anything to get them to untie my hands and to stop them pounding on me." Buckley, too, had confessed and said he had done it under duress, after repeated beatings. Both men described the abuse they had suffered; both had bruises and scars that appeared to back up the allegations. What Monty was used to, in more innocent times, was the hallowed principle that a confession is admissible only if it was made voluntarily. Otherwise, the police would be encouraged to beat confessions out of people as a regular practice, which would be wrong in itself — legalized assault — and confessions given under such duress might, just might, be unreliable; a person will finally confess to anything to stop the abuse. Like Whelan here.

But this gold standard, too, had been tarnished in the North of Ireland. The Diplock commission, which had set up the current system, had decided that such a rule would impede the orderly course of justice. Might impede the success of the forces of *law and order*, yes, but wasn't the course of *justice* something else? Wasn't it? Perhaps not. On the night they first met and drank together, Reddy had informed Monty that it was a feature of Diplock cases that judges routinely allowed "coerced confessions" obtained through "intensive interrogations." And previous courts had ruled this permissible. Monty felt as if he had stepped through the looking glass into a dark and disordered universe.

When the show was over, all three defendants were found guilty. One of them was indeed guilty of the atrocity. Buckley. And it was not his first offence. He was your basic, stock-footage, fanatical terrorist, and Monty wouldn't be the least bit sorry to see him thrown into a cell for the rest of his life. The other two, however, were innocent men. This was clear from Buckley's evidence and other information Monty had gathered about the case. The two men weren't there, didn't do it. But down they went, the latest casualties of Belfast justice. They could expect to be sentenced, alongside Buckley, to imprisonment for life. Addressing the press and the regular crop of protesters outside the Crumlin Road Courthouse, Redmond O'Reilly announced that the verdicts would be appealed.

Back in the office on Friday, Monty was still wired up after his dramatic four days in the courtroom. He felt the need to talk it out with someone, and that someone was Maura. He called her at the

University College Dublin law school and managed to catch her before her class. She let him vent his anger over the wrongful convictions, and the system that allowed — that in fact aided and abetted — such results. He wound down eventually and heard about the fun she and the kids were having in Dublin. The kids missed their dad. His wife allowed as how she too missed old Monty. Monty was seized with the longing to be with his family on the other side of the border, enjoying the *craic* in Dublin and leaving behind the unsettling legal and political terrain of Belfast. He knew that Maura and the children were planning to stay in Dublin for the weekend, which would kick off tonight with a Saint Patrick's Day pageant at Normie's school. But, catching the mood, Maura decided they would take the train up to Belfast on Saturday. Cheered by the prospect of the visit, he said goodbye and told himself to knuckle down and catch up on the work that he, of his own free will, had taken on.

One thing he wanted to look into was the investment company that had been sending payments to Winnie Flanagan. So he went in to see one of the lawyers in the corporate law department, Sandra MacLeod, and asked her if she had ever heard of Day Sure Investments. No, she hadn't. He gave her a bit of the background, and she said she would do a search. He thanked her and went back to his office, did a bit more work, and then headed out for a Saint Patrick's Day lunch and piss-up at McHughs. There wasn't much of a contingent from Ellison Whiteside for the saint's day event, but Monty met up with some congenial souls at the bar and enjoyed the outing.

Muriel Whiteside had a surprise for him after he had returned to the office and brushed his teeth in the men's room. Muriel came into his office and placed a plain white envelope on his desk. "Occasionally," she said, "we need to look into things that have been done sub rosa. We have a man who helps out on those occasions. He has many useful contacts around the city."

Monty picked up the white envelope, which he could not help thinking of as a plain *brown* envelope. He slit it open and withdrew a page of hand-printed notes prepared, presumably, by the investigator. On November 18, 1992, a 1988 Ford Orion had undergone repairs on the front and rear bumpers. There were two small holes in the rear. There was nothing to identify the repair shop or the owner of the car, but the notes did provide a crucial bit of information: the name of an insurance company. Yet, although the car was fully insured, the owner had paid for the repairs himself. The man who did the auto repair work was "quite certain the car owner was UDA. Shots fired at him, doesn't know by who."

The last thing Monty wanted to do was fuel any more of Hughie Malone's conspiracy theories. But wasn't evidence turning up that showed that the old fellow was not as wacky as he had initially appeared to be?

Monty looked up and expressed his thanks to Muriel.

"You're welcome. One thing before I go, Monty. An expenditure like this, we pay out of, well, a bit of a slush fund. Nothing dodgy, just cash we keep on hand."

"Sure. I'll reimburse you. How much?"

"It took quite a bit of time for him to locate the right car."

"I'm sure it did."

"And there's a bit of risk involved for him."

"Right."

"Two hundred fifty quid."

"That's fine. I'll have it for you by the end of the day."

"No rush."

"Oh, and tell him there will be a bonus for him if I get the name of the auto repair shop."

"I'll see what I can do."

On Saturday morning, Monty drove to the train station to pick up Maura and the kids for the weekend. He was anticipating the family visit, but part of his mind was still focused on the image of a 1988 Ford Orion with two bullet holes in its back end.

Chapter XIX

Brennan

On Saturday, March 18, Brennan volunteered to say the five o'clock Mass at Holy Cross for the regular priest, who was said to be ailing. There were a few cracks about the "Saint's Day Effect" but, irrespective of the reason, Brennan was happy to oblige.

"Ah, Brennan," Ronan welcomed him when he got back to Andersonstown. "Good. An old mate just rang. He's back in town after being, well, out of town. We're heading out for a bit of *craic*. You'll come with us."

"I'm always up for the *craic*. Where are we off to?"

"Sure we'll find a shebeen and seek admittance thereto."

"Very sporting of you, Ronan, you being on the dry."

"Thanks for reminding me, Father. I'd almost got myself convinced we were going out on a rip."

"One of us is. I could use a good, soothing pint of consolation. I'm remembering a sad situation. One of Monty Collins's clients — well, a family of six — had to leave the lovely, safe neighbourhood where they grew up to move to a tower block in a very dodgy-looking council estate. Evicted from their house because they couldn't make the payments."

"Ah, what a shame. I hope their fortunes change for the better, God help them."

"Not much chance of that, Ronan. They'll be in my prayers. I don't know what else can be done for them, by me at least. But we'll head out and have a jar or two."

Standing there in the hallway, Brennan reflected on the fact that Ronan had barely mentioned the debacle at Saint Matthew's church after Tom's panicked announcement. Ronan's silence could not be taken as acceptance, Brennan knew. He decided to bring it out into the open.

"Ronan, about that sortie into Saint Matthew's parish house . . . I was the ringleader there, not Tomás."

"Tom's a grown man, Brennan. He's responsible for his own decisions."

Ronan's words were dispassionate, but his expression was that of a father who would never give up agonizing over his son until death did them part. He said, "Tom would have gone in there with or without your assistance, Brennan. I know it, and you knew it at the time. You had the best of intentions; you put yourself at risk to try and save him from himself. And truth be told, I'd have done the same thing if I were in his shoes. I'd have taken the risk of getting the Browning back because the alternative would be to spend the rest of my days waiting for the hammer to fall. Now I guess that's the situation we're faced with, hoping against hope that the peelers won't be able to tie Tom to the secretary's description of the intruder who put the frighteners on her at Saint Matthew's. But it's not going to do us any good to dwell on it now." His words, and the expression on his face, made it clear that the subject was closed.

Ronan went to his front window then and peered outside. "My pal will be here any minute. Gráinne's gone off with some of her friends, so she'll not be here pining for my company." He turned and said, "Will you be joining us, Lorcan?"

His son had just walked into the room with a newspaper in his hand, and he sat down to read. "Can't tonight, Da. Where are you off to?"

"To one of the places where I can still get served."

"Are there some places that won't have you, Ronan?" Brennan asked.

"Aside from the Loyalist bars where they'd blow the head off me the instant I walked in the door?"

"Yeah, aside from those."

"Well, it's an established fact in this town that I'm off the drink."

"So the cash registers don't ring to the extent they used to when you'd take your place at the bar."

"That's right. The local economy has taken a hit. But there are still a few kindly publicans who'll admit me and serve me sparkly water. And Paddy Murphy at the Banned Flag is one of those."

"The Flag, is it?" Lorcan asked, from the corner of the room. He had his head buried in the *Irish News*.

"It is. Join us if you change your mind."

"It's Aoife's sister's birthday. Tom's arranged a bit of a hooley at McCribbon's. There's a session, and Aoife wrote a comical song for the sister, and me and one of my mates are going to sing it for her. Which reminds me I'd better ring him and prompt him about the time. He's not the most punctual man, I have to say."

He got up and went to the phone, punched in the number, and waited. "Oi! You remembered we're on at half nine at McCribbon's?" He listened to the response, then said, "Good. Yeah, sure. Or you could come over here, Mam and Da's place, have a couple of cans beforehand. I've the place to myself. My oul fella's here with cousin Brennan, and they're heading out to the Banned Flag. Unless they suck up everything here before they go, there will be a few drops left for me and you. What's that? Oh, all right. No worries. See you at the hooley." He hung up and returned to his newspaper.

Brennan heard the beep of a horn outside. "That'll be Fegan," Ronan said. "I'll have a word with my men out there."

They left the house, and Ronan waved to the driver of a new-looking grey Jeep — it may have been another model of vehicle but to Brennan anything that looked like a Jeep was a Jeep — idling in the street. Ronan raised the index finger of his left hand, signalling to the man to wait one minute. He walked over to his bodyguards, one of whom was standing outside the security vehicle with his eyes on the Jeep. There was an animated discussion between Ronan and his protector, and Ronan turned and headed towards the Jeep, with the bodyguard at his side.

"Wants to have a look," Ronan said to the newcomer through the driver's window.

"Sure. Go ahead."

The guard took a good long look around the seats before going to the rear and examining the vehicle from there. He returned to the front, took Ronan aside, and spoke to him again. It wasn't hard to get the gist of it: the vehicle looks clean but it's our job to protect you, and you're safer with us. But Ronan was having none of it.

"I'll drop him right at the door," Fegan said, "and then get this parked and go back and join him."

"And," said Ronan, "the fellas at the Flag will know if something's not right in there. They know who's who and what's what."

So they left the house, and Ronan made the introductions.

"Brennan, this is Fegan. I've never heard more than one name for him. Thinks he's a Brazilian footballer, *is dócha.*"

Fegan said, "I took more kicks in the Castlereagh detention centre than I ever managed to execute on the football pitch."

"RUC torture centre," Ronan explained. But there was no need. The reputation of the Castlereagh "interrogation" centre needed no elaboration.

"Nice to meet you, Father."

"Same. Please call me Brennan."

Brennan thought that maybe he should have taken off his Roman collar, but, well, it wasn't as if a priest was an unusual sight in the bars of Ireland. Not even in the North, at least on the Falls Road.

They left Andytown just as the sun was setting and drove on to the Falls Road. Brennan recognized the long-established Republican drinking hole at the corner of the Falls and MacDonough Street; he had been there years before. Fegan pulled up in front of the place, let his two passengers out, and turned left up the next side street to park the Jeep.

Brennan and Ronan entered the bar. Nothing had changed since Brennan had last seen the place. The once-banned Irish tricolour was proudly displayed on the wall, along with photos of the old and new IRA and of the ten men who had died on hunger strike in the H Blocks. The man on bar duty tonight was not Paddy Murphy, but a young fellow who didn't look old enough to legally raise a glass to his lips, let alone purvey the stuff to others. Nearly every one of the punters had a greeting for Ronan.

"Father Mathew! Did my good wife send you forth to get me off the batter?" Father Mathew had been the apostle of temperance in Ireland in the 1800s.

"All hail the Prince of Peace!" someone else said and raised his glass to the man they all knew to be involved in the peace talks.

"Ronan Burke, second in command of the, em . . . how are you filling your time now, Ronan, with nobody to command?"

"I hereby command every man in this room, and every woman, to enjoy a jar on me. Put it on my account, barkeep. You know I'm good for it."

"I do, sir," he responded and began filling the glasses of everyone in the room.

"And when you've filled those orders, Jimmy, the usual for me plus a pint of Guinness for Fegan, and a pint of Guinness and a shot of Jameson for the *sagart* here."

"Coming right up."

There was an ancient man in a tweed jacket seated at a table by the window; Brennan thought he had been in the same place last time. How long was it now, six years? Brennan nodded to him, and Ronan spoke to him on their way to a table in the back. "Keeping an eye on things for us, Shammy?"

"As always, Mr. Burke. All clear out there now."

"Good man."

Ronan chose a table up against a wall away from the windows and sat with his back against the wall. Brennan sat across from him.

"And here comes Mr. Fegan," Shammy announced.

Fegan came in and was greeted by the regulars. He sat down with the Burkes, and Ronan told him his pint was on order.

When all the other drinkers had been served, Jimmy raised a finger to Ronan. "I'll get them," Brennan said and went to the bar. The two pints were ready, and Brennan's Jameson as well. Ronan's libation was *acqua minerale frizzante* imported from Italy. More of a treat perhaps than the local fizzy water? Brennan doubted it. He returned to the table with the glasses, placed them before his companions, then lifted his pint and said, *"Sláinte!"* He took a long, satisfying sip of his Guinness, and Fegan did the same. Fegan and Ronan chatted about people they knew, some of whom would not be free to join them for, it seemed, several years.

Rebel songs played in the background, and a few of the punters sang along. One selection in particular was greeted with a roar of approval and a clinking of glasses. "The Helicopter Song" by the Wolfe Tones. The song celebrated the daring escape of three IRA prisoners from Mountjoy Prison in Dublin back in 1973. A helicopter had been commandeered and the pilot ordered to put the chopper down in the exercise yard of the prison.

"Popular tune, written by Sean McGinley," Ronan said. "It flew up to number one on the charts in the Republic despite being banned by the government!"

"I'll never forget the oul man over in New York watching the news on television," said Brennan. "The story of the escape came on, and the smile on Declan's face! And this even though he was on the outs with the bold boyos at the time, as you well know, Ronan."

"Sure I know it, Brennan. But your da, as a former inmate of the Joy himself, would appreciate the boldness of it nonetheless."

"We arranged for a copy of the record to be sent over for him for Christmas that year. Between him and the rest of the family, we nearly wore the grooves off it. The fact that the warders thought it was somebody from the government touching down in the yard made it even more priceless."

"You heard what one of our lads said in response to that?" Fegan asked.

"No, what?"

"The lad, one of the prisoners, he's standing close to a prison warder and he hears the warder say, 'I thought it was our new minister of defence arriving.'

"So our lad says to him, 'It was *our* minister of defence, leaving.'"

"Good answer, one for the ages! A reference to Twomey, I assume." Brennan knew Seamus Twomey had been chief of staff of the IRA.

The three of them savoured the historic moment, Brennan the Burke deliberately putting out of mind for now what those prisoners might have done to get themselves arrested in the first place. Brennan the priest would wrestle with those thoughts later, as he so often did.

Fegan announced that he had to be on his way. "The wife wants me home early because we're flying out to Spain in the morning and I, well, I'm a little slow when it comes to packing for a holiday. I've not packed a thing, actually, though it has to be said I haven't completely unpacked from my last multi-year sojourn away from home. Anyway I'm under orders to get home early and get it done. I don't want to rush you lads."

"What do you think, Brennan?" Ronan asked him.

Brennan was in no hurry to leave the *ceol agus craic*, the music and the good times in the pub, but he didn't want to put Ronan on the spot. Before he could come up with a reply, Ronan spoke for the two of them. "I think we'll stay on for a bit, Fegan. You go ahead."

So he said his goodbyes and was off. A young couple came in then and looked around for a table. Ronan pointed to the two empty chairs, and the couple joined them. The man offered to buy a round, and the offer was accepted with good grace. The newcomers were from Derry, so Ronan asked Jimmy whether "I Wish I Was Back Home in Derry" was in the pub's collection of recordings. It was, and the Banned Flag's punters gave a hearty rendition, all but drowning out the voice of Christy Moore. Somebody noted that the lyrics had been written by Bobby Sands, who had died in the hunger strike of 1981, so everyone stood and raised a glass to the portrait of Sands on the wall.

When he was seated again, Brennan heard old Shammy at the window. "Ach, now, I don't like the look of that."

"What is it, Shammy?" someone asked.

"That fellow with his cap pulled down. His car's still running and he's coming . . . What the —"

Before he could finish the thought, the door banged open. Something was thrown into the pub and clanked on the floor. The place began to fill with smoke. Brennan could hardly breathe.

"Lads!" Jimmy cried from the bar. "Out! Now! Back door!"

Chairs tipped and clattered to the floor, as every man and woman bolted from the room and ran to the back of the pub. Ronan and Brennan assisted Jimmy in trying to get them all out in a safe, orderly manner. "Here, now, Agnes, you go on ahead," Ronan said to an elderly woman who was well in her cups.

"God bless you, Mr. Burke," she said.

With Ronan, Brennan, and the barman staying behind to man the door, everyone spilled out of the building, some with their glasses still in hand. There was a cacophony of voices as people shouted panicked questions across one another, expecting no answers. A few people ran off into the night; others simply halted, stunned and uncertain, in the alleyway behind the bar.

Jimmy stepped inside again and quickly returned. "Is everybody out?" Brennan and Ronan asked, simultaneously.

"All out," Jimmy answered. "Go! Everyone! Keep going! Get clear of the place!"

Ronan said to Brennan as they hoofed it down the alley, away from the building, "This is exactly the kind of thing I'm determined to —"

He never got to finish. All Brennan heard was the crack of a rifle. He felt Ronan go down beside him. Another shot, and another. Jimmy cried out behind him. Brennan couldn't see the gunman or gunmen, out there in the still, cold night. Ronan was flat on his back, silent, unmoving. Brennan fought down the primal fear, the overwhelming urge to flee from danger. Time slowed down. He dropped to his knees on the concrete beside his cousin. What did he have that was white, that could be waved as a flag of surrender? There, in Ronan's jacket pocket, a white piece of paper. But then he remembered. Priests waving white handkerchiefs had been shot to death on more than one occasion here in Belfast, while ministering to people who were lying on the ground dying of bullet wounds. What could he do? Nothing but stay down beside Ronan and try to keep him alive. With his right hand, he checked for a pulse. He was no medic, but he found it. Slow but present. Blood was oozing from Ronan's gut and his left leg. Shot down on the Falls Road, Belfast. Did you call for an ambulance with guns trained on you? Had the gunmen fled?

"Get the ambulance!" Brennan shouted into the air. As if nobody else had thought of it.

Then he began to pray. He prayed to God to spare Ronan Burke, a man trying to bring peace to his tormented country. But Ronan was fading before Brennan's eyes. He needed Extreme Unction, the last rites. Father Burke had no oil, no holy water. He skipped ahead in the rite: "Almighty and eternal God, raise him up with Thy right hand, strengthen him in Thy might, defend him by Thy power . . ."

He heard shouting all around him. How long had he been kneeling here? Mere seconds? No. He heard sirens approaching. Police, ambulance. It was all a blur after that.

Chapter XX

Monty

Monty had spent Saturday afternoon and evening with Maura and the children, and they enjoyed treats and games and had a fine old time. He had been issued a notice that a number of his fellow lawyers would be meeting to take in a late-night session of traditional music at Morrisons bar, but he told Maura he would decline the invitation and stay home. She, however, urged him to go. His time as a solicitor in Belfast might feel endless to him, but he really had less than two more months here, and he might as well enjoy his new friendships while he could. So he hiked over to Morrisons and got in on the party. As a consequence — actions have consequences, my son — he was a little slow getting himself motivated, or even out of bed, on Sunday morning. His spouse, ever understanding, had left their bed with the words, "No point in trying to haul your sorry arse out into the land of the living, so I won't even try." He had fallen back asleep but now he heard her voice again, from the other side of the bedroom door. She kept repeating the same two words over and over.

"Oh, God. Oh, God. Oh, God."

He bolted from the bed, yanked the door open, and saw Maura staring down in horror at the Sunday paper. Her face was grey. He moved to her side and read the headlines.

Ronan Burke and Barman Shot Outside Pub

Ronan Burke, well-known Andersonstown Republican, was shot at 8:35 last evening outside the Banned Flag pub on the Falls Road. Sources at the Royal Victoria Hospital would not give any details of his condition except to say that it is "serious." James MacColgan, 24, barman at the Banned Flag, was wounded in the shoulder; he was treated in hospital and released. A priest with Mr. Burke, believed to be a relation, attended to the fallen man, as did staff of the Banned Flag until police and ambulance services arrived.

Priest. Lots of priests around, but Monty knew it was Brennan Burke. Maura wasted no time wondering who it was. She knew.

"Hospital?" Maura asked, making an obvious effort to keep her voice steady. "Or should we call Ronan's family first? No, we can't add to their distress."

"Hospital," Monty replied.

He got himself washed and dressed in five minutes, then conscripted a neighbourhood woman, with whom he had become friendly, to take care of the children along with her own three. She had heard about the shooting and assured him he could take all the time he needed. Then he was at the wheel of the car with Maura beside him.

"Do you know where the hospital is, or should we ask —"

"Just off the Falls Road," he told her. "Brennan pointed it out."

Maura opened the paper and read the rest of the article. "Witnesses who declined to be named said a device was thrown into the pub just before the shooting; it was later identified as a smoke bomb. The witnesses say they saw a car speed away from the bar and travel east on the Falls Road. The shooting occurred outside, behind the building, reportedly as people evacuated the premises after the smoking device was thrown inside."

"Jesus Christ," Monty said, "they ran right into the trap. That was probably on Ronan's mind even as he was leaving the building."

"I'm sure it was. But when something's thrown into a bar in Belfast and starts to smoke, what else are you going to do but hightail it out of there?"

"Exactly. You know you're running a risk either way. A bomb or a hail of bullets."

"Please, please, God, let him be all right!" Maura prayed.

Monty echoed the plea, silently, then asked, "What else does it say, anything?"

"At press time there had been no arrests, but an RUC spokesman said the police are following several leads. Mr. Burke is understood to have been, at one time, adjutant, or second in command, of the Provisional IRA's Belfast Brigade. Recently, however, he has been an outspoken advocate of laying down arms and following a peaceful and constitutional path to resolution of the conflict. It has been speculated that he may play a prominent role if and when new governing institutions are established."

There was no need to state the obvious: that not everybody was ready to lay down arms.

"Another headline on the front page: 'Fragile ceasefire: will it hold?' They've got quotes from various factions saying the ceasefire hasn't been broken. It will hold."

The traffic crawled along, stopped and started, and Monty fought down the urge to swerve out and pass. The air in the car virtually crackled with tension. But finally they arrived.

They knew they could not just walk in and see Ronan so they spoke to the nurse on duty, who directed them to a waiting area where the family were gathered. They found the two sons sitting on plastic chairs, knee to knee in intense conversation, oblivious to the newcomers. Gráinne was hunched over in her chair with a set of rosary beads in her hands. She got up when she saw Monty and Maura and came towards them. Her face was grim. Oh, God.

"Gráinne, we are so sorry," Monty said. "What's the word? How's Ronan?"

"He had three bullets in him. He's had surgery. He lost a lot of blood. Of course he's still knocked out . . ."

Monty wasn't about to ask where the wounds were or what the doctors had said. But Gráinne continued her report, "They told me one bullet went through the outside of his left thigh, and that will heal. But two bullets 'perforated' the bowel. That says to me 'ripped through.' But they operated on him. They said the bullets didn't hit the liver or a major artery . . . They tried to sound reassuring, but they always do, don't they?"

Maura put her arms around the distraught woman and said, "We're with you all the way, Gráinne, as you know."

"I know, Maura, thank you. Brennan was here, saying prayers and . . . prayers interspersed with curses. He's gone for a bit of a walkabout. He'll be back soon, I imagine."

"We'll just wait over there for him." Monty pointed to a line of chairs farther up the corridor. He didn't want to crowd the family.

"He'll be needing a bite to eat, Brennan will. He's been with us all night."

Monty and Maura moved off and sat without speaking. Brennan appeared a few minutes later. His face was white, his white collar smeared with blood.

They got up and walked to him. Maura embraced him. "I don't know what to say to you in this situation, Brennan."

He sounded a little hoarse, a little weary, but he came up with a response. "I can't help you with that. The etiquette here is a little different from what you're accustomed to in the peaceable kingdom of Canada. The word 'ceasefire' has shades of meaning here, as well."

A nurse came by then, and Brennan recognized her. He said, "How is he doing, Sarah, really?"

"He received some serious wounds, Father, but he got through the surgery."

To Monty that sounded as if there had been some doubt that he would get through it.

The nurse said, "We're all looking forward to a good outcome. And this is the best place for him, to make that happen." It was well known that, for obvious reasons, the hospitals in Belfast were world leaders in the treatment of gunshot wounds.

The nurse went on her rounds. Monty heard the woop-woop and nee-naw sounds of emergency vehicles outside; another in the long line of catastrophes.

"Have you had anything to eat lately, Brennan?" Maura asked.

"Hospital food."

"So you've had something."

"I said hospital food, darlin'. That means no, I didn't touch anything on offer in this place."

"Right. So let's get some nourishment into you."

They headed out onto the Falls Road, found a café serving breakfast, and had the full Ulster fry. That would keep anyone going for the day. Brennan recounted the events of the night before and then returned to his vigil at the Royal Victoria.

Brennan walked back to the hospital and sat down beside Gráinne. She looked the way he felt, utterly exhausted. She said, "The doctors told me they got the bullets out and said there were no unforeseen complications. Whatever they meant by that."

That, in Brennan's mind, left a whole lot unsaid; surely there were complications that a medical team in Belfast might regard as foreseeable. How had Ronan fared with those? But he didn't have time to speculate further because he saw two men coming towards them. They were in plain clothes but you'd make them as peelers anywhere in the Western world. Here, that meant the Royal Ulster Constabulary.

"Mrs. Burke?"

"Yes."

"I am Detective Inspector Arnold and this is Detective Sergeant Williams. We spoke to Mr. Burke when he was brought in here last night, but of course he was going in and out of consciousness. We'd like to have another quick word if we might. We know this is difficult. But is he . . . is he awake?"

"He's only after having surgery, so . . ."

"All right. We'll wait outside for a bit in case he wakes up soon."

They turned their eyes on Brennan, and there was nothing for it but to make the introductions.

"Ah, yes, Father Burke. We were planning to speak with you today as well. Would now be convenient?"

"Certainly. Let's go down that way." He pointed down the corridor.

When they were out of sight of the family, DI Arnold said, "We'd like you to take us through the events as they unfolded last night."

He told them everything he remembered, from the time they left the house to the harrowing moment when the shots rang out. But he simply could not provide any identifying information about the man or men who had opened fire on his cousin behind the Banned Flag bar.

Inspector Arnold expressed wishes for a swift recovery for Ronan and left Brennan a card with contact information on it. He asked Brennan to ring him if he remembered anything, however insignificant it might seem. Brennan assured him that he would. Arnold and Williams went back to check in with Gráinne. Brennan stood there after the police had left, reliving the horror of watching Ronan fall to the ground, of probing him for signs of life, of knowing that someone out there in the darkness wanted his cousin dead.

Chapter XXI

Monty

Maura came up to Belfast again the following Saturday with the children, hoping to see a big improvement in Ronan. And in fact he had made progress throughout the week. The surgery was successful. The bullets had been removed and the bowel repaired. The wound in his leg was superficial. He was still weak and in pain, and he was being closely monitored for signs of infection, but the outlook was generally good. Monty had brought some work home to the flat, and he tried to concentrate, pushing away the thoughts of Ronan in the sights of a rifle, and Brennan right beside him, of the bullets slamming into Ronan, and the would-be assassins slipping away into the night.

He turned his mind to the file on his dining room table. His colleague Sandra MacLeod had done a corporate search and found no listing for a company called Day Sure Investments in Northern Ireland or anywhere else in the United Kingdom or in the Republic of Ireland. But somebody had been writing cheques using that company name. It looked as if the source of the payments to Winnie Flanagan would remain shrouded in mystery. But there was other financial information he wanted from Winnie. Or from Katie, if her mother was having a bad day. He wanted to know if there were any documents such as paystubs or income tax returns showing what Eamon had been earning before his death. But Monty was not going to have Katie or Winnie come into the city centre from the Heatherfield Villas housing estate, so he called and got Katie on the phone and told her he would take a drive out there in the afternoon.

When Normie caught wind of a visit to the Flanagan kids, she insisted on going along. Maura and little Dominic had plans of their own; there were dinosaurs to be seen at the Ulster Museum, and it was only a short walk from Monty's flat. So Monty and Normie started out for the inaptly named Heatherfield Villas. On the way there, Normie asked about Mr. Burke, and Monty gave her an upbeat report on his condition. "Thank God," she said and went on to talk about her school and friends in Dublin as they drove through the city. She spotted a convenience store on the way and insisted that they stop and pick up some chocolate-coated ice cream bars.

Clusters of bored young guys and girls stood idly by, smoking and eyeing the car as it drove into the compound. Katie met Monty and Normie at the door to the building and sent a fearful look out at the yard before ushering them inside and onto the elevator.

When they were seated in number 705 Monty asked, "Have you had any trouble here, Katie?"

She made a noncommittal sound and moved her head slightly to the side, indicating little Timmy on the sofa. Before they could greet him, he bolted from the room, disappeared into one of the bedrooms, and slammed the door.

"Timmy! Come back and see Normie!"

No more sign of him.

"What's the story?" Monty asked.

"He won't say what happened, but you'll know just by the state of him."

The door to the other bedroom opened then, and Clare emerged, looking pale and depressed.

"Hi," she said to the visitors. Monty and Normie greeted the little girl.

"You can't stay in the bedroom all day, Clare," her sister said. "Not every day. How about we play Scrabble tonight? She's brilliant at Scrabble, spells words I barely knew at all when I was her age."

Monty started to respond but the little girl sank to the sofa and dissolved in tears. "I hate it here! I miss Daddy! How come he had to die?"

There was no need to look at Normie; Monty knew all too well what her reaction would be to such raw pain in another child. Katie wrapped her arms around her sister and held her and whispered softly in her ear. She pointed towards Normie, no doubt trying to encourage Clare to take part in the occasion of the visit, but the poor child was having none of it. She just couldn't do it. She turned and walked back into the bedroom, closing the door softly behind her. Katie looked devastated, and Monty was once again filled with determination to compensate this family of children for their loss. He just as quickly brought himself down to earth; the chances of making a case and achieving a payout in the end were virtually nil.

After a few seconds had passed, Normie nudged Monty and pointed to the bag of treats. Monty nodded encouragement.

Normie called out. "Timmy! Clare! I have ice cream bars. Coated with chocolate."

No response from Clare, but it didn't take long before Timmy caved; the temptation was too great. He sidled into the room with his face turned away from the light. Normie started towards him but Monty put a discreet hand on her arm to hold her back. He wanted to see whatever it was Timmy didn't want them to see. The little fellow gave in and came towards them. He had a black eye, his lip was cut and swollen, and another cut was visible through his short yellow hair.

"What happened to you?" Normie cried out.

The little boy attempted a nonchalant shrug. "I bet up a fella and he hit me back."

Monty decided to go along with the pretence for the moment. "What did he do that made you decide to beat him up?"

He didn't have a story ready, so he improvised. "I went out to kick a ball around. He tried to fuckin' rob it offa me. So I gave him a thumpin'."

There was likely some truth to the tale. Timmy went out with his ball, and the other fella, or fellas, attacked him. Monty didn't ask where the ball was now.

"Here, Timmy," said Normie. "Have a bar. Or will it . . . hurt your mouth? It's freezing cold."

"Won't hurt," he said, holding out his hand for the treat.

"There's one here for you, too, Katie," Normie told her, "and for Clare, and the other kids when they come home."

"Thank you, Normie. I'll put them in the freezer and we'll all have them later."

"But mine will be gone by then! And youse will all be having yours!"

"That's the trade-off you make for enjoying yours now, Timmy. Go ahead, have it now. It will make you feel better."

"I feel good now. Ow!" He gave a little yelp as the ice-cold delicacy hit the delicate tissues of his mouth. But he persevered. "This is brilliant! Deadly!"

"What do you say?"

He turned to Normie. "Thank you for bringing it!"

"You're welcome. I love them, too. Let's go out and we can both kick the ball around."

He looked embarrassed then. "Em, I've got it hidden away, so they won't try to steal it again."

"Okay, we can just go for a walk."

Timmy hesitated, then said, "I'll race you!" And his skinny form rocketed to the door. Normie followed.

"She shouldn't be out there, Mr. Collins."

Monty had been hoping she wouldn't say that. But what should he do about it? His instinct was of course to keep his daughter safe inside. To do that, however, was to acknowledge in front of the surviving members of the Flanagan family that their housing estate was dangerous, not fit for *his* daughter, but that, when he and Normie had made their escape, the Flanagan children were stuck with it. That was exactly the case of course, but he didn't have the heart to make it so starkly obvious. All he said was "Be careful, both of you."

When they had gone, Katie got busy with a kettle and called out, "Mam! Tea!"

Winnie emerged then and said, "Oh! Monty, I'm sorry I wasn't here to greet you."

When the tea was ready they sat down at the kitchen table, and Monty asked Winnie about Eamon's work and earnings. Eamon Flanagan had been working for a well-established company as an electrician and had been doing that work for as long as she had known him, almost eighteen years. Plus he had worked as a contractor, renovating houses.

"Do you have pay statements or tax returns or anything?"

"I didn't keep everything, but I did keep his pay statements close to the time when he died. I'll go get them."

She went into one of the bedrooms and came back a minute or so later with papers in her hand. She gave them to Monty, and he saw that Mr. Flanagan had earned just under £19,000 a year as an electrician.

Katie said, "The amount he made at his regular job plus fixing up houses was enough that we were never without clothes and shoes and schoolbooks and toys and the occasional little holiday. And Mam, you always had the prettiest dresses. You were very fashionable! But I remember the day he first showed me the house in Musgrave Park.

I was only a wee girl at the time, and I told him the house looked as if somebody had broken in and run all through it, making it filthy. The old owners hadn't taken care of it at all. Da told me he had 'got it for a song' and I thought he meant it literally and I asked him what song he had sung to get it. And he put his chin up and his hand on his heart like an old-fashioned singer. And he sang something that sounded like a bunch of nonsense syllables. I later found out it was 'Funiculì Funiculà.' And I remember laughing but at the same time being mortified, and I said to him, 'Be quiet, Daddy, other people will hear you!' And he said, 'Think of all the houses we'll have when everybody hears my song.' But then I asked him if he had paid money instead of singing for it, it would have been nicer, and he assured me that he knew how to do all the work himself to make it lovely. And he did! My da could do everything that needed doing to build or repair a house. Couldn't he, Mam?"

"He could. He was the loveliest man . . ." Her voice broke and she said no more.

Monty now had the foundation of a dependency claim on behalf of the mother and the children, who had lost all the benefits Eamon's income would have continued to provide if he had lived. A comfortable home, clothes, books, sports equipment, music or other lessons, and the opportunity for higher education. Monty did not want to raise Katie's or her mother's hopes with all this talk of earnings. They would surely be crushed when, almost inevitably, the claim died aborning. He tuned in to what Katie was saying, something about Clare having trouble with one of her classes in school.

The door banged open suddenly and Timmy came flying in. "Youse wouldn't believe what we found! And they said they were going to kill him!"

"What!?" Katie and Monty demanded at once.

"Show them, Normie! Here, let me!"

"Just give him a minute, Timmy. He's shaking; he's nervous."

"Who are you talking about?" Monty asked.

"Pebbledash!" both children answered.

"I'm lost here."

"Daddy, look!" And she opened her jacket and gently drew out a little kitten, which must have been around eight weeks old.

"Aww!" said Katie. The universal response to an adorable baby animal.

"Here, let me have him."

"Maybe he's a she," Katie suggested.

"No, he's a boy. You can just tell. Can I have him, Normie?"

"Okay, Tim, but you have to be really gentle because he's so little. And he's scared."

"I know. I did something bad to a kitten when I was a wee lad. I picked him up by his tail and swung him around. I thought he'd like it, flying through the air, like. But my ma killed me for it. So I know that was bad. I know to be careful."

He leaned over the kitten and gently stroked its head. The little thing was mewling and extending its claws, and everyone gathered around to reassure it. Him.

"What did you say his name was?" asked Katie then.

Normie answered, "We called him Pebbledash because he's white with brown spots. Like pebbledash on the houses."

"Good name!"

"Let's get him a dish of milk. He's probably starving."

Winnie looked towards the refrigerator. Her face flushed a painful red. "We, uh, didn't get our milk yet today. I just had a bit for our tea, but there's none left."

No milk in the house for a family of five children. "I'll run out and get some now," Monty said. "But you know, gang, he's somebody else's kitten, right?"

"No, he isn't!" Tim insisted. "They killed his mother, and all the babies are gone except this one."

"Who . . . how do you know what happened to his mother?" Monty asked.

"They showed me, Gary and them!"

"Those sleekit wee skitters!" Katie exclaimed. "Boys on the estate," she explained to Monty, flashing him a significant look.

Dermot came in then and asked, "What are you talking about? Who?"

Katie was about to reply and then saw that he had a couple of boys from the estate with him. "'Bout ye, Missus?" they greeted Winnie.

"Mam!" said Dermot. "We need some Sellotape. There's an old banger of a car out there. No wheels on it. We're making it into a fort! We've a load of rubbish sacs to cover the windows so nobody can see in, but we have to tape them on."

"Well, we've only the one roll, Dermot, so . . ."

"I've a roll with all my old school things, Mam," Katie said, "Youse can have that one. You know where my stuff is, Der."

Dermot ran for the tape, waved it at the room in general, and started out the door.

"Thanks, Miss!" one of the boys called back.

"Yeah, thanks!" the other echoed, and they were gone.

Those young fellows looked all right. Maybe there was hope, after all.

But Timmy resumed his own tale of council estate life. "Gary and them made me look at the dead mammy cat, and they said they . . ." The little fellow's voice caught, and he made a pretence of having to refresh himself in the loo. "I gotta have a slash." He shoved the kitten at Normie and ran from the room.

Normie's eyes had filled with tears. "It really did happen. They took Timmy out to the end of the parking lot and then he came back all upset. They told him they threw her out in front of a car and they showed him the cat lying there, all . . ." Normie's voice broke and it took her a few seconds before she could continue. "And . . . and they said they'd get the kitten, too, and do the same thing to him! You have to keep him in here, Katie!"

"I will." She was clearly worried about the cat. "What do cats need?

Milk? Special cat food? Is it very dear? We have our money all ready to buy our food for the week, but . . ."

"That can be our treat. Right, Normie? After all the pots of tea and hospitality Katie has been kind enough to offer us, least we can do is provide a few snacks for Pebbledash, eh?"

"Ah, now," Winnie Flanagan said, "we can't have you doing that. You've been too kind already."

"No, really," Normie insisted. "You didn't know a cat was coming! We'll just get the stuff this one time. And, um, there's other stuff they need. To poop in."

"Kitty litter. We'll get a bag of that, too. How does that sound, Pebbledash?" Monty tickled the little creature under his chin and got a "mew, mew" in response.

"And you know what we should do?" said Normie. "Katie, you have to come with us and pick out a bed for the kitty!"

"I'm coming, too!" Timmy came barrelling out of the bathroom, fumbling with his jeans.

"Did you wash your hands, Timothy J. Flanagan?" his sister asked.

"Yeah."

"Go wash them again."

"Okay."

Katie drew Clare out of her room and said Dermot was with his mates and they had about an hour before Darren would be home, so the five of them piled into the car and went shopping for pet supplies. Great care was taken to choose the proper bed but there was no contest when Normie spotted, so to speak, one in a leopard skin pattern.

"I'm going to put him on it when we get home!"

"All right, Timmy," Katie cautioned him, "only don't be gutted if he doesn't take to it right away. Cats do pretty well as they please."

"He'll love this bed!"

"He will. It's just that he may do a bit of wandering before he settles on it."

"Aye, all right."

When the mission was completed Monty and Normie bade goodbye to the Flanagans, large and small, two legged and four, and headed out for Monty's safe, lovely flat in tony south Belfast.

"Gary and those guys are really mean. And they're bad. They're always fighting, and they're always scaring Timmy. And they said —" She stopped speaking and stared out the side window.

"They said what, sweetheart?"

"Something gross to me. And something even more gross about Katie. And I'm not going to tell you what it was."

That suited Monty; he didn't want to hear it.

Chapter XXII

Brennan

Lying in bed on Saturday morning a week after the shooting, Brennan wasn't sure whether he had even been asleep. His morning thoughts were the same as the thoughts that consumed him during the night: anxiety over Ronan's condition, and rage over the attempt on his life. Brennan had been spending most of the daylight hours at the hospital, and Ronan was getting better by the day, no question about it. Then another thought jabbed him like a dagger, a selfish thought: what if, in the news coverage of the shooting and of Ronan's recovery, there had been more than a passing reference to Brennan himself. He had avoided looking at any of the news, but Gráinne had told him reporters had been asking her and other family members for interviews. What if there had been a reference to Brennan as one of the people present with Ronan, one of the witnesses to the shooting, and the reporters had obtained a photo of him? What if the secretary at Saint Matthew's church saw his picture and could now identify him? But there weren't any photos of him here in Belfast, were there? Was that his most pressing concern right now? No, obviously not. His most pressing concern was his need for sleep so he wouldn't be prey to this sort of unreasonable, paranoid, self-centred fantasy. He sank into unconsciousness.

When he arrived at the hospital later that morning and was walking towards Ronan's room, he spied one of his favourite people in the known universe. His sister Molly, over from London. She was almost two years older than Brennan but they looked like twins, with the same black hair and dark eyes, though his were black and hers were blue. Like everyone else who'd been in to see Ronan, she was trying to put a brave face on things.

"Molly, *a stór mo chroí*, bless you!"

"God between us and all harm!" They embraced and held on for a good long moment. "Brennan, darling, thank God he lived through it and you weren't hit."

"Pretty grim, it was."

"I know, and him trying to bring peace to this tragic patch of earth. I've been talking to the family, as you might imagine. Mam is in an awful state, and Da would like to launch a rocket from New York Harbour. Terry is looking at flights for himself and Patrick."

"Tell them to hold off. There's no point in them visiting Ronan until he can enjoy their company. And tell them as well to be planning a trip to see me in Rome when I take over the choir in the fall. You and Paddy and Terry and all the rest of them. After all, it's the eternal city; that will make us all feel immortal."

"I'll give them the word. But I'm here till tomorrow and I'm delighted to see you, in spite of the circumstances. Shelmalier is giving a presentation tonight on work she's been doing for her dissertation. I had been planning to attend, but she understands entirely if I miss it under the circumstances."

"What's the subject of your lovely daughter's presentation?"

"Shakespeare and Freud. It's a Shakespeare weekend at Oxford."

"Ah. She'll be brilliant, as she always has been. You tell Shelmalier that you uncovered a deep, unconscious need to hear her speak, in rhyming couplets. And that her uncle Brennan sent you packing. Spend some time with Ronan today and then off with you, back to England in time for Shelly's event."

"Well, maybe that's what I'll do."

So they spent part of the morning beside the sick bed and then enjoyed a few hours together in the city before she left for a standby flight back to England.

Sitting at Ronan's bedside again that evening, Brennan contemplated the excruciating boredom of lying in a hospital bed. This, in addition to the pain and anxiety the patient had to endure. But the boredom: whenever he thought of people serving time in prison, the thing that struck him most forcefully — even more, perhaps, than the loss of freedom, the loneliness, and the fear of violence — was the sheer, unending boredom. He could not bear to be locked up, deprived of his regular life and activities, and left to languish in the day to day, hour to hour, minute to minute mindless tedium of it all. He immediately sent up an Act of Contrition for being ungrateful, ungrateful for his health and for the richness of the life he had been privileged to enjoy. He expressed contrition for his momentary forgetting of all the people in the Royal Victoria Hospital in Belfast who were suffering, whether from wounds or other mishaps or illness.

Ronan and Gráinne's daughter Aideen came in then, greeted Brennan and leaned over her father, kissing him gently on the forehead. Brennan had seen her early in the week when she came to Belfast from university in Galway to be with her dad. She told Brennan she had been here at the hospital in the afternoon, when there had been a steady stream of visitors, including Father Alec Reid and the Reverend Clark Rayburn and some leading lights of the Republican movement. Brennan heard footsteps and turned to greet another well-wisher, but it was one of the nurses. She beckoned to Brennan to step outside.

"There are a couple of gentlemen down in the lobby asking after you, Father."

Brennan felt a surge of apprehension. "Oh?"

"It's up to you of course. If you'd rather not be interrupted . . ."

"No, I'll go down and see who they are. Thank you."

Who would be coming to see Brennan at the hospital, at night? Another family member in town to see Ronan, looking for some advance warning about his condition before venturing up to the ward? That sounded like something Brennan himself would do! But what if this was something about Brennan himself? He was about to find out. He left the room and got into the elevator for the ground floor.

Two men stepped forward when he walked out into the lobby. He had never laid eyes on them before. One was in his fifties, distinguished-looking and well turned out in a jacket and tie. The younger fellow had muscles bulging against his black nylon jacket; he had the look of a boxer who had taken a few too many jabs in the face but was well able to get his own back, in or out of the ring. What were they after?

The older man — Brennan mentally christened him the executive — said, "Father Burke. Sorry to intrude on you here at the hospital, but we were wondering if you would accompany us outside so we can talk for a few minutes."

"Who are you fellas?"

"We're taking care of things for Ronan now," the man replied.

Taking care of what things? Were these new bodyguards? Did the other two get in the soup for letting Ronan go to the bar without them? But it was Ronan's choice, and he's the boss. Brennan didn't know who these men were. And given the unsettling events of the past week, he thought it would not be out of line to make some inquiries. "If you could hold on for a second, I'll be right back."

The executive nodded, and Brennan went back to the elevator, took it one floor up, got out and asked the nurse on the desk if he could use her phone. She agreed, and he punched in the Andersonstown number.

Gráinne answered, and he reassured her immediately. "Nothing to be concerned about, *acushla*. I'm calling from the hospital, and

Ronan is resting comfortably, as they say. But there are two men in the lobby asking me to go off with them for a little chat, and . . ."

"What do they look like?"

Brennan described them, and Gráinne said, "If they are who I think they are, you'll be safe in their company. Not everybody would be!"

He thanked her and the nurse and returned to the lobby of the hospital.

The executive had a look of amusement on his face as if he knew exactly what Brennan had been up to, but he made no reference to it. He merely said, "If you'd come outside with us, Father, we could get into the car and away from this place for a few wee minutes."

One more wee test before Brennan left familiar ground to go off with two strangers in a vehicle. He'd give them a little linguistic challenge to see what foot they kicked with. And he'd do it with a bit of humour, if possible. He looked to the executive and said, "*Chonaic mé ar an Aifreann thú uair amháin, nach bhfaca?*"

The man laughed and replied, in the language of the oppressor, "You may indeed have seen me at Mass, Father, if you were at Saint Paul's in the Falls. You may even have seen me serving Mass for Father Sweeney, if one of the regular altar boys had the football that day."

Brennan smiled and nodded in acknowledgement. With that, he allowed himself to be escorted to the front seat of their car; the exec took the wheel and the boxer sat in back.

The driver pulled away from the hospital and said, "Before we take you back to the hospital or to Andytown, we'd like you to accompany us somewhere else for a few minutes. Won't be long."

"Whereabouts are we going?"

"We're just taking a wee spin and we'll stop in at the house of a friend. We'll take you wherever you'd like to go straight away after that."

Brennan wasn't sure he liked the sound of that. A public place, a *public house*, was likely out of the question, but he'd give it a try.

"We might stop in somewhere to wet our throats before we get to . . . wherever we're headed?"

"That might not be a good idea right now, Father, but I think we can safely assume there will be some cans or a bottle or two on hand at the house we're going to. If not, I'll have one of our lads make a run to the off-licence for you."

"Bless you."

They hadn't driven very far before they pulled up in front of a nondescript brick terraced house. They were still in west Belfast. There was not a soul to be seen in the shadows of the street. He made to open his door, but the driver put a restraining hand on him. "Two seconds, and we'll go." The boxer got out, and Brennan watched while he surveyed the area, while keeping a hand in his right pocket. Then the driver said, "Good. Let's go."

Brennan was led into the sitting room of the house. Everything about the room was dark: the carpet, the walls, the furniture. The only light came from a low-watt bulb in a table lamp. The curtains were drawn. Two new friends rose from their seats when Brennan entered the room. One was short and wiry, in his late forties, with a pleasant, intelligent face and a quick smile; he was dressed in a sweater, shirt, and tie. The other was the equivalent of the boxer who had accompanied Brennan in the car. Muscled and wary. Brennan decided to label him the brawler.

The smaller man spoke up. "Thank you for coming to see us, Father Burke. We won't be keeping you long. Is there anything we can get you? Tea? A drink?"

"What would you have in the way of a drink?"

"Whiskey, cans of Harp, wine, I think."

"A Harp and a good, healthy shot of whiskey would do me the world of good."

The boxer left the room and returned within seconds, carrying a bottle of Powers whiskey and a tray of glasses. He poured a generous splash in each of the glasses and passed them around. He also handed Brennan a can of Harp.

Brennan took his first mouthful of the whiskey and savoured the golden liquid before letting it slide down his throat. *Uisce beatha.* The water of life. He followed that with a taste of the beer.

After his moment of pleasure, he tuned in to what looked like a board of inquiry. All four men had arranged themselves on seats across from him. They placed their glasses on the coffee table and gave Brennan their full attention. The small man in the sweater gave his name as Cathal. Or, rather, he said, "You may call me Cathal." The names of the others were not announced, or invented.

Cathal said, "I understand that your cousin is on the way back to good health, Father Burke."

"He is."

"Is maith sin. The peelers don't have anyone for the shooting yet."

"Chances are they never will," said the executive who had been at the wheel for the spin over. "Not when it's one of ours that gets shot."

"So," Cathal continued, "it falls to us to find whoever it was who tried to assassinate Ronan Burke. We take a greater interest in the welfare of our people than do the members of the Royal Ulster Constabulary."

Brennan felt no need to wonder who "we" were.

"So anything you can tell us about that night, what you saw, who you saw or heard would be most helpful."

"Some of it's a blur."

"Understandably," Cathal conceded. "Let's take it bit by bit. What made you decide to go to the Banned Flag that night?"

Brennan thought back. "We were at the house, Ronan's, and talked about going out. I think Ronan made a little joke about being off the drink, and the fellows at the Banned Flag not holding it against him."

There was knowing laughter on the other side of the room. "It's been low tide for the drinks industry since Ronan took the pledge," the executive remarked. "Lots of men on the dole. He'd best not count on their votes if he gets an elected assembly!"

"I'm sure he won't hold it against them. So anyway, he said that's where we were going, and that's what we did."

"Right. So you went by car, with Fegan at the wheel."

"I didn't catch the fella's name," Brennan lied, in case he might be putting Fegan in danger by confirming his presence.

"Now who else would have known you were going to the Flag?"

"Nobody that I'm aware of. Just family, you know."

"Ronan's family?"

"Right. Lorcan was at the house. Ronan invited him along, but he couldn't come. He was on the phone to a pal of his arranging a birthday party. For his sister-in-law, I think it was."

"Who was he on the phone to?"

Brennan shook his head. No idea.

"All right. Anybody else?"

"Gráinne had gone out, so I don't imagine she knew."

"Did you note anything unusual on your way there?"

"Nothing stood out that I remember."

"So you got to the Flag, and Fegan parked the car on a street nearby? And you walked from there to the bar?"

"No, he . . . we were dropped off right at the door."

"Did you notice anybody around as you walked to the door?"

"You have to remember that I'm a blow-in here. I wouldn't notice anything out of the ordinary. But Ronan didn't react to anything. We just went inside, and there was a roar of greeting for him. A lot of slagging about his being off the drink."

"The lads blackguarding him a little? All in good humour?"

"That's what it was."

"So you sat where?"

"At one of the tables in the back of the place."

"Who did Ronan talk to?"

"I didn't know any of the people there, of course, but he seemed to have a word for everybody. There was an old fella sitting in the window. What was his name now? Seemed to fancy himself a bit of a guardian. I remember seeing him there on a previous visit to the city here."

"That would be old Shammy."

"Of course, yes, that's his name."

"He's permanently planted at that table, takes it upon himself to keep watch on the street."

"Right. And I'm trying to bring it back now . . . He said something just before it all happened, before the smoke bomb was thrown inside. Shammy made a comment about someone outside. Something disturbed him about the fellow, but he wasn't specific. I think he said the man was wearing a cap. And there was something about a car."

"What did he say about a car?"

"I can't . . . maybe that it hadn't stopped. Or the engine was running. If there was anything more than that, I don't recall. I'm sorry."

"No, you're all right, Father. You're grand. Now what else happened?"

"There was a noise, the place began filling with smoke, and everyone bolted for the back door. The . . . device had come in the front door, so . . ."

"So everybody piled out the back. Tell us what happened at that point."

"I heard the gunshots. Ronan fell. I dropped down beside him. Prayed with him, tried to encourage him. He had a white paper sticking out of his shirt pocket. I thought that might serve as a white flag, but then I figured that might make me a target! Like those priests in the massacres a few years back. The ambulance came, and the peelers. We were taken to the hospital. Ronan and the barman, Jimmy, and I went with them."

Cathal looked at the man in the jacket and tie, who gave a slight nod.

"Thank you then, Father. We're grateful."

The boxer spoke up then. "It's well known that Ronan used to drink at the Banned Flag and still pops in for a glass of whatever he takes now. So, if he wasn't followed there . . ."

No one took up his line of reasoning, so he continued, "There may have been somebody inside. In the pub. Saw Ronan and went out and made a phone call."

Cathal and the executive were shaking their heads. "Highly unlikely," the executive said. "Anybody like that would have stuck out like Ian Paisley at, well, the Banned Flag! The lads would have noticed, and we'd have heard about it."

"You never know. Could be a tout in there. Long-time drinker, familiar face, taking the Queen's shilling and passing information to Loyalist scum."

"Not likely," the executive repeated, "but we'll look into it." To Brennan he said, "How long were you in the bar before the smoke bomb was thrown inside?"

"About two hours, maybe a bit less."

"Did you notice anybody getting up and leaving, maybe without finishing his pint?"

"I'm sorry. As I remember it, people were coming and going. I paid no attention."

"Sure, you wouldn't have had any reason to watch them."

"A young couple from Derry came in, and we offered them seats at our table. But they didn't seem to know who Ronan was, and they never got up from the table until the place filled with smoke."

"What did they sound like, the pair who came in?"

Brennan thought about it. "They sounded like Martin McGuinness."

The men laughed, and Cathal said, "Really from Derry then."

A few seconds passed without any conversation, until the executive said, "Peelers questioned you." It was a statement, not a question.

"They did."

"You told them pretty much what you told us?"

"I told them much less. They didn't ask as many questions. Not as skilled at interrogation as you fellas, I guess."

That brought a brief smile to the executive's face. "Not as interested in the outcome as we are."

"All right, now, Father," said Cathal, "we'll give you a spin over to Ronan's place. Unless . . . would you care for another drop before you go?"

"I've a thirst on me, now that you mention it." His whiskey was long gone, and the beer nearly depleted as well.

The boxer rose and replenished everyone's drink. The executive said then, "Father Burke and I had a wee chat about Mass, and Father Sweeney's name came up."

"You've met Father Sweeney?" Cathal asked Brennan.

"No, I haven't. Not yet, anyway."

"Well, if you ever do, be sure to get him going on Ian Paisley." The others in the room chuckled knowingly. "He does a wicked impression of Paisley, so he does."

"Go on, do it," the boxer urged Cathal. "You have to see Cathal doing Sweeney doing Paisley."

"No, you have to see Sweeney himself. He'd be doing Paisley in that over-the-top Ballymena accent, giving out about all us papists and our Saint *Gobnait* and her holy *gob* hanging open waiting for Saint *Brigid* and her lake of *beer*, and on and on like that, and Sweeney would twitch and look over his shoulder with fear and say, 'Is he out there?' Paisley, he meant, and he'd have us all wetting ourselves laughing. Whenever you see Father Sweeney, get him going on it."

"I'll be sure to."

After that, he asked them to take him home to Andersonstown. When they had driven away from what Brennan thought of as the "safe house," the boxer said, "Do you notice anything about our streets tonight, Father?"

Brennan peered out the window but everything looked the same to him: the shops and bars, the side streets with their rows of brick houses, the cars and black taxis, the occasional police cruiser. "Nothing stands out for me," he said.

"No Brits," the boxer replied. "No more soldiers patrolling our streets, as of last night. They pulled them out of other parts of the city a few weeks back. There are still some patrols in the rural areas but, well, now it's our turn to celebrate their departure. It's all to do with the ceasefire and the peace talks."

"That's encouraging news." Not only for the locals, Brennan said to himself, but for the poor devils sent over here to do the job. Some of the army men were thugs, as he well knew, but many were just young foot soldiers going where they were ordered to go, sent into an extremely dangerous theatre of operations.

"Of course only a few hundred of them have left," the boxer explained. "There's something like seventeen thousand of them still here. So it's not *Brits out* yet! It's only the routine patrols they're not doing now, helping out the peelers. Not needed these days, is the idea. But they'll be back in a flash of gunfire if something happens to piss them off."

Brennan nodded. No doubt about that.

The men left him off with wishes for his cousin's full recovery. If these men were who Brennan assumed they were, members of the IRA trying to get to the bottom of the shooting, Brennan could not be faulted for his efforts to help them. He had told them everything he knew. If they were not Provos, if they were some other faction in the bewildering world of allegiances and enmities swirling around Belfast, he had not given away any damaging information about any person. He simply did not have any information that could identify a suspect. But he was ninety-nine percent certain they were genuine IRA.

When he was back at the house, Brennan made a phone call, under the pretext of letting Monty know how Ronan was progressing. Well, he shouldn't say pretext; Monty would want to know how Ronan was doing. But Brennan had another reason for the call, and he would try to be cagey about it. He got to it after delivering the preliminary news.

"Yes, the family are encouraged about his recovery. But they expressed some concern about me," he lied, "about me being recognized by somebody." Of course Brennan knew the same could be said of every other person at the bar the night of the shooting, but he'd started this so he kept it going. "I assured the family that there aren't likely any photographs of my face floating around. There weren't any pictures of me in the papers or on the news broadcasts, I hope." Brennan felt like an eejit, like the sort of person who despite his protestations was really longing for newspaper or television fame.

Monty laughed, as well he might. "There weren't any, Brennan, in any of the coverage I saw. After all, does anyone here have a picture of you? But even if your stoical features had been featured in the tabloids, you can rest easy. Nobody would have recognized you as Duane Ballard. I'm pleased to say there was no resemblance between that southern hick and the Reverend Doctor Brennan Xavier Burke, latterly of Nova Scotia and soon to be of Rome."

Good, thought Brennan. Let Monty think that foolish escapade in the Iron Will bar was Brennan's only perilous adventure. He did not want to think about the lawyer's reaction if he learned of his role in the ill-fated gun incident.

Chapter XXIII

Monty

Monty had two remaining cases that had been put in jeopardy by Emmet Crowley's failure to secure representation for their trials before he fled the jurisdiction. Both clients were members of the Loyalist paramilitary group, the Ulster Defence Association. In one of the two cases, the Crown mysteriously withdrew the charges just before the case was to go to trial. Monty was not clear on the reasons why, but the matter had been resolved, and he put it out of his mind. The last case was that of a young UDA man, Sammy Dean Moffitt, who was charged with planting explosives at a Catholic taxi stand. One driver was killed in the explosion and a passenger severely injured. Two other devices at the stand failed to detonate. Because of the way things had turned out, Monty had not required the services of a local solicitor. He had briefed a barrister, but her services would not be needed for long. Because, at the eleventh hour, Monty had made a deal with the prosecution that his client would grass — inform — on his three accomplices, in return for a promise of immunity from prosecution himself. The Moffitt deal was still under wraps. Moffitt's co-defendants had no idea yet of the trap their comrade was about to spring. He was scheduled to testify at the trial in three weeks' time. Then he would walk out of the Crumlin Road Courthouse a free man. This took some skilful negotiation on Monty's part, not to mention some distaste, and he liked to imagine that his client was grateful. The gratitude was subsumed by a somewhat surly manner during Monty's visits to Moffitt at the Crumlin jail, but Monty would take what he could get. Because there was something specific he wanted to get from Moffitt the tout. And he wanted it now, before Moffitt testified and then blew town to avoid retribution for ratting out his accomplices.

Muriel Whiteside's investigator had come through with the name and address of the auto repair shop where the "hit and run" car had been patched up after the November 1992 incident. The man who had done the repairs was George Ayles, and the shop was in east Belfast. Now Monty was determined to get what he needed most of all, the name of the driver of the car.

So, when Monty was seated with his client in the basement of the jail on Saturday morning and when he had satisfied himself that their conversation was private, Monty put his offer on the table. He began by telling Moffitt what his legal fees would be for all the work he had done to secure the immunity deal. He was gratified to see a look of horror on his client's face. This was going exactly as planned.

"But there's a way out of that for you, Sam. I will consider the debt cancelled if I am provided with certain information that I want. And I know you can provide it."

Moffitt was instantly wary. "What kind of information?"

"There was an incident a couple of years ago. There was a car involved. I know the owner of the car was a UDA man."

"What makes you think —"

"I know, all right? I know everything I have to know about it," Monty bluffed, "except the name of the guy who owned the car. That's what I want: the name."

"I don't know about any incident."

"You will when I describe it to you."

His client exercised the right he would have had, in other jurisdictions, to remain silent.

Monty continued his pitch. "Back in November 1992, late at night, a car was driving along the Ammon Road around the same time a shooting occurred out there. The vehicle was a Ford Orion, not new but not ancient. And somebody fired shots at the car. The owner is reported as saying he didn't know who opened fire. What I want is the name of the registered owner of that car."

"I wouldn't know the owner of some car that —"

Monty ignored him and wrapped up his spiel. "The owner was UDA. An Ulster Defence Association man being fired upon around the time of a well-publicized murder will certainly ring bells with the UDA. Tell me who I should talk to, or work your own contacts in this place. As I say, I suspect that a lot of what went on that night is well known in your organization. And many of its members are here in this institution. However you do it, get me the name." Monty could almost see the wheels turning in Moffitt's brain as he tried to weasel out of his assignment. "And make sure the information you bring me is accurate. If it isn't, I'll know within two days that you screwed me around. And you'll be in the shithouse then; all deals will be off.

"And just so you know, Sam, I am leaving details of this in my desk at work. If anything happens to me, my fellow solicitors will find it. And the whole thing will come down on your head. You'll never get out of this cell or this country. If I return safely to my office after receiving the name, I will be suitably grateful for your assistance and will destroy all references to yourself. And you'll be able to sail off into the sunset with no worries from my end. *And* your legal fees will be paid, and you won't owe a penny."

The financial arrangement seemed to have a bigger impact than the promise that his name would not be associated with Monty's investigation into the incident of November 14, 1992.

Monty would write off his own fees and pay the firm's portion out of his own pocket. It would be well worth it, if this would enable him to make things right for Katie and Timmy Flanagan and their mother, sister, and brothers. Their fate now rested in the hands of a UDA killer who would not have thought twice about blowing the Flanagan family to smithereens if they had been at the taxi stand that day. Monty's scheming of course went way beyond the bounds of solicitor-client propriety, Monty virtually extorting information from a client. He avoided thinking what the reaction would be at Ellison Whiteside, or Stratton Sommers, if either of his firms got a whiff of what he was doing. But Monty had no respect for this client, a killer who was turning on his partners in crime in order to save his own skin. This was a client without scruples, so Monty would dispense with his own scruples in the desperate hope that he could do something for the Flanagans in his short time in Belfast. In reality, though, Monty would not do anything to scuttle the trial or the immunity arrangement, no matter what Moffitt did. But Moffitt didn't know that. Let him think his lawyer was as unethical as he was himself.

Brennan

Brennan went to the Clonard Monastery on Sunday to say a special Mass for Ronan, the warrior turned peacemaker, who was still lying in hospital recovering from abdominal surgery. There was a little gathering in a side room before the Mass was to begin. The monastery, as Brennan well knew, was playing a role in the peace process, and here was the man most closely associated with those efforts, Father Alec Reid. He remembered Brennan and embraced him, assuring him of his continued prayers for Ronan.

The Methodist minister, Clark Rayburn, was there, and he too embraced Brennan. "Thank God," he said, "that Ronan survived that dreadful attack. My congregation has been praying for him."

"Thank you, Clark, very much."

Clark introduced him to the handful of other ministers who, like Ronan, were playing a role in the peace process and who had come to show their support. Clark identified the Presbyterian and other churches with which they were connected. They all offered their sympathy for Brennan's stricken cousin, expressed their admiration for his new role as a man of peace, and wished him an early recovery. One of the churchmen said, "If, the Lord forbid, it turns out that someone from our community, the Unionist community, is responsible for this heinous act, Father Burke, you can be sure we will want to see him prosecuted to the full extent of the law."

The speaker then directed a glance to another man in the room, whose expression did not suggest that he had been saying any prayers for the Burke family. Brennan had seen the intense-looking, wild-haired fellow somewhere, he knew. Then he had it. John the Baptist, a familiar figure from the news pages. The preacher stood apart, glowering at the others in the room. Brennan noted that his more famous colleague, Old Saint Nick, was not present. All this popery must have been just too rich for his blood. As for the Baptist, he looked as if he was suffering from a severe case of indigestion. A steady diet of wild locusts will do that. He finally made his contribution to the exchange. "We don't condone terrorism no matter where it's directed."

Brennan felt that was probably the case for many or most of these rare visitors to the Falls, but he wasn't all that confident when it came to John the Baptist. That same man walked over to Brennan, leaned towards him, and said, "Maybe you should be looking on the Falls Road, in Ardoyne, Andytown, the Short Strand."

"Looking for . . . ?"

"Come on now, Reverend Burke. There are elements in the Republican movement who are none too happy about the peace process, right? Where will that leave them? Sitting on their rear ends with nothing to do, no one to shoot at, nothing to blow up. Well, you've heard them yourself. They say all this peace talk is a sell-out, the end of the dream of a united Ireland. I would suggest you look to some of those fellows before you try to pin it on the Loyalists."

The same thought had crossed Brennan's mind, inevitably, but he was not about to say so. Not in the present company. He had always pushed the thought away. Ronan knew everybody on the Republican side, no matter where they stood with respect to the current peace process. He would know, surely, if someone from his own side was out to get him. Brennan didn't like to dwell on the steps his cousin might have taken to neutralize a threat from within. He brought his mind back to the present.

"We are here for a Mass of peace, Mr. . . . ." Brennan could not for the life of him remember the preacher's real name.

"My name is Geddes. And I only wish we were all on the same page when it comes to a genuine desire for peace in Ulster. Anyway, let's get in there for the service. Gentlemen?"

It was indeed time to head in, time for Brennan to vest himself for Mass, so he excused himself and went into the sacristy to get ready. When he entered the church as part of the procession, he marvelled as always at its beauty. The church was ablaze with light, from the intricately patterned floor to the great vaulted ceiling and the shining golden mosaic above the high altar. Today, the place was packed. And, in a city where mourners had been murdered during a burial at the cemetery, security was tight. Father Reid had come to know Ronan Burke over the past few years, so Brennan had asked him to deliver the homily, which he graciously agreed to do. The sermon was a ringing tribute to Ronan and a cry to heaven for peace. It was a lovely ceremony; especially gratifying for Brennan was the sound of the choir that had been assembled for the occasion. They sang the beautiful *Mass for Four Voices* by William Byrd. The piece was notable for Byrd's poignant setting of the *dona nobis pacem* line, the line that implores the Lamb of God to grant us peace. Then the choir did a selection from the great oratorio that had its premiere performance in Ireland just over two hundred and fifty years before. Handel's *Messiah*.

> He was wounded for our transgressions. He was bruised
> for our iniquities. The chastisement of our peace was
> upon him.

Monty

Monty had been engaging in a bit of B-movie dialogue when he told Sammy Dean Moffitt that he would be leaving an envelope in his desk drawer that would reveal the true facts, if anything happened to Monty as a result of his prodding of the UDA. But after the series of events that unfolded two days later, he felt as if he really was playing a part in a film. And he chided himself for having written off old Hughie Malone as a crackpot. Monday began with a call from the Crumlin jail, a request for him to go and see his client. When he was face to face with Sammy Moffitt, Moffitt told him he would be contacted by somebody who "owes me, big time." Then, late in the afternoon as he was reading about the tensile strength of metals for his Canadian Earth Equipment case, Monty received a cryptic phone call. The caller instructed him to go to a payphone on Waring Street near the Royal Ulster Rifles Museum at five o'clock and wait for a call. Somebody apparently distrusted the phone lines at Ellison Whiteside.

It was a short walk from his office so, a few minutes before the appointed time, he headed out, feeling he should be attired in a trench coat and fedora. He walked to the museum, found the payphone, and loitered, hoping nobody else would come by to use the phone. And of course someone did; an old gent made straight for the booth. Monty took out some coins and pretended to fiddle with the apparatus. He made a "does nothing work at all these days?" gesture and pretended to try again. The man sighed and muttered and moved off. Two minutes after that, the phone rang, and Monty grabbed the receiver. A man spoke to him with a smoker's voice and an accent so thick Monty could barely make out the words. But he got the essence of it: at half eight that night, he was to go to the corner of Sandy Row and the Donegall Road and wait for a black taxi with a patch of body filler on the bonnet. He was to get in. End of instructions. Click. It occurred to Monty that if this was the guy who had the information for him, he could have simply delivered it over the phone. But, then again, maybe not. Who knew where the caller was, or who else was there? And it could be that, before handing over sensitive information, the fellow wanted to see the whites of Monty's eyes, wanted to see for himself "who wants to know." After all this go-ahead, even though he felt foolish doing it, Monty really did write a summary of the situation and leave it in a sealed envelope in his office.

That night at twenty-five after eight he was standing on Sandy Row where it met the Donegall Road. It wasn't left up to the imagination to discern which side of the sectarian division he was on. The murals were fiercely Loyalist. Precisely at eight thirty, a black taxi pulled up. There was a small area of grey body repair filler on the hood. He peered inside. The driver was the only person in the car. He was heavy-set and bald. He didn't speak but gestured with his head for Monty to get into the back seat. With some misgivings, Monty did just that.

The cabbie drove off into the gloom, and Monty lost track of all the twists and turns on the way to a destination unknown. They finally stopped beside a row of dark-windowed buildings. The driver wasted no time on small talk. "Your client told me to tell you this, so I'm tellin' you. Then me and him are square. You can tell him that from me; I've paid my debt to him in full. Fritzy O'Dwyer was a Fenian bigot and a one-man Provie death squad. He was culling Loyalists and innocent Protestant civilians, so somebody — I don't know who — eliminated him. And if you think you're going to do something about that, think again. The RUC won't be happy to see you. It's well known that they had no patrols on in that area that night. Coincidence? No, I don't fuckin' think so. If you want to know the truth of it, I think it was the security forces themselves that leaked to somebody where the psycho Provie bastard was going to be that night. They wanted him gone, a lot of people wanted him gone, he's gone. And nobody's cryin' in their pints over it, despite all the blubberin' that was done over his grave in the Milltown Cemetery."

It was explosive information the guy was giving him, even with the rote denial, the assertion that he didn't know who had killed the IRA man. The implication was that the security forces of the state itself had a hand in the murder, that it was not a routine sectarian killing after all, but a summary execution. This was dangerous information to pass around. No wonder there were so many cloak and dagger manoeuvres leading up to this meeting. How much of this could Monty ever use in his claim for damages over Flanagan's death? He hoped he wouldn't have to go that far. He left that hanging for now and got onto the subject of the car.

"There was a man killed right after that shooting, hit by a car and knocked off the bridge."

"Bad night to be out walking on the Ammon Road."

"What kind of traffic would be out there at that time of night?"

"Nobody would be out there just driving around. There's nothing there, especially that late. A few houses with everybody asleep. Fenian houses. Maybe somebody going to pick up some drunken Taigs from O'Grady's bar. But not a well-travelled road."

"What's the name of the owner of the car that was shot up that night?"

There was a long silence, but the cabbie eventually spoke up. This was the key bit of information he had been told to give Monty, so that the cabbie could pay off his debt to Moffitt. And so that Moffitt could pay off his debt to Monty. "Fellow's name was Colman Davison."

"Was Davison involved in the shooting?"

"Not bloody likely if it was his car that got shot in the arse end by the shooter."

That was Monty's thinking as well. A paramilitary man who had just shot someone to death would have had a gun in the car, not just a flick knife, to point at an interloper like Vincent McKeever. But the bullet holes in the rear bumper suggested that he was there, that he had come upon the scene.

"What would a Loyalist Protestant be doing out on that road at night if there was nothing along there but Catholic homes and a Catholic bar?"

"How the fuck should I know? My work is done here. My debt to your client has been paid in full. Understand?"

"I do."

"And you never breathe a word of this wee spin in my taxi. To anyone, ever."

"Agreed."

The taxi pulled out, travelled a short distance, and stopped at the corner of the Shankill Road and Battenberg Street. The driver said no more, just waited for Monty to get out, and then he drove away. Monty looked around him. Once again in a Loyalist enclave. He had no idea how far he was from home. Where were the taxis when you needed one?

Chapter XXIV

Brennan

The brilliant music at the Clonard Mass for peace inspired Brennan to new heights in his work at Holy Cross Girls' School. What joy it was to return to his work at the church and school after taking a week off to keep Ronan company as best he could. The girls gave him a big cheer on his first day back, and they seemed keen to learn the new pieces he had selected for them: the Byrd *Mass for Four Voices* and some of the most dramatic and poignant movements of Handel's *Messiah*, those suitable for the female voice. If only life could be filled with such beauty every day. On Monday as he listened to the sweet sounds of the girls' voices, he thought ahead to the next adventure, the stint as a choirmaster in Rome. He had reams of great music in mind for that choir. He snapped back to the present and showered the Holy Cross children with the praise they so richly deserved.

He stayed in Ardoyne for a pub supper and a couple of pints, then returned to the house in Andersonstown, where he met Tom and his bride, Aoife, coming out the door.

"'Bout ye, Father Burke?" asked Aoife. "Are you recovering well from the shock of what happened?"

"I'm fine, thank you, Aoife. It's Ronan we're worried about."

Tom said, "I've seen a big improvement in Da these last couple of days."

"Yes, thanks be to God."

"Listen, Father," said Aoife, "we're just heading home, and we're having a few people in. Why don't you join us?"

"Well, now . . ."

"Don't stop to think about it. Just say you will."

"All right. If you call me Brennan, I'll join the party."

"Good, Brennan. It's just a wee walk round the corner."

"I'll go up and change into civvies for the occasion. Be right down."

He was quick but by the time he went downstairs again, Aoife was gone.

"I sent her on ahead," said Tom, waiting by the door. "What do you make of the situation, Brennan? Nobody's come after me. Or you."

"You'd know the ways of the world here better than I do, Tom, but I'd like think we're off the hook."

"They obviously couldn't identify me, or they'd have dragged me out of my bed at gunpoint. I'm thinking they realized that nothing was stolen from the church, nobody was hurt, and they've moved on. They've bigger fish to fry, have the peelers here. So we may be all right."

"*Deo volente*," Brennan replied. God willing.

"That sort of cock-up on my part really pisses me off, though, Brennan."

"None of us can be at the top of our game every time, Tom."

"Aye, I know. But with so much at stake, I mean my entire future! My plan is to go out to work every morning and come home every night to Aoife and our weans like a normal man living in a normal country. I studied accounting, for Christ's sake! I want to buy a house instead of renting one. And we want to have more kids, me and Aoife, a whole pack of them. That's not going to happen if I get lifted for doing something daft and get sent to the Kesh for the rest of my days." He walked ahead and opened the door and waited for Brennan to go out ahead of him. "So I guess my brother is right, that I have *selfish motives* for standing with my old fella and his peace process, instead of keeping the war going till we finally win. If ever we could."

He looked over at Brennan and said, "But I'd be a hero in my own way, when you think about it. Out-breeding the other side, so we'll be able to out-vote them."

"Sure you're right, Tom. We have heroic warriors in our history and heroic drinkers. Why not heroic, em, breeders?"

"Shagging for Ireland!"

"Good on you, my lad. And it will all be done with the blessing of Holy Mother Church and a Thirty-Two County Irish Republic."

"Brilliant! We'll get my mural started tomorrow." They shared a few more laughs, avoided any further discussion of their worries, and arrived at a typical Belfast brick house a few minutes' walk from Ronan's. They went inside and heard Pink Floyd playing on a stereo. A dozen or so people were sitting around with drinks, talking over the music.

"Youse'll have us evicted!" said Aoife, as she went to turn the volume down. "Was it you that turned that music up, wee Brian?"

Her little girl and boy, aged around two and three, stood in the centre of the room. Two pairs of immense brown eyes stared up at the young mother.

"No, Mammy!" the boy said.

"I know, angel," Aoife assured him and gave both children a hug. "Time for bed now. *Suas libh.*" Up with youse. She pointed to the stairs, and up they all went.

Brennan walked over to a side table where there was a display of photos. He recognized many from his own side of the family but he knew nothing about Aoife's first husband, who was shown in a posed portrait with Aoife and the first baby. Tom came up beside Brennan and said, "That's Enda. We were all in the same school, him and Aoife a few years ahead of me."

"What happened to him?"

"He died in a premature explosion."

Brennan was familiar with that expression. It meant the man had died while setting a bomb. A bomb that would have exploded at another place and time, blowing up property and possibly human beings, if all had gone according to plan. He refrained from comment.

"It was right after he died that Aoife found out she was pregnant with their second."

Brennan couldn't think of anything to say that would not be a platitude, in the face of yet another pointless death in the dirty war in Ireland.

"I know," Tom said, reading Brennan's thoughts. Then, "So, what'll you have, Brennan? We've Guinness in the bottle, we've whiskey, wine, pretty well everything."

"A glass of whiskey would go down nicely, Tom."

"Coming right up. Let me introduce you around." He made some introductions and then got him his whiskey. "I hear more people upstairs. You can meet them when they come down."

Brennan chatted with the other guests and enjoyed the to and fro of the conversation. Aoife came back downstairs and poured herself a glass of red wine.

A young man came into the house then, and he looked familiar. A friend of Tom's or Lorcan's, Brennan knew.

"Ah," said Aoife, "here's the shy and retiring Mr. Lalor. We missed you at my sister's hooley, Carrick."

Right, Brennan remembered him now.

"And," said Aoife, "*you* missed the chance of a lifetime, you and Lorcan, to do a lovely duet. A much softer, sweeter song than you fellas used to do when you were punk rockers screaming the house down as the Gobscheiss Militia. This is a song I composed for my sister. 'Poor Oul Soul.' It's going to be top of the charts, and everyone's going to remember where they were the first time they heard it. Except you, because you weren't there. But Lorcan did a heroic job of it all by himself."

"Ah, I'm sorry I couldn't be there, Aoife. Something came up. But I'll be first in line with a fistful of pound notes when the recording hits the shops!"

Brennan remembered hearing something about the party a while back. Lorcan had mentioned it. Right, not easily forgotten; it was the night of the ill-fated outing at the Banned Flag. If only Ronan had crashed the sister's party instead of going to the Flag.

"Well, you're here now," Aoife said to Carrick. "Here's my song if you want to see it, words and music."

She pulled open a cabinet drawer and withdrew a sheet of paper. Brennan could see staves of music and lyrics written in.

Carrick took it from her and looked it over. He hummed the melody and then announced to the room. "This is brilliant, and I can do it justice. Would youse all like to hear it?"

The response was a resounding "Aye, give us the song!"

So Carrick stood with the sheet of music in his right hand, and his left arm out towards his audience, and he did indeed give them the song.

Come all ye old and lonely ones that never were a wife
Take heart from oul Fiona here who ne'r gave up on life.

At this point, he assumed a face of vaudevillian tragedy and clutched his heart. He started up again.

The poor oul soul as you can see has not much to com-
mend her

Weighing in at fourteen stone, you'd need a tractor to
upend her.

His expression was now one of wide-eyed astonishment at the
wide-bodied woman who was the subject of his lament.

With a face on her like a smackèd arse and a shape like
a sack o' shite
She'd lost all hope of a date for the dance, let alone a
wedding night.

His audience began to clap along and stomp their feet.

But just before the clock struck twelve on the day that
she turned thirty
An oul geezer hobbled up to her and said, "My name
is Bertie."

A cheer went up around the room.

So all ye lonely girls out there, don't sit in your room
and hide.
Even poor oul Fiona Mary has been taken for a bride.

Carrick gave a lewd wink and was met with catcalls and whistles
from his listeners. They all joined in the chorus.

Yes poor oul Fiona Mary has been taken for a ride!

Brennan laughed in spite of himself at the doggerel verse and
the antics that accompanied it. When it was over and the roars of
approval had subsided, he approached Aoife and congratulated her

on her song. "I'm a musician myself. My choirs perform the works of Mozart and Handel and Palestrina, but we are always looking for new compositions."

"Ah, now, Father, I'm nothing special. I wouldn't dream of putting myself forward like that."

"How did your sister take it? Not the most flattering portrait, when you think of it."

"Why don't you ask her yourself? I'll introduce you."

He experienced a moment of alarm. And guilt. The poor sister was in the house while the slander was being sung about her. But Aoife took him by the hand and led him upstairs. The door was open to one of the bedrooms and she went inside, with Brennan behind her. "Here she is, the poor oul thing." She pointed to a woman sitting at a desk. "Fiona, this is Father Burke, Brennan Burke, a cousin of Tom's. Father, meet the sad but brave Fiona Mary Davitt."

Fiona rose from her seat. Brennan couldn't help himself. He burst out laughing, right in the woman's face. Far from a fourteen-stone sadsack with a face like a smacked arse, Fiona Davitt was tall, slim, black-haired, and stunningly beautiful.

He said to her, "Where are my manners, Fiona? Let me assure you and Aoife that I would not have been laughing if you in any way fit the picture your sister painted in her verse."

"Consider yourself absolved, Father. Isn't she bad?" She inclined her head towards her sister. "Just wait till you turn thirty, you little minx. And see what I'll have to say about you!"

"You'll get me back, I know it. Just promise me you won't do it on live television!"

"I may do it at the BAFTAs or on Oscar night. Ye won't know till the day comes, will ye?"

Aoife turned to Brennan. "Fiona is an actress. She's performed on the stage here in Ireland and in London, and she's made two films as well!"

"Ah. Congratulations, Fiona. Good for you."

"Thanks, Father. It's loads of fun while it lasts. But I have other plans now."

Aoife said, "She's managed to land herself a man in spite of it all, as I acknowledged in the song. You may have heard of Bertie Breannacht?"

"Blondy fella? In a recent film about spies?"

"That's him. He and Fiona are getting married next month."

"Lovely," he said. "Congratulations." Then he remembered something from his childhood, something his mother always said. It was bad manners to congratulate the bride-to-be. Why was that? Something about maintaining the image that the man had done the chasing. Well, whatever the case, Fiona had not taken offence.

"And we plan on having a family," she said, "so that will cut into my swanning around on the stage. Small price to pay. Who was doing the honours with your wee bit of libel this time round, Aoife? It wasn't Lorcan."

"Carrick. He missed the night of your party. And he missed his calling. He should be on the stage."

"Can't you see the reviews? IRA bloke slays them in the aisles!"

"Fiona, for feck's sake, keep it down!"

"Everyone in the room down there knows it, or Lorcan wouldn't have let them past your door. Lorcan! That brother-in-law of yours . . . if I were a casting director . . . 'Yon Cassius has a lean and hungry look!'"

"He let you past the door."

"I told him I'm the quartermaster of the Ballyobarmy Brigade, Second Battalion. But I was only *acting*." She threw out her arms like the quintessential ham actor.

Her sister laughed and said to Brennan, "Isn't she a terror? You can see why we banished her up here by herself. What *are* you doing up here by yourself?"

Fiona pointed to a bunch of papers on the desk. "Answering my fan mail. I just can't keep up with it."

"Really? It could be true," Aoife said to Brennan.

"No, I'm planning the menu for the wedding. Porridge and a few lumps of mutton. Can you think of anything else?"

"No, you've got it covered. Now we'll leave you to it."

"Lovely to meet you, Brennan. I hope meeting us won't put you off seeing us again."

"I'd be charmed to see you again." He'd have been content to just stay on in the room and gaze at her, but he dutifully left her to plan her marriage to another man. Damn his eyes.

He returned to the party and when he saw Lorcan alone, he approached him and asked if they could speak privately. Lorcan led him into a tiny room that had a desk and chair and computer, and little else.

"Who do suppose tried to assassinate your father, Lorcan?"

"If I knew, you'd have read the news of a fella with his head blown off and a sign pasted on his corpse saying, 'This is for Ronan Burke.'"

"You must have some suspicions."

"The Loyalists would be terrified of someone like my old man gaining power in this place. He's brilliant, he's popular; someone like that would gain power and influence by the force of his personality. He'd put the rest of them in the shadows. And Nationalists would benefit as a result. The Loyalists see any benefit to us as a loss to themselves. They're terrified of that."

"But wouldn't feelings run just as strong on the Republican side, among those who don't accept the peace process? Those who want to finish the job, overthrow the government of this illegitimate little state, and unite the six counties with the twenty-six in the South? Those who feel they're being sold out?" Like Lorcan himself, Brennan refrained from adding.

"You're suggesting one of our own lads did this."

"Not suggesting. Asking if there is anything to it."

"There isn't. Nobody in the Republican movement would take out my father. And you can be sure we're going to track down the bastards who did this. We won't have any more trouble from that lot, whoever they are."

Monty

It was time to gather more evidence in the Flanagan case. After dutifully attending to some Canadian Earth documents and a couple of his Ellison Whiteside matters, Monty turned to the Flanagan file and did an inventory. He had the autopsy report on Eamon Flanagan and the time of the shooting of Fritzy O'Dwyer. He had spoken to the cop who had investigated Mr. Flanagan's death, not that he'd got much from him beyond an estimate of the time when Flanagan must have fallen. He now had the name of the driver, Colman Davison. He had Vincent McKeever's account of his run-in with Davison. McKeever had heard shots just before Davison's car came flying down the road and turned in to the woods, Davison's car with the bullet holes. The next move was to go and talk to the man who had done the repairs on the Ford Orion. Monty had already performed a little experiment on that model of car himself. He knew from the autopsy report that Eamon Flanagan had been around the same height as Monty himself, so he had gone in search of an Orion of the same era, had spotted several over the course of a few days, and found one parked on a street in the city centre. He walked up to it, stood with his leg against the front bumper, and confirmed to his satisfaction that an impact with the bumper could indeed result in a fracture of the kind sustained by Flanagan.

Monty got into his car and drove across the Lagan to east Belfast, out to the Upper Newtownards Road, and then turned off. The shop wasn't hard to find, and he pulled in. There was a man out in the yard, and Monty asked him whether George Ayles was around. George was just putting the finishing touches on a job and would be available in a wee minute. Monty could go inside and have a seat by the parts desk.

Ayles came in about fifteen minutes later, wiping his hands on a rag. "You wanted to see me?"

Monty stood to greet him and said, "Yes, Mr. Ayles. I'm hoping you can help me." He explained who he was and why he was there and could practically see the man closing down on him as the context became clear.

"There is of course no problem with your work, Mr. Ayles. I'd just like a few details to help me get some compensation for the widow and the five children."

No problem from the point of view of the law, or the quality of the repair job, but maybe a problem with local paramilitaries who wouldn't appreciate George Ayles or anybody else grassing to lawyers about things that went bump in the night in Belfast.

"We know it was Mr. Davison driving that night," Monty said in an effort to reassure him. "All I need is the details of the damage to the car." He would want a formal statement later, one from George Ayles and another from Vincent McKeever, and they would be served with a subpoena if the case went to court, but he didn't get into that.

It took a bit more persuading, but Ayles finally relented and said he would go and look at his records from November 1992. He returned a few minutes later with a sheet of paper. He read off the details. The shop repaired the rear bumper where there were two bullet holes. No, he didn't remember finding the slugs embedded in the bumper; if so, he would have disposed of them. There was a dent in the left front bumper, and that was repaired. Monty kept a poker face when he received that crucial bit of news, evidence that the car had run into something. Driving on the left-hand side of the road, hitting something with the left side of the bumper. Something at the side of the road. He tried to sound casual as he asked, "What did Colman have to say about that? The dent in the front?"

"Said he veered off course when the bullets hit, and he ran into a tree. Then he got back on track and kept going on his way."

"Any sign of that? Bark, splinters?"

Ayles merely shook his head. Finally, though, he said, "Left head-light was smashed and had to be replaced." This was getting better by the minute! More good evidence of an impact.

"Did he say anything about anybody else being in the car with him?"

"I don't know if I ever asked him." Ayles looked at the paper in his hand, thought for a second, then said, "I know we had a bit of a conversation. I think I said something like, 'Good thing you were able to get back onto the road, with all that going on.' And he said, 'It's times like that when you're glad you're alone.' Or 'At least I had nobody screeching at me from the passenger side and adding to the stress.' Something like that, anyway."

That confirmed what McKeever had said, that Davison was alone in the car.

Monty asked for a photocopy of the work record and, again, George Ayles was leery. But Monty again brought up the plight of the five fatherless children. And the auto repair man, being a decent sort in spite of his fear of retaliation, took the page to the copier in the corner of the room and made a copy while Monty looked on. *I, Montague M. Collins, QC, do say and I do verily believe that this is a true copy of the original document that I saw on the premises of the George Ayles Auto Repair Shop on the 28th day of March, 1995.* Monty thanked him and let him get back to his work.

There was something to check back at the office, so Monty set out for the city centre, trying not to get his hopes up. He would be looking for a little piece of evidence that, if it had been there at all, probably had not survived the fall to the rocks below the bridge. The police had found Flanagan's body during their search of the area fol-lowing the anonymous call about the shooting. They called for an ambulance — the second ambulance to be deployed to the Ammon Road that night — and Eamon Flanagan was taken to hospital. As soon as Monty got into his office, he dug out the medical informa-tion on Flanagan. One of the things that had been noted was the clothing he had on, and the parts of the clothing that were torn or damaged. He scanned the report until he found a reference to the front of the left leg. He had been wearing blue jeans and the jeans were torn below the knee where the leg was broken. Was it possible that . . . *Eureka,* there it was! Two tiny slivers of glass stuck in the threads of the left leg of the jeans. The slivers, some of them at least, had been driven in so hard that they stayed in place through the trauma of the fall.

The smashed left headlight of Colman Davison's Ford Orion had left its evidence on the leg of the late Eamon Flanagan.

Chapter XXV

Monty

Ronan Burke was released from hospital on Friday, March 31, nearly two weeks after the attempt on his life. He was weak and in pain, and he would require nursing care at home, but he was out. Ronan was front-page news in Belfast, and the story was covered in the Irish Republic and on the BBC. One paper described Ronan as "one of the future leaders of a new era in Northern Ireland, an odds-on favourite to be elected to a new assembly with power shared between Unionists and Nationalists." Gráinne decided to hold an open house that evening to celebrate. Drinks and tea and some snacks, nothing too elaborate. Brennan invited Monty to join in. "It's not an all-night hooley. She's having it early, so she can get him tucked into bed early. Otherwise, he'll be shattered." An early night was fine with Monty. He had been in the office since seven that morning, working on the papers for the Flanagan case. He was ready to down tools by four o'clock. He headed for Andersonstown.

He could hardly get in the door, there were so many on hand to welcome Ronan back to the land of the living. There were some serious-faced, muscular men in attendance and out on the street. It looked like several sets of bodyguards. That was all but confirmed when Monty spotted Martin McGuinness and Gerry Adams in the gathering; no doubt there were other major figures Monty didn't recognize, who also required protection.

At one end of the room were two young guys with guitars. Monty recognized the shorter, leaner of the two as Ronan and Gráinne's younger son, Lorcan. Monty, a musician himself, took note of the full, warm sound of Lorcan's Gibson J-45 guitar. The other fellow was bigger and had a schoolboy kind of haircut, but a closer look at his face revealed a harder edge. They played some patriotic songs but nothing overly militant. They took a break, and the bigger fellow went off somewhere, leaving Lorcan playing softly on his Gibson. Monty went over to introduce himself.

"Hi Lorcan. I saw you at your brother's wedding, but we were never introduced. I'm Monty Collins."

Lorcan gently laid down his guitar and shook Monty's hand. "Right, you're Brennan's mate from Canada."

"That's right. Beautiful sound, your J-45. Buddy of mine has one. We have a blues band back home."

"Oh, aye? I love the blues. We don't hear enough of it around here. Of course you could say we *live* the blues around here!"

"True enough."

"What do you call yourself, your band?"

"Functus."

"Doesn't get any bluesier than that, whatever it means."

"It's a legal term."

"Me and Carrick there, and a couple of other fellas, had a punk band. Called ourselves the Gobscheiss Militia."

"That's great, even better than Functus! You guys aren't playing anymore?"

"We're on hiatus. Until the other two finish doing their whack out in the Kesh."

It took a second before it sank in; people here were so casual in the way they referred to the prison terms their friends and family were serving. He merely said, "I don't envy them."

"Tell me about it. I did a wee stint out there myself. You may not have that crime in Canada. It's called 'getting in with the wrong crowd.'"

"Nothing in our Criminal Code like that, no, or half the teenage children in our country would be locked behind bars."

"Maybe I'll emigrate over there. But my work is not finished here." He gave a little laugh, but there was no humour in it. Monty assumed that "getting in with the wrong crowd" was a euphemism for being a member of a proscribed organization, that being the Provisional Irish Republican Army. And his work for that organization was yet to be completed.

"So," Lorcan was saying, "with my mates in the H Blocks, it could be awhile before anybody hears the Gobscheiss Militia again."

"I'll keep checking in *Rolling Stone* for the announcement of your reunion."

They talked music for a few more minutes until Monty saw a break in the line of well-wishers approaching Ronan. Tom and Aoife and their two little kids were saying goodbye, so Monty waited, then excused himself and crossed the room.

"Welcome to the throne," Ronan said when Monty reached him. "I feel I should have people kissing my ring!"

"And well you should, Ronan," Monty replied. "According to the press, you'll be the Holy Irish Emperor once the Holy Irish Empire is put in place here in the North. So how are you feeling?"

"No complaints. I must get up and circulate like a normal human being." It took him a couple of attempts, but he got up on his feet and stood. People broke into applause.

Brennan came over then, with the politician from Dublin. Monty tried to remember his name and got it just in time. "Hello, Mr. Cagney," he said, putting out his hand.

"Dinny," the man said as they shook.

"Dinny has some good news for us, Monty," Brennan announced.

"Oh?"

"The information gathered by Father Burke here has turned up aces," Cagney told them. "I understand there was a bit of undercover work involved, Father."

"Call me Brennan. Or, as some folks in a certain east Belfast saloon call me, Duane."

"A job well done, Duane."

"I didn't act alone, but my co-star is away at the Grand Ole Opry." Or whatever the equivalent might be in Dublin, where Maura and the kids were staying this weekend.

The politician said, "Brennan's information from America shows that MacAllan's papers were falsified. And I handed over those details, along with his photo and the statement of the witness who saw him in one of the bomb cars, to Garda Sullivan in Dublin. And, after doing some more work on the file, he personally provided the RUC with copies of everything. The officer he is dealing with here in Belfast was impressed with the evidence and told Sullivan he will be looking into it."

Brennan said, "It's about time, seeing as the peelers have had incriminating evidence against scads of suspects since 1974."

"I know, I know. But Sullivan tells me this RUC man is a good, honest copper. So there's hope that somebody will finally be arrested and brought to justice for the Monaghan and Dublin massacres. And it's not stretching things to picture MacAllan grassing on the others to get a better deal for himself. But one way or another, once the police take action against one of the killers, this could provide the momentum for a reopening of the investigation into the rest of them. Even with only one going to court, the shameful inaction of the police and security forces, and their collusion with their favoured terrorists, will be made public all over again. So, there's hope, thanks to you people."

"Well, of course, it was Ronan who got the whole thing going."

"Oh, his name will be high indeed on the roll of honour."

Brennan raised his eyes to the firmament. "Paddy, my dear old friend, for you and the thirty-three other innocent souls who were taken that day, the waiting is nearly over."

Cagney then said his goodbyes because he had to get back to Dublin. He called out to Ronan across the room, "It won't be long, Ronan, till you and I meet at some kind of official hooley as members of our respective parliaments, as soon as they set one up here. Or, better still, one parliament for the entire island. Whatever it turns out to be, I've no doubt you'll be elected in a landslide. *Tiocfaidh ár lá!*" Everyone in the room raised a glass and repeated the Republican rallying cry. Our day will come!

Eventually, McGuinness and Adams departed with encouraging words for Ronan, and the crowd thinned out. Then it was just family gathered in the sitting room, plus Monty and a small group of young fellows Monty didn't know. They spent most of their time huddled with Lorcan.

During a lull in the conversation, Monty broke his own good news to Brennan. "You'll be pleased to hear this, Brennan. The Flanagan children are going to have their day in court. I have an expert who will give an opinion that Eamon Flanagan was hit by a car, and I have confirmation that the car was fully insured. I shouldn't get too cocky; all my years in the practice of law have taught me to look for a bad moon rising over any case I take on."

"Yeah, I can see that."

"Anyway, I'm just at the stage of filing the claim right now. So early days yet. But if things go as they should, the mother and children will be in line for a substantial award of damages, which will allow them to get the hell out of the housing estate into a safer, more comfortable home and get their lives back on track."

"Well done, Montague!" said Brennan.

Monty heard a tea kettle whistling in the kitchen, and Gráinne said she had a couple of plates of scones and biscuits left if anyone was still hungry. Brennan offered to assist in the serving and got up and followed her out.

"How did you manage to pull that off?" Brennan called out from the kitchen.

"Some cloak and dagger stuff with the UDA. All in a day's work for a Belfast solicitor!"

Monty sat back to savour his drink and his accomplishments so far on the case. When he looked around, he saw Lorcan Burke and his comrades staring at him intently. Ronan was gazing into the middle distance, his face suddenly pale and drawn.

Monty was taken aback. Was it something he said? Must have been the reference to the UDA. "I'm not working *with* the UDA," he tried. "I know how *that* would go over in this room. The UDA guy is the defendant. He was driving . . ." Monty wound down. Nobody had cracked a smile.

Chapter XXVI

Brennan

Brennan had remembered nothing about the assassination attempt except the sound of the shots, Ronan falling, Brennan dropping down beside him, prayer after prayer, then the police and ambulance screaming to the scene. But the morning after Ronan's homecoming, while he was thinking of something else entirely — that being the sixth book of Saint Augustine's *De Musica* — the sound of a voice came into his head. A peculiar voice. And he realized with a start that he had heard it the instant after he fell to his knees. A man had said, "That won't save you, you papish fu—" And he clammed up, as if someone had given him a clout to shut him up. And then footsteps and they were gone. The voice had a rasping sound to it, a damaged sound. So Brennan now had information that he had not consciously possessed before. Whether it would be of any use in identifying one of the attackers, he didn't know, but he wanted to pass it along. To someone. The peelers? That would be the responsible, civic thing to do. But the blood running in his veins was the blood of the Fenian Burkes of Dublin and Belfast. And the instinct of a man born to generations of rebellion was to inform his own side only. He had no idea how to contact the men who had questioned him after his release from the hospital.

"Does that narrow things down for you at all?" he asked Ronan across the breakfast table. "Know anyone who sounds like that?"

"Not straight away, I don't, but . . ."

"Now it could simply be someone disguising his voice, or someone jittery with nerves, or someone with a sore throat."

"Or," said Ronan, "someone with an injured throat."

That was Brennan's thinking as well. A man who had suffered an accident. Or a wound. "So where do I go with this information, Ronan? The fellas who came for me at the hospital, asked me some questions, I wouldn't know how to reach them."

"You leave that with me, Brennan. You'll be hearing from them."

Gráinne answered the telephone that evening, said, "He is," and handed Brennan the receiver. A man greeted him and said a car would come by to pick him up in half an hour's time.

Precisely on time, a new-looking grey car pulled up. As Brennan watched from the window, a man got half out of the driver's side, made some kind of hand signal to the two bodyguards on the night shift, and then settled back into the seat. Brennan went outside and approached the car. He recognized the driver as the man who had given his name as Cathal and the passenger as the other nattily dressed IRA man who had questioned him. He opened the back door and got in.

"Good evening to you, Father Burke," said Cathal. And the other man nodded and said, "Father."

"Perhaps we can put ourselves on a first name basis and you can call me Brennan," he said. "Ahem."

The unnamed-till-now man gave a good-humoured little laugh and said, "I'm Francis. Now I understand you've remembered something about the shooting."

"Just one thing, and it won't take long to relate. After the shots were fired at Ronan and he fell, I moved towards him. He wasn't far from me. I knelt down and began to minister to him. Initially all I recalled after that was fear and rage and confusion, and the effort to keep praying and keep Ronan from slipping away. Then, today, in a moment of calm when my mind was on something else, I remembered the sound of a voice coming from the direction of the shooter or shooters."

"Yes?" Francis prompted.

"The man said, 'That won't save you, you papish fuck.' Or fucker. But he never finished that last word because, I'm thinking, someone else hit or nudged him to shut his gob. Not too bright. Anyway, he shut right up. And they took off."

"Two of them, then," said Cathal.

"Seems so. But the distinctive thing about this is the fella's voice. It was breathy, ragged, raspy. It sounded to me like the voice of someone whose throat was, well, damaged. I knew an opera singer once who had an injury to his larynx, and his vocal folds, or vocal cords . . . well, I realize I'm drawing a conclusion here that might not be justified."

"No, Brennan, you're grand," Francis assured him. "That's good information."

"And that's all I have."

"All right, then, we'll let you go. We'll be looking into it."

Brennan had no doubt about that. "All right, lads. I'll leave it in your hands."

Both men thanked him, and he got out of the car. His questioners drove away.

Monty

On Monday there was a break in Monty's tripped-and-fell-in-the-pub case. This was hardly on a par with the fatal injury claim on behalf of the Flanagans or the multi-million-dollar products liability suit that had brought him to Belfast, let alone the murder cases he had tried back home, but Monty had a duty to pursue all the claims that crossed his desk, no matter how humble. And now here was a "without prejudice" offer from the defendant pub owner to pay a cool £650 to the plaintiff who tripped on a loose flagstone in the floor of the darkened pub. "Without prejudice" meant there was no admission of liability that could be used against the defendant in future proceedings if the thing didn't settle. Monty called the client, gave him the facts, and told him the wee packet of money would change hands tomorrow. The client was not impressed, but Monty drove home the fact that he was fortunate to be getting anything at all. And he'd be lucky to get a pint in the pub again. Monty would likely forget all about it by the end of the week.

It was getting dark before he got to the work he really wanted to do: draft the papers for the estate of Eamon Flanagan and his dependents. Winnifred, Kate, Clare, Darren, Dermot, and Timothy Flanagan, the plaintiffs in the lawsuit. The defendant of course was Colman William Davison. Monty had worked with a medical expert to confirm that a front-on strike by a motor vehicle could have caused the injury to Mr. Flanagan's leg and propelled him to his death below the Ammon Road Bridge. He had the evidence of glass in the jeans. Also confirmed were the whereabouts of the insured driver, Davison, so the writ could be served on him and notice given to his insurance company. Once Monty got a response from the solicitor representing the insurer, he would serve the statement of claim on the lawyer and wait to receive a defence. Monty considered which witnesses he would be calling if the matter went to court. His medical expert and the pathologist who prepared the autopsy report, and Vincent McKeever and George Ayles, the auto repair man, for sure. Monty knew there was more to the incident than a guy exceeding the speed limit late at night on a country road. The driver had pulled a knife on McKeever. McKeever would be a reluctant witness, to put it mildly, and Monty would have to issue a subpoena to get him before the court if the case didn't settle.

And then there were the bullet holes in the rear bumper, which put the car in proximity to the shooting of Fritzy O'Dwyer shortly before McKeever encountered the car. And there was Monty's covert operation, the furtive nighttime taxi ride, where he heard of paramilitary and possibly even official involvement in the killing. This meant a whole other can of worms. Monty hoped he would not have to peer down into whatever was writhing around at the bottom of that can, but it might be unavoidable. It might be necessary to involve the Royal Ulster Constabulary, because he might need a police witness to testify about the shooting, to give a context to why Davison might have been in such a hurry that he either failed to see Flanagan on the bridge or saw him but failed to stop after hitting him. There was a whole host of unanswered questions about the events of November 14, 1992, including: what was Colman Davison doing at or near the scene of the crime?

Night had fallen by the time Monty had completed the drafts of his papers and left the office. A couple of other late-working keeners were emerging from the building and he exchanged a few words with them, then headed out to his car. It had started to rain, and his shoes made a squishing sound on the pavement. There weren't many people out and about. It was cold and windy, and a blast of wind blew the rain into his face as he strode along, head down, wishing he had worn a raincoat with a hood. Suddenly, he heard the sound of another pair of feet splashing through the rain behind him. He reached the curb and was about to cross the street when a car came roaring out of the intersection. Monty turned so the wave of water from the wheels wouldn't get him face-on, but the car slowed as it approached him. Thoughtful driver, slowed and veered away to lessen the impact. After it passed, Monty crossed the street. He was in sight of his car now and increased his pace. The footsteps behind him speeded up as well. He turned to look over his shoulder, and a man in a hooded windbreaker closed in on him. Monty backed away and the man put his hands up in the air, as if to say *I'm not armed.* Then he reached up and pulled his hood off. He had dark, neatly combed hair and a muscular build. There was something familiar about him.

"Mr. Collins," the fellow said.

He tried to place the guy. He had seen him recently. Where?

"I have to speak to you."

"You mean you . . ."

"I did, yeah. I waited for you at your office, but there were people around. So I followed you."

"You're familiar. Right. Ronan's party. Band mate with Lorcan."

"Aye."

Monty remembered his name then. "Why didn't you just phone me, Carrick?"

He shook his head. "Is that your car?"

He knew it was Monty's car. He followed as Monty headed towards it. Monty didn't like what was happening here, but he wanted to find out what it was all about. He knew full well that Lorcan Burke was IRA — he had served time for membership — and this fellow likely was as well, but so were half the other people he had met at Ronan's. He wanted to believe there was no reason for anyone in the Burkes' circle of acquaintances to wish him harm. Wanting to believe something didn't make it so, but he would play it by ear and hope he was not making a big mistake by remaining with this person in the darkness of the street. He unlocked his car doors and gestured to the other man to get into the front passenger side. When they were both seated, Carrick pulled out a pack of smokes and offered the pack to Monty. Monty shook his head, and Carrick lit one up for himself.

Carrick got right to the point. "This case you have going against the UDA man. I'm here to warn you to drop it."

Monty felt a chill that had nothing to do with the cold Belfast rain. "And what happens to me if I don't?"

"Nothing."

"Well, then . . ."

"Nothing happens to *you*."

What was he getting at? Was this a threat against Monty's family? Surely not. This guy was a friend of the Burkes. Whatever could be said about the Burkes here in troubled Belfast, they were strong family men. Monty could not imagine any of them threatening harm to someone's wife and children. Would their friends and comrades-in-arms be as sensitive to family sanctity? What did Monty really know of their murky world of warring paramilitaries?

"Nothing happens to you," Carrick repeated. "But something happens to people you know in this city."

"How? What are you saying, Carrick? My case is a hit and run. It occurred right around the time of the shooting of an . . . of a Republican named O'Dwyer. I know that. But the guy I'm taking to court is a member of the Ulster Defence Association. Why would you care what happens to a UDA man? Your people have been at war with the Loyalist paramilitaries for more than twenty-five years."

Carrick's gaze was intense behind the smoke in the car. "There is way more to this than you know, Mr. Collins. Step away from it. Drop it."

"What you have to understand here, Carrick, is that I owe a duty to the family of Eamon Flanagan. Those children and their mother are going through hell right now, and it's not going to get any better for them unless they get compensation for Mr. Flanagan's death, compensation for the loss of his support of the family."

"Maybe something can be done for the family. Money could be found, maybe not in the amounts you have in mind, but —"

"There is only one way for them to get the level of support, the amount of compensation, they need and deserve, and that is through a finding of fault on the part of the defendant driver and a payout by his insurance company."

"All I can do here is urge you, again, to back away from it. For the sake of others who could be hurt . . ."

"If you'd just explain —"

"Including your friend, Father Burke."

"What? You can't be serious. Nothing about this could possibly affect Brennan Burke. It all happened over two years ago."

Monty knew Brennan would not involve himself in any violent activities, so what was Carrick getting at? Then it came to Monty with a pang that Brennan had in fact got involved in something and that Maura had got herself mixed up in it, too. That ridiculous episode when they tarted themselves up like a pair of yokels from the American South and questioned some Loyalist hard-ass in a bar in east Belfast. But that was about what? A bombing that took place back in 1974. How could that be related to the events of November 1992? And they had got away with their little charade, as far as anybody knew. Well, Monty knew it himself. There had been no fallout coming Maura's way, so not likely any for Brennan either.

This fellow Carrick might well have a motive of his own for wanting the events of November 14, 1992, kept under wraps. So Monty was not about to fall for this obvious play on his sympathy, on his friendship with Brennan Burke. Brennan could not conceivably have any connection with the murder of an IRA man more than two years before.

"Carrick . . ."

"There is a whole lot more to this than you know. I'm sorry. Truly. But give it up."

"I don't appreciate you strong-arming me like this, Carrick. I have a client with a righteous case, and I intend to see justice done for them. No matter what."

"You want to tell that to Father Burke when —"

Monty pictured the scene in Loyalist east Belfast. Father Burke, posing as a hick, an anti-Catholic bigot. Him with his doctorate from Rome and his appointment as choirmaster in that holy city. He said to Carrick, "What to tell Father Burke? Tell him to say three Hail Marys and if that doesn't do the trick, call the papal crisis line, one-five-five-five-VATICAN!" Monty imagined Burke making the call, using the southern drawl he had affected as Duane Ballard. He had to smile.

Carrick shot him a look of disgust. He opened the car door, threw his cigarette to the pavement, and ground it out with his heel. Without another word, he pulled the hood up over his head and walked away into the night.

Chapter XXVII

Brennan

It didn't take long for the 'RA to find a suspect to match Brennan's description of the raspy voice. He gave them the information on Saturday morning and on Monday night Brennan was in the car with Cathal and Francis, heading across the city to the east bank of the Lagan. Cathal was the wheelman, Francis was the front seat passenger, and there was a third man present, sitting beside Brennan in the back. It was the fellow who looked like a boxer. He introduced himself as Mick.

"We put some feelers out to our sources," Cathal said, "asking if they know of a Loyalist paramilitary with a raspy voice."

Brennan wondered if there were any dissident Republicans with a voice defect. How could Cathal and his men be so sure it was someone on the other side?

"Could have been any number of the Orange fuckers," Mick replied to Cathal. "Wearing their voices down belting out the 'Famine

Song' over the Lambeg drums in front of Saint Patrick's holy Catholic church on the twelfth of July."

"He's right," agreed Francis, "but we eliminated all of them. Except one."

"Eliminated . . ."

"Not literally, Brennan. Eliminated them from consideration in our search, with one exception. We eventually got a name. Willie John Craig. Vicious wee get, member of the Ulster Red Hand Commando. And connected with the UDA. Took a bullet in the throat two years ago. We had a couple of false starts trying to find the bastard, but we're acting on a good tip right now as to where he is tonight."

"Em, what's going to happen now?" Brennan asked.

Mick answered. "We're going to lift him, engage him in conversation, and you're going to tell us whether we have the right man. I hear you're an expert in singing, choirs, all that, so you know voices, right?"

Brennan allowed as how he did, but . . . "What happens if it's the right man?"

"We'll take things as they come," said Francis.

They drove along the Newtownards Road and then turned into a side street, pulled over, and turned off the engine and the lights. "All right now, Mick," said Francis. "Our man is going to try and lure Craig out of the bar with a promise of a bonnie wee lass who's going to bestow unspeakable pleasures on him in the back seat of this lovemobile. When he opens the door, Mick, you grab him, get one hand over his mouth, the other over his eyes. We can't be sitting here in public view with balaclavas on, so we want him hauled in, his eyes covered. Our contact out there will shut the door. I'll lean over and shove this hood down over his head and push him out of sight before he can register our faces, and away we go."

What in the hell had Brennan got himself in for? How many crimes, how many sins, was he going to be party to before he got out of Belfast? Brennan's misgivings were not lost on Cathal, who looked at him in the rear-view mirror and said, "Keep in mind, Brennan, that this is almost certainly the hateful wee bastard who tried to take Ronan's life."

"Go round the block," Francis said to Cathal. "We can't be seen sitting out here."

Cathal started the car up and drove at normal speed down the street and around a corner. They made this and other journeys for the next ten minutes until Mick whispered. "They're out. There they are."

The car pulled up beside two young men who were lighting up smokes a few feet away from the window of a bar. One of the men was short, wiry, and nervy-looking. The other was tall and fit and had his eyes on the car. He laughed and said something to the smaller fellow and moved towards the rear passenger-side door. The wiry lad looked apprehensive, until his companion gave him a shove and whispered something in his ear, yanking the door open as he did so. Mick reached out and circled his arm around the man's head at the level of his eyes and pulled him inside. There was a muffled cry as Mick covered the fellow's mouth. The man outside slammed the door shut and took off at a clip. Francis leaned over from the front seat and tried to get a black hood onto the captive's head, but the captive was surprisingly strong for his size, and he kicked out at Mick and bashed the side window with his fist. Mick took hold of the hood and got it on him, but the captured man lurched out of his grasp and tried to lift the hood. Brennan partially rose from his seat and grabbed the man's two arms, wrenching them behind his back. The man cried out in pain. Brennan held him until Mick got a good grip on him, shoving him down to the floor and holding him there.

By this time, Cathal had manoeuvred the car through a number of twists and turns, and it looked to Brennan as if they were heading to north Belfast. Francis spoke down to the man pinned across the floor of the back seat. "Willie John Craig. Tell us now, how much did that pimp take off you for the wee hoor you were planning to meet in the back seat here?"

What? Brennan wondered. Of all things . . .

"What hoor? I didn't give him nothing. He just asked me for a fag, so I lit one up for him. Let me the fuck out of here!"

Ah. Just a question to get him talking. And, yes, Brennan realized with a shiver, this was the same voice he had heard as he knelt to tend to Ronan. No room for doubt. He caught Cathal's eye in the rearview and nodded his head.

Cathal reached over to the stereo and put on a little mood music, the Wolfe Tones' rousing version of "Rifles of the IRA."

"Where are youse taking me?" The voice was raspy, damaged, and terrified. "I didn't do nothing. Let me out!"

"Don't be wasting your breath," Mick said to him. "You'll be needin' it later."

"You're going to regret this. They'll be out looking for me."

"Well, they won't find you. Not where you're going."

"What do youse want?"

Craig's fear was palpable. You could smell it off him. Little wonder.

Francis turned and addressed Brennan without using his name. "We'll be dropping you off before we have our meeting with this fella."

No, Brennan was not going to leave them to it, not going to beg off and pretend he didn't know someone was going to face interrogation at the hands of the IRA. God knows Brennan did not want any part of it, but to weasel out of it would not absolve him of responsibility now that he had knowledge of the plan and had in fact become a party to it.

"No."

"Yes, we'll take you to —"

"I said no."

Francis gave him a long look, caught Cathal's eye, and shrugged, and he said no more on the subject.

They were soon out in the country. Brennan did not know where. Wind whistled through the trees, and clouds scudded past a pale half-moon. Cathal turned into a rutted road, and the car rattled along until it came to a house that sat in dark isolation. There was a barn in an advanced state of dilapidation. What was going to happen here?

Nobody said a word, but Francis got out of the car and waited for Mick to haul the prisoner out into the farmyard. The two of them hustled him up to the door. It was unlocked. Cathal and Brennan followed the other three inside. Brennan looked out the kitchen window and spotted another car sitting at the side of the house. He heard something moving below them, in the basement. Another sound, of a chair being moved. Whoever it was, he was making no effort to stay under the radar.

The hooded man, by this time, was trembling. Mick opened a drawer and took out a length of rope, which he used to tie Craig's hands behind his back.

"Down the stairs with you," said Francis. "We've some questions for you."

There was a whimper of fear from their captive. Cathal grasped one arm, Francis the other, and they manoeuvred him down a set of stairs.

Mick reached over and closed the door. "Me and you will wait upstairs," he said to Brennan.

"What are they going to do?" Brennan demanded to know.

And, he wondered, why is the muscle — Mick the boxer — staying up here? Why is it Cathal and Francis who will be handling the interrogation? Who else is down there?

"Come on upstairs with me now, Brennan," Mick said. Brennan hesitated, looking at the basement door. Mick shook his head. "Come on now."

Brennan followed him along a short hallway and then up to the second floor. Mick led him into a room that had a sofa, two armchairs, a phone on a table, and a television set. Mick switched on the TV and found a replay of a hurling match played earlier that day between Wexford and Waterford.

"Look in the press there, Brennan. There should be a bottle inside."

Brennan went over to a cabinet set above the table and opened the door. There were bottles of Jameson and Powers whiskey and a package of plastic cups. He poured himself a Jameson and looked questioningly at Mick. "A drop of the Powers for me." He filled a glass for the man and handed it to him. They both sat facing the hurling match.

Brennan was jolted in his chair by the sound of a shout two floors down. Mick affected to ignore it and addressed the TV screen. "Have ye lost the plot entirely there, Griffin?"

"What are they going to do to that man, Mick?"

"Not what that man was going to do to Ronan."

The hurling match ground on, punctuated by the occasional raised voices from the basement of the farmhouse. Brennan tried to imagine the finely dressed Francis and the gentlemanly Cathal interrogating a suspect; he did not want to dwell on the image. Brennan and his companion had been watching the hurling for just over twenty minutes when Brennan heard a mechanical whirring sound from below. He could not place it. Some kind of machinery. Then he heard an ungodly scream. He bolted from his seat.

"Brennan, sut dyne."

"What's going on? The man is screaming."

"They're throwing a scare into him, I expect. Nothing to worry about."

"Nothing to worry about?! A scream of sheer terror and the sound of a . . ." He had it then. An electric drill. Sweet suffering Jesus! Surely they're not . . . Then came a scream of agony, the like of which Brennan had never heard in his life. "I'm going down there! This has to stop!"

"You're not going anywhere, Brennan."

Brennan got up and Mick jumped up and blocked him. "I said I'm going down there. I will not be party to the torture of a man, no matter what he's done."

"Sit down on that fucking chair, Brennan. You had your chance to be let out of the car. Now you're here, and you're here for the duration."

"Fuck you! Get out of my way." He grabbed Mick by the shoulders and made to shove him aside, but Mick broke free, reached into his pocket, and Brennan was suddenly looking into the barrel of a gun.

The house erupted in screams of pain and the sounds of someone retching. Brennan thought he was going to be sick on the floor, just from the sound of it. He could hear the whirring of the drill again, on and off, on and off. The sounds of thumping and screeches that sounded more animal than human. This is what we are reduced to in the face of hideous pain.

"Get that gun out of my face. I'm going down there and putting a stop to that. What kind of men are you?"

Mick lifted the gun with both hands and pointed it at Brennan. "If you step outside this room, Father Burke, I will have no choice but to use this to make sure you can't move. There is nothing you can do to save that murdering Orange bastard downstairs."

Brennan understood. There was nothing he could do to help the victim. He could make a pointless, meaningless gesture of defiance here and be gravely wounded or die a pointless death. It would do nothing to change the unspeakable events unfolding in the basement of the house. If he thought he could make a difference, he would defy his captor and try to leave. But it would make no difference at all. There was nothing he could do. Now he knew why the muscle was assigned to stay with him. He felt like a hollow man sitting there, a man without substance.

Then he was jolted by the sound of a gunshot; it reverberated throughout the house. It was followed by a crashing sound and then utter stillness. Brennan glared at the man opposite him; Mick avoided his eyes.

A few minutes later, Brennan heard footsteps on the stairs. Cathal entered the room looking as if he didn't have a care in the world. He took the seat facing Brennan and Mick and lit up a cigarette. He offered the pack to Brennan, who didn't acknowledge him.

"What did he say?" Mick asked Cathal.

"Good soldier that he was, he refused to give us anything. He insisted he wasn't anywhere near the Banned Flag on the night of March the eighteenth. And suggested that maybe we should be looking out our own back window for whoever tried to kill the peacemaker and the peace process. I took issue with that and told him our back garden was clean. And that we hadn't just gone out looking for Loyalist pricks at random, that we knew it was him and that things would go a lot easier for him if he just admitted it now, rather than admitting it later — which he inevitably would — after a whole lot of aggravation. He tried to keep up the defiance but he was looking a little shaky at this point."

As well he might, Brennan thought.

"I don't know if you've ever heard the way a grown man screams when the whirring point of an electric drill penetrates a part of his body."

"For the love of God! How can you live with yourself?"

"Brennan, he's the bastard who pulled the trigger on Ronan and that poor young barman, Jimmy. Either of them could have been left dead or crippled for life. Now, as I was saying, even the sound of a power drill coming towards you is enough to give you the squitters in your brand new kacks. But when it grinds into your flesh —"

"God forgive you! Because I certainly —"

Cathal spoke over him. "The sounds of a man suffering that kind of horrendous pain are torture enough. It's torture even to hear it. He no longer sounds like a human being. He is reduced to the state of a mindless animal, bellowing and screaming and crying for his mammy and retching and boaking up all over himself."

"Are you enjoying this, Cathal? How could you do that to a person, no matter who he is, no matter what he's done?"

Brennan thought he himself was going to boak up all over the place. The scene he had just heard described was so horrible, so brutish, that he could not believe he was sitting in the same room as a man who could blithely commit such an atrocity upon another human being. He made no effort to hide his revulsion.

"We had him well terrorized. And he gave us what we wanted."

Who would not, under such duress?

"He admitted being the gunman."

Mick asked, "Who tipped him off that Ronan was in the Banned Flag that night?"

"He told us the UDA have a fella watching that part of the Falls Road."

"They've the entire British Army watching it!"

"Well, they've a man of their own on the job, as well."

"Who?"

"He doesn't know. Under the circumstances, I think he'd have coughed up the name if he had it. We'll find the wee spy ourselves. He operates out of one of the buildings with a view of the Flag. Rings his masters in the Shankill if anyone of interest comes by."

"They'll pull the fella out of there now."

"We'll be checking into that. Now the other main point of interest was the motive for the hit on Ronan. Wait till Ronan hears this."

"What?" Mick demanded.

"The man who ordered the execution of Ronan Burke was one of his fellow peacemakers, one of his colleagues round the table during the talks."

"Who?"

"Our witness claimed he didn't know which one, Old Saint Nick or John the Baptist. But something he let slip later in the conversation points to it being the Baptist."

Brennan broke his silence then, in spite of himself. In spite of his question giving legitimacy to the way the information was obtained. "So, it was to derail the peace process after all. They sit at the table with Ronan and say they want the violence to stop, and behind the scenes they're planning to take him out and abort the whole process."

"No, that wasn't it."

"No? What do you mean?"

"It was about Dublin and Monaghan."

"Jesus!"

"They were desperate to stop anything that might force the hand of the peelers and open the whole thing up again. Somehow they got wind of the fact that there's been some movement with this, and they know that with Ronan's personality and popularity behind it, it might not go away this time. And here's what was especially intriguing about the information Craig gave up. In his words, 'It wasn't supposed to . . . He's not a mass murderer, him a minister in the church! He said it himself: he never thought there was going to be all those people killed!' We happen to know it was John the Baptist who, in what he thought was a private conversation, said that."

"So," Brennan said, seeking clarification, "this Craig was quoting a minister of the church . . . and the man said he had never expected all those deaths to come from the Dublin and Monaghan bombings. In other words, he knew in advance about the plan to send car bombs into those two cities in the Irish Republic."

"Yeah."

"God almighty. Ronan always said there was collusion with the security forces. Now we've got churchmen in on it."

"You got it."

"So," Brennan said, bringing himself back to the present, "you've succeeded in extracting this information from young Craig. Now, what are you going to do with the body?"

"Body?" Cathal laughed. "We'll be releasing him into the wild."

"I can't find anything humorous in this, Cathal or whatever your real name is."

"Rest easy, Father. We'll be releasing him unharmed."

Brennan rocketed out of his seat and stood over Cathal. "Unharmed! You just told us you tortured the man with an electric drill!"

"I may have left you with that impression. But in fact, aside from some initial pushing and shoving, we didn't lay a hand on him, let alone go at him with a drill or any other such implement."

"But you just described the torture of a fellow human being.

Whatever he had done, if you lower yourself to that level, then you are no better than —"

"Ah, but I am better than that, Father. There's no denying that some of our people have done ferocious things to punish or extract information about traitors in our ranks, but nothing like that has ever been done by my men or by me. As for young Craig, we've allowed him to live. Live in fear, for definite, because he knows we can come for him any time. But we do not want a murder that could be traced back to us, so we're letting him go. He has served our purposes. And —" he held up a hand to ward off whatever Brennan was about to say next "— we did not harm him at all during the interrogation. What I referred to in my description of the events in this house tonight was the *sound* of someone screaming. And that's what our boy was subjected to. We told Craig we had picked up one of his fellow paramilitaries, and we had him in an adjoining room, and he was giving us a lot of very interesting information. And sure enough we did have a lad in the adjoining room, a dedicated young Republican. And that young fellow should be given an award for his performance. He could have a career on stage or screen. He had an electric drill in there with him, and he turned it on, so Craig could hear it. Then our performer began screaming and crying, and making the most terrifying sounds you could ever imagine coming from man or animal. Several long minutes of listening to that was enough to make our witness tell us everything we wanted to know. Hell, I was ready to tell *him* anything he'd want to know about *our* side. I wouldn't have been able to hold out against that level of terror myself. So, as they say in the films, nobody was harmed in the filming of these scenes."

Brennan was all but weeping with relief. It was psychological torture, undoubtedly, but it was an immense relief to learn that the person who had tried to kill Ronan would walk away unscathed. Of course, now Ronan would have to come to terms with what Brennan had just learned: one or more of his partners in the peace process had

advance knowledge of the 1974 bombings and was prepared to kill —
to kill Ronan — to cover it up.

"And by the way, Brennan," said Mick, turning to face him, "I was
never going to shoot you, no matter what you did. But we knew you
would try to stop what was going on, and we didn't want you, well,
walking onstage and interrupting the play."

"All right, lads, let's get rolling," Cathal said and walked out of the
room, followed by Mick and Brennan.

When they got down to the kitchen, Francis was standing in the
middle of the room with his hands like vises gripping the arms of the
captive. Craig was still hooded but there was no sign of injury.

"*Amach leat*," Francis said to him. Out with you. He propelled
him out the door. He and Mick eased the man into the back seat.
Everyone else got in, and Cathal started the engine. Brennan heard
the sound of a door being closed and looked back to see a man leaving
the farmhouse. Brennan had never seen him before. He walked
towards the other car in the yard and got in.

No one spoke on the drive back into Belfast. Somewhere on the
east side of the city, Cathal turned into a dark side street and pulled
over. Mick opened the door and helped the captive out. He untied
Craig's hands. Francis leaned out the car window and said, just in
case a warning was still necessary, "You're alive because we let you live.
You'll stay alive as long as we allow you to go on living. Remember
that and govern yourself accordingly."

Thank Christ, if Christ was still listening, that they had let the
man live, in spite of what he had done. Craig yanked the hood off
his head and took off like a bat released from hell, like a still-healthy
young man. He did not look back.

Chapter XXVIII

Brennan

The morning after the interrogation, Brennan awoke with a fierce need to get away from Belfast. He knew just where to go. After a couple of phone calls that Tuesday to make arrangements, he scribbled a note to Ronan and Gráinne, packed his things, and headed for the train station. It would be a long journey, not by North American standards but certainly by Irish standards, from the North of Ireland to the southern tip of the island. He took the train from Belfast to Dublin and another from Dublin to Waterford; he then boarded a bus to Dungarvan and hired a taxi to take him to Cappoquin. He gazed through the cab window at the Knockmealdown Mountains. Dominating the slope above him was the tower of a grey stone Gothic Revival church. As the car climbed the hill, the other stone buildings came into view.

He would be spending the next couple of weeks in silence and prayer at the Cistercian abbey of Mount Melleray in County Waterford.

Brennan could feel the tension melting away as he shook hands with the guest master and was welcomed into the contemplative community of monks. The serenity of the interior of the church, the sublime chanting of the Divine Office, the stillness outside — all this combined to provide him with the peace, rest, and spiritual renewal he sorely needed after the past tumultuous weeks in Belfast. After witnessing the attempt on his cousin's life, and having a hand in the ghastly interrogation of the suspect, this was exactly the way to restore himself physically and mentally for the welcome challenge ahead of him in Rome, at the church of Sancta Maria Regina Coeli, Mary Queen of Heaven. Father Burke sent a fervent prayer of thanks to the God of love and mercy for delivering him from the turmoil and danger of Belfast, and he prayed for those who would know no rest until the much-needed peace was established. Yes, he thought in gratitude, this was the way to glide gently to the end of his sojourn in Ireland.

Monty

Monty would have to tell Brennan about his night-time encounter with Carrick in the car park, but that would have to wait. He had received a voice message from Brennan saying, with no detectable trace of irony in his voice, that he was entering a monastery and he would be out of touch for a while. He didn't know how long. Well, Monty couldn't blame Brennan for getting out of Belfast. But Brennan wasn't the only one who was having a break. Monty and Maura had come up with a half-formed plan to spend some time travelling around the country south of the border. Easter was coming, and Maura and Normie both had holidays. By bringing along a box of documents and a Dictaphone, Monty was able to get away for a few days with the family. So a little tour of the Irish Republic ("such as it is at this moment in history," his Burkean acquaintances would surely add) would be just the thing.

But first he had a job to do. As soon as he got to the office on Tuesday morning, he arranged to have the writ served and notice given to the insurance company in the Flanagan case. This would set in motion the lawsuit over the hit and run. He beamed up a prayer of thanks that Colman Davison had had insurance on his car at the time of the incident. Davison had fourteen days to issue a memorandum of appearance, stating that he would be defending the claim. Monty assumed that Davison, or his solicitor, would get his papers in on time, in order to avoid a summary judgment being entered against him. As soon as Monty saw the memorandum, he would have his statement of claim ready to go.

After sending out the initial paperwork — firing the first shot, as it were — Monty turned his attention to the bigger picture, the situation surrounding him in Belfast. In the wake of the "Framework for Agreement," the news was filled with talk of peace in the war-ravaged North of Ireland. Voices that formerly thundered across the sectarian chasm, like that of Old Saint Nick Sproule and John the Baptist Geddes from the Loyalist side and, well, people Monty had met in the company of Ronan Burke from the Republican side, were speaking in courteous and cautious tones about coming to an accommodation. There was a peace rally scheduled that evening in the gymnasium of a west Belfast school, and Ronan would be giving a speech, the first since his injury. It was just getting underway when Monty arrived, and there was standing room only at the back of the gym. Security was tight all around the gathering, and Monty noticed that Carrick was part of the security detail. But the mood was upbeat.

A good-looking blond fellow in his thirties stepped out of the wings and took centre stage and was greeted with expressions of surprise and enthusiastic applause. Two young girls near Monty looked at each other, eyes wide, and one said, "Did ye know he was comin'?"

Her friend shook her head. "Nobody did!"

The man gave a warm and witty introduction to Ronan, which was met with more applause and roars of approval. Ronan got up to speak, and there was an anxious moment when he looked as if he were going to fall. He put his hand on the back of a chair to steady himself and then walked to the microphone and greeted the crowd. "Thank you, Bertie." Ronan looked out at the audience and said, "Sorry, folks. He's not going to be speaking my lines." And everybody laughed.

Monty leaned towards two men standing nearby and said, "Excuse me. Who was that?"

"Ah, you're not from here. America?"

"Canada."

"Toronto?"

"No, about an eighteen-hour drive from there."

"Whoa! Right, big country. Anyway, that's Bertie Breannacht. You may have seen him in the fillums. Ronan's slagging him about being the stand-in for Gerry Adams."

"Doesn't look much like him!"

"No, no, he'd read out Gerry's words when Gerry's voice was banned."

"Banned?"

"Aye, they only lifted the ban a few months ago, after the ceasefire."

Monty had heard about media censorship here and in England as well, but he had obviously missed the details. "What's the story? I hope you'll excuse my ignorance."

"Sure you're grand. They had a ban on the radio and television. Wouldn't let certain people's voices be broadcast. So for some, they brought in actors to say their words. Like Breannacht there. The ban covered a dozen or so groups, including Loyalist paramilitaries, but nobody was fooled by that. The real targets were Republicans. The Shinners. The Provos. That's who they were really after."

Monty felt as if he had lost his bearings. "Who placed the ban on all these groups? When?"

"It was the Iron Lady and her government who put the ban in place, back in 1988. Thatcher. It covered all of the U.K., and the radio and television had no choice but to obey it. You'd not be hearing Sinn Féin, Gerry Adams, Martin McGuinness."

Up on the stage, Ronan was saying kind words about the other luminaries involved in the peace process. Monty said to the man beside him, "But Adams is the president of Sinn Féin, a political party with elected members. It's their job to speak, even when it's not election time. Anyone who doesn't agree — and their numbers are legion! — talks back to him. It's . . ." It was unthinkable that a political party back home in Canada would be forbidden to speak.

"They really had it in for Gerry. Even before the ban, when the BBC was still allowed to interview him, the reporters were instructed to make sure they sounded hostile!"

"Sounds positively Stalinist."

"But it wasn't just here. They were banned in the Free State, too."

"The Republic of Ireland went along with Thatcher on this?"

"They did it first."

Monty shook his head and turned his attention to Ronan's talk. He had just asked Gráinne to stand, which she did with good grace, and he thanked her for her support, political and personal, over the years. "And I wasn't always the easiest man to live with. I was an awful bollocks with drink in me. But I'm trying to be a wee bit more civilized now!" This was met by gentle laughter around the room. He then turned to the documents that had been released on February 22, the framework that had been hammered out by the Irish and British governments. The documents spoke of a permanent end to violence; they promoted forbearance and reconciliation. The acknowledged differences among the various traditions were to be negotiated exclusively through peaceful political means. There was talk of a new assembly.

One man called out, "You'll have my vote, Ronan!" And this was greeted with another round of applause. If a representative assembly could be created in this battle-scarred little territory and if this audience was any indication, Ronan Burke would be one of the front-runners in the first election.

When it was over, and everyone was filing out, Monty heard a clacking noise and turned to see a trainload of little kids coming towards him. A clacking of the train wheels and the "Choo-choo get out of the way, youse!" from the children. It was in fact a wheeled trolley, the kind of thing you'd use to move a supply of books from place to place in a library. Pushing this conveyance was none other than Tomás Burke, with a little kid's engineer cap on and a repertoire of train sounds to complete the picture.

A little boy turned to a much smaller girl and said, "Your da's name is Thomas so he's Thomas the Tank Engine!"

"Nah, I'm just Tom the *Caboose*!" The way he said it made it the funniest-sounding word the children had ever heard. They squealed with delight and repeated it over and over, "Caboose! Caboose!" then collapsed into fits of laughter.

"What are youse blackguardin' me about, ye wee skitters? Caboose just means the train's bum! Nothing funny about that!"

In case there was a child so young that he or she had not yet had the word "bum" added to his or her vocabulary, the oldest boy on the train made sure there was no misunderstanding. He bent over and pointed to his own rear end, and this set them off in hysterics again. When the train pulled into the station, Tom gently lifted the children off one by one, whispering to each that he or she was going to be the *caboose* from now on. So, even as they grumbled about the journey ending, they couldn't help dissolving into giggles. Tom put two fingers in his mouth and emitted a loud whistle, which brought the parents around to collect the passengers. He then departed the station with two dark-haired little kids, a girl and a boy, one hoisted up on each shoulder. Monty had seen them before: Aoife's kids, Tom's stepchildren.

Monty gave a moment's consideration to approaching Tom and hinting around about the warning delivered by the family friend, Carrick. But this was not the time; he was not going to interrupt the children's fun. And he wasn't about to approach Ronan himself to fish for information, not at this celebration of Ronan's recovery from an attempt on his life. If there was nothing to Carrick's insinuation, Tom or Ronan would wonder what Monty had been smoking. If, on the other hand, the family knew something about the events of November 1992, they would hardly open up to Monty about it. So that left Carrick. As much as Monty dreaded bringing the matter up again with this rather dubious individual, he didn't see any alternative. He walked to the back of the room where Carrick was standing watch. Without preamble, Monty said, "I'd like some clarification about that warning you gave me, Carrick."

Carrick looked around him, then leaned in and said, "I'm trying to protect people, not inform on them."

"But you mentioned Brennan. That makes no —"

"I haven't seen him. If you're in touch with him, tell him to pack up and get the first flight out."

"Out of where?"

"Off this island. Easy enough for him, maybe not so easy for somebody else."

"But —"

Carrick looked past Monty to the door and raised a finger as if to say, "Just one second." To Monty all he said was, "I've work to do here."

Monty shook his head as he walked away. What is going on here? Brennan should flee the jurisdiction? He's already south of the border, in the Republic. And who did Carrick mean by somebody else? Maura? Is that what he meant, that he knows she's tied to work, and our daughter is in school in Dublin? Does he know all that? But there are extradition treaties, so a flight from the jurisdiction would be no guarantee . . . And anyway, Maura and Brennan didn't do anything illegal, so this wouldn't be a case of fleeing the law. Had their identities been revealed? Were they in danger from Loyalist paramilitaries? From people involved in those bombings over twenty years ago?

Chapter XXIX

Monty

Monty made an effort to put his misgivings aside, as he and Maura carried through with the plan to enjoy some holiday time in the Republic. They did not neglect their Easter duties, at least not entirely, and attended Easter Sunday Mass at Saint Fin Barre's Cathedral in Cork City. And the Easter Bunny found them, to the delight of little Dominic and his older sister, who did nothing to discourage her little brother's belief in the altruistic and indefatigable bunny rabbit. And there was something else about the trip, too, above and beyond the Easter egg hunt in the hotel room and the Easter chocolate binge. Brennan Burke had been trying for years to light a fire under Monty, figuratively speaking, to get him to look into the Irish side of his heritage. After touring various Michael Collins sites in Cork and in Clonakilty, and enjoying a pint in the Four Alls in Sam's Cross — the pub where the Big Fella drank — Monty was keen to establish some kind of link, however tenuous, with the Collins family of West Cork. He would certainly be investigating the matter. From County Cork, he and the family made their way up through the middle of the country, through counties Tipperary, Laois, Kildare, and on to Dublin, delighting the kids — and not just the kids — with stops at numerous castles along the way. Some were in ruins, some had been restored, all were standing wonders of the medieval age.

Normie, as always, had a plan. "We'll move here, Daddy, and buy one of those castles and put the stones back up on it, fix it all up, and live in it, and invite everybody we know to come and stay with us. Right, Dominic?"

"Yeah! Live in a castle!"

"There's one right in Dublin," Normie said. "We've been to it loads of times."

"We go there!" her brother boasted. "It's up the hill!"

They eventually arrived in Dublin, north side, not castle side, and Monty stayed on for a while before returning to Belfast. And now was the time for the questions he had put off during the family trip. He steered the conversation in the direction he wanted it to go, hoping not to raise any alarms in doing so. "I wonder how Brennan is getting along in the monastery."

Maura snickered at that. "Him, of all people, living as a monk!"

"Let's hope it's one of the monasteries where they make their own brand of liquor."

"It is now, I'll bet."

"And maybe he's slipping in some country and western hurtin' tunes along with the Gregorian chant."

"Somehow I doubt it."

"I can't believe you two went off and did that Ruby and Duane routine in east Belfast."

"Neither can I. It was a little unnerving but we enjoyed the comedy of it."

"But you could have been dragged out of there and never seen again, if any of those guys had caught on. That's a Loyalist heartland."

"Yeah, but nobody twigged to us. We pulled it off. I could be looking at a new career. Undercover spy with MI5. Or country music gal with my own TV show."

"Did anyone seem suspicious of you, though? Seriously."

"Not at all. You know how you can feel that something is off? There was nothing like that. Nobody in the Iron Will bar had a clue that we weren't a pair of bumpkins from Kentucky. I'm sure they've seen gauche tourists before."

"Any police on the scene?"

"Police? What do you mean?"

"Just wondered if there were any patrols or coppers stopping in for a wee dram."

"And if there were, so what? It's not illegal to dress up like yokels and talk in a matching dialect. But there weren't any cops on the scene. Why are you asking about this?"

"Well, you were in there talking to a man who planted a car bomb and killed and injured a great many people. That caused me some concern."

"He had no idea what we were up to, Monty, and neither did anybody else. Get it out of your head."

She was right. If Carrick thought there would be any fallout from that incident, his worries were groundless. Monty did not see how it could rebound on Brennan or anyone else. And the scheme had been designed to ferret out information about bomb attacks that occurred twenty-one years ago. It had no relation, as far as Monty could see, to the events of November 1992.

Monty was back in the office on the Tuesday after Easter and, just as he was about to leave at the end of the day, he received the memorandum of appearance from the solicitor representing Colman Davison's insurer. Monty had his statement of claim all ready to go. But warning bells were ringing in the back of his mind, and he formed a picture of Carrick materializing out of the mist with a set of bells in his hand. Monty did not quite know what to make of Carrick. But he had questioned Maura nonetheless and had been reassured by her answers.

He knew he owed it to Brennan to check with him as well. He tried to call him at Ronan's place, in case he had found monastic life a wee bit too quiet and had come back to Belfast. The ostensible reason for the call would be Monty's acknowledgement that he had finally seen the light and would be tracing his Collins genealogy. But Brennan had not yet emerged from seclusion. He asked Ronan for the phone number of the abbey in County Waterford, and he made the call. A kindly sounding man told him to hold the line whilst he went in search of Father Burke. Brennan's voice betrayed concern when he came on the phone.

"Everything's fine, Brennan, and I'm sorry to interrupt your serenity there."

"No worries, Montague. What can I do for you?"

"We were in County Cork and I traced my lineage back to a night of drinking and carousing on the part of Michael Collins. There was a blond involved and a secret marriage."

"Sure, isn't that always the way?"

"Just wanted you to know, so you could say 'I told you so.'"

"Consider it said."

"And while I have you here I just wanted to ask you something." Monty didn't care to mention that Carrick had followed him from work one night and issued a bizarre warning about Brennan, given that Monty had — not unwisely, he hoped — laughed it off. But he would go about it another way. "Have you any concerns, Brennan, relating to my lawsuit on behalf of the Flanagans?"

"What do you mean?"

"Just, is there anything you can think of about my case that, well, could cause problems?"

"Well, I wasn't driving the car. It happened long before I arrived here." There was a slight pause and then, "You don't have anyone else by the name of Burke in your claim, do you?"

"No. Far from it."

"Well, then, how could there be a problem?"

"There couldn't. I'm just checking all angles. Never know in Belfast!"

"True enough."

Monty steered the talk to lighter fare after that, and they shared a few laughs. Then, "All right, I'll let you go. How long do you expect to be cloistered down there?"

"I don't know. It's so peaceful I may never emerge at all."

"I hear ya."

The conversation left Monty with a feeling of relief. But, he knew, his suit on behalf of the Flanagan family had to go ahead no matter what. The family deserved justice, and he would do his utmost to make sure they got it. Still, it was good to know there was nothing behind the strange encounters with Carrick.

He read over his statement of claim for the Flanagans one last time and headed home.

First thing the next morning, Monty arranged to have the statement of claim served on the other side. Less than a week later, he received the defence. A circumstance in the Flanagans' favour was that Davison's insurer was a relatively new company, started up in London in 1990 and aggressively pursuing new business. The company was billing itself as a caring collective of insurance professionals who would expedite the paperwork and pay out claims without delay. How long the good feeling and timely payments would last was another question but, while the company was still in the process of attracting clients away from the older, established insurers, this would work to the Flanagans' advantage.

The statement of defence drafted by the defendant's solicitor was a masterpiece of denial, but that was not unusual. Monty himself used the same boilerplate phrases, bits of text that were used over and over again, in his defences at home.

> The defendant denies that he struck the deceased with his motor car as alleged in the statement of claim or at all.
>
> The defendant denies that he was in the area of the Ammon Road or the Ammon Road Bridge as alleged in the statement of claim or at all.
>
> Further, or in the alternative, if the defendant was present in the said area on the date in question, which is not admitted but specifically denied, he was in the area under duress and not of his own free will.
>
> Save as hereinbefore specifically admitted, the defendant denies each and every allegation contained in the statement of claim as though the same were herein set out and traversed seriatim.

Yes, just about what Monty himself would write if he were representing the defendant. But he was interested in the part that said "under duress and not of his own free will." Was this more boilerplate, or was Davison going to claim he had been forced to go to the Ammon Road that night?

The following day he decided to find out. He called the defendant's solicitor, and they set up a meeting in Monty's office. Royden Barrett was tall, slim, and white-haired. They shook hands, and the two sat down at Monty's desk. They exchanged a bit of small talk and then Monty got down to business. "Royden, I was interested to read in your pleadings that Mr. Davison claims to have been under duress on the night of the incident. Yet I know from witnesses that he was alone in the car."

It was clear to Monty that if Davison was pleading duress, he had admitted to his lawyer that he was on the scene that night.

Barrett asked, "If he was out there, alone, who are you saying is your witness?"

"I have spoken to a man who was present on the Ammon Road that night and saw Davison in the car." He wasn't about to add, not yet at least, that Davison had pulled a knife on Vincent McKeever. He didn't know where his information might lead, so for now he wanted to keep it to himself.

Barrett replied, "I'm not at liberty to say any more right now, except to tell you we will be issuing third-party pleadings in this matter."

Well now! This meant they would be making a claim against somebody else, to try and shift the blame on to that other person or persons. Who was the third party against whom Davison would be making a claim? He was obviously taking the position that someone else was responsible for what happened on the road that night. Be that as it may, it was Monty's task to hold Davison responsible and extract payment from his insurance company for the damages sustained by the Flanagan children. If Davison hoped to recoup some of that from another party, good luck to him, but Monty's interest was in the impact of Davison's car on Eamon Flanagan's leg. He outlined for Royden Barrett the evidence from the doctor, the pathologist, and the auto repair man, linking the injury and death of Mr. Flanagan to Davison's actions behind the wheel. He also described as eloquently as he could the Flanagan children, their personalities, their grief over the loss of their father, the frightening place where they had been forced to live, Winnie's depression, Katie's dashed hopes of becoming a solicitor, her uncomplaining acceptance of her role in helping to raise four younger children.

Monty was laying it on thick about Katie and her family, and both of them knew it, but there was no denying the fact that Davison had brought all this down on the family by his reckless driving, regardless of whatever had set him hightailing it down the Ammon Road in the middle of the night. Recently there had been a story in the press and on television about a family in Coleraine who had been burnt out of their home. It had not been a criminal attack but an electrical fire or something of the kind, and their insurance company was, so far, denying the claim, leaving the parents and the three children homeless. The negative publicity would not have been lost on the insurance industry. And it would be a boon to a new company portraying itself as a new kind of insurer. Accepting liability and lifting the Flanagan family out of poverty would be good for business. The two lawyers talked for a while longer, and then Barrett left, saying he would be in touch.

Brennan

Brennan found the periods of solitude and the times of companionship with the monks at Mount Melleray so peaceful, so spiritually rewarding, that he felt like a new man, a new priest, in the mountain sanctuary overlooking Cappoquin, County Waterford. There are no grounds theologically or geographically, of course, for feeling oneself closer to God up on a mountain. But the profound silence he found there brought him to an almost mystical state of union with the Absolute, the omnipotent, all-loving God. This feeling intensified when he said or attended Mass, and the lovely interior of the church resounded with the chanting of the ancient tones. He recalled a saying he had heard years ago: "If you have lived your life without touching the sacred, you have done nothing." On a more earthly plane, he found friendship, intellectual stimulation, and a surprising (to him) amount of wit and humour among the men who had retreated from the world to live and pray in the abbey.

True, he'd had a moment of unease following that call from Monty. What had Monty been talking about? He wouldn't know

— thank God! — about the gun fiasco at the church. The farce at Saint Matthew's arose out of the shooting of an innocent backpacker from the Netherlands. It had nothing to do with the Flanagans or their father being hit by a car.

But tranquility soon reigned again. So he found himself making one excuse after another to delay his return to the turbulence of Belfast. That didn't mean he wouldn't leave his monastic devotions for a little trip to Dublin. After putting off his brothers Patrick and Terry earlier in the spring, telling them that Ronan would be more receptive to visitors after a bit more healing, he now welcomed his brothers' offers to fly over from New York and enjoy a quick visit with Brennan in the South and Ronan in the North. He rang his sister Molly in London and beckoned her over again, too. They all planned to start off in Dublin, so they agreed to an early evening get-together at the family bar, Christy Burke's.

But Brennan didn't wait till evening to come to the city. He had another plan for the afternoon. He took the train from Waterford to Heuston station in Dublin, and then caught a bus through the city centre and across the Grand Canal to the Rathmines Road. His first stop was a large classical stone building with columns and a stately green copper dome. Brennan, like so many other Catholics in Ireland — even those who were lapsed — automatically made the sign of the cross when he came even with the church. He smiled as he read the familiar inscription: *Sub. Invoc. Mariae Immaculatae Refugii Peccatorum.* This was the church of Mary Immaculate, Refuge of Sinners. Brennan's mother, Teresa, had made much of the name when she uprooted the family from their former home close — too close, in his mother's estimation — to Christy Burke's bar on the north side of the city and planted them here on the south side in a house identical to their old one. The move was made when Brennan was not much more than a toddler and his father was serving a sentence in Mountjoy Prison, not far from the pub and the old house. Brennan entered the church and admired its bright, elaborately carved interior and arched ceiling over the altar. He knelt and said a prayer for Ronan and Tomás and for the families who had been devastated when the cars blew apart on the streets of Dublin and Monaghan.

A few doors away from the church was his own door, or that which had enclosed his early life in Rathmines. And three houses up from that was the Healeys' place. Both were Georgian houses with demilune fanlights above their yellow doors, their brick exteriors bathed in the glow of the springtime sun. There was nothing unusual about visiting his old neighbourhood, and nothing unusual about calling in to see his old neighbours. But this time his visit to the Healey family would be charged with a significance that Brennan would have to keep to himself. He did not want to get their hopes up about a possible arrest and prosecution of one of the Dublin bombers, when there was so much that could go wrong. He lifted the brass knocker and rapped on the Healeys' front door.

Margaret Healey was short, thin, and tired-looking. It took a couple of seconds before she recognized the man on her doorstep. Then her eyes widened in surprise. "Brennan! Come in, come in. Isn't this grand now? Come in. Jackie! You'll never guess who's here. It's Brennan! Father Burke, as he is now. Come inside, Father."

"Margaret, it's so good to see you." He followed her inside, shut the door, and put his arms around her.

"You'll have a cup of tea, Father."

"I will, as long as you call me Brennan. Remember, the little gossoon who used to peg stones against Paddy's window to lure him outside when he was supposed to be doing his lessons?"

"Sure I remember. And mind the time your father brought the two of you here by the scruff of your necks after you mitched off school and went swimming in the canal with your uniforms on? You sit down now. I'll wet the tea." She got up on her tiptoes to whisper in his ear, "Jackie's using a walking frame these days, but don't let on you've seen it."

"I won't."

He entered the sitting room and saw Paddy's father in the corner, with a TV remote control in his left hand and a plate of biscuits on his knees. There was a walking frame beside his chair; Brennan affected not to notice. The old fellow was thinner of hair and more bent over since Brennan had seen him last. But his face lit up when he saw he had company.

"Brennan! Welcome home. I won't get up or I'll knock all this stuff onto the floor."

"Sure you're grand, Jackie. What's the *craic*?"

Jackie gestured with the remote. "I'm after watching the highlights of the hurling. The senior club championship. Brilliant goals by a couple of lads named Murphy and O'Neill for Birr."

That gave them the opening to talk sports until Margaret arrived with the tea. When they were all settled with their teacups, she filled him in on the whereabouts of members of the family. "Now, will you be stopping with us for a bit, Brennan? Patsy is only over in Ranelagh." Paddy's second son. "He's got a young one working with him now; he can leave the shop whenever he likes. You know he has a shop that sells computers?"

"That's something new for him then. So I suppose youse have a roomful of computers here now."

"Divil a one," said Jackie. "Wouldn't even know how to turn one on."

"I'll ring him now," Margaret said.

Patsy came in the door twenty minutes later. Greetings were exchanged, and Patsy was handed a cup of tea and joined the others in the sitting room. He was tall and fair-haired, a young-looking thirty-one; he was ten years old when his father was killed. The four of them chatted for a while, and then Patsy said he had to get back to the shop, and would Brennan like to see the place? Sure he would. So they took their leave of Jackie and Margaret, Brennan making a promise to keep in touch. He said not a word about his hopes for a breakthrough in the bombing case.

When they were out in the street, Patsy said, "I don't have to be back in the shop at all. I've an assistant there who can handle it. What I'd really like to do is go down the pub for a pint. Join me?"

"Wouldn't say no."

So they headed for Slattery's bar, greeted the barman, ordered their pints of plain, and sat down to savour them. "You didn't know my father only as a little boy in short trousers, Brennan. You kept in touch with each other in later years."

"Yes, we did. Now, if we were girls I might have a lovely batch of letters carefully preserved and tied up in ribbons. But, boys that we were, I don't think there were any letters after maybe one or two the first year after I emigrated. And those have not been preserved."

"Right."

"But I called in any time I came over here to Dublin."

"I may have met you then, but I don't remember. My first memory of you is right after he died."

"I was in Dublin a couple of weeks after it happened." He was not about to recount the tales of horror he had heard, or the dreadful images he had seen, or the wreckage it had all made of Paddy's wife, his parents, sisters, brother, and his bereft and bewildered little children.

Something else, mercifully, came to his mind. "I remember meeting you a couple of years before that, Patsy."

"Yeah?"

"Yeah. And you gave out to me in front of an entire congregation on the steps of a church."

"What?!"

"Do you happen to recall your auntie's wedding? Noreen's?"

"Was that the one at the Pro?" The Pro was the Pro-Cathedral on Marlborough Street in Dublin, "pro" meaning "provisional" because the Catholics had lost their "real" cathedral, Christ Church, to the Anglicans at the time of the Reformation. Still provisional after nearly five hundred years. "I remember a picture of me in my First

Communion suit, which had been handed down from my brother Jack and was still too long in the legs and arms."

"Well, that did not deter you from being an authoritative figure that day as a member of the wedding party."

"Really?"

"Here's how it happened. Warning: Paddy Healey and his pal Father Burke do not come out of this story looking like angels. Or even grownups."

"Tell me!" Patsy leaned forward in his seat, as wide-eyed as the little boy he had been when these events occurred.

"Well, your aunt Noreen was getting married at the Pro on a Friday evening in June, 1972. I was a young priest at the time. Your grandmother thought it would be nice if I would perform the ceremony, and she got in touch with me in New York. I would love to have accepted but I had obligations at the home parish that I couldn't weasel out of. I could fly over on the Friday and attend the wedding, but I didn't feel I should officiate if I hadn't had time to meet with the bride and groom. And what if something came up and I couldn't make my flight? So, I regretfully turned down the invitation but said I'd try my best to be there as a guest. Great opportunity to see all the family. The regular parish priest would perform the sacrament. Father Egan."

"I remember him! A long streak of misery, he was. Still is, I expect."

"A stern man, as I recall."

"Officious prick."

Brennan laughed. "That, too. So anyway, I had an overnight flight and landed here early in the morning. Your da collected me at the airport and dropped me off at my uncle Finn's place to catch a few hours of sleep. Paddy and I were delighted to be together again and made a plan to meet that afternoon at Finn's other premises: Christy Burke's bar, which Finn had taken over after old Christy's death. And this is the fork in the road where if Paddy had gone right and done what he was supposed to do, everything would have gone as planned. But he went left, neglected his brotherly duties, and joined me in lifting a few jars at Christy's."

"What was he supposed to do that day?"

"He had undertaken the responsibility of getting the wedding program printed up. You know, a little brochure setting out the music, words to the hymns, the names of the people doing readings. Photo of Noreen and Aidan on the cover, that sort of thing. Paddy was supposed to have got this done well in advance of the wedding day but somehow he hadn't managed it."

"That sounds like him! I can remember my ma pestering him to get this or that done. He had a tendency to put things off."

"He did. And that came back to bite him in the arse on the day of his sister's wedding."

Patsy took a good long pull of his Guinness and said, "Let's hear it."

"Noreen had done up the program and had it on five sheets of paper. The printing company would put it together, make a little booklet of it, and run off eighty copies. So Paddy had the sheets of paper on him, and he had lent his car to someone in the family, so he caught a bus here in Rathmines to go over to the north side to Christy's. Another thing: it was bucketing rain that afternoon and windy as hell. So, Paddy takes the bus and gets off wherever the closest stop was to Mountjoy Street. He's standing in the street and he pulls out his wallet, to make sure he has enough for a couple of pints, and with the wallet out come the pages of the wedding program."

"Oh, no."

"Oh, yes. The wind catches the pages, all but page one, and whips them out of Paddy's hand and into the street."

"Jesus! Noreen's going to murder him."

"Oh, yeah, he's in the soup and he knows it. There's water running in the street and one of the pages goes off and down a drain. Two attach themselves to one of the wheels of the bus, and they go off out of sight. He doesn't know what happened to the last one. Yer man is well and truly fucked."

"Christ, I feel as if I'm standing there in the pissing rain watching that bus go off!"

"So, as the story goes, a man walks into a bar. Poor Paddy comes into the pub looking like something that was left off Noah's Ark in the flood, and he rattles the story off for me and Finn, and Finn pours him a pint of consolation, and we sit at the bar and try to figure out what in the hell we can do to salvage the situation. And there's another complication in this. The missing pages contained the names of the hymns, and the words, so everyone could sing along. Problem was, Father Egan was a bit prissy about what could, and what could not, be sung at a Catholic wedding. Noreen and Aidan had decided on two songs in addition to the liturgical pieces, and that's where you come in."

"Me? Wait . . . yeah, I got stuck singing at the wedding. I couldn't carry a tune, still can't. But I don't remember the details of that little bit of hell. Must have blocked the memory of it!"

"You and your brother and sister were going to sing a little pop song, 'Chapel of Love,' with two or three of your older cousins. It was a song by a girl group called the Dixie Cups. Noreen had taught it to you, and you had rehearsed it. Reluctantly, as you say. But then Father Egan decreed that a pop song and the haunting old love song, 'Coinleach Glas an Fhómhair,' were not appropriate, and he substituted 'Immaculate Mary' and 'On This Day O Beautiful Mother.'"

Patsy rolled his eyes.

"So there we were in the bar and we had our pints and shots of whiskey, and Finn gave us pens and sheets of paper, and we sat there trying to reconstruct the program. And Paddy's got the janglers, knowing he has to get it right and have it printed by the end of the afternoon. And he's scribbling things down, and we're drinking, and we start going into fits of laughter over the whole thing.

"Finn has an old typewriter back in his little office but of course he's the classic two-finger typist, and so are we, which means the thing will take hours to type up. And will be filled with errors. No personal computers in those days. So he calls in somebody he knows, a retired secretary. And gently she asks, 'Did your sister not make a carbon copy?' And your da says she didn't. Presumably because the printing shop was going to make the copies. 'Could you not just ring your sister and ask her what to put in it?' the woman says then.

"And Paddy looks down and mumbles, 'Em, no. You see, she thinks I have it all done. I sort of told her that it's already in the print shop, and that I'll be collecting it today.'

"So Paddy is sitting there, downing the Guinness and the whiskey at a furious pace, and I'm trying to get him to ease off the stuff. I'm having a few myself, of course, but . . ."

"I didn't know Da was a man for the drink. But maybe everyone played that down, you know, after he died and all."

"No, he really wasn't. It was just the nerves going on him that day. Which of course made it worse, him not being used to skulling pints at such a rate. 'She'll have me bollocks for this,' he's saying. Noreen, he means. He sits there in a funk for a bit, then his face brightens like the morning sun. 'No, she won't! She'll be covering me with glory!'

"'How's that now, Paddy?'

"'The music! I'll give them back the tunes they want!'

"And he starts in on Father Egan, how crabbed he's being about the music, and why can't Noreen and Aidan have the songs they picked? 'What do you think as a *sagart* yourself, Brennan?'

"And I say, 'Let them have the music they want. It's their day. It's not going to negate the sacrament to have a beautiful, haunting old love song in Irish and a, well, sugary little pop song.' Now I'm a stickler about music myself, Patsy. For me it's Gregorian chant and the great Latin hymns. 'Chapel of Love' would not have been my choice, but they were a very young couple, and why not? Finn picks up the phone and rings a musician who appears frequently in trad music sessions in the pub, to try and get the words to the Irish language song. We know we're making a hash of the spelling, but it's the best we can do. Then we get on to 'Chapel of Love,' and we start singing it to make sure we have the lyrics. And other punters join in and a couple of young women stand up and do a little dance. It's great gas."

"Jesus, wouldn't I give anything to be there right now seeing my father in such a fix!"

"Oh, you'll have your moment, when we get to the church." Brennan drained the last of his pint and went up to the bar for two more. He resumed his tale. "So yer one is there with the typewriter, a good-natured lady anxious to help us out, and Paddy dictates the names of the people doing the readings as best he can. Of course he's lost when he comes to the chapter and verse of the scripture selections, so he settles for 'Readings from Holy Scripture.' He remembers that there were a couple of standard hymns in there but can't for the life of him recall what they were, so I come up with substitutes. We finally get the thing finished, and we thank Finn and the typist and we bolt from Christy's with the new program in a brown envelope and we make a joke or two about that. We get to the printing shop, and Paddy pleads with the fellow to do this right away, and the man laughs and agrees to drop everything else and print the thing up. So we have the programs, and Paddy runs off home to get changed and ready for the wedding."

"And they all lived happily ever after."

"I'm sure they did, eventually. I of course wasn't on the scene when Paddy presented the family with the new edition of the program. But I was in the church for the wedding, and it was lovely for the most part. Father Egan had a puss on him when 'Coinleach Glas an Fhómhair' was sung, beautifully, by the groom's sister. And I thought he was going to bust a vessel when you little ones got up to do 'Chapel of Love.' His expression was matched only by your own, Patsy. You glowered out at the congregation and barked out the lyrics in a less than romantic tone of voice. There was chuckling in the pews over that. So you made a hit in spite of yourself.

"Then, when it was all done, and everyone was gathered on the steps of the Pro for photographs, Father Egan lit into your poor father over the changes to the program. So I stepped up in his defence and made the argument that the sacrament was in no way diminished by the songs. I wasn't wearing my collar. I was just in civvies, so the priest whirled on me. 'And who are you, may I ask?' So I told him my name without adding 'Father.' He said, 'Is that liquor I'm smelling off you, Burke?' He cast his eyes on Paddy then and jerked his thumb in my direction. 'So this is the *bastún* who had you out in the shebeens on the afternoon of your sister's marriage! Inserting rock music into a wedding!' Imagine classifying 'Chapel of Love' as rock. You'd think it was Black Sabbath, not the Dixie Cups. Anyway, he told us we were a disgrace, the pair of us.

"And then you got in on it. You understood that your father and I were responsible for your having to sing. You'd obviously learned your Catechism that week. You gave out yards to me about the dangers to my immortal soul."

"I didn't!"

"You did. You glared daggers at me and condemned me in a loud, clear voice that all could hear. '*You* have great dirty spots on your soul! You aren't going to heaven when you die. You are going to purgatory and you're not going to like it! And I'll not be saying any prayers for your soul to get out of there!' You turned to your oul fella and said, 'Da, don't be mates with him. He'll have you on the drink and singing bad songs!' Oh, you were full of fire and brimstone that day, my boy."

Patsy stared at Brennan, astonished. "I can't believe it. I can't remember ever thinking that way!"

"It was priceless, this little lad of eight years togged out in his little suit, with the authority of the One True Church to back him up. Everybody loved it. But then you extended your loving mercy to poor old Paddy. He was standing there, mortified, and you saw that and said something like, 'Da, it's not your fault.' You pointed a finger at me and said to Paddy, 'Stay away from *him* and you'll be grand. He's a bad —' you wanted to say *influence* but you weren't sure of the word and it came out as *effluent*. So that sobriquet stuck to me, so to speak, for the duration of the weekend."

Brennan and Patsy enjoyed a laugh and finished their pints. They walked out of Slattery's, and Patsy shook Brennan's hand. "You know, Brennan, that may be my favourite story about my father. It's the only one anyone ever told me that didn't portray him as a man of saintly perfection. It makes me even more . . ." His voice faltered and he turned away.

And that's when Brennan threw caution under the bus. "Patsy, if there is one sentence in the English language that has the opposite of its intended effect, it is 'Don't get your hopes up.' But I can tell you in confidence that there may be a chance of a breakthrough in the bombing case." The young man turned and stared at Brennan. "It's far from a sure thing. But someone in my family has uncovered evidence that a certain man was in one of the bomb cars coming into Dublin that day; there is a witness who can identify him."

"Oh, God."

"And the man in the car has documents stating that he was out of the country on May the seventeenth but we know those papers were forged."

"Jesus, Brennan. After all these years! Who is the fucker?"

"I don't know his name," Brennan lied. "But the evidence has been passed on to the police on both sides of the border. And if this man is charged, he may well give up some of the others in order to get a better deal for himself. But, given the history so far, it's very possible that nothing will come of this, Patsy. Please understand that."

"I do." But of course he didn't.

✝

It was another attack that had Finn Burke scowling from his place behind the bar and behind the lenses of his dark glasses. Brennan had arrived at Christy Burke's and had given his uncle an update on the situation with Ronan. If it were up to Finn — and, Brennan suspected, if he were able to cross and re-cross the border without being detected — the fuckers who had tried to kill his nephew would be sent kicking and screaming to the everlasting flames of hell. Brennan had no desire to get his uncle started on the connection between the assassination attempt and the car bombs in Monaghan and here in Dublin. He did not reveal that one of the best-known preachers of God's word in the North of Ireland, John the Baptist Geddes, had known of the bomb plot in advance.

But there was something he hoped to find and it was related to those bombings. "Finn, there used to be some photos in here, showing the lot of us as kids before our midnight departure from these shores all those years ago. There were a few of me and my brothers and sister, the crop of us born in Ireland, and there was one was of me and some other lads in our football jerseys. I would have been nine or ten at the time."

"Go back there into my office, and you'll see a stack of the old pictures. You're not about to rob them off me, I hope, Father."

"No, I just thought I'd bring some of them to a photography shop and get copies made."

"Sure, go ahead."

Brennan went behind the bar and into the office. He found the pile of photos and picked out a few for copying. He took a couple of his family as it was constituted the year they left Ireland: his mother, father, Molly, Brennan, Patrick, Francis, and Terry. Their youngest, Brigid, was born in New York after their hasty emigration. And he took the one showing his Gaelic football team, with him standing flank to flank with Paddy Healey. He waved the pictures at Finn and set off walking until he found a photography studio in Dorset Street. He asked for copies and was told they would be ready the following morning. He walked back to the cream-coloured building bearing the name Christy Burke and stood at the bar savouring a lovely, rich pint of Guinness.

His sister and brothers arrived soon afterwards. It was made clear by Patrick and Terry, newly arrived from New York, that their old man Declan was in a fury over the attempt on his nephew's life. He groused that he should "sign up again" and take up arms in Belfast.

Brother Patrick, psychiatrist and smoother of roiling family waters whenever those waters were a-roil, offered his love and healing power at any time, any place. He said, "All you have to do is ask, Brennan. And if you don't ask, I may interpret that as *a cry for help!*"

But brother Terry declared that Brennan had come through it all in his usual imperturbable manner. "He'd walk through flames and all you'd hear from him would be 'Would you ever be turning the heat down, lads?'"

"You're not a man to be rattled yourself, Ter," Brennan told him, "keeping jumbo jets aloft through all weathers, fair and foul."

"Neither snow nor rain nor heat nor gloom of night keeps our man Terry from his duties," said Molly.

"You'll find that inscribed on the New York post office building, not my aircraft. I don't have to get my brogues wet when I go to work."

"The New York post office and Herodotus speaking of the Persians in 500 B.C."

"Leave it to you to know that, Bren," his sister said.

"Ah, now," Brennan replied with modesty.

"What Father Brennan Xavier Burke — licentiate, Gregorian University, doctorate, Angelicum — doesn't know could be written on a tiny piece of paper this big," she said, her fingers delineating a small scrap of paper.

"A bar coaster," suggested Terry.

"In old ogham script."

And it went on like that.

The next morning, he collected his photos and took care not to crease them. He would keep the picture of himself and Paddy in view in his room, as a talisman of sorts to bring on the prosecution of one of the many men responsible for the slaughter of his friend and all the other victims twenty-one years before.

After completing that errand Brennan spent a relaxing day with his siblings before he returned to Mount Melleray, and they took themselves off to Belfast.

Brennan reflected on the fact that he had been away from Belfast for just over three weeks by the time he turned his mind to a departure date. He was anxious to see how Ronan and Gráinne were doing, though he felt they had probably benefitted from having their house to themselves for a while. And he would have a few pints with Monty before he headed back to the law courts of Halifax; he knew Monty had planned to finish his work on the tractor case and fly home to take up the local end of the job in early or mid-May. Brennan also wanted to make up for the time he had lost from the Holy Cross girls' choir. The girls had had Easter holidays and then they were pre-paring for a play to be staged later in the spring, but now it was time to see how they were progressing with Palestrina, Byrd, Handel, and Mozart. That would inspire him for his next adventure, which would begin in September: the gig as choirmaster at Sancta Maria Regina Coeli in Rome. He told himself he would enjoy another week of quiet and contemplation, then pack his bags for the North.

But that night as he drifted off to sleep, two conflicting notions came over him. One, his determination that he would move heaven and earth to bring to justice the men who had ripped the hearts out of the families of '74, and two, a fear that the entire shaky edifice of this plan, and any hope the families might have, were destined to fall to the ground in a smoking ruin.

Monty

The closing of the month of April brought some fine sunny weather but also an element of stress as Monty tried to wrap up his work on the Canadian Earth Equipment matter. He had cartons full of statements and documentary evidence from the manufacturing plant and engineering reports that bolstered his case. He believed he had everything covered from this end. He also had to deal with his Ellison Whiteside files, either complete the work or pass them over to other solicitors. He would have to leave Belfast as planned in early May. He was not looking forward to leaving an ocean between himself and Maura, Normie, and Dominic, but the children were better off staying till the end of June, Normie to finish out her school term and Dominic to be with her. He tried to shut out the image of his children saying goodbye to Orla Farrell after she had been taking care of them, and having loads of fun with them, for all their months in Ireland. His own goodbyes would be traumatic enough.

But the first of May brought some very good news for the Flanagan plaintiffs. Monty had just received word from Royden Barrett that Colman Davison's insurance company would be making a "without prejudice" interim payment of £25,000. The defendant was making the payment without admitting liability. But, between the lines, Barrett made it clear that in fact there would be more to come. They were going to be naming some other persons as third parties to the action and presumably going after them for compensation. Monty didn't know the details, who these people were, or how the Davison insurer hoped to collect from them, but his concern was with his own clients. They would be getting the £25,000 immediately, with more to come later. And the first thing Monty was going to do was move them out of that terrifying tower block and into a nice, friendly, safe neighbourhood. Monty had one of the assistants at Ellison Whiteside scan the real estate pages, and she found a townhouse not far from the house where the Flanagans had been living before their eviction. The monthly rent was reasonable and the place was available now, so the move was on.

Another thing the family needed was a new solicitor to take them through the rest of the doubtlessly long, drawn-out litigation/negotiation process. He had gathered from his conversations with Muriel Whiteside that this lawsuit, with the taint of guns and bullets, was not the sort of thing the solicitors of the firm would want to dirty their hands in. He had little doubt they would step in if need be, but he had another idea. He left Ellison Whiteside and walked to Reddy O'Reilly's office just a few blocks away. Monty waited until Reddy finished with a client and then was admitted to his quarters. They had a good gab about the never-ending news cycle in Belfast, and then Monty told him about the case and asked if he would be interested in taking it on. Reddy's reaction was not what Monty had hoped for. The solicitor's expression darkened and he shook his head. "Sorry, Monty, can't do it."

Monty nodded, said he understood, although he didn't, and directed the conversation to less controversial subjects. He then returned to his own office. He knocked on Muriel's door and asked her how she would feel about the firm staying on the record for *Flanagan v. Davison* with its whizzing bullets and unknown third parties out there in the mist. If she had any qualms, she didn't let on and suggested one of the firm's other solicitors for the case. So that was taken care of. But Monty couldn't help but wonder what it was about the case that caused Reddy O'Reilly to turn it down.

Chapter XXX

Monty

Wednesday, May 3, was once again moving day for the Flanagan kids, but this time it was a joyous occasion. Brennan Burke had done a lot of the heavy lifting the day the Flanagans had been forced to leave all they knew and loved in order to move into the tower block in the Heatherfield Villas housing estate. Monty remembered how he and Brennan had stiff-upper-lipped it as young Timmy said goodbye to his best friend, how Brennan had cast a sombre eye on the family's dismal new surroundings and the threatening gangs of toughs hanging out in the yards. It was only fitting that Brennan should be on hand to see the children reunited with their friends and neighbours in the world they had loved and lost. Monty called Ronan's number and heard the voice of a young woman, maybe Ronan's daughter. She told him Brennan was still in the South. He was expected back before too long, but she wasn't sure when. Monty regretted the fact that Brennan would miss the homecoming scene and that he and Brennan had not seen each other for the last month of Monty's sojourn in Ireland. There should at the very least have been a Collins-Burke "Farewell to Ireland" pub crawl before Monty flew out, but it was not to be.

He thought again about the claim by Carrick that the Flanagan case could have repercussions for *people Monty knew in this city*, including Brennan. He remembered, too, the subdued reaction at Ronan and Gráinne's house party when he announced that he was ready to commence his lawsuit on behalf the Flanagans. But Brennan hadn't even known what Monty was talking about when he made that call to the abbey. Not for the first time, Monty wondered whether the person who really had cause to worry about the November 1992 incident was Carrick himself. Well, the whole thing had made no sense to Monty when he heard it and it made even less sense in the light of a bright May morning and £25,000 cash in the hand.

Monty had no trouble finding a substitute for Brennan as a lifter of heavy objects and mover of well-worn furniture. One of the Ellison Whiteside secretaries volunteered her teenage son for the job. The young fellow, Robert, was agreeable, even more so when Monty handed him twenty quid in advance for his efforts. So off they went to the tower block to collect the kids and their furniture and transport them to a far, far better place. Once again, all the Flanagans piled into a taxi van that followed their load of belongings. All except Timmy, who pleaded to ride in the front of the cargo van with Monty and Robert. Once again, they made the journey across the city. But this time they were going home. It wasn't long before they arrived in the Musgrave Park area, and Monty turned in to the family's old street. "Drive up there! Drive up there!" Timmy urged. "They're playing football!"

His old football buddies were on the pitch, and Timmy made a lunge for the van door before Monty had even stopped.

"Hold on there, Tim. Wait till I stop. Don't want you on the disabled list for the final."

But seconds later they were stopped, and Timmy was out the door.

"'Bout ye, lads?!" he called out to them, and play was stopped. The boys all gaped at him, then abandoned their positions and came at their old pal in a rush. There was a mad scramble, which ended in a gleeful clump of boys on the field.

Monty could imagine the joy with which Normie would have viewed the scene; he looked forward to reporting to her after the move was complete.

A door opened across the street and a woman emerged. Monty had seen her before.

"Merciful God! Is that —?"

"We're back, Mrs. Hamill!"

She spied Katie on the pavement. "Katie, God love you! Are you moving back?"

"We are! Different house, but really close to home! You can see it from here."

"And that's wee Timmy I saw out my window, under that pile of lads?"

"It is."

"Welcome back to youse all! Now let me go in and put some chocolate biscuits in the oven. I'm thinking Timmy has been missing my biscuits."

"He has. You've no idea, Mrs. Hamill. Thank you!" Katie turned to Monty. "I'm going up to see a couple of the girls and then I'll help you unpack. The other kids . . ." By the time she thought to look for them they, too, had made a beeline for their old friends' houses.

Monty said, "Robert and I can take care of this stuff, no problem, Katie. Go off and enjoy yourself."

"Are you sure?"

"Absolutely."

When the stuff had all been placed in the new house, at the gentle direction of Winnie, Monty gave Robert a lift into the city centre, returned the van, got into his car, and drove back to the Flanagans' place for supper. Everyone had returned to the house, and they all crowded around the table, sitting or standing, with take-out pizza and fish and chips and Mrs. Hamill's chocolate biscuits. Timmy and his best mate Barry exchanged playful punches and competed for the goodies on the table. Katie and Clare, Dermot and Darren, all had pals in for the happy occasion. Dermot was telling his mates about a couple of new friends he had met in the housing estate, and his mother assured him they would be welcome to hop on the bus and come for a visit.

Hughie Malone arrived then, obviously in his cups, and beamed around the room at one and all. Monty went over to him and shook his hand. "Thank you, Hughie, for getting all this started. I have to confess I was a bit skeptical when I first heard your story."

"You and all the lads in McCully's bar." His speech was a little slurred. "They never believe a word out of my mouth, but I speak only the truth."

Winnie came towards them with a bottle of wine in one hand and a glass in the other. "A wee glass of red, Hughie?"

"Thank you, Winnie. Here, I'll pour it. You go on with your other guests."

Winnie laughed and handed the bottle and glass to Malone. She went off to speak to Mrs. Hamill. Malone filled his glass to the brim and said, "Monty, I could tell you stories about this part of the world that would —" He stopped, and Monty followed his gaze. He saw Assumpta Flanagan coming in the door, dressed for spring in a pale pink dress and a short white jacket. She was carrying a bouquet of Easter lilies wrapped in paper. She caught the eye of someone, smiled and raised the flowers in salute. That's when Hughie made his move.

He rushed at Assumpta and said, "How about a kiss for your favourite oul rascal?"

Next thing Monty heard was a crash, the sound of breaking glass, a loud *reeeooowwr* from the cat, and a louder curse from Malone, who had tripped and toppled to the floor. The lilies lay beside him in a pool of red wine. This inspired Monty to deliver a line of verse, from one of Ireland's patriot poets, "I see his blood upon the rose."

The line got a laugh, even from Assumpta, who had grabbed hold of the door frame to keep herself upright. Like the lilies, her white jacket and pink dress were splashed with red.

Winnie rushed over, mortified, and then glared in the direction of Pebbledash, who had streaked across the room and was watching from the safety of a dark corner.

"Will somebody put manners on that cat? I'm so sorry, I can't count the times I've nearly fallen to my death tripping over that creature."

"Oh," Assumpta replied, "I think we can give the wee moggy a pass." She looked down at Hughie, prostrate at her feet. "This oul *baste*, though . . ."

Hughie didn't even lift his head, just muttered out of the corner of his mouth, "Och, I was cursed by the other crowd the day I was born."

"The other crowd?" Monty asked.

"The fairies," Assumpta explained.

Darren and Dermot cleared away the wine and the broken glass, Clare rinsed off the lilies, found a vase for them and placed them on a side table, Assumpta and Winnie disappeared into a back room together. Winnie emerged a few minutes later with the stained clothing and took the bundle to the kitchen sink. Assumpta was now dressed down in a bright green track suit.

Katie said the only thing that could be said. "Tea, anyone?"

When everyone was seated with their teacups, including a subdued Hughie Malone, Katie looked over at Monty. She spread her arms out, indicating the new surroundings. "We owe all this to you, Monty. I don't know how to say a big enough thankyou. Right, lads?" All the kids joined in a round of applause. Except Timmy and Barry, who were wrestling under the dining table by that time.

Winnie said, "We all owe you so much, Monty. I don't know where to begin."

"It's been my pleasure, Winnie. And a certain Mr. Malone deserves some credit here, too. Let's not forget Hughie."

"Hughie is now, and ever shall be, unforgettable," Assumpta said, turning to him. "Bless you, Hughie."

A flush crept up Hughie's cheeks. He raised his teacup in rueful acknowledgement. "I'd best be counting my blessings, in case they don't come my way again!"

Katie said, "We're going to really miss you, Monty. And Normie!"

"She won't be leaving for another two months, so she'll have the opportunity for some visits before then. And she loves to write letters. I know there's a new thing now. People can write to each other by computer. One person writes, sends it, and the other person receives it instantly!"

"I know," one of young fellows piped up. "Electronic mail. Everybody's talking about it."

"They must be if even *I've* heard about it." Monty laughed. "So, Katie, I'm going to speak to your new solicitor about making sure you get a computer, for fun and for *electronic mail.* And of course for your school work, *if* you promise to go on to law school." Katie's eyes filled with tears, and she came to Monty and gave him a great big hug. She wasn't the only one who teared up.

This was why he did what he did, to bring justice to people like Katie Flanagan and her mother and the little kids. True, it wasn't often that he had clients so clearly deserving as the Flanagans, nor was it often he got a result worthy of celebration all round. After all, how many citizens celebrated the old standby, the *killer getting off*? Well this was a far cry from that. Get it while you can!

Two days later, Monty had said his goodbyes and managed to maintain once again that stiff upper lip that would earn him approval from the English side of his family, and he was on the plane to Heathrow. He would stay overnight and catch the morning flight to Halifax on Air Canada. The working holiday in Belfast had been a turbulent one, with Ronan Burke being shot, Maura going undercover to flush out a mass murderer, and Monty himself extorting information from a client and having a secret rendezvous with a hostile paramilitary.

At the end of it all, right had prevailed for the family of Eamon Flanagan. But what about Ronan Burke? What about the families of the 1974 bombing victims, who meant so much to Ronan and Brennan? Would anyone ever see the inside of a prison cell because of those crimes?

Chapter XXXI

Brennan

Brennan had delayed his departure from the peace and felicity of Mount Melleray even longer than anticipated but finally, on the second Saturday in May, he embarked on the journey from County Waterford back to Belfast, after more than a month away. He was still basking in the beauty and peace he had found with the monks at the abbey. When he returned to his lodgings in Andersonstown, he heard that his sister and brothers had made a big hit during their visit and had promised to stay in touch with the Belfast branch of the clan. Now Gráinne and Ronan were packed and ready for a night in Derry. They didn't say but Brennan had the feeling that the purpose of the trip was to do a bit of political campaigning with Republicans and other Nationalists in that city, to promote Ronan as a future candidate in an elected assembly for the North of Ireland. Ronan was in good spirits when he left the house and was getting around quite effectively in spite of his pain. Gráinne, too, was clearly looking forward to the excursion. Brennan made a call to Monty's place but the phone was answered by a new tenant; Brennan had missed Monty by a week. Well, Brennan would be back in Halifax for the summer, before heading to Rome in September, so he and Monty would have plenty of drinking time at the Midtown Tavern.

With no prospects for company, Brennan decided to go into the city centre to try out an Italian restaurant he had noticed before he went away. Two doors from the restaurant was a music shop with a display of classical compact discs in the window, so he made that his first stop. He wandered around inside, coveting everything in the shop. He settled on a new recording of Vivaldi's *Gloria* and an old, but cherished, rendition of the Monteverdi *Vespers of 1610*. Then he went into Pannacci's and savoured a wonderful meal of antipasti and pasta al forno and a couple of glasses of Chianti. He topped it all off with the best pistachio gelato he had ever tasted outside of Rome. The couple who ran the place had recently arrived from Perugia, and Brennan got into a conversation with them in Italian and had a thoroughly enjoyable time. It was after ten when he got to Andytown and let himself into the house. Now for the music. He started with the Monteverdi. Almost without thinking, he found himself at the drinks cabinet reaching for the Jameson, but then decided to hold off a bit before getting into that.

He lit up a smoke and flaked out on the sofa in the sitting room and let himself be transported as the early Baroque masterpiece moved from the dramatic to the prayerful to the ethereal. He lay there enthralled for several minutes after the final note. Then he rose, poured himself a whiskey, and put on the Vivaldi. It was late and he had an early Mass to say in the morning, but there were parts of the *Gloria* that always filled him with *gaudium quod est immensum atque probum,* the joy that is immense and good. So he pressed play again, cranked it up, took a sip of the Jameson, and sighed with pleasure.

Just at the end of the *Et in terra pax* — and peace on earth — his own peace was shattered by a loud hammering at the front door. He considered ignoring it, but then thought that might not be the thing to do as a responsible guest in his cousin's home. A knock on the door at midnight: whatever it was about, it didn't bode well. He knew he had no choice. He got up and turned off the music and headed to the door. Before he reached it, the pounding began again. He looked out the window and saw a police car. Oh God, what had happened now?

He pulled the door open and was met by two burly coppers. He began to speak, to ask what was wrong, but one of the peelers talked right over him. "Are you Brennan Burke?"

Oh, Christ. How would they know that?

"I am."

"Brennan Burke, I am placing you under arrest for possession of an offensive weapon in a public place, and for criminal damage, attempting to pervert the course of justice, and making a threat to kill."

"Threat to kill?!"

"Does that mean you're admitting to the rest of the offences?"

"No! Of course not."

Sweet suffering Jesus! This can't be happening. How many people had said the same thing when faced with some unexpected, outrageous misfortune? But it was happening. He hadn't even seen the gun that day at the church, but this was happening. They put him in cuffs and shoved him into their car and drove off with him. He was too bollixed to map out where they were driving, but he knew they'd crossed into east Belfast and kept going. They pulled up beside a long, rectangular building and dragged him out of the car. Before he could get his bearings, they took him to a small, harshly lit room with a table and three chairs and sat him down across from a giant of a peeler, not one of the two who had arrested him. This fellow was balding and had the rest of his hair shaved off. His eyes were a flinty grey. He pulled out a pack of cigarettes and lit one up. Brennan was nearly shaking from the need of one himself, which he suspected was the point of them being flaunted in his face. He fought down the urge to ask, to beg for one.

The cop wasted no time on pleasantries, not that pleasantries would be expected in such an environment. "What made you go for the gun in the cellar at Saint Matthew's?"

Brennan made no reply.

"What made you decide to get that gun?"

No reply.

"You do realize that things will go a lot easier for you if you answer our questions. A lot of flexibility with the charges you're facing. Answer the questions. Be good to us; we'll be good to you."

Brennan said nothing. He knew from years of listening to Monty Collins that he always, without exception, told his clients — pleaded with them — to keep their mouths shut when questioned by the police. But Brennan had imbibed the same lesson like mother's milk from his family. His father, his uncles, his cousins, all who were or had been in the Irish Republican Army: give the peelers nothing. Stonewall them. Don't cooperate. Don't give them legitimacy. Don't open your mouth.

"Who told you where the gun was?"

Silence.

"This is your chance right now. Help us, and help yourself while you're at it. Who told you?"

Brennan kept his gob shut and stared at the wall above the man's head.

"Just like all the rest of the Provie scum, thinking that stonewalling us will win you the day. Well, guess what, Burke, you fuckin' terrorist? You lose!" Suddenly, the peeler charged at him, grabbed him by the throat, and slammed him against the wall. Another man materialized then, and Brennan could smell the booze on his breath. The second cop drove his right fist into Brennan's gut, and Brennan reeled from the pain. He longed to grab this hate-filled bigot, this sorry excuse for a policeman, and beat him to a pulp. But even in the pain and stress of the interrogation his mind was working clearly: hit one of them, and the story would be that Brennan had struck first, had obstructed the investigation, had assaulted a police officer. More charges on the sheet.

But, perhaps as a hangover from all his years of studying and teaching in the universities, he attempted to deflect them by engaging them in a seminar. He tried to make them see reason. "You call me a terrorist."

"Nothing wrong with your ears, Burke."

"I am not a terrorist. But say, for the sake of argument now, that I am."

"You call this an argument? Yeah? Well, we're going to argue you a lot more before this is over!"

"So. I'm a terrorist. And you are not."

"Right. You take the cup for brilliance."

"The thing to do with me as a terrorist is to arrest me, follow the procedures of the world-renowned British justice system, let me get a lawyer, let me out on bail or possibly keep me in custody until my case is heard in court and then, if I am found guilty, I serve my time in prison to pay for my crime. Right? I'm the terrorist. You are not. You are better than that. You are the forces of law and order, hired to keep the peace and maintain order, not conduct a reign of terror in this hellish place. So why are you allowing yourself to be carried away in a frenzy of violence? Who's the terrorist now?"

This infuriated them even more, as Brennan might have predicted.

"Would you like some more, ye Fenian bastard?" And with that, the first cop slammed his fist into Brennan's left jaw. He heard a crack. A back tooth. He prayed to God to give him the patience and strength to endure this without losing the rag and fighting back. That would make it infinitesimally worse for him. The second peeler delivered another punch to the abdomen, and Brennan crumpled to the floor. He made what felt like a superhuman effort not to let them hear his gasps of pain.

"Maybe you'll be a wee bit more cooperative next time I invite you in for a chat."

He was then yanked up and taken to a cell, which contained an iron bed and a chair, which were chained to the floor. The door was banged shut. He either passed out or fell asleep. He had no idea how much time passed while he was out, but he found himself in the interrogation room again. It was two different cops this time, and they were both demented with drink. Their questions were slurred at him, and his refusal to answer set them into a fury of violence. He tried to pray for survival, for deliverance, but the prayers wouldn't come. The soul, the intellect, was unreachable. He had been reduced to the basest of animals, with only one instinct remaining: to avoid annihilation. He twisted and turned to evade the blows. The last thing he remembered was a savage kick between his legs, and him falling over in agony, vomiting onto his shoes. The last thought he recalled was that he had to have a shower. Immediately. And his clothes had to be washed. Cleanliness was, well — he had been slagged about this all his life — an obsession with Brennan. As painful as it would be to stand in a shower, he simply had to . . .

He regained consciousness in his cell and wished he hadn't. He was filthy. His clothing stank. And he was sick with pain from all the pounding. Snatches of conversation somewhere beyond his cell told him he was in the Castlereagh detention centre. Thinking of the beatings he had endured at the hands of the RUC barbarians filled him with a murderous rage. How many others had suffered the same abuse and worse in this and other detention centres? Torture chambers. All the stories he had heard over the years had horrified him; how many times had he said he could not imagine what the prisoners had gone through? How many times had he said that no matter what the prisoners might have done to get arrested, they deserved a fair trial and humane treatment by the authorities? Because once the authorities of any state sank to the level of what they thought the prisoners had done, then there was no order left. No civilization. Just what Hobbes had warned of: the war of all against all.

Brennan knew he had to tamp down the pain and the rage and humiliation. And the longing for revenge. He tried to free his mind. He was a musician; he tried to call up that gift to comfort him now.

A line of plainchant, a motet by Mozart, a Mass by William Byrd. But it was another piece of music that came into his head. What was it? A song that asked the question who the terrorists really are in this conflict. "Joe McDonnell," that was it. Brian Warfield of the Wolfe Tones had written it after McDonnell died on hunger strike. He wished the Wolfe Tones would materialize in the yard of this hellhole and belt out the song at the top of their lungs. Who indeed should be included in the word "terrorist" here?

But Brennan understood that he was only in the early stages of a long and terrifying ordeal, the end of which nobody could predict, least of all Brennan himself. He had to gather his wits and make a phone call. Even in this place, he was permitted to do that. But who would he call? A lawyer. Who? He didn't know any. Well, he knew Monty Collins, but Monty had left for Halifax. Brennan knew he would have to humble himself and confess to Monty what an idiot he had been. Another criminal client picked up for a boneheaded scheme that — inevitably, as Monty would see it — went horribly wrong. He would have to let Monty and Maura know where he was and what had befallen him. But what he needed was a lawyer who knew this legal system from top to bottomless pit, and he needed that lawyer now. Ronan Burke and sons likely had an entire stable of solicitors who had assisted them over the years. Brennan would ask his cousin to find someone for him, and get this sorted.

Gráinne answered the phone. "Hello?"

"Gráinne, it's Brennan."

"Brennan! Where have you been?"

"I'm sorry, *a chroí*, I can't talk now. Is Ronan there?"

"He is. You don't sound good at all, Brennan. Are you all right?"

"Em, no."

"Oh, God. I'll get Ronan."

Two seconds later, Ronan was on the line. "Brennan?"

"They lifted me last night. The peelers."

The reduction in the volume of Ronan's voice did nothing to hide his alarm. "What?"

"I need a lawyer. I'm locked up. I'm in fucking Castlereagh."

"Jesus." There was a pause during which Brennan could almost hear Ronan telling himself to keep his reaction to the minimum necessary. "Brennan. I'll try to get Reddy O'Reilly. One way or the other, I'll have someone there for you today." Then, in Irish, "*Ní déarfaidh mé a dhath eile anois.*" I'll say nothing else now.

"*Tuigim. Go raibh maith agat.*" I understand. Thank you.

By mid-afternoon he had a solicitor, the fellow Ronan had mentioned. Redmond O'Reilly. The name sounded familiar. Had Monty mentioned him, or had he read about him in the news? He was an impressive-looking man, tall with longish dark-red hair streaked with silver. They met in a prefabricated hut on the grounds of the Castlereagh interrogation centre. A cop watched them through a window.

O'Reilly introduced himself, narrowed his eyes at whatever Brennan's face looked like now, and then jerked his head towards the cop at the window. "How bad was it?"

"Bad enough," Brennan acknowledged.

"I'll take the details of that before I go."

"It seems everything you hear about the system here —"

"Everything you hear is true. Amnesty International got involved in all this a few years back, found that the 'safeguards,' whatever they might be, were 'inadequate to prevent the ill treatment of detainees.' One of the things they looked at was the case of a young lad who had been abused here at Castlereagh. Now it's you. Tell me what happened from the time they came for you."

Brennan filled him in on the arrest and the charges. O'Reilly listened without taking notes, then outlined what Brennan could expect now. He would be taken to another police station, the Musgrave station, and he would be charged with the slew of offences arising out of the hare-brained gun escapade. Then he would be taken from there into a courtroom, a low-level court of some kind. He would apply for bail. Bail would be refused.

"Refused? But if we apply and I meet the qualifications for —"

"You'll not be getting bail. You'll be transferred to the Crumlin Road Gaol . . ."

"The Crumlin jail!"

"I'm sorry, Brennan. There's no point in me trying to sugarcoat it; this is what you'll be facing. You'll be on remand in the Crum. There will be some procedures to attend to at the courthouse across the way — at the other end of the tunnel — and we'll try to get you a trial as soon as we possibly can."

"Jesus the Christ who died on the cross and descended into hell!"

"I know. But I'll do my utmost to make the best of a very bad situation. Now. Tell me what they did to you." He told O'Reilly what they did to him, and O'Reilly wrote it down.

"Now, Brennan, this is going to look like a spoof of a bad spy film, but see this other pen I have. It's a camera. I know, I know. But I'm going to take a picture of your face. Not that it will do any good. But it will be documented: yet another detainee subjected to abuse."

"Another hunk of meat in the slaughterhouse."

"Standard procedure, unfortunately, Brennan. All our lads are beaten on arrest. All of them."

Brennan found himself in another circle of hell the following day. Bruised and wracked with pain in face and body, he sat perched on an iron-framed bed, the upper of two bunks, in a cell in the Crumlin Road Gaol. He had, as O'Reilly predicted, been refused bail. He could not believe he had ended up here, in the Crum. High in the narrow wall of his cell was a barred window, which provided the only evidence of reality, of a real world outside this place. Or at least the city of Belfast. The massive Victorian prison in north Belfast was constructed of basalt rock and had four wings radiating out from the centre building, all contained within a five-sided wall. Wasn't there some kind of occult nonsense about five-sided figures being evil? Maybe there was something to it after all. He tried to recall what the theory was, but he was unable to concentrate. He had more immediate concerns. There was his cellmate, snoring away in the lower bed.

Brennan was the quintessential "private person," so sharing a tiny, cramped cell with another person after living in solitary contentment his entire adult life was a trial in itself. But that was not the worst of it. The worst of it was there on the floor, the stuff of nightmares for such as Brennan Burke. A chamber pot! A shit pot, overflowing and stinking of another man's waste. Brennan had been slagged without mercy for being the most fastidious person in the known universe. But he came by it honestly. He had read somewhere that the Celts invented soap. If this was a matter for debate — and how could it not be, given how old the story was — it was said that they were a fastidious lot. And he embodied that quality. Now he was expected to — no. This could not be happening. Just the thought of it made his flesh crawl. And where the fuck would he be having his showers? And how early in the day could he get in there, and how long would he have to soap himself thoroughly and luxuriously as was his habit? And if he had an active day in the exercise yard and felt like having a second shower . . . Would he be forced to perform his ablutions in some communal, slimy . . . *De profundis clamavi ad Te, Domine. Domine, exaudi vocem meam.* Out of the depths I have cried to Thee, o Lord. Lord, hear my voice.

After seeing his cell and his very own shit pot under the bed — in other words, after seeing that life as he knew it was over — he was taken to the basement of the Crum to meet with his solicitor. And now Brennan had a look at the first piece of evidence against him: O'Reilly had obtained a copy of the statement the police had taken from Mrs. McNally, the secretary at Saint Matthew's parish house.

Brennan took the piece of paper and read the words that were going to condemn him.

"He had lost his voice or, well, he must have pretended he lost it. He mouthed some words at me. Pointed to his throat and he was sneezing. Had a bad cold. Then he took out a holy card from his wallet and wrote a note asking me to ring for a taxi."

"Do you have that note, by any chance?"

"No, he put it back in his wallet."

"The pen?"

"I don't think so. But it was all wet, so I wiped it off. Oh no!"

"That's all right. You couldn't have known."

"I believed him! How could I have been so foolish as to let him in there?"

"Now, Mrs. McNally, you have nothing to be sorry for. Just take your time now, and tell us what else happened."

"Well, he seemed to be a very nice fellow, even though he couldn't talk to me. A lovely priest. The first time he came, that is. But then the second time, when he came all covered up in a raincoat with a hood over his head, well, there he was, bounding up from the cellar, the priest with a gun in his hand! And, as we found after, dust and dirt everywhere from the ceiling being torn open!

"When he came up and into the hallway I didn't know what to do. I was terrified he would shoot me! So I said, 'I heard you down there. I called the police on you. They're on their way now!' And of course that was a foolish thing to say; he knew straight away I had made it up. I hadn't had time to call the police. And he said, 'No police, and you won't get hurt.' And him with a gun in his hand!"

"What was he doing with the gun at that time?"

"Well, he was holding it, kind of out like this."

"Pointing it at you."

"Well, kind of. I'm sorry, I'm just too confounded to tell you properly."

"And he said, 'No police and you won't get hurt.'"

"Right."

"And did you feel threatened, him with a gun in his hand telling you not to call the police?"

"Well, yes, in a way. A man with a gun. You know. A man who had impersonated a priest and come in under false pretences! God only knows who he really was! One of the Provos or something! I went back into the office and then of course I really did call the police."

And now Brennan was tasting the bitter fruits of that encounter. The fear and trepidation grabbed hold of him again. That ridiculous episode, him sneezing and miming words, and Tom checking out the basement, and Tom going in there again and making a bollocks of it with the ceiling and the dust. And had Tom been pointing the gun, unintentionally, at the dear little secretary? Had the poor soul really thought he was threatening her? Threatening to kill her? And how had the police come to identify Brennan? How closely did he resemble Tom, if Tom's face was mostly hidden by a hood and scarf? There was a vast difference in age, but Tom said the light in the corridor was dim. They were pretty well the same size, with black hair and dark eyes. The police must have learned Brennan's name after the shooting of Ronan. And they'd had a good look at him that night. But that was two months ago. Why now? How long would he be in this dreadful place? Could he really be convicted of any of those charges? Convicted and banged up here for years? Reddy O'Reilly tried to sound reassuring, but Brennan was far from reassured.

Back in the cell, Brennan pulled one of the two chairs as far as he could from the head of the man still lying uncovered on the lower bunk. The fellow appeared to be in his mid-twenties, with unruly dark brown hair and a few days' growth of beard; he was dressed in a grubby blue sweatshirt over a pair of baggy pajamas. Brennan was still in the clothes he'd been wearing when they arrested him, blue jeans and a light grey cotton sweater that was now soiled and stained with his blood, shoes that he had thrown up on. He was in desperate need of a change. And he needed to have a slash; could not avoid it any longer. And there it was, his fucking piss pot. He had to beat down the temptation to unzip his jeans, stand at the bars of his cell, and piss all over the floor of the Crumlin jail. God knows, the floor looked as if it was no stranger to bodily fluids. But he took a deep breath of the fetid air and stale smoke, dismissed all thoughts of dignity, and pissed in the pot.

The other fellow stirred in the bed, then awoke with a jolt. "Wha? Who are you?"

"I'm your partner in misery."

"Lots of that to go around."

"My name is Brennan."

The young fellow got up off the bed and said, "Dónal. Who did that to you?"

"Peelers in Castlereagh."

"Fuck! They had my wee brother in there. One of the Orange peelers kept jumping on his leg. The bastards broke his fuckin' leg!"

"God save us. If this was happening in some other part of the world . . ."

"Like El Salvador or someplace! The death squads they had down there! The U.S. would be sending in the marines!"

"Em, no, the death squads and the Salvadoran military and the U.S.A. were all on the same side."

"Jesus! They're as bad as the Brits being on the side of the Red Hand Commando!"

"I know. I'm sorry to be the bearer of bad news. But I take your point. When all this torture and abuse —" a streak of pain shot through his groin, and he had to stop himself from crying out "— was being carried out by the Russians in the Soviet days, we heard about the evil of it, no end."

Brennan assumed there was a protocol discouraging one prisoner from asking another what he was in for, so he searched for another topic of conversation. He spoke of the matter uppermost in his mind.

"Dónal, I'd like to have my shower now. How do I get the screws to come and take me to the shower room?"

"Did you say you'd like to have your *shower,* Brennan? *Now?*" Dónal's face registered incredulity, then softened to pity. "You'll likely be waiting several days for that."

"*What?!*"

Then he began to pray, for deliverance from this nightmare and for the strength to endure whatever was to come. His prayer, as it often did, took the form of a hymn, and on this occasion it was the "Ave Verum Corpus." He sang it softly to himself. Brennan noticed, halfway through the piece, that his cellmate's eyes were on him, wide open. But Brennan finished his hymn to the true Body of Christ: "*Esto nobis praegustatum in mortis examine.*"

"You've a fine singing voice, Brennan. What song was that?"

"It's Mozart's setting of the 'Ave Verum Corpus.' It says, 'Be for us a foretaste in the trial of death.'"

"Yeah, we need all the help we can get for the trials we go through in this place."

"Exactly."

Brennan climbed up to his bed and tried to get comfortable on the damp-smelling, lumpy mattress. He willed himself to turn off all his thoughts and fears, so he could fall asleep. Of course he knew that telling yourself you have to sleep is a surefire recipe for a sleepless night. But, somehow, he drifted off late, late in the night. When he awoke at the crack of dawn, he craved a cigarette and a shower. He knew he wasn't about to get either. But one thing he did know: he had to squat over his chamber pot. And he was going to have to slop it out.

Chapter XXXII

Brennan

Brennan had to endure long hours of excruciating boredom in his cell in the Crumlin jail. There was exercise time and time allotted for associating with other prisoners, but this was limited by the fact of self-segregation. Republican and Loyalist prisoners, mortal enemies in the streets outside, did not mix within the prison walls. A few years ago, he learned, Loyalists had fired upon a bus carrying Republican prisoners' families in for a visit, and two wives were injured. A few months after that, Republican prisoners managed to detonate a bomb in a C wing canteen when the Loyalists were having a meal. Two were killed, several others injured. Sometime later Loyalists retaliated by launching a rocket-propelled grenade at the Republican wing from outside the prison, but it failed to detonate. Little wonder the fellas who had committed run of the mill, everyday crimes were known to the authorities here as ODCs. Ordinary decent criminals.

With only so many hours slated for time in common areas, and two groups who did not associate with one another, the out-of-cell time was severely restricted. So Brennan found himself wasting away in a tiny concrete cell with another man. A complete loss of privacy, showers limited sometimes to once a week, and — Brennan tried and failed to shut out the memory of what he had seen scuttling around some areas of the old Belfast dungeon — cockroaches. These revolting creatures infested his nightmares; he had images of them hissing and scrabbling over his body and in his clothing, and he often awoke batting at himself and his bed and the walls, trying to fight the imaginary vermin off. And they weren't just imaginary in the daytime.

Ronan and Gráinne came to see him in the visiting area and brought him a change of clothes. Ronan was distressed about Brennan being jailed after doing a favour for the family, and he was apoplectic about the way Brennan had been mistreated after his arrest. Gráinne tried to be as encouraging as possible about his eventual acquittal and release. Ronan turned to his wife and said something Brennan couldn't hear. Gráinne stood up, said her goodbyes, assuring Brennan of her love and prayers, and left the two men alone. Ronan said then, "Tom is gutted about your arrest, Brennan, absolutely distraught. I hope he'll be in to see you, but em, I'm not sure . . ." Brennan waved that off. "He's confident, though, Tom is, that you'll be acquitted." Then Ronan mouthed the words, "After all, there is no evidence connecting you to the gun."

Brennan's visitors brought him cigarettes. This was of great interest to his cellmate. "You've the snout and I've the papers." Dónal produced the papers and suggested that he redistribute the snout, the tobacco, into skinny, prison-style cigarettes. Brennan hoped it wouldn't come to the point where this would matter. But he suspected it would.

A few days later he got word of another visitor. The MacNeil! He felt a momentary flash of elation, but it was followed immediately by a spasm of anxiety. No. He had been reduced to a dirty wretch who lolled about in a prison cell accompanied always by the smell of shite. Gráinne had brought him fresh jeans and a dark blue sweater, but it wasn't long before the clothing took on the grime and stench of his surroundings. Maura MacNeil had come all the way from Dublin, but he simply could not allow himself to be seen by her. Even worse was the mortification he felt about taking part in that stunt with the pistol, even though he had only acted as a decoy. He remembered reasoning it all out beforehand: he would not be touching the gun, would not be seen with it. And he had done it for Ronan's son, and for those parents in the Netherlands who had no idea what had befallen their boy. The point remained, though, that Brennan had taken part and had been caught. Like thousands of other dim, doltish offenders. He could not look the MacNeil in the eye. He told the warder no, he would not be seeing any visitors.

Monty

"Monty, you're not going to believe what's happened here!" That was Maura on the phone to Halifax, and she wasn't wasting any time on small talk.

"What is it?"

"Brennan has been arrested!"

"Arrested?! For what?" He tried to process this information. "Was there more to that Duane and Ruby night at the bar than I was told? Did you get involved in something else there? Are you yourself —"

"Monty, listen to me. He's been arrested and charged with a string of offences relating to a gun. Possession of a weapon, attempting to pervert the course of justice, uttering threats. It's unbelievable."

"Brennan wouldn't do anything like that, for Christ's sake. Are these some kind of trumped-up charges relating to his family over there? Was he present for something they did?"

"No, it's just him apparently. I went to talk to Reddy O'Reilly."

"He's representing Brennan?"

"Yes."

Monty remembered the last time he had seen O'Reilly. The solicitor had turned down the chance to represent the Flanagan family in their suit against the UDA man, Davison. And he remembered the eerie warning from Carrick. Monty would rather have his fingernails pulled out than admit he'd received a warning and laughed it off. He felt more and more uneasy as the conversation went on.

"Reddy told me what Brennan was charged with, but he wouldn't say much more. Which is only right. So then I went to the Crumlin jail —"

"Brennan in the Crumlin jail? This cannot be happening. Is he going to get out on bail?"

"Yes, the Crumlin jail. No, he's not going to be released. I went to arrange a visit. And he wouldn't see me!"

Monty didn't want to ask, but he had to. "Why not?"

"I haven't a clue."

Brennan

Brennan's nightmares became more extreme and terrifying as the days went on, and he fought not only against the ugly creatures that invaded his consciousness but the ugly fact that his deterioration was partly the result of something he had always refused to acknowledge about himself. Sure, Brennan Burke was fond of a jar. Anyone could tell you that. Fair enough. But he could not recall ever being physically and psychologically debilitated by going a few days without a drink. To be honest, he could not remember the last time he had gone a few days without a drink. Even in the abbey, he had a bottle or two on hand. Now, though, he could not avoid the suspicion that the shakiness he felt, the disrupted sleep, the nausea, the sweating were caused by withdrawal from alcohol. A few days ago, one of the lads — Frank, a heavyset man with the broken facial capillaries of a heavy drinker — had slipped him a quart bottle of *poitín*. Homemade, smuggled in, or concocted somewhere on the premises of the jail, Brennan didn't know. He had bought it from the man in exchange for a fistful of skinny, prison-grade, hand-rolled cigarettes — yes, it had come to this, that he was jealously guarding hand-rolled cigarettes to satisfy his own cravings and to use as currency. He had taken the bottle of homemade brew and tried to make it last, by taking little sips. The delicate sips of a gentleman in his club. But then he simply opened his gullet and poured the stuff down. He spent the night after that boaking up all over his bed. Poor Dónal was a saint about it. Not so the screw on duty that morning. "Clean that filthy mess up, you fuckin' drunken Taig bastard!" There weren't many Catholics on the prison staff, so it was a slur heard frequently by the prisoners, one of many instances of humiliation and intimidation the inmates were subjected to by the staff of this wretched place.

His symptoms continued to worsen in the wake of the bad brew. Never one troubled by stress or doubts in the past, he now found himself riddled with anxiety about every little sound or rumour or alteration in the routine of the prison. His heart raced, he had the shakes, he had headaches, he felt sick to his stomach, and he was bathed in sweat. And had to wait for days before he could shower it off. He was hardly better than the bugs and grotesque creatures that populated his booze-withdrawal hallucinations. A fine sight he must have been trying to stumble through his daily, solitary Mass with a scrap of prison-issue bread and cup of apple juice — *apple juice* for the sacramental wine!

His image of himself was confirmed when, unshaven and grubby, he received more visitors at the Crum. Father Alec Reid on one occasion, Lorcan and Gráinne's sister Éilis on another. And the Reverend

Clark Rayburn. Brennan saw how they reacted to his appearance and tried to cover their reaction. Clark Rayburn prayed with him and did his best to utter words of encouragement. Brennan was more grateful than he could ever express for the Protestant minister's kindness to a Republican prisoner in the Crumlin Road Gaol. Molly flew over from London again, followed by Terry and Patrick from New York. They could not mask their shock at the look of him. Patrick, the psychiatrist, was clearly alarmed at what he saw. Brennan was relieved about one thing, anyway: at least he had not shamed himself by wheedling his family into trying to smuggle whiskey in for him.

Then he had another caller. The MacNeil, trying again, not giving up on him. He felt the same impulses warring in his soul again this time. The mortification over what he had done and what he had become in prison battled with his longing to see her face, hear her voice, glom onto her and . . .

How soon would she be here? Was he still going to have the shakes when he was sitting across from her? Would a cigarette fix him up? He had only three left. Should he have one now, and one closer to the visit? If he smoked them both before, he'd only have the one for the letdown after her departure. And Christ! He was grimy and sweating and he hadn't had a shower! Or a shave. This was almost as horrible as those weeks on the ship that had taken him from Ireland to America as a child, that storm-tossed, vomit- and shite-sloshing journey across the Atlantic when he nearly jumped . . . This visit couldn't happen. The MacNeil couldn't see him like this. But he got the word: she was here and she wasn't leaving.

He was escorted to the visiting area, and there she was, her brown hair shining, her summery yellow blazer and white shirt immaculate. As soon as he saw her, he had the urge to run into her arms and cling to her, weeping. Naturally, that was not on, and he liked to think he was still, barely, man enough not to do anything so needy and pathetic. Not to mention the fact that any contact with him, with what he was now, would leave her contaminated. He knew instantly, from the look on her face, what she thought of the state of him. Her mouth opened, no doubt to make a wisecrack of some sort, but it closed again without emitting anything but a stifled little cry. For the first time since he had known her, Maura MacNeil of the quick, sharp, lacerating tongue was without words. That alone spoke volumes to Brennan.

"Professor MacNeil. Have you come to study the Norn Iron justice system at firsthand?"

"Brennan, you don't want to hear me on the subject. What in the name of God have they done to you?"

He knew he had lost weight. How long had it been since his arrest? Three weeks? It felt like three centuries. The bruising in his face had gone from black and blue to a bilious green; it was fading but still visible. He said to Maura, "I can tell you this: anything that's been done to me in this place, or the place I was before, has not been done in the name of God."

"What has Reddy O'Reilly said about getting you out of here?"

"You're the law professor, MacNeil. And this is Belfast. So you know I'm not getting out of here. And who knows when in the hell my trial will be. O'Reilly tells me it can take a year, or even longer, to get to trial."

Once again, Maura MacNeil could think of nothing to say.

"Entertain me here, MacNeil. Tell me something that will make me forget for a few minutes where I am, and what I've become."

He watched as she made the effort to come up with a couple of stories about the children, Normie and Dominic, and tried to keep up a line of patter for the duration of the visit. He told her a bit about his life in the Crum. He looked at the lovely face, listened to the familiar voice, and wished the visit would never end, regardless of what she was saying. When she was gone, he had never felt so lonely in his life.

"I went to see him in the Crum." It was Maura on the line.

"Jesus, Maura, I can't believe we're having this conversation."

"*You* can't believe it? I saw him and I can't believe what that place has done to him! I hardly recognized him when they brought him in. His face has obviously been battered. His hair is dirty — Brennan with dirty hair! — and he hasn't shaved for days. He looks like either a God-crazed saint or, well, what he's accused of being: a stereotypical Irish terrorist! I'd be terrified of him if I met him in a dark street. He just sat there with a hollow look in those black, black eyes."

Her voice broke, and Monty tried desperately to find something positive to say. "It's an awful situation, for sure, but you know Brennan, how strong he is. He'll tough it out. He'll be saying Mass for the other inmates, ministering to them the way he does in his prison ministry here in Halifax . . ."

"You didn't see him. He is falling apart. This is absolutely destroying him. He's reduced to fretting about how many cigarettes he has left to get him through the day, and when the next batch of potcheen or moonshine or whatever it is he's been nipping in there will be safe for consumption!"

"Christ, that stuff can kill you, can blind you, if you don't do it right."

"Tell me about it. A girl I grew up with in Cape Breton, her father died after drinking bad shine. But no wonder Brennan has sunk to drinking prison hooch. As if all this wasn't bad enough, there was the call from Rome." Oh, God. Of course. "The priest from Sancta Maria Regina Coeli called Ronan's place looking for Father Burke. I got this from Gráinne. I know Ronan would have tried to put a good face on a disastrous situation: 'There's been a mistake. Father Burke is facing false allegations. He'll be cleared. Let's all just wait till it gets sorted.' But you can guess the rest. Father Brennan Xavier Burke is not going to be directing the music of the spheres in Rome in September."

There was one aspect of prison life to which Brennan had managed to adapt instantly: the prisoner's difficulty in adapting to change. Any change or rumour of change was met with fear, on the principle that things could always get worse. And almost certainly would. An alteration in routine, a new cellmate, a new screw on the wing, all brought on waves of stress. So Brennan's own anxiety spiked to the sky when, in the middle of June, he got the news that he was being moved. Not to another cell, not to another wing, but to Long Kesh, also known as the H Blocks. Officially, it was Her Majesty's Prison Maze. The H Blocks were where ten hunger strikers died for the cause, where the blanket protests were held, where history had been made.

Long Kesh was where Brennan would be held while waiting for his trial, and he now knew the date: September 18. Three months stretched ahead like an eternity to Brennan, but this was in fact a very early trial date; he could have been waiting on remand for years. Reddy O'Reilly explained that another trial, which involved several defendants and which had been forecast to last for weeks, was not going ahead. O'Reilly didn't say why, and Brennan didn't ask. So a number of other cases had been rescheduled. O'Reilly did some finagling and managed, because Brennan's trial was expected to be a short one, to get an early date. Brennan dreaded the trial but dreaded a long prison stay even more. The sooner he got to trial, the sooner . . . but no, there was no guarantee that he would be acquitted and set free, although the alternative was unthinkable.

Brennan had absolutely no control over the direction his life would take. It was as if he were no longer a subject, an independent human being, exercising his free will and acting in the world. He had been reduced to the level of an object, acted upon and moved at the will of others. And so there he was, being transported out of the city to the Kesh. The sight of it was familiar from his visit to Lorcan's friend back whenever that was, a lifetime ago. The watchtowers, the walls, the razor wire. After all the rigmarole of getting admitted, the warder led him down a corridor lined with cells that were shut in by massive steel doors, each with only a narrow, horizontal slit of an opening. The screw opened one of the doors and ushered him into a concrete cell with his new roommate, a red-faced man of middle age who sat on his bottom bunk and glared at Brennan. He looked as if he would explode with rage at any minute. And there on the floor was the dreaded chamber pot. Brennan turned his attention to the outer wall but found little relief there. Long vertical openings in the concrete provided the only view out. Not much better than the arrow slits in the wall of a medieval castle. The limited view was of the exercise yard and iron fencing, not the earth and moon and stars above.

The afternoon after his first night in the Kesh he had to face down the temptation to grab his cellmate by the throat and throttle the life out of him. He gave his name as O'Morda, an enormous, surly fellow who wore a dingy brown muscle shirt that displayed tattoos all over his arms and shoulders. O'Morda of course was present for every second of Brennan's existence. A screw came by to tell Brennan that a visitor had come for him but she would only be able to stay for a few minutes. Was this the MacNeil, on a flying trip to Belfast and all the way out to Lisburn to see him? His anticipation must have been evident, because the screw laughed and said, "I'll take that as a yes."

Brennan fought the urge to sprint to the visiting area. When he arrived at the cubicle, though, it was not Maura. It was the parish secretary, not from Saint Matthew's — God knows — but from "his" parish of Holy Cross in Ardoyne. He hoped he had succeeded in masking his disappointment that it was not Maura. He was filled with gratitude that Mary Pat had come all the way out to this frightening place to see him, and he thanked her profusely.

When he got back to his cell, O'Morda was lolling in bed smoking a cigarette. "So who is she, Burke, the one who had you blasting out of here with a big fuckin' grin on your face?" As far as Brennan knew, he had never had a big fucking grin on his face at any time in his adult life. But the odious creature went on, "Give me all the details so I can enjoy them after lights out tonight."

It took all the patience Brennan had — and he had never been renowned for his patience — to refrain from falling on this gouger and pounding the face off him.

"What's her name, Burke?"

He refused to rise to the bait. All he said was *"Ar Éirinn ní neosainn cé hí."*

"What the fuck does that mean?"

"You haven't been working on your Jailic, mate. It means 'for Ireland I'd not tell her name.' I'm surprised you don't know that, O'Morda. Maybe you're on the wrong wing. More comfortable on a Loyalist wing, would you be?"

"Fuck off."

Thank God for small mercies, not everyone on the wing was as unpleasant as O'Morda. And the prisoners were not confined to their cells all day, which meant that Brennan was sometimes able to avoid the round white "convenience" on the cell floor. There were times when the prisoners could go outdoors to exercise and they could socialize with one another in the evenings. So Brennan roused himself from his torpor to sit in on a session of music on his third evening in the place. He walked down the corridor to a spacious room where his fellow remand prisoners were gathered. The walls were decorated with political cartoons and pictures of the ten dead hunger strikers. There was a photo of the scholar and politician Eoin MacNeill, who had been imprisoned during the War of Independence seventy-five years before. Brennan tried to draw courage from MacNeill's defiant words: "In prison we are their jailers, on trial their judges, persecuted their punishers, dead their conquerors."

The *céilí* was well underway when he sat down. Two men were playing guitars, one a bodhran, another a mandolin. The fellow in the seat beside him looked to be in his late thirties, with thick brown hair and a good-humoured look about his eyes. He introduced himself as Turlough.

"I'm Brennan Burke. Father Burke in better times."

"Oh, aye? Have they made the Church a proscribed organization again?"

Brennan had to laugh. "Yeah, we're back to penal times. They caught me saying a Mass out behind the trees."

"Were you at the rock?" Turlough sang. It was an old Irish song, about the days when Mass had to be said at midnight at a "Mass rock" and there was a bounty on priests the way there was on wolves.

"No, in my case, I wasn't picked up for my religious duties."

Turlough offered him a cigarette and lit it for him. Brennan and his new friend smoked and listened to a set of rebel songs. When the current performer bowed to applause and went off for a smoke of his own, a man called out from across the room, "Turlough! Do Maggie for us!"

"Ah, no . . ."

"Do it. Or the only spuds you'll be getting in this place are the unfermented kind your mam used to boil for yer dinner."

Brennan perked up at the word "unfermented." Discounting the prefix "un" implied the existence of an in-house distillery. He wouldn't ask about it now; he would bide his time and then make a casual inquiry. Tomorrow, or maybe tonight.

"Turlough, give us Maggie on the Blanket. I'll be Denis."

"You always get to be Denis," another man groused.

"Where is my hairstylist, gentlemen?" It was Turlough's lips that were moving, but the voice and accent were that of Britain's former prime minister. Brennan had oft heard it said that she was the most hated person in Ireland after Cromwell. "I don't go *on* without my hair being perfect!"

Someone handed Turlough a comb, and Turlough bent forward, shook his hair and then used the comb to do what Brennan's sisters used to call teasing. He managed to shape it into something resembling a Thatcherite helmet of hair.

"My bag! My bag! What is the matter with you people?"

"Yes, Prime Minister!" one of the men said and handed the PM what appeared to be a camera case with a strap. The Iron Lady now had her handbag, which she looped over her arm. She announced to the world at that point that she had been taken prisoner. "The terrorists have won the battle but not the war! Never the war. Now that the Irish Republic's expansionist policies have led it to invade and occupy this great kingdom of ours, I hereby vow that I shall wear nothing, nothing at all — will be bare-arse naked — until this occupation ends! And Denis will do the same. Denis!"

"No, Margaret, my little love führer, please no."

"Denis, what did I say? Strip! Now!"

The man whimpered and began unbuttoning his shirt.

But the PM's minions cried out in horror, "No, Prime Minister, we beg you! Anything but this! The television cameras are here." Someone produced a dishtowel. "Take this blanket, and cover yourself, Mrs. Thatcher. Modesty demands it."

"I shall bow to no demands. I make the demands around here."

"The blanket, Prime Minister. How about we all go on the blanket to show solidarity? You know, like that Irish rabble did a few years back."

"I shall not hear of it." By this time the Iron Lady was down to her skivvies, as was a quivering Denis by her side.

One of the other fellows then held his fist in front of his mouth like a microphone and announced to the world, "We interrupt our regular programming for this news bulletin. The Irish Republican Army, having recently invaded and occupied all of the United Kingdom, was seen today scrambling to get off our island. They commandeered every ship and every little boat, raft, and water-wing to make the voyage back across the Irish Sea. Their commanding officer said, 'We have the best fighting men in the world, but our men have been frightened and terrorized by the horrors they witnessed on English soil. The Thatchers, both of them, naked as the day they came into the world! I pray to God and Mary and Saint Patrick that I never again see —'"

"What are those men doing with their clothes off?" The question was barked from the edge of the room.

The prisoners all turned to see a shocked warder standing there, his eyes out on sticks.

"Show some respect for the prime minister, Dickson!" one of the prisoners demanded. "And the poor wee man at her side."

"Are ye stark, raving mad, the lot of youse?"

"Set us free, Dickson. It's life in this dungeon that has us demented."

"Get your clothes on and act like normal human beings, why don't youse?"

"Ordinary decent criminals, you mean, sir?"

"That would be an improvement." The warder shook his head in bafflement and moved off.

All the foolishness helped take Brennan's mind off his plight, for a while at least. And it had another benefit. It gave him something to talk about a few days later when it really was the MacNeil who came to see him. Her first visit to the Kesh. Her last visit to Brennan. She and the children were leaving Dublin for home the following week, the last week of June. He had fretted about the visit all night. Now here she was. He avoided the subject of her departure by amusing her with the Iron Lady naked protest skit. She responded with a tale about protesting against Ronald Reagan years before, when he visited Ottawa. She had made the trip from Halifax to the capital to join a demonstration against the American president and his policies. As the president and his entourage made their way towards the House of Commons, Maura rushed forward so Reagan would see her protest sign. Her sudden movement alarmed the security men and Maura, being a typically polite Canadian, blurted out "Sorry, sorry!" which served to take the edge off her tough-on-Reagan stance.

"Ah," said Brennan, "the MacNeil unmasked as nothing but a Reagan apologist. A tool of the military-industrial complex."

"And a lackey running dog of the corporate bourgeoisie!"

But their stories had to end, and they sat there looking at each other. "Brennan, I'm sorry — there I go again, so Canadian! — I'm so sorry to be leaving you in here. As you can imagine. But you've got a great lawyer in Reddy O'Reilly. He'll do his very best to see that justice is done, and you're let out of here."

He made no reply. They both knew there were no guarantees in the Belfast courts. Visiting time was up. They stood, and she opened her arms to him. He fastened onto her. Clung to her like the weak, pathetic man he had become. She was weeping; he was doing his level best not to. Then she turned and was gone.

He returned to his cell and lay on his bed, for hours and hours on end, staring up at the ceiling and hearing nothing as prison life went on around him. As the night wore on he was once again afflicted with the DTs, once again afflicted with regret for his imprudence and the consequences of his actions.

There were a few bright moments that week when he attended a class in the Irish language, though there was a shadow of darkness even over that. Brennan commended an older man next to him for his skill with the language.

"So much better now when we can have classes openly," the man said. "I was here in the late 1970s, when we weren't even allowed a pen or paper and had to shout our lessons from one cell to another, and scratch our words on the walls with the broken edge of a toothpaste tube."

Another of the men piped up, "We weren't even allowed to receive Christmas cards with Irish greetings. Irish was forbidden as a 'foreign language'! In our own country! They're still censoring letters we get in Irish."

The first speaker responded, "That's right. Hard to believe so many of our lads have the Jailic now. In some of the other blocks, you'll hear Irish spoken all day."

There was a *céilí* that evening. Brennan forced himself to get up and attend, knowing it would distract him at least temporarily from his plight. He saw Turlough in the room and greeted him.

"You're not looking all that well, Brennan."

"Ah . . ." Brennan tried to brush it off.

"You can't let yourself be defeated by this place. If you can't hold up now, what will become of you if you have to spend years in here? You have to think about that, as much as you don't want to."

"I know. I appreciate your concern, Turlough, really." Then he said, "A wee drop would fix me up."

Turlough's answer was unexpected. "No, it wouldn't. Stay off the stuff, Brennan. It's a cycle you should try to break now, rather than later. I speak from personal experience; I'm trying to get off it myself."

Brennan nodded; he couldn't think what to say in response to the man's kindness and his wisdom. But he was saved from having to reply by the other prisoners once again calling upon Turlough to provide the entertainment. "Give us a song, would you?"

So Turlough fetched a guitar from a corner of the room and gave them some rabble-rousing songs that had them all shouting and pumping their fists in the air. He had a strong, rich voice and was a dab hand on the guitar as well. He switched then to a couple of slow, poignant ballads and was even more effective singing those. There was a reflective silence in the room after his final song, followed by a thunderous ovation. He came and sat down beside Brennan.

"That was brilliant," Brennan told him. "I'm something of a musician myself. I can carry a tune and I've directed a number of choirs, so I appreciate genuine talent when I hear it. You were a ballad singer in your former life, perhaps, Turlough?"

"I was a bomb maker in my former life, Brennan." Brennan was surprised at the candour. His surprise must have been obvious, because Turlough said, "It's no secret. It's been in the news then and now."

"Right."

"But yeah, I sang in the bars from time to time. Was all set to make a recording with some other lads when I got lifted and banged up in here."

"You're fairly new in the place, too, then."

"No, I've been accommodated here before. Spent some of what would otherwise have been the best years of my life here. Is Ronan Burke a relation of yours?"

"My first cousin."

"We need more like him. I'm not sure he's on the right path now, but he's been a patriot for a quarter of a century. Nobody can take that away from him."

"Somebody tried."

"Aye, I know. Ronan and I go way back. I've known him since the internment-without-trial years. My father was dragged out of bed by soldiers of the British Army and kicked unconscious in front of my mother and me. I was fifteen years old at the time. I wanted to sign up, join the IRA that minute. Me and all the other lads I knew. The Brits' policy did wonders for IRA recruitment. Ronan was the fella we had to talk to. He told me to come back when I turned seventeen, and to keep my nose clean in the meantime. They had me checked out, made sure I was sound, not a criminal type."

Turlough gave a little laugh and said, "I passed muster. But I've been designated a criminal by our opponents. I blew up buildings. Military installations, barracks, things like that. That's against the law; it's criminal. Fair enough. But what those soldiers did to my father was criminal. What the peelers in Castlereagh did to you — I know what they did, because they did it to all of us — is criminal. But nobody locks them up. We are all fighting in the same war, all committing acts of war. In here we are prisoners of war. Our protests over the years have had the desired effect. We wear our own clothes now; we're not locked up all day. The prison authorities know they have to deal with our own OCs and staff. This entire complex is a prisoner of war camp in all but name."

Brennan looked at the man beside him. Ballad singer, wit, bon vivant, wise counsellor, bomb maker: Turlough was all these things, and Brennan liked him immensely, as he did so many others in this part of the world. The mix of outsized personality and violent history was a feature of many people in Brennan's own family, and he got on with them famously. Did this mean he glossed over what they had done, or might have done, during the dirty war that had raged here for over twenty-five years? No.

"I can guess what you're thinking," Turlough said then. Brennan didn't bother with a rote denial. They were both silent for a few moments and then, "Could I speak to you in your other capacity, not as a fellow H block prisoner but as Father Burke?"

"Certainly."

"Let's go over there." Turlough pointed to the end of the room where there was some private space. They both sat, and Brennan waited. Turlough said nothing.

Eventually, Brennan prompted him. "You wanted to talk to me?"

"I do. It's just that I don't want the other lads . . ."

"There's no need to go through the ritual." No need to make the sign of the cross and recite the words and make it obvious that he was in the confessional. Then somebody picked up a mandolin and launched into a song, and nobody was paying attention to priest and penitent at the back of the room.

"First of all I have to confess, Father, that I confessed this before." Brennan merely nodded. "And it didn't take."

Brennan had to smile at that. "How do you know?"

"Because the priest refused to give me absolution."

"Did he say so?"

"He did. I killed two civilians. Two Protestant men with no para-military involvement. I thought the barracks had been cleared, but in fact it hadn't been. Two innocent people died. I never got caught for that, by the way. I'm here on unrelated charges, other explosives offences. But that other disaster, I confessed it to my priest, and he said I had spent so much time justifying myself and explaining how it happened that I wasn't taking responsibility for it. Said he was forever hearing stories about phone boxes not working when warnings were meant to be given before the bombs went off, or the men ringing the authorities with genuine warnings but the peelers didn't pass the warnings along. All of these things have happened, of course, but my priest said he had heard this all too often. In my case, I didn't know there was a delivery man on the premises. And I thought the cleaner had ended his shift an hour before. The priest said I was denying responsibility, that I wasn't remorseful. But I am! I have the deaths of those two people on my conscience."

"Some people are not as scrupulous as you are when it comes to casualties."

"Aye, I know. Civilians are not targeted but they end up being killed and injured anyway. That should never happen."

"Even if not intended, civilian deaths are inevitable when bombs are exploded on the streets of a town or in shopping centres, as they have been during this conflict."

"Well, Father, I can assure you that mums with shopping carts, or fellows delivering newspapers, have never been my targets. I never go near those places, exactly for that reason."

"I believe you. And I know you are genuinely sorry for what you did. Here's your penance: someday, somehow, do something to help the families of your victims. Or other victims. Anonymously. I understand that. I'll leave it to you to sort out. Will you do that?"

"I will. You have my word."

"*Ego te absolvo a peccatis tuis in nomine Patris et Filii et Spiritus Sancti, amen.*"

†

Back in his cell that night, Brennan prayed and hoped with all his heart that Turlough and others would find ways to bring even a small portion of solace to victims of attacks perpetrated by the Republican side, just as Brennan and Ronan were trying to do for the victims of the Loyalist bombings in Dublin and Monaghan.

And then the spectre of a moral philosopher arose in Brennan's consciousness, as it so often did. The question to be debated yet again was the question of a just or an unjust war. *Ex nihilo nihil fit.* Out of nothing, nothing comes. Or to turn it around, this war, these Troubles didn't arise fully formed out of nothing. The statelet of Northern Ireland was formed not from the nine counties of Ulster but of the six with a Protestant majority. That way, there was no fear of Catholics voting it out of existence. And the loyal-to-Britain majorities were maintained by gerrymandering, rigging the boundaries of districts to make sure the majority stayed that way. There was no universal franchise here in the times leading up to the Troubles; the only people who had a vote in local elections were a man who either owned or rented a house, the man and his wife. Any other adults living in the house, such as lodgers or grown sons and daughters who could not afford houses of their own, could not cast a ballot. And public housing was given out by elected councils; if you gave someone a house, you were giving them two votes. Same with jobs: give a man a job and he might be able to buy a house and thus become eligible to vote. So, don't hire him. Oh, and there was a "business vote," whereby nominees selected by the business could vote more than once. This was not the situation in mainland Britain of course, just here in the North of Ireland.

All of this was incontrovertible fact but, even so, Brennan hated thinking like this: Nationalist and Unionist, Republican and Loyalist. Us and them. And he particularly hated thinking in sectarian terms, of Catholic and Protestant. When he was anywhere else on the planet he never thought of his fellow Christians in that way; he respected and admired the freedom and the culture that Protestantism had brought to much of the world. But in this small part of the world, the minority had been denied that freedom. And that was what had led to the civil rights movement here. Then, when the people attempted to end discrimination by peaceful means, what happened? The marchers were beaten by the police, shot and killed by the army. So what do you do if peaceful protest is met by violence? You fight back. People had not just started throwing rocks and petrol bombs and real bombs for no reason. *Ex nihilo nihil fit.*

But even if you had a just cause, a justifiable reason for taking action, what kind of actions were justified in carrying out that struggle? What or who was a legitimate target? Military installations? Government buildings? Commercial property, on the theory that if it got too costly, London would no longer prop up the local regime? And could killing ever be justified? Civilians? Never, not even if their deaths were unintended, were "collateral damage." Soldiers? Well, they were just the poor devils who were sent out to fight for their country. Or do its dirty work. Was it fair to target them? Some would say that's the risk they signed up for. But did that justify the actions of a sniper taking out a soldier from a rooftop above the fray? And what about the situation when soldiers went far beyond the code of the soldier and acted as terrorists themselves? What about soldiers and intelligence spooks who colluded with one side in killing the other?

These notions had been warring in Brennan's soul for as long as he could remember, ever since, as a child, he had come to understand what it meant that his family was a "well-known Republican family." He was no closer to resolution now than he had been then, no closer to certainty even in here, where he was locked up with alleged soldiers — or, as the authorities would have it, terrorists — in this long and terrible war.

Selfish concerns took over then. While he was talking to Turlough and hearing his confession, Brennan had momentarily forgotten his own plight. He had been back to his real self, Brennan Burke the priest, performing the sacraments and ministering to his fellow man. Now in his bed in the middle of the night, though, he reverted to Brennan Burke the physical, mental, and neurological wreck, bedevilled by drink and nicotine and raging against his misfortune.

†

Brennan had a brief, painful encounter early in July. Tomás Burke came for a visit. Before going out to meet him, Brennan gave himself over to a fantasy, an imaginary scene in which Brennan grassed on young Tom in return for his own freedom. He imagined himself walking away from the H Blocks, boarding a plane out of Belfast, leaving all this behind him forever. There was no mystery about why people in desperate circumstances turned on their co-conspirators. But he knew he would never do it. Brennan was a Burke. Burkes were not informers; they sure as hell did not turn in members of their own family. He walked out to the visiting area to meet his cousin's son.

They sat across from one another in the cubicle, both of them knowing why Brennan was in here, neither of them knowing what to say. Finally Tom spoke up, with the only words that could possibly be said, "You'll be acquitted, Brennan. I know you will. Reddy O'Reilly is brilliant; he'll get you out of this."

Brennan wanted to sound hopeful, wanted to ease the young man's distress. They both knew that whatever sentence Brennan might be facing if convicted would be less onerous than what Tom would face if he were in Brennan's place. The charge against Tom would be murder, the sentence imprisonment for life. A young man with a wife and family . . . But what about Brennan? Surely his life was of value as well, and if he lost years of it . . . He chastised himself; Tom would not be thinking of Brennan as expendable. Brennan felt compelled to reassure him. He took a glance around to make doubly sure no one was listening. "Even if they'd nabbed you, there's no guarantee they wouldn't have lifted me as well, for my part in it. My willing participation." Tom's expression was bleak. Brennan said then, "You don't have to come back, Tom."

"I can understand why you wouldn't want to see me, Brennan. I —"

"No, that's not it. But it won't do either of us a bit of good. Stay away from it all."

And that's how they left it. By the time Brennan raised his hand to bless his young relation, Tom had turned away, despondent, didn't see it.

At the *céilí* that evening Brennan gave them a song. He stood and apologized to the audience for the fact that it would be Brennan singing this aria and not the incomparable soprano, Kiri Te Kanawa.

Turlough responded, "Kiri broke out of here in the great escape of 1983. Hasn't been seen here since. So you go ahead, Brennan."

"Thank you, Turlough. This is 'Vissi d'Arte' from Puccini's *Tosca*." Brennan put his entire heart and soul into the song, every word of which resonated with him more painfully than ever.

> *Sempre con fè sincera la mia preghiera ai santi tabernacoli*
>   *salì.*
> *Sempre con fè sincera diedi fiori agli altar.*
> *Nell'ora del dolore perché, perché, Signore,*
> *Perché me ne rimuneri così?*

> Always with true faith my prayer rose to the holy
>   shrines.
> Always with true faith I gave flowers to the altar.
> In the hour of grief why, why, o Lord,
> Why do you reward me this way?

When Maura and the kids returned to Halifax from Ireland, Normie decided to go to her regular school to spend the last two days of the term with her friends. At the end of the second day, she called Monty's office and said, "You guys have to come and get me after work." So Monty and Maura walked over to Saint Bernadette's Choir School just before five o'clock. Their daughter had been watching for them and met them at the door. "Guess what? We have a surprise for Father Burke! He's coming home soon, right?"

Monty had a sick feeling in his stomach. Maura had obviously been able to keep Normie away from the papers and the news broadcasts when they were in Dublin, and he had no desire to bear the bad tidings now.

Normie was nearly beside herself with excitement. "Come on in and see! We made a great big poster showing an old-fashioned church like they have in Rome. Then we drew a whole bunch of angels with hymn books and their mouths open. They are his new choir in Rome. Except guess what? We cut out our own faces from our school pictures and put them on as the angels' heads, even though we can't go to Rome with him."

She led them into the art room where a bunch of the other kids had gathered. She showed her parents the poster. "See? They're all angels except one. There's a little red devil in the back row. Guess who it is? Not me! It's Richard Robertson!" Richard was well known as a character in the school.

"And we looked up something in Italian to write on it. It's a blessing. Listen to me say it: *Il Signore ti benedica e ti custodisca.* It means the Lord bless you and keep you. Mummy? What's wrong?"

"Nothing, sweetie. I just . . ."

"So anyway when we bring him in we're going to show him the poster, and then we're going to sing two songs for him. 'Regina Coeli,' which means Queen of Heaven, which is the name of his church, and

'The Lord Bless You and Keep You,' because of the saying on the poster, and it was written by Saint Francis of Assisi. He was Italian. Father Burke's going to love it, right?! And he went to school over there and got a degree from a college in Rome called the Angelicum. Remember when I was little? I thought he was an angel himself!" She leaned towards them and confided, "I still do!"

Monty could not bear the thought of telling his daughter what had befallen her angel now. Could not bear the thought of telling her that Father Burke, with his outstanding musical talent, his lifetime of service to God, his doctoral degree from the Angelicum in Rome, was now languishing in a prison, dirty, depressed, and afflicted with delirium tremens, charged with being a terrorist.

Chapter XXXIII

Brennan

Brennan looked upon Redmond O'Reilly the way he had hitherto looked upon the risen Christ. In O'Reilly resided Brennan's every hope of a future life. O'Reilly would be — would have to be — his saviour. That this trial might only be the beginning was simply unthinkable. The solicitor's handsome face was lined from a lifetime of experience in this state and its system of trial and retribution. The shining hair brushed back from O'Reilly's forehead gave him a fearless but dignified appearance. Brennan did not think he, himself, would be able to project a dignified image when he entered the courtroom. If he looked the way he felt — seedy, soiled, depressed, and sick from occasional jars of illicit drink and delirium tremens when the stuff had run out — his appearance would likely convey "This sad bastard must surely be guilty" to judge and jury, press and public.

"So, Brennan," O'Reilly said to him at the Kesh two days before the trial, "let me apprise you of what you can expect in the Belfast

Crown Court on the Crumlin Road. First and foremost, of course, there will be no jury."

Brennan had of course heard of non-jury trials here but wasn't that just for . . . "I'm not a paramilitary. I'm not charged with blowing up a bar full of innocent people. Wouldn't I have a right to be tried by a judge and jury if —"

Reddy O'Reilly shook his head. "You're in Belfast now, Brennan. You are in a different world from the justice system with which you are likely familiar."

There went Brennan's slim put persistent hope of explaining to a box full of jurors, as earnestly and reassuringly as he could, that he had not had a gun in his hand, had not behaved in a threatening manner in any way, had not caused any damage. He didn't know quite what he would say about the motive for his visit to Saint Matthew's, what he would say in order to save his own hide and that of Tomás. But he would work it out with O'Reilly. Lawyers couldn't knowingly let you lie on the stand, but . . . now there was no jury. A judge might not be so easily charmed.

"This is a Diplock court, remember, Brennan. The system was formulated more than twenty years ago by Lord Diplock, a Law Lord, member of the House of Lords. I shall spare you the details but juries have been abolished for trials on charges relating to terrorism."

"Terrorism! I may be guilty of bad judgment, stupidity, sentimentality, in agreeing to distract the secretary, but surely even in this jurisdiction I cannot by any stretch of the imagination be considered a terrorist."

O'Reilly looked at him with something close to pity and laid a hand on his shoulder. "Brennan. The threat charge and the possession of a firearm in a public place are enough to bring this into the Diplock court. Judge alone. The stated reason for this is that jurors can be too easily intimidated and threatened in the current climate of sectarian violence."

"But doesn't the same argument apply to judges? Can't they be threatened as well? And their families?"

"They can be and have been. Not merely threatened but murdered. Judges who hear these cases are under twenty-four-hour protection. What you have to understand about the Diplock courts is that they act more like an arm of the security forces than courts of law even-handedly dispensing justice. That's easier done by a judge than by an unpredictable box full of jurors."

"Are there any conscientious judges who come to the trial with no preconceived notions or alliances and who weigh the evidence, try the cases fairly, that class of a thing?"

"There are."

"But there are many who do not live up to those lofty ideals."

"There are."

"What you're saying, Reddy, is that I'm fucked."

"Notwithstanding all the odds that are stacked against us, we shall do our utmost to see that you are not fucked, Father Burke."

†

That hope dimmed further on the morning of the trial, when O'Reilly outlined for his client what to expect.

"The prosecutor will be calling six witnesses."

"Six? The church secretary, obviously. Who else?"

"That's how many they need to nail it, the way they see it."

"To nail *me*. Who are the witnesses?"

"The parish secretary, a couple of peelers, an eyewitness who saw suspicious behaviour at a rubbish skip, a ballistics expert, and a pathologist."

"Pathologist? Nobody died on my watch. What am I missing here?"

"The doctor will testify about a man who died of gunshot wounds. And one of the RUC peelers is a ballistics expert. He'll say that the bullets dug out of the murder victim were fired from the gun you took from Saint Matthew's. That goes to motive of course, your motive. The reason you took the gun out of there was to pervert the course of justice with respect to a murder investigation."

But that couldn't be! There was nothing to which the bullets could be matched, because the body of that poor young backpacker was still buried. Wasn't it? None of this made sense, least of all the idea that he would threaten to kill a defenceless woman in a church office.

"Well," he said, "let's hope the judge will see that I am sincere and credible when I get up there and explain —"

The look on O'Reilly's face stopped Brennan in his tracks.

"What now?"

"Brennan, we are not putting you on the stand."

"But then we only have the word of the coppers and poor Mrs. McNally who must, understandably, have been terrified. And she thinks it was me. But of course it wasn't. If I can explain . . ."

"If you were to take the stand and testify in your own defence, you would be asked why you were at Saint Matthew's setting up a plan to retrieve the gun, how you knew it was there, *and* whom you were retrieving it for. Would you really want to get up there and implicate that person or those people, whoever they are?"

Of course Reddy O'Reilly, the "well-known Republican solicitor," knew perfectly well that the gun was connected with Brennan Burke's family members in Belfast. Brennan said, "Well, obviously I wouldn't answer any questions about, em, you know . . ."

"How do you think that would look for you in the eyes of Mr. Justice Rupertson Pound?"

"Right, right, I know." What had Monty Collins been telling him all these years from his experience in court? The defendant is not required to testify. He can decide not to take the stand, and the judge is not allowed to use that against him. "So," he said to O'Reilly now, "I exercise my right to remain silent, not testify, and not incriminate myself. I get it."

O'Reilly laughed. "No, you don't get it, Brennan."

"Eh?"

"You cannot be forced to testify. That much is true. But the judge is entitled to draw a negative inference from the fact that you chose not to do so."

Brennan was nearly sputtering at this point. "But isn't that a right an accused man has, and it can't be used against him?"

"That right has been abolished here with the stroke of a pen. Legislated out of existence. As we say here, 'If your punter decides not to the take the stand, chooses not to incriminate himself by speaking, that by itself can incriminate him.' What did I tell you, Father? You are no longer in the world you once knew."

†

On Monday, September 18, 1995, Father Brennan Burke's trial for terrorism-related offences got underway in the Crumlin Road Courthouse. Brennan was showered, shaved, and dressed in a dark grey suit with a snowy white shirt and navy tie. Redmond O'Reilly assured him that the barrister he had briefed for the trial, Pearse McKendrick, had a vast amount of experience in these courts. And McKendrick certainly looked impressive and unflappable as he took his place at the barristers' table in the courtroom. O'Reilly explained that he, O'Reilly, would continue to confer with Brennan; McKendrick's job was to conduct the trial.

The prosecutor was a whippet-thin man with the imposing name of Osborne Wickersly Hull. He, like the defence barrister, was decked out in a curled grey wig for the performance.

The judge sitting alone in the Belfast Crown Court did not inspire a great deal of confidence in the man whose life was in his hands. O'Reilly had been circumspect when Brennan had asked him about Mr. Justice Rupertson Pound. "He's been known to acquit." Acquit whom? Acquit how often? When was the last acquittal? One look at the bewigged, cold-eyed, hatchet-faced oul bastard who was to preside over Brennan's fate gave Brennan a chill.

Seated slightly below the judge's bench were the clerks. Next were the lawyers at a large table in the well of the courtroom. The Crown and defence barristers faced the judge's lofty bench; the solicitors sat opposite them with their backs to the judge. Redmond O'Reilly nodded at Brennan, whose place in life now was the prisoner's dock. Behind him was the public gallery. There were armed police at all the entrances. There were no Burke relations in the gallery. Nobody had to spell it out: everyone in the family knew that a public association between the accused "terrorist" and a "well-known Republican family" in full view of the judge would not serve any of them well. And, of course, Tomás could not show his face anywhere near the courthouse. Or the witnesses.

The first witness was the parish secretary, Mrs. McNally. The poor woman clearly had the janglers; she did not want to be there. As distressed as he was about his own situation, Brennan's heart went out to her. She was sworn in, and the prosecutor, Osborne Wickersly Hull, asked her to identify herself. Then the questioning began.

"Mrs. McNally, please tell the court what happened at the Saint Matthew's presbytery on the twenty-seventh of February of this year."

Her eyes darted to Brennan and away again. "I was working in the office, straightening things away before going to our noon Mass, and he came in."

"Who came in?"

"The priest. Or, I mean, the man who was dressed as a priest."

"Do you see that man in the courtroom today?"

She nodded her head without looking at anyone.

"We need you to speak your answer, Mrs. McNally."

"Aye, he's here."

"Could you point him out to us, please?"

She pointed a trembling finger at Brennan.

"Let the record show that the witness has identified the defendant, Mr. Burke. Now, Mrs. McNally, how was the man dressed?"

"In clerical clothing. Roman collar, under his jacket. He certainly looked like a priest to me."

"What happened after he, Mr. Burke, arrived?"

"Well, he did some play-acting, or I assume now that's what it was. Pointed to his throat, pretended he'd lost his voice. He seemed very pleasant, really. Good-humoured. Or so I thought at the time."

"What did he say, or communicate to you?"

"He was soaking wet and sneezing, and he mouthed words at me that he'd lost his voice. And I invited him in, and he took a holy card with the Blessed Mother out of his wallet, and wrote a note on it saying he'd come to look at Samson and Goliath and could I ring a taxi for him. I said I would, and then I had to be off to twelve o'clock Mass. I said he could stay and dry off a wee bit until the taxi came. I left for Mass and was wishing I'd offered the poor man a cup of tea."

"And then?"

"He was gone when I got back after Mass and I never saw him again until . . . until the time with the gun!"

"Now you say you saw him a second time. What day was that?"

"The seventh of March."

"And what happened that day?"

"I went in to the office early as I always do. I work from half six in the morning to half two in the afternoon, so I can see my grandchildren after school. And I'm up early anyway, and we have a seven o'clock Mass in the morning."

"Right, so that morning . . ."

"I got to the door, put in the code to turn off the alarm. He must have known I would do that! So I was working at my desk and all of a sudden I heard this crashing noise in the cellar. And I was afraid because I thought I was alone in the building, and I heard that noise. As if somebody was there."

"So what did you do?"

"I ran out into the hallway and I heard footsteps pounding up the stairs from the cellar. And then he was just there! Right in front of me."

"And did you recognize the person as someone you knew?"

"Well, not right away."

"What was the person wearing?"

"He had on an anorak. Or a raincoat with a hood pulled up over his head. And his face was covered up to his eyes."

"What did you notice, if anything, about his eyes?"

"That they were very dark."

"What else can you tell us about his appearance?"

"He was tall. And I could see black hair under the top of his hood."

"How was the lighting where you were standing?"

"Well, of course the sun had not come up. And even when it did, you'd not be able to find it for the rain! When he was there, the hallway was a wee bit dark. But I could still see him!"

"Was there any light on at all?"

"Yes, in the office behind me, so there was a bit of light."

"Now who did you think this person was?"

"At first I didn't know. Only later on after I'd called the police and thought things over, I remembered that priest coming to the office. And I thought to myself, That's him!"

"And why did you think that?"

"He was the same size, big and tall, and the black hair and the dark eyes on him. And I started wondering if he came that first time for some other reason besides getting out of the rain. Maybe he wanted to find out how to break in!"

Pearse McKendrick was on his feet. "Objection, My Lord. Speculation."

The judge turned to the witness. "Just tell us what you saw and heard, Mrs. McNally."

"I'm sorry, Your Honour!"

The prosecutor resumed his examination. "Did you go down to the cellar after this person left?"

"Only after the police came."

"And was there anything you noticed in the cellar?"

"Dust all over the floor. Or, well, on parts of the floor. And I looked up, and a few of the ceiling tiles were crooked. Out of place. The dust was under those tiles."

"Had you seen the tiles out of place like that before?"

"Never. I go down there to file things away and never saw anything like that."

"Now about the gun you mentioned earlier, Mrs. McNally, is there anything you can say about the type of weapon it was?"

"I wouldn't know one from the other, so."

"Big gun, little gun? Long? Short?"

"A handgun, not a rifle or anything like that."

"If Your Lordship pleases, I should like to show the witness a handgun that we shall be entering into evidence through another witness later in the trial."

And there it was. Where had they found it? Tom said he had buried it deep in a rubbish bin. Now here was Hull cradling it in both his hands and holding it up before the witness.

"Does this look like the gun you saw that day?"

"Sure it does but, as I said before, they all look alike to me."

"Fair enough, but you would say it is similar?"

"It is."

"Just for the record, had you ever seen that gun before, at Saint Matthew's or anywhere?"

"No, never."

"You didn't place it in the cellar or anywhere else at the church?"

"No, of course not!"

"Now what position was the gun in when you first saw it? Where was it?"

"It was in his hand."

"In the hand of . . ."

"The priest. Or the man that came in."

"The man you identified at the start of your testimony? Mr. Burke here in the courtroom?"

"Aye, him."

"And he was holding it how?"

"Well, just, you know, the way you'd hold a gun."

"The handle of the gun was where?"

"In his hand, the normal way it would be."

"And the barrel?"

"It was pointing out."

"Out towards what?"

"In my direction."

"What was your reaction to that?"

Her eyes ventured in Brennan's direction for a split second, then refocused on the prosecutor. "I was afraid."

"What did you do or say?"

"I tried to make up a story. I pretended I had called the police. I know it didn't make any sense that I could have called them that quickly, but that's what I told him."

"Did Mr. Burke say anything to you?"

"He said something like, 'No police and you won't get hurt.' Or 'I won't . . .' Oh, I don't know exactly. My nerves were going on me. Like they are in here today."

"That's understandable, Mrs. McNally, with someone pointing a gun at you and having to come to court and —"

"Objection, My Lord." Pearse McKendrick was on his feet.

"On what grounds, Mr. McKendrick?"

"My learned friend is misquoting the witness's testimony."

"I don't see how, Mr. McKendrick."

"She did not say he was pointing the gun at her."

The prosecutor took up the argument and said, "The gun was pointing in her direction, My Lord. With all due respect, I think my friend's objection is off the mark."

"Objection overruled. Continue, Mr. Hull."

"What happened next, Mrs. McNally?"

"He came towards me."

"Still holding the gun."

"Right. And I was terrified, and I jumped out of his way. And he left."

"Please describe your feelings to us, the feelings you had when he was standing in front of you holding the gun."

"Well, as I said, I was terrified. I thought he must be . . ."

"Yes?"

"One of the . . . terrorists."

"Would you say you felt threatened?"

"Objection!" McKendrick was on his feet again. "Leading!"

The judge said, "Just describe your feelings in your own words, Mrs. McNally."

Which was a cinch now that she had been given the right word to use. "I felt threatened by him, with that gun."

"Thank you, Mrs. McNally. My friend may have some questions for you."

Pearse McKendrick stood and spoke gently to the witness. "I won't keep you long, Mrs. McNally. I know this is difficult for you."

"Thank you," she said.

"I'm going to take you back to the first few minutes when you were in the office with a priest on February twenty-seventh. What kind of conversation did you have, if any?"

"Well, it was conversation on my part, and mouthing on his part. But it all seemed friendly. He'd come to see the cranes, was all wet, needed someone to ring for a taxi. And he saw our church, so . . ."

"Did that man give you any reason for concern? At that point, I mean."

"Well, no, not then. He was . . . I thought he was very nice."

"And did you have any concerns about leaving him in the office when you went to Mass?"

"No, I didn't see any reason to be worried then."

"Now eight days later, on March seventh, you heard a noise in the cellar and you went out and saw a man in the corridor. A man with a gun."

"I couldn't believe my eyes!"

"Now I'd like you to do something if you would, Mrs. McNally. Just close your eyes and pretend none of this is here." His hand took in the judge, the prosecutor, the courtroom. "I know it won't be easy to wish this all away!"

She laughed and said, "I wish I could!" Then she turned to the judge in alarm and said, "I'm sorry, Your Honour!"

He made a dismissive gesture with his hand, and McKendrick resumed the exercise. "Just unclench your hands." She laughed a bit again and eased her hands apart. "Close your eyes." She did so. "And think back. Take your time. Try to picture the parochial house at Saint Matthew's and the man and the whole scene as it unfolded. I'll give you a few moments to do that."

The prosecutor's impatience was obvious, but he restrained himself from commenting.

After thirty seconds or so, McKendrick spoke in a calm, quiet voice. "Just describe to us what you are seeing and hearing, Mrs. McNally."

Her voice was quiet as well. "He's standing there, with the gun and a surprised look on his face. I mean, what I can see of his face. His eyes and eyebrows. He looks nervous. Upset, like. And I'm telling him the police are coming, and he says they're not. Or there's not going to be any police. Something like that. And then he says, 'I'm not going to hurt you.' And when I think of it now I realize I believed him! After the first shock of it, I felt sure he wasn't going to hurt me."

"What about his voice? Is there anything you can tell us about that?"

"Just normal. He'd got his voice back."

"Accent? Anything about that?"

"I'm sorry, I just can't remember."

"Nothing stood out in that regard?"

The prosecutor rose with an objection. "Question asked and answered, My Lord."

"I'll allow it. You may answer, Mrs. McNally."

"I just don't remember, so I guess nothing stood out."

"How long were you in the corridor with the man, can you estimate it at all?"

"Not long. Only a few seconds, and he was gone in a flash."

"Now tell us again about the lighting."

"There was no light on in the hallway, so it was dim. But there was a light coming from the door of the office."

"Is the door to the office directly opposite the door to the cellar?"

"No, the cellar door is down a ways. Not right opposite."

"And where is the gun when the man is standing there?"

"Well, he's just holding it."

"And the way he is holding it?"

"Just the normal way. I mean, he isn't going to give it to me, so he isn't holding the handle out towards me to take it. The barrel end of it is kind of hanging down."

"Thank you, Mrs. McNally. I know this hasn't been easy for you. Those are all my questions."

Right, thought Brennan. He had had enough conversations with Monty Collins to know that one of the most important skills acquired by a trial lawyer is to quit while you're ahead. He remembered Monty saying younger lawyers sometimes don't have the confidence to leave well enough alone and abandon the rest of the questions on their lists. But that was obviously what Pearse McKendrick was doing here. He now had the witness on record saying the barrel was pointing down. Not directly at her. Thank God and Mrs. —

Brennan's train of thought was interrupted by the judge. He leaned towards the witness and said, "You told us earlier that he was pointing the gun at you, Mrs. McNally. Do I have that right?"

"Well, I guess so. I . . ."

"How tall are you, Mrs. McNally? Approximately."

Brennan could see the sudden tension in Pearse McKendrick's posture. And that of Reddy O'Reilly, facing him across the room from the solicitors' bench.

"Tall? Not very!" Mrs. McNally replied. There was some laughter — not unfriendly laughter — in the courtroom. "But I'm over five feet!"

"Thank you. Any redirect, Mr. Hull?"

Of course there would be redirect. If the prosecutor hadn't had new questions for the witness two minutes ago, he certainly did now.

"Could you be a wee bit more specific for us about your height, Mrs. McNally?"

"I'm five feet, one and a half inches tall. I got measured at the doctor's surgery when she took my weight. I hope you're not going to ask me about that!"

"No, certainly not, Mrs. McNally. So when the defendant, Mr. Burke, arrived at the office that day, you would have had to look up to engage in a conversation with him, look him in the eye?"

"Yes, I suppose I did. I do with most people! Men, anyway."

"Thank you, Mrs. McNally. Those are all the questions I have."

Hull, too, had the tactic down cold: quit while you're ahead. Now that you have, with the judge's thoughtful prompting, established the difference in height between Brennan Burke — Tom Burke! — and the secretary. Now that you have set up your argument that the gun would of necessity be "pointing down" when the man was pointing it "at her." Brennan could see the anger in Reddy O'Reilly's face, but the solicitor held it in check.

The second witness was an officer of the Royal Ulster Constabulary. Detective Inspector Glenn Hobson formally entered the Browning pistol into evidence as Exhibit One. He testified that this was the same gun that had been found on April 19 during a search of a landfill outside the city. Hull asked him what had prompted a search of the landfill on April 19. The officer said that reliable and confidential information had come into the possession of the Royal Ulster Constabulary about a paramilitary incident that had occurred some years back. And the information indicated that the gun used in that incident had been taken to the property of Saint Matthew's church and concealed there. The officers recalled the report of a gun being brandished at an individual at Saint Matthew's in early March of this year. That prompted questioning of residents of the area around the church, and a witness recalled seeing someone behaving suspiciously around a rubbish skip. The witness was not a local resident but a businessman heading to the building site. He had not given it another thought until he was questioned.

"So we knew which skip and which landfill area to search. It was a huge operation with metal detectors and other means, and we eventually unearthed the pistol."

The prosecutor told the judge that he would be calling other witnesses who would corroborate the evidence that this was the gun at issue.

After Hobson came the businessman who was walking to work in east Belfast early on the morning of March 7, and saw in the distance a man in rain gear climbing down from a rubbish skip beside the building site. He assumed the fellow was a skip diver, someone who roots around in skips and rubbish bins for articles of interest. Could he describe the man? No, he was too far away to see anything but the dark-coloured rain jacket with a hood up.

After that was another member of the Royal Ulster Constabulary. Constable Orville Smith identified himself, was duly sworn, and Osborne Hull began his examination.

"Constable Smith, could you tell us about an incident you were called to on March eighteenth of this year?"

"Yes. I was called to respond to a shooting in west Belfast."

"Where exactly in west Belfast?"

"The Falls Road."

"Tell us about that."

"I was dispatched to the scene of a shooting outside the Banned Flag bar just after half eight at night."

The Banned Flag? The assassination attempt? What did that have to do with this gun, with the charges against Brennan here?

McKendrick was on his feet. "Objection, My Lord. Irrelevant!"

"I'll allow it. Proceed, Mr. Hull."

"Go ahead, Constable Smith."

"When we got to the Banned Flag we found Ronan Burke on the ground outside the bar. He had been shot and wounded."

"You knew that because . . ."

"He had blood coming out from his body onto his clothing. And witnesses described a shooting. They told us two men had just fled the scene in a vehicle."

"Now, you said the man on the ground was Ronan Burke. Could you tell the court your understanding as to who Mr. Burke was? Who he is?"

"Objection, irrelevant!" McKendrick protested again. To no avail. The judge directed the cop to respond.

"He is known to us, well known here in Northern Ireland, as a leading figure in the Republican movement. And as a former high-ranking person in the Provisional IRA. Second in command in Belfast."

Pearse McKendrick was furiously scrawling notes on his legal pad.

Hull continued the questioning. "Were there other people with Mr. Burke that night, Constable?"

"A priest was tending to him after he was wounded."

"Were you able to identify the priest?"

"Aye. He was Brennan Burke, cousin of the IRA man, Ronan Burke."

Pearse McKendrick tried again. "My Lord, the defence objects to this obvious and irrelevant attempt to link my client with paramilitary activity."

The prosecutor responded, "The purpose of this evidence, My

Lord, is merely to demonstrate how the police knew the name of the man they later arrested on the charges before this court today."

"Objection overruled."

The peeler then told the court how they had put two and two together and determined that the man at Saint Matthew's fit the description of the man who had been seen alongside Ronan Burke, and the arrest was made after that. The cop entered into evidence papers that documented Brennan's family's immigration to the United States from Dublin when Brennan was a young boy, his work history in the U.S. and later in Canada, the times he had travelled to Ireland, and his entry into Northern Ireland earlier this year.

The judge announced that the court would adjourn until two o'clock that afternoon.

"All rise."

Everyone stood as the judge left the courtroom and the trial broke for lunch.

Reddy O'Reilly abandoned his courtroom sangfroid and let loose when he and Brennan were in a room together, unobserved. "That performance with Mrs. McNally! Fucking outrageous! Not that I haven't seen it in this court before."

"The judge cross-examining the witness, you mean."

"It's one thing for a judge to ask for clarification of an uncontroversial point. But here was His Lordship taking on the role of prosecutor, helping Osborne Hull get the job done, wiping out the advantage we had just gained when the woman said the gun was pointing downwards. She virtually admitted that the man was just holding it, as she said, 'in the normal way.' He was hardly going to hold it by the barrel, so he held it by the grip and of course the barrel was pointing outwards. Now the judge has enabled Hull to project the evidence in a way that has a man over six feet in height, if he's the same height as you, pointing the weapon down at wee Mrs. McNally. What do you think of Belfast justice so far, Brennan?"

"It's everything I thought it would be. But more so."

"And then there's the evidence of the Banned Flag incident, the entire purpose of which was to connect you to the 'RA." O'Reilly took a breath and started to speak again.

But there was a knock on the door, and a man appeared, asking to speak to Reddy. The solicitor excused himself. When he came back, his rage had escalated from atomic to thermonuclear.

"What now?" Brennan asked.

"Surprise witness."

"Fuck. Who is it?"

"Someone who is going to speak to the 'perverting the course of justice' charge. Someone who, according to Osborne Hull, was unknown or at least unavailable until this very afternoon. Hull ever so thoughtfully offered to adjourn until tomorrow or the next day if we wish."

"Should we do that?"

"There'd be no advantage in doing that. No advantage either way, I mean. Today or tomorrow, it's all the same." He plopped down in his chair and put his head in his hands. He ran his fingers through the copper and silver hair. "The same fucking shite, no matter what we do."

After a minute or so, he pushed himself up and said, "I have to go and discuss this with McKendrick, Brennan. You'll go and have your lunch, and, as they say, I'll see you in court. I'm sorry I have to leave you like this, but —"

"I know."

Brennan was taken to a holding cell to eat his lunch. He could barely look at whatever it was they had slopped on his plate. All he could think of was the new development in the case, the new and unexpected witness — whoever he was — and the hopelessness he had seen on the face of his lawyer.

†

Back in the courtroom, O'Reilly came over to Brennan and whispered, "This is an individual who has turned Queen's evidence."

"That doesn't sound —"

"Doesn't bode well at all. He's turned on his fellow conspirators and is now assisting the Crown and has been promised immunity from prosecution."

"Which, for us, means . . ."

"He'll say whatever they want him to say."

"Jesus the Christ who suffered and died on the cross!"

"And when the curtain rings down on this charade, they'll whisk him away, put him in hiding somewhere with a new identity, and he'll never be seen in these parts again."

Sitting there waiting for the inquisition to resume, Brennan wondered, What conspirators? What conspiracy?

"All rise!"

Court was now in session, and security was even tighter than it had been before, as a twitchy young fellow was brought in to testify. He had a narrow face framed by long, lank, dark hair; his eyes were fixed on the middle distance in front of him. He swore to tell the truth, the whole truth, and nothing but the truth, and the questioning got underway.

"Please state your name for the court."

"Colman Davison."

The name meant nothing to Brennan.

"Mr. Davison," the prosecutor asked, "have you had any involvement with paramilitaries in this city?"

"I have."

"Could you expand on that for us, please?"

His eyes flickered over the assembly, and then he steeled himself before saying, "I've been involved with the Ulster Defence Association and the Ulster Red Hand."

There were mumbles throughout the courtroom in response to the admission.

"And these are Loyalist paramilitary groups?"

"Aye."

"Did you know a man named Francis O'Dwyer, sometimes called Fritzy?"

"I didn't know him personally, but I knew who he was."

"What was your understanding of who O'Dwyer was?"

"One of the hard men with the Provos."

"The Provos being . . ."

"Provisional IRA."

"And Mr. O'Dwyer's role as you believed it to be?"

"Enforcer, killer, that sort of a bloke."

"Were you involved in an incident on fourteen November, 1992, connected with Mr. O'Dwyer?"

"I was ordered to shoot Fritzy."

There were gasps throughout the courtroom. Brennan, from long practice, was able to conceal his reaction. But this trial was spiralling even further out of control than it had been in the morning. What in God's good name did the charges against Brennan have to do with the murder of the IRA man back in November of 1992?

"And did you carry out those orders?"

A long silence. "I had to."

"Who ordered you to shoot Mr. O'Dwyer?"

Davison's eyes flew up to the gallery, then down again.

"Shall I repeat the question? Who ordered you —"

"The boys from Andytown."

"Who do you mean by 'the boys from Andytown'?"

"Andersonstown IRA."

Oh, God. It was all Brennan could do to maintain his composure.

"So you're telling us the IRA ordered the murder of one of their own number and hired you to do the killing?"

"I wasn't hired; I was forced."

The prosecutor paused to take a drink of water. "Now, Mr. Davison, what kind of weapon did you use to carry out the shooting in 1992?"

The answer was as predictable as a forecast for rain tomorrow in County Down.

Lord, have mercy on me, Brennan prayed silently.

"A Browning Hi-Power nine millimetre pistol."

"I am going to show you Exhibit One." Hull held the gun up before the witness. "Is this the gun you used on Mr. O'Dwyer?"

"Aye."

"How do you know?"

"I can tell by the look of it. Those scratches around the barrel. And, besides, they tested it and found that it was the gun that fired —"

"Objection," said McKendrick. "This witness is not competent to testify to that."

"Sustained."

But of course it didn't matter. The court would be hearing all about the bullets, all in good time. Meanwhile, the damning testimony continued. And then it was Pearse McKendrick's turn to cross-examine the witness. He held a whispered conference with Reddy O'Reilly before facing Davison.

Brennan wondered what kind of strategy had been discussed. But what was consuming him now was the reference to the boys from Andytown. The Burkes of Belfast were boys from Andytown, and it was Ronan's son Tom who had set the wheels in motion for the return of the gun. For now, though, all Brennan could do was listen to whatever this man Davison was going to say next.

McKendrick asked the witness, "Mr. Davison, how did it come about that you, a Loyalist paramilitary, were selected by the Irish Republican Army to carry out this assignment?"

"Fritzy was a psycho and a killer, and he was a liability to them. They wanted him dead."

"That's not what I asked you. Shall I repeat the question? Why you?"

"They knew me."

"Yes, go on."

Davison swallowed and seemed unable to speak.

"Mr. Davison. What was your connection to the IRA that resulted in you being chosen for this assignment?"

Again, even though he had been assured of immunity from prosecution, the man could not bring himself to state the obvious. He was not immune from whatever retaliation would be meted out to him on the streets of Belfast, should he ever be spotted in the city again. But someone else favoured the court with the answer.

"You're a fookin' tite, Davison! A fookin' tite!" A ruckus erupted at the back of the courtroom as those who had denounced Davison as a fucking tout rose in their seats and were swiftly grabbed and hustled out of the room by the police.

"No further questions, My Lord." And McKendrick sat down.

It was Colman Davison's turn then to be taken from the court surrounded by a phalanx of armed police officers. His work was done. And everybody now knew that he, a Loyalist, had been an informer for the enemy, the IRA. Colman Davison was about to begin a new future as *persona non grata* in the country of his birth.

Davison was followed by a pathologist, who testified that O'Dwyer had died in the early morning hours of November 14, 1992, of multiple gunshot wounds. He described the effect of the various wounds. Brennan tuned him out. McKendrick did not bother to question him.

The final witness was a ballistics expert who confirmed that the five bullets taken from the body of Francis O'Dwyer on November 14, 1992, had been fired by the gun that was in evidence before this court.

"And," Osborne Hull asked the witness, "can you tell us anything about the circumstances of Mr. O'Dwyer's death?"

"Only that he was shot multiple times with that weapon." He pointed to the gun, Exhibit One in the trial. "Other aspects of the case are subject to a current and active investigation."

"Thank you, Inspector."

"Mr. McKendrick?" the judge inquired.

"No questions for this witness."

"That concludes the case for the prosecution, My Lord," Hull announced.

McKendrick rose then and announced that the defence would not be calling any evidence.

Court broke for the day and would resume the next morning for the Crown and defence summations.

When Brennan was back in the H Block, he had no desire for company. Even O'Morda, his cellmate, was able to sense the mood and spent every permitted free hour out of the cell. All Brennan could do was pace back and forth in his tiny dungeon and ruminate over and over about the events that had unfolded in the courtroom. The gun had been used to kill O'Dwyer, the man who was shot just around the time Monty Collins's client, Mr. Flanagan, died in the river. Ronan hadn't said a word about this. But of course he wouldn't. He wasn't going to own up to knowledge of a premeditated murder and a connection between that event and the pistol he — no, his son, Tom — wanted recovered from its hiding place at Saint Matthew's. And, fair play to Ronan, he had done his best to dissuade Brennan from making the fateful trip to the church to act as Tom's decoy. Brennan had brushed off his cousin's attempts to keep him out of trouble. Now, in the prison, he needed a cigarette or he felt he would come apart in pieces all over the room, yet he couldn't bring himself to go out scavenging for a smoke. Couldn't bring himself to make conversation with the other men. And he craved a drink. It took a superhuman effort to control the shakes and the sweats. When it was time to sleep, that proved to be impossible.

When morning dawned, painfully, the only mercy that came Brennan's way was a cigarette handed him by one of the screws on the wing. He could not remember when a gift had been more welcome. He could not remember anything at all, except the horrors of the trial.

He was transported to the city to the courtroom again, and the two barristers wrapped things up with their summations. Osborne Wickersly Hull for the prosecution reiterated all the testimony that, he said, proved beyond a reasonable doubt that Brennan Burke was guilty of all the charges brought against him.

When it was Pearse McKendrick's turn, he meticulously went through the testimony and the conclusions to be drawn from it and made a passionate plea for his client's innocence. "The Crown called only one witness on the question of identification of the man with the gun. Mrs. McNally. She was confronted by the man on March the seventh. She saw him in a dimly lit hallway, with no direct lighting on his face. His face was covered by a scarf up to his eyes, and he had a hood over his head. All she saw was a tall man with dark hair and dark eyes. It goes without saying that there are many men fitting that description."

Brennan wondered how his barrister was going to skate around the fact that a priest looking exactly like Father Burke had wormed his way into Mrs. McNally's office with a ruse about a lost voice.

"Mrs. McNally, when questioned by police, recalled a visit by a priest who had lost his voice and hoped she would ring a taxi for him. She says that was really Father Burke. The defence submits that there is nothing to link the arrival of a priest with a throat ailment and the gun incident eight days later. The defence further submits that this memory of a priest coming to the office coloured her perception of what the gunman *must have* looked like; she got it into her mind that the two incidents were related and this led her to project the priest's appearance onto that of the gunman whose face was all but concealed.

"Moreover, when Mrs. McNally was asked whether she noted anything about the second man's accent, she answered that nothing stood out. I suggest that this is because the accent was the same as her own Belfast speech, which would not stand out to her at all. She did not say the man had a foreign or a Dublin accent. Father Burke is originally from Dublin and he has lived in America and Canada throughout his adult life. Again, more evidence that this was a different man.

"We do not know what the brief February twenty-seventh visit was about, but we do know there was no gun that day, no threatening behaviour, no concern on the part of Mrs. McNally, no damage.

"Then we come to the Crown's star witness, a man who testified in return for a promise of immunity from prosecution for the murder he has admitted to, the shooting death of Francis O'Dwyer. And yet here is Father Brennan Burke, being prosecuted for an alleged attempt to pervert the course of justice in connection with that same crime. There is no evidence Father Burke was even aware of that killing, and certainly no evidence he knew about a gun, let alone a gun connected to that incident.

"Colman Davison has given us no explanation of why he would commit a murder for and on behalf of the IRA, the longstanding enemy of the Loyalist paramilitaries with which Mr. Davison is affiliated. So his story makes no sense."

It was obvious to Brennan and to everyone in the courtroom that Davison, for some unstated reason, had become a tout, an informer, for the IRA. But that was not part of the testimony; McKendrick had not put the question to him, had not specifically asked him whether he had been an informer, and Davison sure as hell had not admitted it on his own. So it was open to McKendrick to argue that there was no explanation properly before the court that would explain Davison's actions.

"We know the gun was used in the murder of Fritzy O'Dwyer. We know Mr. Davison committed the murder with that gun. In other words, what we have is a Loyalist who admittedly killed a member of the IRA. That's all we have. It is not credible to say that Father Burke, a Catholic priest, would retrieve a gun with the intention of perverting the course of justice, to protect a member of the Protestant Loyalist paramilitary groups and prevent that man from facing justice for the murder of a Catholic Irish Republican like Mr. O'Dwyer. Father Burke is merely visiting our city from his home in Canada. There is no evidence that he knew any of this history between Mr. Davison and Mr. O'Dwyer.

"There was no evidence called on the criminal damage charge, apart from Mrs. McNally's observation that there was dust on the floor of the cellar and a few ceiling tiles out of alignment. Hardly the stuff of criminal damage. As for the threat charge, Mrs. McNally's testimony is that the man, the unidentified man, was merely holding the gun in the normal way one would hold a gun. And that in fact the barrel was pointing downwards; the man was not holding it out towards Mrs. McNally in a threatening manner at all. And, according to her testimony, the man said, 'I am not going to hurt you.' And he did not. He left the parochial house without hurting anyone. I respectfully submit therefore that there is no evidence of any offence being committed by Father Burke, and he should be acquitted of all charges."

Mr. Justice Rupertson Pound thanked the two barristers and said the court would break until three o'clock, at which time he would give his verdict. Brennan was trembling. His heart was racing and he thought it might give out on him. That might be best. He sent up a prayer beseeching the almighty and merciful God to deliver him from this torment.

✝

When he was brought back into the courtroom, Brennan's thoughts flew to all the men he had heard of through the years, all the men — women, too — charged with crimes, brought to trial, and facing the verdict of the court. One thing he had always understood, whether the defendant was a petty criminal or a mass murderer, was the debilitating stress and fear of waiting for that verdict. He knew it all too well from his own past, and now here he was again. He felt as if his head was going to explode.

And here it was. Mr. Justice Rupertson Pound swept into the courtroom and took his seat. He didn't require notes to say what he had to say. He spelled out the charges and got down to business. "Mr. Burke was on a mission on those two days in February and March of this year."

Brennan knew without hearing another word that he was going down. One glance at Reddy O'Reilly's face showed that he knew it, too.

"Mr. Burke had knowledge of a Browning Hi-Power nine millimetre pistol hidden in the presbytery of Saint Matthew's church in east Belfast. We have not been told why the church office was selected as the hiding place. I accept the evidence of Mrs. McNally that she had not placed the gun there and had not been aware of it until this incident with Mr. Burke. So either someone entered the office surreptitiously and opened up the ceiling and slid the gun in above the tiles, or someone at Saint Matthew's hid it as a favour to the owner or possessor of the gun. The evidence of the expert witnesses and of Colman Davison, which I accept, proves that this gun was used in at least one terrorism-related shooting in the past. Then, on February twenty-seventh, Brennan Xavier Burke comes on the scene.

"Mr. Burke, even though he did not speak aloud, misled Mrs. McNally, who had shown him nothing but kindness, deceived her about his reason for being there. He won her trust with a ruse designed to allow him to be alone in the building when she went off to the noontime church service. He was 'casing the joint,' as the expression goes, finding out about the alarm system, the door to the cellar, whatever else he needed to know to go in later with his face covered and retrieve that murder weapon. He planned to retrieve, and did retrieve, the Browning Hi-Power pistol that had been used in the previous terrorism-related offence or offences. Mrs. McNally recognized him when he emerged from the cellar on March the seventh. The pistol he took, if recovered by the police, would form part of the evidence in future court proceedings related to those previous offences. Clearly, therefore, Mr. Burke attempted to pervert the course of justice in this jurisdiction. In committing this offence, Mr. Burke caused damage, criminal damage, to the property of Saint Matthew's church in east Belfast."

Brennan heard the two convictions the way he would hear a bell tolling the end of his life.

"And then," the judge continued, "there is the possession of an offensive weapon in a public place. A public place is any place where the public have, or are allowed to have, access. Nothing more need be said about that. Now: the threat to Mrs. McNally. The evidence shows that Mr. Burke pointed the gun at her. The court takes judicial notice of the fact that Mr. Burke is over six feet tall and Mrs. McNally just over five feet. A gun held by Mr. Burke and pointed directly at Mrs. McNally would, obviously, be 'pointing down.' Mrs. McNally tried to protect herself from Mr. Burke by telling him she had called the police, and the police were on their way. His response was that there were to be no police and she would not get hurt. In other words, if the police did arrive or were really on their way and Mr. Burke was in danger of being caught or reported, she *would* get hurt. Now, what does one do with a gun that is pointed directly at another person? If one fires, we can take judicial notice of the fact that people very often die from a shot or shots fired so close and so directly. It was a threat, and not just a threat of scratches or bruises. Given the nature of the weapon, it was a threat to kill."

An involuntary gasp came from Reddy O'Reilly at this interpretation of events. Brennan himself was long past surprise.

"If," the judge went on, "if Mr. Burke had another interpretation of these events to offer us, presumably he would have testified in this trial and told us so. From the fact that he did not testify, I am left with the inference that he has no defence to offer with respect to his words and actions that day. In light of all of the foregoing, I find Brennan Xavier Burke guilty of all charges."

Brennan had known it would come to this, but he felt he had taken a bullet to the heart nonetheless. He could scarcely breathe.

"I assume, Mr. McKendrick, that you would like some time before you speak to sentence? You may arrange a time and date at your convenience."

O'Reilly came to the dock, leaned over and hissed in Brennan's ear. "There is no fucking point in delaying the inevitable. He knows exactly what he's going to do and nothing we say is going to make it any better. The sooner we get the sentencing done, the sooner we can file the appeal of verdict and sentence."

Brennan somehow found his voice and said, "Agreed. Let him condemn me, and you start the appeal."

"We'll finish this off first thing tomorrow."

O'Reilly returned to the front of the courtroom and had a word with his barrister, who got to his feet and said, "I shall be ready to speak to sentence tomorrow morning at nine."

Once again when they were alone, O'Reilly expressed his outrage. "That pointing of the gun downwards, the height differential, that was evidence the judge set up himself! And then he weaves it all into a threat to kill! And of course the negative inference from your not taking the stand; the lawmakers in this statelet were kind enough to provide that for him in the Criminal Evidence Order of 1988. Which applies *only* to the North of Ireland, by the way. They weren't getting enough convictions when the hallowed right to silence was in place. Forgive me, Brennan. Forgive me, Father! But every day I spend in these courts fills me with a boiling rage."

Brennan was sitting with his head down, massaging his temples. "Little wonder," he muttered, "that we have people, known to you and to me, who have spent the better part of their lives trying to overthrow this state!" He looked up at O'Reilly. "He's going to send me away for how long?"

"We'll be filing the appeal before the close of day tomorrow."

†

If ever there was a dark night of the soul for Brennan Burke, it was the long, black, torturous night between the verdict and the sentence. The next morning he sat in the courtroom, virtually catatonic, while the prosecutor portrayed him as a terrorist or, failing that, a violent, deceitful man who aided and abetted the terrorists who had caused so much death and destruction in this country, a man who threatened and aimed a gun at an innocent woman, et cetera, et cetera. Pearse McKendrick made every effort to rebut the Crown's submissions on sentencing, to put the best spin he could on the findings of the judge. Father Burke was a priest who had served in Rome, South America, the United States, and Canada. He was a choirmaster who ran a choir school in Halifax, Nova Scotia. He had no criminal record; he had in fact a stellar academic record and a lifetime of service to God and community. McKendrick did his best, God bless him.

But the steely-eyed judge was having none of it. He knew a lying, murderous, unrepentant Fenian terrorist when he saw one. He sentenced Brennan to six years in prison.

Brennan wished for something he would otherwise never have desired in a thousand years; he wished he was in the Royal Victoria Hospital, sedated. Permanently.

Brennan did not live up to the long Irish tradition of making a resounding speech from the dock. But Reddy O'Reilly did, not from the dock but from the steps of the Crumlin Road Courthouse. Brennan, a convict starting his sentence in the Long Kesh prison, watched the speech that evening on the television news. There was a gathering of press and regular protesters outside the courthouse. O'Reilly declaimed, "What we saw in this building yet again was the courts of this state carrying out anti-insurgency policy rather than upholding the rule of law. The rule of law and civil liberties have long been abrogated during the war that has raged across the North of Ireland. Cicero recognized the problem two thousand years ago in Rome. A poetic translation of the statesman's words: 'The laws are silent amid the clash of arms.' But Lord Atkin, in the House of Lords, begged to differ. Answering Cicero in a case heard during wartime in 1941, Lord Atkin famously declared, 'In this country, amid the clash of arms the laws are *not* silent. They may be changed, but they speak the same language in war as in peace.' He went on to say that it is 'one of the pillars of freedom' that a judge must 'see that any coercive action must be justified in law.' The Diplock courts have once again failed to live up to the ringing words of that illustrious member of the House of Lords. We shall be filing an appeal immediately, an appeal of the verdict and the sentence handed down here today."

✝

Back in the Kesh once again, this time as a sentenced prisoner, Brennan felt a deep, black despair that he could never before have imagined. Here he was in prison with men who, many of them anyway, had had a rough, rocky road through life before winding up here. Brennan had enjoyed a full and blessed life. Oh there had been some low points, some trouble spots, some sacrifices. He had given up the chance to have a wife and a family of his own, had signed on to a life of chastity and obedience. He had not always lived up to the promises he made, but he had done his best. The Almighty God had given him the gift of music, had shown him at times the sublime and ineffable love that waits on the other side of the veil that shimmers between this world and the next.

With all this, why was Father Brennan Xavier Burke not able to rise to the challenges that had been handed to him here in Belfast? Look at the grotesque and terrible suffering endured by the saints throughout the ages. And here was Father Burke, unable to function because he was locked up in prison. And why was he not able to minister to his fellow inmates the way he had done in his prison ministry back in Halifax? Shouldn't he put his own misery aside and place himself at the service of the other men? It didn't help that he kept coming back to how careless he had been. He had tried to be as clever and as careful as he could, having no contact with the gun. And he had not had an inkling that the pistol had been used in a premeditated murder. He thought it had killed a tourist, somehow

395

in self-defence. Whatever the facts turned out to be, one thing was indisputable: what Brennan had done, he had done for the benefit of others, not for himself. But still . . . how could he, a priest, a teacher, a professor, a PhD, have been so fucking thick?

Chapter XXXIV

Brennan

"I didn't know any of this going into the trial, Brennan." Reddy O'Reilly was sitting across from him in one of the H Block meeting areas. "I was aware of two incidents out on the Ammon Road and thought they were likely connected, given the close timing. But I didn't know about any connection between the Browning pistol and the hit on O'Dwyer until we were sandbagged in the courtroom by Davison. Now that Davison's role in that incident has been made public and his solicitor has started third-party proceedings against the others involved, documents are being filed and tongues are being loosened. Here's what I've been able to piece together so far."

Brennan waited, with a sense of foreboding, for the unwelcome tale to unfold.

"Fritzy O'Dwyer was a psychopath, a vicious, heartless killer. Unpredictable and out of control. A definite liability to the Army. The Irish Republican Army, I mean. They wanted him out of their hair. But nothing was done about him until a small group of IRA volunteers came up with a plan of their own, a plan that would not have been authorized from the top.

"The Browning nine millimetre is a weapon typically used by the British Army, so the idea was to have O'Dwyer executed by a UDA man using a British Army type of gun, creating the suspicion that someone in the military was a party to the plan. The information I have is that the boys who orchestrated this scheme told Fritzy to drive out to the Ammon Road. They knew the road was almost certainly deserted in the wee hours, and they could pull their cars over to the side of the road, and the trees would obscure the view of them. The bait they used to lure Fritzy out there was a story that they had a possible informer in their midst and they wanted him interrogated. I don't mean Colman Davison, the Loyalist whom the IRA had black-mailed into informing *for* them. I mean they pretended there was someone who had betrayed them, made up a name. They said they would transport the alleged traitor out to this remote site and consign him to the tender mercies of Fritzy O'Dwyer. This was O'Dwyer's forte, extracting confessions from people under — let's call it duress. So he was keen. But he was a paranoid, suspicious fucker as well.

"There must have been something that raised O'Dwyer's suspicions that night. It wouldn't take much. So he brought someone else along with him in the car. I can only conclude that this was a hostage of sorts. If the lads, his own people in the IRA, tried anything with Fritzy, he'd use this young fellow as a shield. Or so the thinking goes. The hostage was a tourist, a blow-in from the continent, here for an extended ramble around the countryside. O'Dwyer was seen talking with him in a bar earlier that night and being uncharacteristically generous with drink. Plied the poor devil with liquor until his judgment was gone. We can't even speculate on what kind of story Fritzy gave him to get him in the car, but he did."

The unwelcome truth was dawning on Brennan now. The young rambler would be the Dutch backpacker. Brennan had known his name; what was it? Van der Meer. And Tom Burke was there, too. Must have been. The incident on the Ammon Road and the incident involving the Dutchman turned out to be one and the same.

"So the three cars converge on the scene. Davison's, O'Dwyer's, and that of the rogue IRA unit who are going to have O'Dwyer whacked. Three cars, all these people, the whole thing has the makings of a major clusterfuck. You just knew it would go wrong. And that's why a young IRA volunteer who would not normally have anything to do with an execution — more of an intelligence officer type man — had been brought to the scene that night. This young fellow had occasionally acted as Davison's 'handler.' He met Davison from time to time and collected the information Davison provided about the UDA. The presence of this person, a fellow with a pleasant, calming manner, was intended to reassure Davison, so Davison would not be spooked and bolt before the plan could be carried out. I don't imagine this lad was told what the real purpose of the mission was that night."

This, Brennan reasoned, was how Tom had ended up in the midst of the shambles on the Ammon Road. Tom's name would probably not escape the lips of Reddy O'Reilly, but now that Davison had pulled the pin on the Ammon Road conspirators, Tom Burke's name would be one of several on the casualty list.

Reddy resumed his narrative. "From this point on we have the evidence provided by Davison after he was named in a lawsuit for personal injury. I think you know what I'm talking about. Once he was identified as the driver of the car that hit the man and knocked him off the bridge, Davison knew he was fucked. So he turned Queen's evidence, as we know all too well. So. November 1992. They all arrive on the Ammon Road. The boys get Davison in the car with them. He doesn't know why he's been summoned. They've got the Browning pistol all cleaned up for the hit, and they're going to put it in Davison's hand and force him to shoot Fritzy O'Dwyer. But across from them in Fritzy's car, something happens to alarm the young, drink-sodden tourist in the passenger seat. For whatever reason, he comes flying out of the car. And he's got a Stillson wrench in his hand, a pipe wrench. Something Fritz would have in the car for his work. This item in the dark could easily be mistaken for a gun, the jaws of the thing looking like a grip, and the long barrel of it. We'll never know what was going on in his mind, what he was trying to do. Fritzy has his window open and shouts something at the tourist. Davison doesn't know what he said. But anyway, the men in the IRA car see this fellow running towards them. So one of the men grabs the gun, aims it at this out-of-control stranger coming at them, and fires. In self-defence, in defence of the lads in the car. Puts three bullets in him, kills him. Only later does the shooter realize this is a completely unconnected individual. An innocent bystander, so to speak. The tourist likely had no clue that Fritzy was IRA or even what the IRA stood for. But he'd met Fritzy and now he was dead.

"So the IRA contingent have a dead body on their hands. But before they can deal with that, they have to deal with Fritzy. They pile out of their car, hand the gun to Colman Davison, and force him to go and blow Fritzy away. How do they get an armed man to do their bidding? One of them has a weapon of his own trained on Davison. So Davison gets to Fritzy, who's trying to turn his car around. Fires one bullet through the open window and hits him in the neck. A couple of the other fellows pull Fritzy out of the car and make Davison shoot him again, to make sure he's dead. He fires a few more rounds. But then Davison whips around and manages to knock the gun out of the hand of the man who has him covered. Knocks him off his feet long enough for Davison to get in his own car and take off. With the Browning.

"Davison reasoned that if anyone tried to pin the shooting on him, he would take his IRA handlers down with him, by directing the police to this gun. He drove away as if the furies were after him. Which they were. They fired a couple of shots at his car, trying to stop him, but then they had other things to take care of. They left O'Dwyer by the roadside, but they had an innocent victim that they had to take away and bury. Which apparently they did. And they got rid of O'Dwyer's car somehow; it's never been seen again.

"So Davison got away and he kept the pistol as his insurance policy. I heard he had a confrontation with somebody on the road that night, pulled a knife on him. If he settled for a knife at that time of night after what had just occurred, that tells you how protective he was of that Browning pistol! He was thinking straight enough that he didn't want anybody to see that gun on him."

Brennan had many questions, most of which he had no desire to ask. But he gave voice to one. "How did a Loyalist end up stashing a gun with a Catholic priest?"

"I can't quite imagine the conversation between the two of them, but Davison could not lodge the weapon with the Loyalists, because he'd be terrified they'd find out he'd been an informer for the IRA. And he no doubt figured that if the priest told the authorities about the gun, it would spell trouble for the Republicans. Davison told someone in the IRA that he had placed the gun with a trusted person as insurance. If they protected him, he'd protect them by keeping the gun — and its history — out of sight. I know enough about the former priest there to know he wouldn't do anything to stir up trouble for anybody, on either side. For him, it was probably 'out of sight, out of mind' with respect to the Browning.

"Sometime this past winter one of the lads here in the Kesh found out — there was an informer or a slip of the lip — about the hiding place. He passed the word to someone on the outside. And of course that's when the fates converged on you, Brennan. The course of justice in bringing the shooters of November 1992 to court was the course of justice you have been convicted of trying to pervert."

Brennan's mind reeled with the enormity of what he had been part of, however unwittingly. And his experiences with the police and the courts and the prisons illustrated all too starkly what lay in store for Tom. And Aoife and their children.

Reddy said, "It's ironic, given the chaos out there on the Ammon

Road, but these rogue Republican plotters almost pulled off the attempt to portray this as another instance of collusion. The investigation went nowhere. Many people believed that the RUC were simply letting it slide. It was just the murder of another IRA terrorist." The lawyer suddenly looked exhausted. "If word gets out of this ham-fisted effort to make the killing look like a Loyalist hit with a gun supplied by a member of the British Army — and word surely will get out — it will be a major setback for the claim we have been making for years, about the very real collusion that has gone on here. The authorities will say the IRA faked this and all other instances of apparent collusion!"

He paused and then looked intently at his client. "Brennan, I know it wasn't you who went into Saint Matthew's the second time and retrieved the gun. But it was someone who is the same size as you, the same colouring, and someone you were willing to take an enormous risk for. I'm not the only person who will have figured that out. If, as seems likely, a member of Ronan Burke's family was involved in the shooting of the Dutch tourist and the conspiracy to kill Fritzy O'Dwyer and pin it on the UDA, that individual will be charged with murder. And Ronan will go down in the fallout from the actions of his family. If Ronan actively took part in a cover-up, or an effort 'to pervert the course of justice,' there will be criminal charges as well as political consequences."

Brennan was heart-scalded hearing this. He said, "After all Ronan has tried to do to bring peace to this country. If there is a new elected assembly and if the Republicans are to be represented, he'll get the votes. He's a shoo-in for the position. He's vastly popular in Nationalist areas —"

"*Was* a shoo-in, Brennan. It's over for Ronan."

†

The stark fact of Ronan's downfall sent Brennan into a new spiral of despair, which inevitably resulted in another bout of drinking, and, when the *poitín* ran out, another onset of the DTs, the shakes, the sweats, and the night terrors. He hardly had the energy to walk to the visitor's area to see Ronan and Gráinne for their scheduled visit. What on earth could he say to Ronan, knowing what he knew from Reddy O'Reilly?

But Ronan wasn't there. Gráinne had come by herself. Brennan began a greeting as he approached the cubicle, but he was brought up short by the appearance of his cousin's wife. She looked grey, haggard, older than her years. No wonder, given what her son and husband were going through.

He sat across from her and said, "Gráinne, *a mhuirnín,* you must be going through hell. This is the last place you should be. You look as if you need a good, long rest. Even better, a holiday far from this bitter place." He knew he wasn't making any sense. Rest? A holiday? Shut your gob, Burke, before you make things any worse.

"No, no, I wanted to see you, Brennan, God be good to you."

She chattered away about Aideen's studies at university, about the ceasefire holding, about the changes in Belfast city centre, where some of the imposing steel gates had been replaced with less intimidating barriers. Then she faltered into silence.

"Where's the oul fella today?" Brennan tried, in an effort to lighten things up.

She looked at him without replying. Her eyes had a haunted look. Brennan was alarmed. But he couldn't bring himself to speak.

Finally she said, "Ronan is . . . He's not the man I took back into my life four years ago."

Oh, God of mercy and compassion. Brennan knew. Ronan had gone back on the drink.

There wasn't much to the visit after that. It was unbearable seeing her walk away, promising gamely to come and see him again soon.

Brennan was about to leave the cubicle when he got word of another arrival. Lorcan's friend Carrick. The young fellow sat down and started gabbling away, and Brennan could hardly follow him. He was still poleaxed by what he had learned about Ronan. He made a superhuman effort to nod and mumble occasional replies to his guest. Finally, Carrick got up to leave.

"It pains me to see a man like you in a state like this, Father Burke. You have my full sympathy. And it didn't have to fucking happen. If only your pal Monty had been open to finding another solution to that family's problems, the Flanagans. Or at least waited till you had flown back to Canada."

Brennan forced himself to tune in. "What are you saying? Monty wouldn't have known what the fallout would be for starting that lawsuit. He wouldn't have known about my family's involvement. Certainly not *my* involvement."

"He knew. I told him."

Brennan was silent.

"I tried to warn him off, slow him down at the very least, said this would all blow back on you. Your mate Monty only laughed."

"What?" Brennan could not have heard him right. "Are you telling me he laughed?"

"Yeah. He made a joke. Said something like, 'Just tell Brennan to say three Hail Marys and ring the Pope's help line.'"

What?! Brennan remembered Monty's call to the abbey. What had Monty asked him? Whether Brennan had any concerns about the Flanagan lawsuit. And Brennan had told him no. He had wondered about the question — it made no sense to him — but he had put it out of his mind. He sure as hell didn't know that Monty had been warned. Brennan knew that Tom Burke had, at some place and some time, killed an innocent man in what he thought was self-defence. Brennan had no idea then that there was any connection between that and the debacle on the Ammon Road. And if he had known, what then? Monty would have proceeded with the lawsuit anyway. How could he do otherwise? Brennan would never have tried to block a righteous lawsuit for a deserving family.

But could it have been delayed until Brennan was safely away?

Monty had a deadline and had to be back in Halifax, but he would have handed it over to another lawyer. He would have done that at some point anyway. So maybe it could have been postponed. In the end, though, what burned into Brennan's soul was the fact that his best friend had been warned that this would bring grief down on Brennan and had laughed and blown him off with a joke.

And here he was in Long Kesh, after enduring beatings and an unjust trial. Here he was for six long excruciating years.

He spent a sleepless night shaking, sweating, and gasping for a drink. At the very lowest point, at the dread-filled hour of three o'clock when all defences are down, what he wanted more than a drink, more than a smoke, more than joining his body and soul with that of a woman, more than any of this, Brennan wanted revenge. Revenge on the unjust judge who had condemned him, on the violence-crazed police at Castlereagh who had beaten him black and blue, on the government in London that permitted this to happen to Irishmen day after day after day, and on the security forces that kept the system in place. And what about Monty Collins, his closest friend? Till now. Till Monty had dismissed out of hand any concern for Brennan, flipped him off with a laugh. Should he, too, feature in Brennan's fantasies of revenge?

Gone from Brennan's mind were the doubts and scruples that were the usual cause of sleepless nights for him, misgivings about the way the IRA — and his family — had prosecuted the war against the occupying forces of the North. Deaths caused by the IRA were regrettable just as were deaths caused by the other side, even if the IRA had not "started it," had not been the ones to initiate sectarian attacks against the people of the North in the late 1960s. But the respective responsibilities of the various factions, and the subtleties of just causes and just methods, were not what occupied his tortured mind tonight. If

Brennan were able to get up and walk out of this prison camp, he would head for the nearest . . . what? IRA safe house? Or Ronan's place? Could Brennan support what his cousin had worked so hard for, détente with the regime that had brutalized him and so many others like him? Or would Brennan be a dissident Republican? Would he have to side with the diehards who believed that anything less than a complete victory would mean that all the patriots in times past had died in vain? Fuck it; he wanted revenge. That's all there was to it.

He then turned his mind to his new cellmate, Owen, who was a prince among men compared to O'Morda on his former wing. Owen had something Brennan dearly wanted: two big bottles of prison-made hooch. *Poitín* stashed under the lower bunk. It was half six in the morning. Brennan had degenerated to the point where he would start drinking at half six in the morning, but not to the point where he would steal the stuff from a fellow prisoner. There was only one thing to do: wake Owen out of a sound sleep for Brennan's own selfish needs. So that's what he did. Owen said to take one bottle and leave him the other. Brennan spent the next two hours nursing the foul-tasting, mule-kick-strength brew and then got dressed and ready to perform the sacraments.

Some of his fellow prisoners had asked him to say a Mass for them so he headed to the chapel. As the clock struck nine, he stood at the altar raising a trembling hand to make the sign of the cross. *"In ainm an Athar agus an Mhic agus an Spioraid Naoimh. Amen."*

The men were respectful and attentive. It was not as large a congregation as there would have been back in the days when Mass was the only occasion when the prisoners could get together and pass notes, exchange information, and hatch conspiracies, but it was a decent turnout. Brennan did his best to sing the Mass parts in Irish and to perform the ancient ritual with dignity and reverence. But the reality was that he was nearly paralytic with drink, and the effects became more pronounced as the Mass went on. He didn't trust himself to say much of anything by way of a homily; he wasn't of a mind to get up and hector his fellow prisoners about living an irreproachable life. He managed to slur his way along until he got to the consecration. It was the most sacred moment of the Mass, a moment that often transported Brennan to another state of being, a communion with the Absolute, a moment of ineffable peace. But today, as he raised the round white host and began the words of consecration, he felt his legs give out beneath him. The next thing he remembered was waking up and looking into the face of a man. It was Turlough, picking him up off the floor, carrying him in his arms. "Father," he was saying, "God bless you, but you've had a wee fall."

Chapter XXXV

Monty

Maura's anguished reports of Brennan's arrest and imprisonment had thrown Monty into turmoil. He and Maura had made regular calls to Ronan and Gráinne over the course of the summer. Brennan's cousins tried to sound reassuring; everyone was hopeful that when the case went to trial Brennan would be found innocent of all charges. What Monty had seen in the Belfast courts gave him no reason to be optimistic. But surely in this case there would be no evidence, no evidence at all, that Brennan had committed the offences with which he was charged. Monty had also called Reddy O'Reilly a couple of times, but the conversations were awkward; Brennan was the client, not Monty, and there was only so much O'Reilly could say. He, too, tried to be reassuring. But Monty could read between the lines; O'Reilly would have no trouble raising the reasonable doubt that should stave off a conviction, but the judges in the Crumlin Road Courthouse knew a bloody Fenian terrorist when they saw one. When the word came that he had been found guilty and had been sentenced to six years in prison, Monty was dumbfounded. He was, quite literally, sick to his stomach.

He could barely concentrate on his day-to-day work at Stratton Sommers in Halifax. He came to a decision: he would fly over to Belfast again and make as many prison visits as he could in the few short days he would have available. Before making his flight reservations, he would call Ronan and find out about Brennan's condition and the visiting policy for sentenced prisoners at Long Kesh. Gráinne took his call and sounded hesitant to bring her husband to the phone. But Monty was patient and Ronan eventually came on the line. He sounded strange, not like his usual self. He was courteous as always, but Monty sensed an undercurrent there. Well, who wouldn't be distressed if his cousin, his guest, had been arrested, convicted, and thrown into prison? Ronan told Monty he would speak to Brennan and call Monty back.

The call came two days later. And if Monty was troubled before the call, he was distraught afterwards. The message was blunt: "Don't come." And Ronan sounded even worse on the phone this time. His speech was a bit slurred, almost as if he had been drinking. Maybe just exhausted. Surely the man Brennan had extolled as a "heroic non-drinker" had not fallen into his old family-destroying habits. Ronan had been tactful while putting Monty off. "Ah, Brennan's going through a bad patch these days, as you can imagine, Monty, so it's best that you don't come to see him now." But Monty didn't buy it. Brennan's life had gone almost as far down the toilet as one's life could go. Monty would have expected Ronan to make this point, certainly, but then say something like, "Don't expect much from him, Monty, but he needs all the support and encouragement and friendship he can get. So hop on the first plane out, and come see him." Instead, it was plain that neither Brennan nor Ronan wanted him in Belfast.

Any talk about the situation upset Maura so much that Monty now avoided the subject at home. And after his experience on the phone with Ronan, he was not about to call on any of the Burkes for enlightenment. He had often picked up foreign newspapers at Atlantic News on Morris Street, so he called to see if they had any of the Belfast papers in. They did; they had the *Telegraph*. Monty got up and left his office and said to the receptionist, "Darlene, I'll be back in a bit. I'm going over to Atlantic News for some Irish newspapers."

Kyle, the law firm's computer guy, had just come in with a large box under his arm. He always came in these days with a large box under his arm. "Did you say you're going to buy a bunch of foreign papers, Monty? Pretty soon you'll be able to get all the information you want on your desktop computer. Information from the world wide web."

"*World wide web*, right. I won't cancel any subscriptions yet, Kyle."

Darlene said, "You'll be back for the lunch, eh, Monty? The Canadian Earth Equipment people are coming in."

Lunch with the big client, right. The company had issued its third-party claim against the metals supplier, and all indications were that Canadian Earth would be successful in avoiding losses in the hundreds of millions of dollars. The client was delighted with the work Monty had accomplished in Belfast, and he was scheduled to give a talk to personnel from the company's various offices across the country. But he had other things on his mind.

He hoofed it down Barrington Street to Morris and turned right, walked to the corner of Queen, and went inside for his papers. When he got back to his office he closed the door and spread the papers out on his desk.

All hell had broken loose in Belfast.

He looked at page one of the *Telegraph* and what to his wondering eyes should appear but Old Saint Nick. Gideon Sproule, the Ulster firebrand, was in the paper holding forth on the latest turn of events in his native land. Monty read his words and heard in his mind the harsh, razor-wire Norn Iron accent of the famed preacher.

"What kind of peace talks can they be, if the main nego-
tiator the Republicans put forward, the best man they can
offer up in the cause of peace, is nothing but a *supposedly retired* IRA man with a whole band of still-active IRA
terrorists hiding behind his back? Including at least one
member of his own family. We call upon the Republicans'
man of peace to come clean about the cover-up surrounding the murder of one of his fellow terrorists."

What was this? Ronan and a cover-up? And was his son implicated too? Lorcan? Monty flipped the paper, and directly below the
fold were side-by-side photos of Ronan Burke and not Lorcan, but
Tom. Monty stared at the page with growing apprehension. There
was more from Gideon Sproule.

"No loss to the world, you might say? Live by the sword,
die by the sword, Fritzy O'Dwyer the gunman and multiple murderer is no loss to the world? Aye, maybe not.
Maybe he's no loss to decent society. But that's not the
end of it. Now we know there was more to it than the
elimination of one rotten apple. Because when the IRA
decided back in 1992 that Fritzy O'Dwyer had to die, it
wasn't just a case of the IRA terrorists executing one of
their own."

Oh, God. The O'Dwyer murder on the Ammon Road. Ronan's
son Tom connected with it. Was this why Reddy O'Reilly, Republican
solicitor, wouldn't take the Flanagans' case?
This was what the warning had been about. Monty had spoken to
Maura and reassured himself that nothing about the Kentucky tourist
impersonation was going to come back to haunt her or Brennan.
Monty hadn't known about any other misadventure. But he had

called Brennan himself. He hadn't come clean with Brennan about the warning, and he had to admit to himself it was because he had brushed it off. But he had asked if Brennan had any concerns. Maybe Brennan himself didn't know the whole story. If Monty had known there was something else going on, he would have tried harder to pin it down. But he hadn't known. And the papers had to be served to get the Flanagan lawsuit safely underway before Monty left Belfast.

His mind flew back to Katie Flanagan telling him about mysterious payments to her mother after her father's death. Was it money from some kind of IRA slush fund? Were the payments engineered by the Burkes or others involved in the calamity that night to try and do clandestinely what they could not do openly, support the widow and her children? Why did the money stop? Did somebody notice the finances taking a hit?

And where did Colman Davison fit in? Monty focused again on the paper with a feeling of dread.

> "What did they do, the young bloods of the Andersonstown IRA? They hatched a conspiracy to make the murder look like a killing by a Loyalist group, the Ulster Defence Association. Fit up an innocent Loyalist for a murder he didn't commit!"
>
> As previously reported in this newspaper, a UDA man testified that he was not "fitted up" for the murder but was actually "forced" to pull the trigger.

There. That's where Davison fit in. Forced, somehow, to do the killing. And maybe he panicked afterwards, perhaps afraid he was next. So he took off, and his car was fired on as he drove away. There was more in the paper from Old Saint Nick.

> "The whole vile business was arranged so it would look as if there was 'collusion' — aye, you've heard that word

before from our Republican friends — *collusion* by the Royal Ulster Constabulary, the British Army, the intelligence agencies, and who knows who else? The FBI and the CIA, perhaps, too! Maybe aliens from outer space! Well, I am here to tell you, men and women of Ulster, that the forces of law and order and security who are doing such a magnificent job, under very difficult circumstances, to maintain law and order and security in this province had nothing whatsoever to do with this sordid crime! They are innocent, and no amount of IRA conniving and conspiring can change that!"

And if the news suggesting Ronan's son's involvement in the Ammon Road shooting was not bad enough, Monty found more bad news in the next day's edition of the *Telegraph*. The story was about the bombings of Monaghan and Dublin in 1974. A man was interviewed, a man named Patsy Healey.

Mr. Healey is the son of Paddy Healey, who was killed in one of the bomb attacks in Dublin. He was asked for his reaction to the Royal Ulster Constabulary's statement that they will not be investigating any leads in the bombing case.

Will not be investigating! Will be stonewalling Dublin. Monty sank back in his chair, deflated.

Patsy Healey told this reporter that the facts of those bombings were known to the authorities. "No matter what is going on in the North, no matter what other cases the police are dealing with, we know they have always had the identities of the terrorists who committed these atrocities. And we also know that the police have new and solid evidence against one of the bombers in particular. We demand that they act on this evidence and arrest this man."

An RUC spokesman, Detective Inspector Glenn Hobson, said, "I do not know what Mr. Healey is referring to or why he is talking about new information."

The cop was lying. Monty knew perfectly well that the Northern Ireland police force had received new information. They had very specific evidence about Brody MacAllan, the man Maura and Brennan had tag-teamed in the bar.

"There have been no new developments in the Monaghan and Dublin bombings," the spokesman stated. "The RUC takes every criminal act seriously and investigates every lead. Every lead is examined, if it comes from credible sources. Occasionally we get so-called tips from people with another agenda, with an axe to grind. Sometimes these people try to manoeuvre the police into laying charges against someone who didn't do it, someone these people don't like, so they try to fit the person up. Well, I am here to remind everyone that we are a professional police force, and we are not here to be manipulated or tricked by people out there trying to settle scores."

There was no need for the cop to spell it out any more clearly. Even though collusion had been a reality of life in the North for years, the police had now turned the tables on their accusers. All they had to do was point to the Fritzy O'Dwyer fiasco and say, "See? They're trying the same thing again. Making it up." Monty knew how important it was to Brennan to have uncovered the truth about MacAllan, to give new hope to his old friend's family all these years after Paddy's death. He would be devastated by this announcement. The Ammon Road revelations had torpedoed the chance to find justice for the Monaghan and Dublin families and maybe also the chances of Ronan Burke to be elected to the new institutions that were expected to be set up in a new, peaceful Ireland.

This, and Brennan Burke tried in a Diplock court and sent to prison for six long, agonizing years. Father Burke, his brilliant friend, in a prison cell! And it had all come about because of Monty's lawsuit, Monty's unquestionably righteous lawsuit, against the man who was forced to pull the trigger. It had taken down Brennan Burke as one of its victims, and Monty might have prevented this simply by holding off a bit, if only he had heeded that sinister warning.

There was a racket outside Monty's office, and he looked up. A posse of lawyers and staff members were calling to him, mimicking the raising of a fork and the hoisting of a glass. Lunch with the big corporate client. Then the group lapsed into silence.

A few moments passed before the senior partner, Rowan Stratton, said, "My dear fellow, are you all right?"

"Monty, what's wrong?" asked one of the secretaries. "Are you sick?"

He was looking in their direction but he didn't see them. All he saw was the concrete cell of a prison and a man inside, lying motionless on the floor. There was another man, in shadow, at the door of the cell. He had a gun in his hand. He replaced it in his pocket and turned away. Colman Davison? Tomás Burke? No. The face he saw on the gunman was that of Monty Collins himself.

Chapter XXXVI

Brennan

Falling in a drunken heap on the floor with the Holy Eucharist in his hands was the most shameful failure in Father Brennan Burke's long and not always exemplary life. The kindness he had seen in the face of Turlough at the moment of his disgrace was something that would stay with Brennan until the day he died. Turlough was a bomb maker. He would be labelled a terrorist by many, a soldier by others, a man fighting a war against uniformed soldiers who, like Turlough himself, had killed in the course of the conflict. Brennan was a consecrated priest, and yet he was the lowest person in the chapel on that day. He had disgraced himself, disgraced his church, in the presence of all those who had gathered for the consolation and blessing of the Mass.

That night, he smoked a cigarette before going to bed but denied himself a flask of prison-issue *poitín*. As the shakes began, he drove his mind back to the time before everything fell apart, before the universally feared knock on the door at midnight had set him hurtling towards the abyss. And into his mind came the exultant music of the *Gloria* by Vivaldi, which he had been enjoying when the knock came on the door. This music had always elevated Brennan to a state of pure and shining bliss. The piece had been performed by the girls at the orphanage where Vivaldi worked as a musician in eighteenth-century Venice. And here was Brennan — no Vivaldi, but a musician of some ability — here was Brennan who had lost his choir of girls at Holy Cross, and who had banjaxed his opportunity to direct the choir at Regina Coeli in Rome. And what about his choir school in Halifax? He pictured their angelic (at times) little faces, Normie Collins foremost among them. He heard their sweet voices. He heard them in his memory singing the *Gloria* as it was meant to be sung. And he longed to be with them, to hear them again. How old would they be by the time he got out of here? Long gone from the choir school. Unbearable to think of.

But if his appeal was successful . . . Reddy O'Reilly had told him the Court of Appeal overturned Diplock convictions more often than it did jury convictions. Brennan tried to focus on that slim hope instead of on the brutish police and the unrighteous judge who had reduced him to an embittered wretch. He directed his mind to the possibility, however remote, that his sentence might be reduced, or some of his convictions overturned.

He kept coming back to music. He recalled a quotation attributed to Giuseppe Mazzini, the nineteenth-century Italian patriot: "Music is the harmonious voice of creation, an echo of the invisible world." At times in Brennan's life, music had given him unmediated communion with that invisible world. Following an earlier crisis in his life, Brennan had returned to his church in Halifax and, in the hour before a concert at the church, he had sat in his room and found his pen flying across the empty pages of his music dictation book. He later had no conscious memory of writing the piece, a setting of the *Agnus Dei*. He handed copies to his choir sight unseen, and they performed it to near perfection. They asked him afterwards when he had composed it. But he hadn't composed it; he felt as if he had been taking dictation. From an unseen power.

With all that God had given him, *this* was how Father Burke repaid him? Sinking into despair. Failing to appreciate his gifts, failing to use them for the benefit of others. A piece of music came to him then, inevitably, but not a sacred piece. An old Neapolitan song, "Core 'Ngrato." Ungrateful heart. He was the ingrate here. He vowed that he would mend that ungrateful heart, starting now. If he could wean himself off the drink, he would. If not, he would not let it keep him down. He would be priest and musician. He would use his gifts to endure his imprisonment and to help lift his fellow prisoners from their misery.

He saw Turlough the following day and said to him, "Do something for me, Turlough. If you ever again see me in a self-involved or drink-fuelled funk, take me to your OC and have me disciplined."

"Ah now, Father, there will be no need of that. You can think of me as, well, your provisional altar boy. From here on in, I've got your back."

It was going to be difficult, it was going to be painful. But never again would Father Brennan Burke be the one who had to be picked up off the chapel floor.

Epilogue

Concluding Paragraph of the Decision of the Court of Appeal:

"We accept the judge's finding that the parish secretary correctly identified the appellant Brennan Burke on the February 27 visit to the presbytery. The finding that she recognized the appellant as the man who came up from the cellar with a gun on March 7, however, is not sustainable. The man's face was mostly covered, and the lighting was poor. The man with the gun had no particular accent that she noted. Appellant's counsel made the point that this suggested a man from Belfast, who would sound similar to Mrs. McNally. The appellant on the other hand is originally from Dublin and has spent his adult life in America and Canada. There is no question that his actions on February 27 were peculiar, and that they give rise to suspicion. But suspicion is not enough to support a conviction. The standard of proof is reasonable doubt. There is a reasonable doubt that the appellant was involved in what happened on the 7th of March, 1995. With the identity of the gunman not established, there is no evidence of the appellant possessing a gun, making a threat, or causing damage. Those charges are not made out. As stated above, there are suspicions that he was part of a conspiracy to obstruct justice with respect to the murder of Francis O'Dwyer in November 1992, but not proof beyond a reasonable doubt. The appeal is allowed."

Acknowledgements

I would like to thank the following people for their kind assistance: Joe A. Cameron, Rhea McGarva, Joan Butcher, Pádraig Ó Siadhail, Jim Sheridan, Charlotte Jones, Dr. Marnie Wood, Declan Finn, David Byrne, the people at Coiste (the organization for former Republican prisoners), and the CAIN (Conflict Archive on the INternet) Web Site. I am grateful also for the contributions of a few people who cannot be named here. Thanks as well to my astute and sharp-eyed editors, Cat London and Crissy Calhoun.

This is a work of fiction. Any liberties taken in the interests of the story, or errors committed, are mine alone. It should be noted that some streets, locations, and bars are fictional, i.e., the Ammon Road, MacDonough Street, Clarkson Terrace, the Heatherfield Villas housing estate, Pannacci's restaurant, the Iron Will bar, Phelim's, the Banned Flag, O'Grady's, McCully's, McCribbon's and the Flute and Drum. All other bars and locations are real. The one Dublin Monaghan bombing suspect named here, and the bereaved Healey family, are fictional, but otherwise that story is all too real.

At ECW Press, we want you to enjoy this book in whatever format you like, whenever you like. Leave your print book at home and take the eBook to go! Purchase the print edition and receive the eBook free. Just send an email to ebook@ecwpress.com and include:

Get the
eBook free!*
*proof of purchase
required

• the book title

• the name of the store where you purchased it

• your receipt number

• your preference of file type: PDF or ePub

A real person will respond to your email with your eBook attached. And thanks for supporting an independently owned Canadian publisher with your purchase!